King of Wands

Death's Handmaiden Book 2

Zoey Lee

Copyright © [2022] by [Zoey Lee]

All rights reserved.

No portion of this book may be reproduced in any form without written permission from the publisher or author, except as permitted by U.S. copyright law.

Contents

		VI
1.	Chapter 1	1
2.	Part 1	3
3.	The Road Less Traveled	4
4.	A Letter to Time	15
5.	Phantom Love	26
6.	Into the Unknown	38
7.	Toxic Thoughts	50
8.	Good For You	62
9.	Armor	76
10.	Fire and Ice	87
11.	Monster Hunting	98
12.	Family Reunion	109
13.	Whispers	120

14.	Remember That Night	131
15.	Comatose	142
16.	Part 2	153
17.	The Search For Sprin	154
18.	The One	166
19.	Dragons	178
20.	The Cure	190
21.	Visitors	203
22.	Haunted	215
23.	Tide's Change	226
24.	People's Choice	237
25.	Sophie	248
26.	Forget Me Not	260
27.	Part 3	271
28.	Hell Hath No Fury	272
29.	Lessons	283
30.	Rebellion	294
31.	Ghosts of the Past	305
32.	The Boy King	317
33.	Sanctuary	329
34.	Lithiara	340
35.	Dragon Bone	351
36.	Nightshade	363
37.	Return to Eralia	374

Epilogue	385
38. Bonus Chapter	388

For mom, who kept supporting me,
even when we didn't always agree.

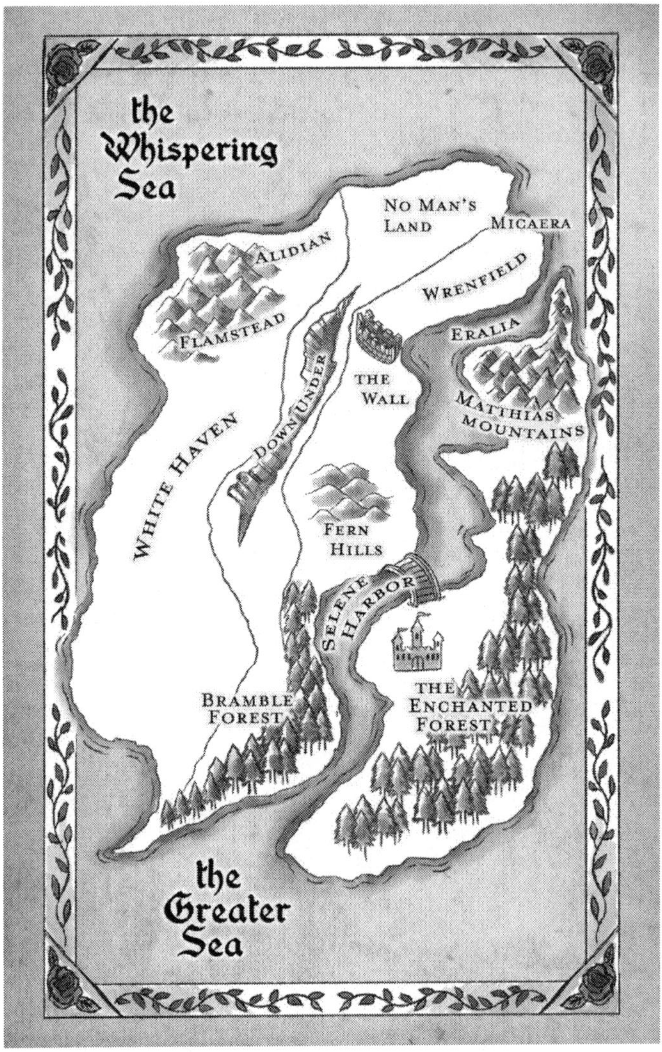
the Whispering Sea
No Man's Land
Micaera
Alidian
Wrenfield
Flamstead
Eralia
The Wall
Down Under
Matthias Mountains
White Haven
Fern Hills
Selene Harbor
Bramble Forest
The Enchanted Forest
the Greater Sea

PART 1

Runaway Bride

"Any man who must say, 'I am the king,'
is no true king."
-Game of Thrones

The Road Less Traveled

> "It's not the world that's cruel,
> it's the people in it."
> -Nora Sakavic, The Foxhole Court

As soon as the sun came up, Telyn was making her way out of the palace. Piran had been ordering everyone around and making preparations all night. They hadn't gotten any sleep at all because he'd insisted that they leave at daybreak. It was too dangerous for them to stay in a compromised location he'd insisted. And the well trodden path to Eralia was "too open," so he was taking them through an alternate route. One that included a longer sailing time.

The land and sea to the west of Alidain had been left uncharted and it made Telyn uneasy to have to go through such a vaguely documented area. It could be even more dangerous than staying where they were, simply because they didn't know what to expect.

Piran kept Telyn close to his side as they left the palace with Zerina, Colton, and Cordelia trailing along behind them.

Zerina and Colton had insisted on coming along because they were family.

As for Cordelia, the thought of an adventure excited her so much, it was hard to tell her no.

Nolan had been strongly against the idea of letting her go, but Zerina had promised to look after her, and none of them could find a good reason to crush the little girl's hopes as long as she had someone looking after her.

Pip was waiting for Telyn at the gates. They nodded curtly at Piran as he passed, but held Telyn aside.

Telyn took their hands in hers with a grim smile. "Thank you for being willing to look after them while I'm gone."

"Anytime, I just hope everything works out for the better." They smiled. "We'll be waiting for your return."

"Sometimes hope is all we have." Telyn sighed.

"It's time to leave." Piran looked back at Telyn and Pip.

Pip grimaced. "Good luck."

"Think of it as an early honeymoon." Piran smiled as Telyn caught up to him.

Contrary to what he may believe, that didn't make her any more excited for the journey. If anything, it made her want to stay at the palace even more. She didn't want to think about her impending doom or anything that might follow the wedding. The attack hadn't given her enough leverage to get him to push the wedding back. If anything, he wanted it done sooner after her life had been threatened.

The light pressure of her bag on her back felt much heavier than it should have been. She knew it was only a few pairs of clothes, and just enough supplies to get her to Eralia, but it felt like she was carrying the responsibility for it all.

It didn't help that she was leaving Alexander behind on bad terms. Not that he seemed to mind. He'd done nothing more than glare at her on her way out.

But in a way, despite being trapped by Piran's whims and feeling Alexander's hatred burning into her back as she left, she felt free. The pull that begged her to go north eased the further she got from the palace. It was like the trip was a stepping stone that pulled her closer to the intoxicating wonder that had her wrapped around its finger.

With her feathers at her back, Telyn felt safer. She knew realistically they could still be injured, but they provided a sort of barrier between her and the things she so desperately wanted to leave behind.

She knew that they were sending her off in hopes that she would learn to manage fire the same way she did her shadows and water, but that wasn't her reason for not putting up more of a fight. She didn't think she would be able to control any more than she already did, and she didn't want to find out if she could.

This world wasn't hers to save, and she was far from a hero.

Nox had been silent throughout this whole ordeal. He had nothing to say about his champion almost being slaughtered in her palace. She wasn't expecting to receive any guidance from him at this point, no matter how desperately she wanted it; she knew he couldn't directly interfere.

It was times like this when her mother's absence was the most painful. Maria would have known what to do. She would have come up with some elaborate scheme to save Telyn and hidden her away from the chaos until it had passed. She would have told her it was going to be alright, even if it was far from it.

Now, there was no caring mother to protect her from the horrors of the world. There never would be again.

You are capable of everything your mother was. You can build yourself a new home. Ice crept into her thoughts and she welcomed the familiar voice that spoke to her.

I'm far from ready to be a homemaker and mother. Even if I was, it's not as if I have the time between staying alive and saving the world. Telyn thought back wryly.

That is not what I meant. You don't need children to be the woman your mother was. And home is often not a place, but rather the people you love. You just have to find them. She replied wisely.

Have you decided if you're going to grace me with your presence in these coming weeks? Telyn asked, eager to change the subject.

She didn't want to think about how the people she loved always ended up leaving her.

And beyond. She promised.

Will I get to see you in Eralia? Telyn pressed. She'd been dying to meet her stranger ever since she'd learned she was more than just a figment of her imagination.

It's doubtful. She answered slowly.

In Eralia? Telyn pushed stubbornly.

I do live there... She conceded.

Telyn sighed. She would have preferred to meet the woman before her husband-to-be was likely to murder her for looking at Telyn too long.

Your wedding is in three weeks. Telyn felt the vibration of the conversation drop to a sadder pace.

It is. It dimmed even further.

She was silent, but Telyn could feel the sadness buzzing around her brain. *You know I don't want to go through with it.* Telyn told her.

I know. Her tone was dejected. *I'll be there.*

What? Telyn blinked in surprise. She knew the voice in her head wouldn't see it, but she couldn't help herself.

You're marrying my prince, it would be disrespectful if I didn't come. She pointed out.

I suppose you're right. I just wish there was a way out of it. She sighed.

Things still have time to change.

It seems all I have left now is time.

Usually immortals are a bit older before they start saying things like that. Telyn felt a flicker of amusement. *You haven't even settled yet.*

If i'm lucky, I never will. One lifetime with this psychopath is already going to be too many, Telyn said bitterly. She knew she shouldn't be talking bad about Eralia's crown prince, but she couldn't stop herself. This was just between her and her stranger, right?

She wished she was allowed to spend her last three weeks of freedom the way she wanted. Instead she would be spending a week trekking through unmapped woods, another week on a ship across waters no one had documented, and then yet another week walking the rest of the way to the palace of Eralia. And it would all end with her in a gilded cage across the world from everything she'd ever known. A world away from any reminders of her mother or Kassian.

She reached for the ring on her finger and felt her heart sink as her fingertips met nothing but smooth skin. It was hard to get used to remembering that Piran had lost her ring. Thrown it out into the vast landscape of No Man's Land. It was probably buried under several feet of snow by now.

You'll escape before you're ever truly trapped. The ice promised.

How can you be so sure of that?

Because I'm the one that's going to get you out.

"Telyn!" Piran barked gruffly. Judging by his irritated tone, he had been trying to get her attention for some time now.

"What is it?" She asked.

"You aren't at all tired?" He asked, the others were a few feet ahead of them.

"There's no point in wasting time," She grumbled. "Let's keep going."

She really didn't see the point in spending more time out here, when there was the possibility that she could get some time to herself if they arrived in Eralia early. Even if it was only by a few hours, she would be grateful for the extra time to grieve the life she was about to leave behind and the girl that would die standing in front of that altar in three weeks.

"Are you doing alright?" Zerina asked as she fell back to walk beside her sister.

Zerina knew how much Telyn had been dreading this trip.

"Just trying to figure out how I'm going to survive this." Telyn sighed. "I'm not sure I'll even be able to see next month."

"Don't talk like that!" Zerina admonished.

"It's only the truth. This whole situation has been slowly killing me." Telyn shot back.

"Because you're still in love with Alexander, even though he hates you?" Zerina guessed.

Telyn hesitated. "I'm not." She wished so badly to be able to tell her sister the whole truth. Even if it wouldn't put Zerina, she would have still kept it to herself.

"It's alright that you still care for him," Zerina said gently.

"No, it's not." Telyn shook her head. Though Alexander was no longer a threat to Piran, and therefore not in danger, it still felt wrong to believe in the feelings she'd tricked herself into having.

But she had more pressing matters to worry about than her love life. In fact, it was the least of her concerns right now. What with the demonic shadow that was hunting her down.

So no, it wasn't alright that she still cared for Alexander.

The week that it took to get to the coast was already wearing on Telyn's patience. Piran had been demanding her attention at very inopportune times, and it was difficult for her to convince him to leave her alone long enough to relieve herself.

Zerina tried her best to keep Piran occupied long enough for Telyn to catch a break when she could, but the prince was stubborn and insistent.

Telyn wasn't sure how much longer she could handle his every whim before she snapped at him. And if she snapped, he likely wouldn't be the only one caught in the crossfire. She had been trying to be patient for Zerina, Colton, and Cordelia's sake.

Telyn could smell the salty sea air before she saw the ocean that stretched out on the west side of her kingdom, the sea that would lead her all the way to the only continent she'd never seen before.

Under different circumstances, she might have been excited.

But since she was going under the pretense of marrying the one person she absolutely could not stand, the concept was much less thrilling.

There was already a ship waiting at the dock for them. This place had clearly been used before, and recently judging by the thoroughly cleaned boards that made up the dock itself.

Telyn would have to remember to keep track of who came and went from this place when she came back. It was an area that could easily be used against her if the wrong person found out about it.

The captain of the ship was a tall fae woman. Her ears stuck out of her hair and under her hat. Her dark hair was in a braid that fell to her back and her grey eyes were narrowed on Telyn. She stood with a hand on her hip before she scanned the rest of the group.

"Your Highness, this is more people than you told me to expect." Telyn could hear the slight irritation in the captain's voice that she struggled to hide as she addressed the prince.

"We had an unexpected tag-along. Or three," Piran said. He waved his hand nonchalantly, as if feeding three extra people wouldn't be a problem when they had nowhere to stop and restock on food for a week.

The captain's eyes drifted back to Telyn. "Your Majesty." She nodded curtly.

"It's just Telyn." She shook her head.

"Sorcha."

"It's nice to meet you." Telyn smiled.

Telyn wasn't about to let the irritation Piran had caused ruin her aquanticeship with the captain.

After all, she may end up needing to seek Sorcha's help in escaping if things in Eralia went belly up.

It didn't take long for Telyn and her companions to board the ship, they had all packed fairly lightly. Only a bag or two each. Though Piran had five or six that he was carrying.

Not even the crew offered to help him as he waddled up the gangplank and onto the deck. Telyn took up a post on a bench out of the way of the crew and watched the waves that crashed against the hull of the ship below her.

Within a few minutes, Sorcha's crew had the anchor pulled aboard and the sails unfurled. Then they were off, putting a strip of ocean between them and Alidain.

Telyn had never been on a boat before, she'd only ever dangled her feet over the edge of the dock by her old house, but it didn't bother

her. The gentle sway of the boat as it rocked on the waves was oddly soothing.

The water was what Telyn had always known. It was where she had always felt safest. It always came to her when she needed it to.

But even with nothing but water surrounding her, she still wasn't completely at ease.

She knew she was capable of drowning this whole ship, and Piran with it, if she wanted to, and she could even probably manage to save the rest of the people on board, but it wasn't a risk she was willing to take.

Not with so many lives in her hands and the risk of failure so high.

She didn't want to be responsible for any more deaths than she already was.

Before long, the others filtered below deck to situate themselves for the coming week.

Piran had been the first to go. His face had grown pale and green as the ship rocked beneath his feet and he nearly hurled when he'd looked over the edge of the ship at the indigo waters that thrashed below them.

Telyn had no intention of going below deck. She knew it would be dark and damp, and that was something she didn't want to experience again. It would get warmer the closer they got to Eralia, so she wasn't too worried about freezing, but her little bench wouldn't be very comfortable.

Yet she still preferred it over staying below deck with the others.

"Not keen on dark spaces, are you?" Sorcha came to lean on the railing beside Telyn.

"A few bad experiences have tainted the atmosphere." Telyn admitted.

"You're safe here. I know you probably haven't felt that way in a long time, but I won't let anything happen to you while you're on my boat."

Telyn knew that the dark skin they shared meant they had probably had some similar experiences outside of Eralia. Telyn was familiar with the strange looks and accusatory glares from those who feared and hated what they didn't understand.

"Thank you." Telyn's voice was quiet.

Sorcha was likely older than her and had probably experienced far worse. It made Telyn glad that it hadn't spoiled her kindness. She was still kind and willing to help despite the uncomfortable situations she must have had in similar situations.

Especially as a woman running her own ship. She had likely been looked down on her entire life, and despite that, she had still made it here.

And Telyn could see it in the gleam of her eyes that she loved being out at sea with the wind in her hair and the sea spraying in her face. She had found what she loved and she'd fought to be where she could live a life she wanted.

The two girls weren't so different.

Telyn smiled to herself. This week might be less difficult than she had originally anticipated.

With Piran's sea sickness and preference for below deck, and Telyn's aversion to it, it was unlikely that he would be up to bothering her. Which meant she might get a bit of peace and time to herself.

For the first time since he'd dragged her back to Alidain after she'd rescued her people.

She had accomplished so much without him, and she had felt so much more herself without him hovering in her shadow.

And he had ruined that by trapping her. He knew there was nothing she wouldn't do if it kept her family out of danger. And he had taken advantage of that.

Telyn couldn't find a way out of it, a way to turn around and say she hadn't meant what she said. That she would rather die than marry him.

But she knew she couldn't protect her family from him if she was dead.

So she would stay.

For now.

She was still clinging onto her stranger's words. That one sentence echoed around her head every day and every night. The sincerity had been surprising, and Telyn hoped it wasn't just her imagination. If she had help, she might be able to get them all out of this safely.

Her words bounced around once again, reminding her that not all was lost.

Not yet.

Because I'm the one that's going to get you out.

A Letter to Time

"Nothing really dies as long as it's not forgotten."
L. J. Smith, The Forbidden Game

Telyn found even more solace in her sleep, where not even in her dreams could Piran reach her. Nothing could reach her there. With Nox silent and her stranger plotting her escape, Telyn was left alone with her thoughts and her dreams. Whether they were good dreams or nightmares depended on the night.

Some nights, her worst fears returned to haunt her. The memories of the deaths that surrounded her life. Dying words and screams echoed in her ears and she didn't know how much longer she could pretend that they didn't bother her. Because they did. She wasn't sure she would ever be able to forget the way her mother's words rasped with her final breaths, the last conversation she'd had with Kassian, or the way Time had worn a smile as the life drained from his eyes at his own hands.

She'd hoped that with the sea under her, she'd be able to have a peaceful night of sleep as she settled down under her bench on the deck. Telyn could hear Piran's whiny voice drifting up from below deck. She tried to ignore him going on and on about meaningless plans for when they reached Eralia. Of all the things he wanted to do, the celebrations he wanted organized. Things that she hoped she didn't have to live through. She closed her eyes and let herself slip away until reality was nothing more than a memory burning in the back of her mind.

She opened her eyes to a familiar setting. Dark woods, broken branches, and blood-splattered leaf litter. This forest, this scene, had been haunting her dreams for weeks now. She'd been hoping they would go away with time. But here she was. "Why am I back here again?" *Her voice echoed in the silent forest.*

Only one thing had changed since the last time she had been there. A letter sat in the brush, droplets of blood had seeped through the paper and blurred some of the words. That letter way always there, and it was always the same.

And she was always stuck. But she read it again anyway.

Dear Time,

I wrote this to ask when you'll leave,

I hate you for all you've taken from me, and I still can't seem to breathe.

The rest of the words were unreadable, smeared with blood, and stained with tears. It was the letter that Telyn had detailed out in her head so many times. The words she wished she could scream at her uncle.

'You're gone, I watched you die. Just like I watched the people you killed die.

But I can't shake the feeling that there was something more to it.

Like you had something against me personally.

I can barely remember them now.

The memories I had are fading, but they wouldn't be if you hadn't taken them from me.

You ruined my life, and didn't even let me fix it myself. You did that too.

You took my revenge away from me.'

That's what the rest of it was supposed to read.

"You never would have been able to do it. You don't have the blood of a killer yet."

She didn't expect the voice that came to her in the silence.

"Part of you will never truly leave this forest." Time was before her, as he was before he'd died, and come back as a shadow demon.

"At least I can *leave*." Telyn scowled.

He was the last person she wanted to talk to.

"Then why haven't you?"

That was the question she'd been begging herself to answer. Why?

"Because I have nowhere else to go." Telyn felt her voice falter. "And it's all your fault." She could feel the warm tears that swelled in her eyes as she glared at him.

"How is it my fault?"

"You took them from me, you killed them, and made me run away from everything I have ever known." She answered, despite knowing full well he'd read the note and knew how she felt.

"I didn't force you to do anything. You chose to run. I may have made it the easier option, but ultimately, it was your choice."

"Oh, yes, what a wonderful choice here. Run and live to avenge my mother, or stay and die for who I am." Telyn threw her arms up.

"Your actions were your choices." It infuriated her how calm he appeared. He was dead and only existed as a shadow of himself, and yet he still acted like he was better than her. Like she should have known better.

"You killed my mother. I've started to forget what her voice used to sound like. I can't remember the exact color of her eyes anymore, but you're still here. You're still messing with my head! Even though you're *both dead, you're the one I remember. It shouldn't be like that. I started to doubt she loved me at all, and it was only because you killed my father and drove her from her home. It's your fault she could barely stand to look at me!"*

"I wanted what was best for our family."

"No, you wanted what was best for you. You killed Kassian too, and you kept Zerina from me in hopes that I would fall, and break, and just give up and die like the rest of them. If you wanted what was best for our family, more of us would still be alive."

"That was what we needed. Without having you separated, the world would have hunted you down."

"For what it's worth, I still held onto the hope that you could change..."

"Why would I change?"

"Because deep down, I was still hoping that you were at least partly human. That part of you might realize you had taken everything from the only family you had left and you would stop. I was hoping that maybe you weren't a complete monster."

"I was never human."

"No, of course you weren't. You were one of the ones who always loved the fact that your blood put you higher up on the food chain. Now, you're the only one here. You saw me at my worst, in the depths of my grief. Even if you stayed in the shadows, you saw what you had done, and you still kept taking them from me. You kept trying to break me. There wasn't even a drop of sympathy or guilt for doing this to your own flesh and blood, was there?"

Telyn was sobbing now, and she couldn't stop herself.

"Give up on me." She begged. "Let me go home. Let me find some way to cope with all you've done. Please."

"This family failed me. I owe you nothing. And to answer your question, you were Corbin's daughter, not mine. So no, I felt no remorse. You were never mine." Time scowled.

"You are dead!" Telyn screamed.

She crumpled to her knees and clutched her head in her hands. Her tears blurred her eyes, rendering Time as nothing more than a human-shaped blob of darkness. The same way he was when he'd come back as the shadow.

"So why... Why are you still here? Why are you haunting me? Just let me go." Telyn squeezed her eyes shut, trying to stop her tears from falling to the ground that was already wet with blood that should have dried ages ago.

"Let me go..."

There was no response and Telyn looked up.

Time was gone, but the feel of his presence lingered.

And once again, Telyn was left alone in the cursed forest.

It seemed that not even her dreams would be enough of an escape from reality.

Not if she kept having such an unpleasant visitor.

Telyn woke up curled up under her bench, tears streaking her face in a reminder of what she'd fought to forget.

"Are you alright, lass?" Sorcha's voice came from above the bench. Telyn glanced to the side and saw her boot clad legs crossed at the ankle as she leaned against the side of the ship.

Telyn rubbed the remaining tears from her face and took a deep breath before she emerged from under the bench. "I'm fine." She forced a small smile onto her face.

"I am no stranger to the horrors of the world. If something is bothering you, you can talk about it. This crew has seen its fair share of bloodshed and betrayal." Sorcha's eyes were on the horizon as Telyn pulled herself up onto her bench.

"I'm afraid there's going to be much more of it soon." Telyn sighed.

"What do you mean?" The suspicion that crept into Sorcha's tone didn't escape Telyn.

"Carling has grown more active. He wants bloodshed."

"And nothing can stop him?"

"Nothing short of death." Telyn shook her head.

"How does one kill a god?"

"With more luck than I seem to have."

"Things will all work out in due time, lass." Sorcha gave her a sad smile.

Telyn wondered how many times she'd said that over the years, and out of those times, how many of them had been to reassure herself.

It was still early, but more than just the crew were up and moving around. Colton was helping out where he could, carrying buckets and ropes.

Zerina sat with Cordelia, the two of them were discussing something that had a big smile on the little girl's face as Zerina illustrated the story with animated hand gestures.

And Piran was just pacing around. He got in the way of several crew members, and was entirely unapologetic when he ended up tripping people up or spilling water buckets.

Typical.

Telyn sighed and rolled her eyes. She was almost tempted to slip over the edge of the boat and not have to deal with the absolute wreck that was supposed to be her husband.

"Don't try anything, he'll have my head," Sorcha muttered.

And the unfortunate truth of the matter was, she was right.

Piran was just deranged enough to take it out on someone who wasn't even involved in the situation rather than realizing he was the problem.

Telyn looked out over the water as it lapped against the hull of the ship. Shadows danced under the surface of the water, a playful pod of dolphins kept pace with them.

It reminded Telyn of when she used to look out over the dock near her house. It felt like such a long time ago even though it had only been a few months. She'd promised herself then that she would leave that city one day.

And now she had, but it didn't feel as freeing as she thought it would. She felt just as stuck as before, if not more.

The restriction on her magic wasn't there anymore, but other bonds had taken their place.

She hadn't found the freedom she'd sought on the other side of that muddy harbor. Instead, she'd found more responsibilities that should never have been hers. Though these waters were clearer and more lively, she couldn't help but feel she was only allowing the chains around her to tighten.

But what other choice did she have?

She couldn't just let Piran kill everyone she cared about.

I may have made it the easier option, but ultimately, it was your choice.

Telyn shook her head as she realized how wrong Time had been.

He hadn't made anything an easy choice.

There had been no easy choices since her mother died.

There had only been making the decisions necessary to survive. The decisions that kept the people she'd come to care about safe. They had been easy to make because they had been the right ones, but they weren't easy at all.

Marrying a man she hated would not be easy.

But she would do it for the sake of the people around her. As long as they were safe, she was willing to do anything to keep them that way.

Even if that meant she would have to be miserable for the rest of her life.

She knew that if she were to refuse, her friends and family would be dead in seconds. Piran didn't know things like mercy and kindness. All he knew was manipulation and power. And that had been allowed to fester for far too long.

Which meant he was just another responsibility she shouldn't have.

She didn't think the king and queen would be inclined to believe her if she told them how much of a monster their son was.

If they hadn't been paying enough attention to see it by now, they wouldn't care enough to change him now.

Even if they did have the heart to try, she wouldn't be surprised if he just killed them as well.

His solution to everything seemed to be murder. It was infuriating. If he couldn't kill the person causing the problem, he would just kill someone close to them, which put his own sister at risk as well.

It was disgusting behavior, but Telyn couldn't see it changing anytime soon. She couldn't see it changing at all.

This was just the way Piran was.

And though she wasn't ready to accept the fact that in a short amount of time she was about to be chained to him for the rest of her life, she had already accepted that if she made one wrong move, he would tell the world that he lost his wife in a tragic accident.

What they wouldn't know was that he was the one who staged the accident.

She wondered how long these people had been living with the monstrocities he'd comitted without realizing he'd done them on purpose.

They may very well end up going their entire lives without knowing what their crown prince did when no one was watching.

She could find a way to tell them...

She could expose him to his own people.

But at the same time, that would be putting her own at risk. And that wasn't something she was willing to do. She wouldn't put someone else's people before her own. Eralia's king and queen could handle their people how they saw fit. Telyn wanted no hand in it.

Not while she had her own people to worry about.

Not even when those people were supposed to merge with her own.

Piran wasn't so different from her uncle.

They both wanted the same thing. Complete and unchallenged power over the entire world. What they had wasn't good enough for them.

They weren't interested in the well being of the people they wanted to lord over, or the safety of their families. All they did was only for their own gain. It was all just what they wanted.

And people like that should never be handed the power they seek.

In fact, they shouldn't be handed power at all.

But all too often, there were times like this, where the greedy jealousy of an heir was left unchecked, allowed to fester and grow. Until eventually, there was no stopping them. They had no morals, no lines they refused to cross in the name of living honestly.

Piran had reached that point. Where all that mattered to him was what he wanted.

Unfortunately for Telyn, right now what he wanted was her.

Or rather the power she had.

And he had trapped her between threats and a debt he demanded be repaid.

She would do what she could to keep him from getting what he wanted, but there was only so much she could do before she jeopordized everyone else. She would have to be smart and find a way around it.

It would take time and planning, but she could find a way out of it all eventually.

She had to.

Because she knew for certain that she couldn't let herself be trapped by this man forever. Not as he stomped around, knocking over buckets, without any regard for the people around him that he was inconveniencing.

He thought the very world revolved around him.

She would have to find a way to show him that it didn't. That if anything, he was the one stuck in its orbit, and when he died, the world would go on. There would be the grief from his parents and his people, but they would survive, and they would be better for it.

It was kinder to let them grieve for a son they didn't know had no soul than it was to let them see the monster he'd grown into. To spare them from everything he'd done. Because Telyn was sure she wasn't the first to have to deal with his antics.

The less they knew the better.

But at the same time, what would happen when they came looking for answers?

If they were stubborn enough, it would lead to everything he'd hidden from them.

If they knew before hand, they might not grieve as badly.

But with him still alive, he hung a threat over Telyn's head constantly. She might not be able to warn them before she could manage the concequences of doing so.

She could either risk losing the people she cared about or tell everyone the truth.

That's what it always seemed to come down to.

Zerina, Colton, and her court were always on the line, and they were the one thing she couldn't give up.

So she made what Time would have called the easy choice.

She would go through with the wedding, and she would stay silent. She wouldn't be happy about it, and she certainly wouldn't make it easy, but it was all she could do.

She would walk down that aisle to her death.

She knew that was exactly where it would end.

But she would rather it be just her than them. They were all she had left, but they had each other. They would survive without her, but she wasn't sure she could if the tables were turned.

Phantom Love

"Hope is the only thing stronger than fear."
-Suzanne Collins, Hunger Games

By the time they reached Eralia, they were caked with dust and dirt, and it left Telyn wishing, not for the first time, that they'd never gone on this trip. *Help.* She thought feebly as they reached the cobblestone paths that crisscrossed the capital city.

You've arrived. The voice that answered sounded vaguely amused.

I have. She confirmed.

Is the city really that terrible? She asked.

It is when you've been walking for three weeks towards your death and only slept for about three of those nights. Telyn answered.

I told you I would rescue you from your fiance's clutches, She said gently.

Telyn cringed. *Please don't call him that.*

No matter what we call him, you won't have to deal with him much longer. She assured.

How do you plan on pulling that off? The wedding is tonight.

She hadn't gotten the extra time to grieve as she had wanted. No matter how many times they walked through the night, there were always setbacks. There was always some problem that wasted all the time they'd gained.

Telyn suspected Piran was to blame.

So now, Telyn had mere hours before she was shackled to the prince forever.

Unless her stranger pulled through and managed to rescue her. Unless, against all odds, Nox was finally answering her cries for help.

Telyn had lost track of how many times she'd broken down and begged the god of death for a way out.

She hadn't asked to save the world, she hadn't asked for a kingdom to lead, but she had to do it anyway.

Because no one else would.

So she'd take on the cursed path she'd been given, but she was still fighting the part that required her to marry, quite possibly, the vilest man she'd ever met.

As much as she knew it was a bad idea, she was still clinging to the hope that her stranger would be able to rescue her before things fell much further.

"Two hours." Piran gave her the unneeded reminder in a sing-song voice that made her want to vomit.

Zerina gave Telyn a discreet look. Telyn knew her sister was worried about her, but she also knew that Piran would kill Zerina the second he suspected she was interfering. So as badly as she wanted to break down and tell her sister everything, she couldn't risk letting Zerina know anything more than she already did.

"My mother should have everything arranged. We just need to get to the palace and get ready," Piran said cheerily.

It wasn't long before the servants had scrubbed Telyn clean and dressed her in an uncomfortably intricate wedding dress. The floor-length white silk seemed to burn where it touched her skin, and the rough embroidery on the bodice scratched against her ribcage every time she took a break. Crystal beads glistened along the hem and sides of the dress, and the long narrow sleeves were too tight.

Once they left her to wait, a voice she hadn't heard in a very long time spoke up.

Listen carefully. The shadow of Nox's voice spoke quickly. *Ceremonial marriages are very dangerous for your kind. The properly worded vows and binding ribbons will give him access to your magick.*

Panic sparked in Telyn's chest and she waited for a solution, but Nox wasn't providing one.

If it was possible for Telyn to be any more panicked about this evening, she was now. She couldn't go through with it. She couldn't give him that kind of power. She couldn't give him *her* power. He would use it for nothing but destruction.

"It's time." Queen Tara smiled from the doorway.

No voices in Telyn's head came to her rescue.

Telyn followed the other queen through the intricately designed hallways, her hands twisted nervously in front of her.

"I was nervous when I married His Majesty as well." Queen Tara smiled. "But I never regretted it. It's been over five hundred years, and never once have I thought about what would have happened if I hadn't married him."

Telyn knew she was only trying to help, but the gentle words were far from comforting.

They entered a room that looked as if it was dedicated to royal weddings. The decorations were so vintage and frail-looking that Telyn suspected they'd been up since King Bran and Queen Tara had gotten married.

The room was full of people and slow music was playing. Pink flower petals had been scattered along a white silk carpet that matched Telyn's dress. A small girl with blonde hair and green eyes stood beside Cordelia on Piran's left, with a big enough gap for Telyn to slip in between them and stand beside Piran in front of the altar.

Queen Tara led Telyn down the silk carpet and up to the altar. Then she took a seat in the front row.

Telyn's hands were clenched together in front of her and she forced herself to smile.

"Today, we are joined together to witness the joining of two wonderful monarchs." A priest, whom Telyn had never met, started. Silence fell over the hall. "Today will mark a new era when Piran Thomas joins Telyn Tate in eternal union"

Telyn wasn't sure she wanted to know how this priest knew her middle name. It was the least of her worries right now. She could feel her panic rising once again.

The priest tied a red ribbon around Piran's wrist and secured the other end around Telyn's. "May Arion bless this marriage," He said solemnly. "Piran Thomas Greyhorn, do you take Telyn Tate Ramirez to be your wedded wife under the twelve realms?"

"I do," Piran replied.

Telyn suspected she was the only one who saw the cold cruelty in his smile.

"And do you, Telyn, take Piran as your wedded husband, so long as you should live?" The priest asked.

Piran had had her vows changed...

He wanted to ensure she was shackled to him forever.

She hesitated. The ribbon on her wrist felt like it was lined with tiny razors. Both Piran and the priest were looking at her expectantly.

She assumed their audience was waiting too. Her mouth was dry, her tongue like sandpaper in her mouth. She couldn't say it. This was as far as her lie could go and keep her alive. Even if she did go through with it, she knew it wouldn't be long before Piran staged an "accident" for her.

"I object!" A familiar voice yelled as the door slammed open.

Telyn whirled, the ribbon on her wrist tightened with the movement.

Skylar Morris stood in the entryway to the hall, a dark cloak clasped around her shoulders and a defiant look on her face.

Telyn heard Piran snarl beside her, but her heart leaped to life in her chest.

I'm here. Skylar said grimly in her head.

She'd come to rescue her.

"We, uh... We haven't got to that part yet." The priest mumbled.

"And you won't because it's clear that the bride objects as well!" Skylar said tersely.

"Is this true?" The priest asked.

Telyn nodded numbly and the priest cut the ribbon that tied her to Piran. She quickly took a large step away from Piran.

"Now, if you'll excuse us, we have business to attend to."

Telyn hefted up her skirts and hurried around the altar to get to Skylar. "Telyn, you can't do this," Piran warned. She knew what he would do, and she would find a way to stop him, but there was no way she would survive marrying him.

"You know what will happen." Piran tried again as her feet brought her in front of Skylar.

"No, I know what you want to happen, and I won't bend to your will," Telyn said coldly as she took the arm that Skylar offered her.

Skylar led her out of the palace before Piran recovered his senses and did more than just yell at her from the altar.

"Thank you," She said quietly as they walked through the courtyard. "But my sister, my court. They won't make it in there."

"I've already made arrangements to have them brought to the Winter Court." Skylar assured her.

"The Winter Court?" Her eyes snapped up to study her face.

"You're not the only one with secrets, Majesty." Sklyar grinned at her.

"You mean-"

"Yes, I'm the High Lady of the Winter Court, and very much not human." Skylar wore the same charming smile Telyn had grown accustomed to on their quest last month.

Telyn studied her. She couldn't find any oddity that marked Skylar as anything other than human. No strangely colored eyes like herself. No wildly pigmented skin like Senekah and Parsifal. She looked completely human. Telyn's mind wandered to the grey speckled feather she'd been carrying around with her since Kassian died.

"You're like me," She said quietly. Her wings shivered in response.

"Bingo." Skylar grinned.

"We traveled together for over a week! How did I not realize you had wings?" Telyn demanded.

"I was very good at hiding them." Skylar shrugged. "You couldn't know who I was yet."

"Why exactly not?" She asked.

"There were things you needed to do. My interference would have prevented that." Skylar made it sound as if it was simple.

Telyn couldn't even begin to count the number of times she'd desperately needed her help. "Who told you that?" She asked quietly.

"It's complicated. There are bigger forces at play here than us." Telyn could tell she was beginning to get uneasy.

"Nox told you to leave me alone. Didn't he?" She asked. She couldn't help but feel a sting of betrayal when Skylar nodded.

Nox had been supposed to protect her, but he'd withheld help when she needed it. At least up until now. And even now, she suspected it was only to protect her power, not her. Never her. She'd had too much faith in the god when she thought he'd cared about her.

She was only a pawn in the stupid war the gods were playing out.

"You have to trust us."

"I don't *have* to trust anyone!" She snapped. "In fact, I'm not sure I can. Not with everyone lying to me."

"We're not lying, we're trying to keep you safe!" Skylar raked a hand through her dark hair.

Telyn was torn. She could stay with Skylar, who was hiding gods knew how much. Or she could brave Piran's wrath back in the palace.

She knew it would be wiser to trust Sklyar. Her heart wasn't screaming for her to fly away to a place she'd never been. It never did when she was with her. She knew that should mean something.

Her chance to make a decision was stolen when an explosion rocked the palace grounds. Telyn turned to see the wedding hall crumble to ruins.

It was like she forgot how to breathe. She could feel the color drain from her face as she stilled. Her heart was pounding in her ears, far too quickly.

Her family was in there.

Before Skylar could get a word in or keep her out and away from the danger, she took off running. The sickening feeling of de ja vu clung to her skin like cobwebs. Similar cobblestone streets filtered into her mind and her steps faltered. She couldn't lose Zerina and Colton the same way she'd lost her mother.

Keep going! Skylar yelled in her mind.

She sounded almost as panicked as Telyn felt.

When she was running again, she realized two things.

First, Skylar cared about someone in there as much as she cared about her family.

Second, she wouldn't hold her back.

She wouldn't try to shield her from danger. She would let her handle herself.

There were still billowing dust clouds when she got there. She wove around chunks of plaster and stone in her hurry to get to the cluster of people who had gathered.

Everyone looked nearly the same with chalk-white dust covering every square inch of them. She spotted a pair of bright green eyes on a little girl and made her way over.

"Cordelia?" She knelt in front of the little girl, ignoring the grime that would surely get on her dress.

"Telyn..." The little girl sounded shell-shocked.

"Where are Colton and Zerina?" Telyn asked.

"I-I don't know. Zerina was arguing with the prince. And-and it just-"

"Shhhh." Telyn soothed. "It's okay. Get on my back and we'll go find them."

Cordelia stiffly climbed onto Telyn's back. Telyn stood up and scanned the area, but there were no other familiar faces in the crowd.

Telyn was sure any unnatural in the crowd could hear her heartbeat pounding in her chest. It was almost the only thing Telyn could *feel*.

It beat in time with the panic that surged inside her every minute she wasn't able to find her sister.

Telyn noticed Colton and Zerina weren't the only ones missing. Piran, King Bran, Queen Tara, and Brea were missing as well.

"Over there!" Cordelia pointed a dust-coated finger to a hostile-looking standoff a few yards away.

Relief washed over her as she recognized Zerina's defiant stance. But it was short-lived as she saw the other two figures. Familiar cobalt eyes were wide with fear, and meeting those eyes were a pair of angry green ones.

"Stay here," She said quietly to Cordelia.

The little girl slipped to the ground and Telyn stalked over to the group, her hands curled into tight fists.

In one fluid movement, she closed in on Piran and punched him as hard as she could. The prince was so startled, he dropped Colton. "What *is* it with you and trying to strangle the people I love?" She demanded angrily.

Zerina pulled Colton back, out of Piran's reach.

The prince's cold, angry eyes narrowed on Telyn. "You knew what the consequences would be, and you still walked out." He growled.

"Can you blame me? All you've done is hurt and manipulate the people I care about!" She retorted.

"I can blame you all I want. That captain of yours certainly does." He gloated with a cruel gleam of amusement in his eyes.

She knew now that Carling had done it for his champion.

"I'll stay, just let them go." She knew she had to make amends before he turned her family against her as well.

"What makes you think you're in any position to make demands?" He seethed.

"Because you need me. If you didn't, you wouldn't be trying so hard to pin me down," She replied. "So you'll let them go."

"Fine," Piran growled. "They can go, but *you* are going to find my sister."

"What about your parents?" She asked.

"They're dead," He answered bitterly. "Crushed in the explosion."

Telyn's gut told her something was wrong, but she couldn't put a word to what it was. "I'll find Brea." She agreed.

"Do it quickly." He snapped.

Zerina pulled her sister away from the prince.

Skylar was waiting beside Cordelia. Her blue eyes were rimmed with red. She had a gentle hand on Cordelia's shoulder and she had her small arm wrapped around her. It looked like Cordelia was comforting Skylar as much as Skylar was her.

What happened? She sent the question down their odd little bond.

They're all gone. Her eyes locked on Telyn's across the distance between them.

That mournful expression was all it took for Telyn to forgive her. When she reached her, she wrapped Skylar in a hug.

"Told you so," Zerina said, her eyebrow quirked towards her hairline as she watched Telyn's reaction.

"I'm so sorry," Telyn whispered, choosing to ignore her sister.

"They knew it would be dangerous." Skylar looped her arms loosely around Telyn's waist, but her words were numb and distant.

"Don't forget your duties." Piran hissed as he whisked by.

Telyn shuddered and Skylar held her tighter.

"We should get going." Colton feebly rubbed at his neck, where a ring of bruises was beginning to form.

"I have to find the princess." Telyn agreed.

"I'll come with you." Skylar offered immediately.

"You don't have things you need to attend to?" Telyn asked.

"None of them are more important than you. I'll come along," She answered.

"Alright, what exactly happened when I sent you two off together?" Zerina asked.

"We knew each other long before our paths crossed," Skylar said quietly.

"Romantic, but please refrain from being mushy around me. I already miss my girlfriend," Zerina groaned.

"We weren't-" Telyn's voice faltered. Skylar's arms were still around her. She was still holding on to Skylar as well. She almost hadn't realized it.

Skylar's embrace wasn't rough and possessive like Piran's. It was so light and gentle, she'd forgotten it was there.

Colton cleared his throat.

"Right, things to do," Telyn said quickly. "Where do we start?"

"Siluria," Skylar responded, "It's the safest place to go during a crisis in the mortal realm."

"Do you think she made it?" Telyn asked skeptically.

"She's one of us." She winked at Telyn. "We all have our default home tricks." Her playful smile contrasted their situation so much that Telyn almost smiled herself.

Zerina, always the sensible one, asked, "What do you mean?"

Skylar's blue eyes flicked to Zerina's left and the air beside her warped until it seemed to swirl. "Portals are hard to master, but the easiest one to tame is the one home."

Home.

The word settled over Telyn like a warm blanket. Home had never been the little cottage she'd lived in with her mother. It had never been the grand palace in Alidain that she'd inherited. It had always been somewhere else, somewhere where nothing was supposed to exist.

It was Silura.

Siluria was the home she'd been chasing for so long. But now that she'd caught up with it, she couldn't make sense of it. It seemed her butterflies had caught up with *her*.

"So what's the deal?" Zerina eyed the warped space warily. "We step in, and then *boom*, we're in Siluria?"

"In a basic sense, yes," Skylar admitted. "If you ever want to be able to create one, you'll need to know the technical and magickal bits."

"So who wants to go first?" Colton asked.

Telyn couldn't blame him for being hesitant. The only times he'd seen active magick, it had always been violent and wild.

It had been used to abuse and manipulate those closest to him. It was easy to see why he only saw a slim chance that the same power that had caused so much hurt, could be used for anything good.

"I'll go," Telyn said quietly.

"Are you sure?" Colton asked.

"It's home." Telyn nodded. "I'm going home," She said firmly. She knew she meant the words as she said them. They were the first *right* things that had been said or done in months.

She looked up and ice met her eyes.

Go on. You know what to do. She told her. *Go home.*

Telyn wrung out her hands and took a deep breath.

She was ready. She was going to go home. She was going to be alright.

With a final look at the people who mattered most, she stepped into the portal.

INTO THE UNKNOWN

"Sometimes the truth is a secret you're keeping from yourself because living a lie is easier."
-Adam Silvera, They Both Die at the End

On the other side of the portal was a beautiful grey fog swirled with snow. Telyn almost couldn't see the beautiful stone-cast castle that loomed above her up ahead.

It wasn't long before Zerina stumbled through the portal and came out beside Telyn, brushing snow and ash from her clothes. Next was Cordelia, then, after a brief pause, Colton came through looking like Nox had been chasing him. His ash covered face was even more pale than it had been before they'd come through.

Skylar was last, with an amused smile at Colton, she said, "Welcome to the Winter Court."

Telyn could only stand in awe at how perfect it was. The cold air brushed against her skin, but it wasn't too cold. The snow swirled in different patterns, almost like it was trying to tell a story, and the quiet air was only broken by the wind and the occasional rustle of wings overhead.

This was home.

This was *her* home.

"C-can we go ins-side?" Zerina's teeth chattered as she wrapped her bare arms around herself.

"Of course." Skylar briskly took the lead, headed for the castle, and the others were close behind her.

Colton and Zerina shared a look of relief when the warm air of the castle settled over their chilled skin. Telyn kept close to Skylar as she led them through the bustling hallways. It reminded Telyn of the first time she'd walked into the Academy.

Only this time, she didn't have to find her own way.

The flurry of activity here was so different from the slow, almost stagnant, pace of Alidain. It looked like it brought a new adventure to each day unlike the bland repetition of the walls in Telyn's palace.

"Welcome to Ceris, the royal estate of the Winter Court," Skylar said with a flourish. "First thing's first, tea. Then we can work out the details of this search and rescue mission."

She took them to a drawing room, where warm tea and scones were already waiting. "Take a seat." Skylar gestured to the various chairs and cushions spread out around the room.

She plopped down on a velvet green love-seat and picked up a cup of steaming tea.

Zerina and Cordelia eagerly followed her lead. Cordelia snuggled into Zerina's side on a couch, a scone clutched in her tiny hands. Zerina wrapped her arm around the little girl's shoulders and took a small sip of tea.

If Telyn thought about it, with her red hair and green eyes, Cordelia could easily pass for Lilith and Zerina's daughter. Zerina had certainly developed a fond relationship with the youngest member of the court.

Telyn took a seat beside them, but Colton remained standing. Skylar noted this with a small shrug before she took a sip of her tea.

"You know Siluria and the princess best, where should we start?" Zerina asked.

A flicker of pain flashed across Skylar's face. "Brea... She's like a little sister to me..." She hesitated. "I can't imagine how terrified she must be right now."

Telyn's heart constricted in her chest and she moved to Skylar's side. She could smell the jasmine wafting off of Skylar's cup of tea as well as the underlying scent of snow and juniper that Telyn had come to associate with her. "We'll find her." She promised and gripped the other girl's hand lightly.

Skylar gave her a grateful smile. "It wouldn't be the first time we've had to track someone down," She agreed.

"So where do we start?" There was a pained look in Zerina's eyes.

Telyn was beginning to feel guilty for not insisting that Lilith come with them. She would have to make it up to Zerina later.

"In a panic, it's hard to focus enough energy for an exact location," Skylar explained, she set her cup down and steepled her fingers in front of her. "But the Enchanted Forest exhibits a stronger pull of magick, so most of us end up there."

"That's where we'll start." Colton's eyes were narrowed, as if he wanted to say something but wasn't quite sure how.

"Will Princess Brea be okay?" Cordelia asked quietly.

"Why wouldn't she?" Zerina pulled Cordelia into her lap.

"The big man said the forests were dangerous. He said there were monsters!" Cordelia clung to Zerina.

Cordelia had seen monsters before. Telyn could understand why she was so afraid. If Telyn was being honest, she was a little afraid too.

"The forests have all kinds of creatures, but most of them are nice." Skylar gave Cordelia a kind smile.

"We should leave now." Colton was pacing, leaving dusty, white footprints on the carpet.

"We won't do Brea any good like this. We should clean up, and rest. We can begin our search tomorrow," Skylar said.

Colton paused.

He seemed to have forgotten that they were all coated in grey-white dust from the debris of the palace.

"Yes, of course," He agreed quietly.

"You are all welcome to use the estate as you wish. Everything is at your disposal," Skylar said.

"You're too kind." Zerina smiled.

Telyn didn't know what had passed between her sister and the girl that sat beside her, but it was beginning to make her wonder. She was unsettled by how quickly Zerina had seemed to change from being love-sick to being completely fine with their situation.

And something was bothering Colton, but he seemed hesitant to voice it. They were never going to be able to get through this if they kept secrets from each other.

But then again, Telyn was keeping secrets of her own.

Skylar let them choose if they wanted to share rooms or not. Cordelia and Zerina chose to stick together. Colton and Telyn, on the other hand, opted for more privacy.

Telyn needed time to think. She'd pulled her family from danger's grasp for now. The part she was uneasy about was what Piran would do once Brea was back. What would he demand she do next?

And how could she keep everyone safe?

Whatever Piran chose to do next wouldn't be anything rational. It never was. So Telyn had to be sure he couldn't trick her into anything. She had to stay one step ahead.

She liked to tell herself that she'd already seen his trickery and she would recognize it. But if she was being honest, she didn't know if she would. He'd already done such a convincing job of making her think he was a good person, there was nothing to say he didn't have something else up his sleeve.

There was nothing to say that there wasn't some other hidden facet of his personality. There could be a side of him that was even worse.

With Queen Tara and King Bran gone, there was no one to stay his hand. He was the king now. He was one step closer to his goal of world domination.

All she could hope for now was that she and King Roland wouldn't fold under the pressure.

There was a soft knock at the door. "Come in," Telyn answered.

"You're still awake?" Skylar opened the door.

"I usually am." Telyn looked up.

"I'm sorry." Skylar stood in the doorway and narrowed her eyes at the carpet.

"For what?" Telyn asked, her confusion written on her face.

"For letting Nox stay my hand instead of rescuing you sooner," She replied.

"You had things at stake too. I wouldn't ask you to sacrifice everything for me." Telyn shook her head.

"You wouldn't have had to ask."

Telyn looked at Skylar for a long moment. She could hear the erratic beating of her heart. She had no doubt Skylar could hear hers as well.

"Who did you lose?"

Skylar's gaze shuttered.

So she had been right. There was someone involved in their little heist that she cared for. Someone who hadn't made it out.

"He was my best friend. He and I had been through everything together," Skylar said as she leaned heavily on the doorframe. "It seems you and I have that in common."

"Not getting the chance to say a proper good-bye." She agreed.

"Speaking of which, I have something for you." Skylar cleared her throat and pulled something out of her pocket. "I figured you might want this back."

Kassian's ring sat in the palm of Skylar's hand.

"You found it..." Telyn gently reached out to take it, afraid that if she moved too fast, it would disappear.

"I knew it was important to you. When His Majesty threw it, I saw how shattered you were over it," She said quietly.

Telyn fought back the urge to cry.

"Thank you."

Some of the weight lifted from her shoulders when she slipped the ring onto her finger. It felt like Kassian was with her again. It made her feel stronger. She knew it was silly that the presence of the ring made her feel like she could make it through the storm that raged around her.

"It's not silly. Objects hold power. Especially objects that are close to our hearts or those of the ones we love." Skylar retreated back to the door frame.

"I forgot how easily you could get in my head." Telyn's laugh was light.

"You should laugh more often." Skylar suggested.

"Perhaps when the war is over."

"The war hasn't even begun yet. The tension is building, but it hasn't snapped yet." Skylar frowned.

"Maybe not amongst the gods, but Carling declared war on me and my people when he messed with Alexander's head," Telyn's voice was cold.

Skylar shifted and looked out the window. "You're rather fearless, aren't you?"

"I spent my whole life being afraid. I don't want to be that girl anymore," Telyn replied.

"You aren't. You've grown. You're stronger. But no fear at all can be a dangerous thing."

"I am afraid, but I know what I need to do, so I'll do it." Telyn plopped down on the floor.

"Most people would still run from it." Skylar cautiously took a step into the room.

"I did run." Telyn pointed out. "I didn't go through with marrying Piran."

"Things would have turned out worse if you had. He's power thirsty, and though your power is greater than anything we've ever seen; it wouldn't be enough for him," Skylar's voice was bitter.

"We have to stop him." Telyn looked up at Skylar.

"He'll run Eralia and Siluria into the ground in his obsession for power," She agreed. "But we have to stop the war first."

"Piran is Carling's pawn, the same way I am Nox's. If we incapacitate the king, we at least inconvenience the god," She explained.

"Which gives us time." Skylar nodded. "So how do we dethrone the king?"

"From inside the castle."

The next evening, Telyn was the last one out of bed. She'd finally crashed for an hour or two before she woke up after dawn. Her conversation with Skylar the previous day had sparked the flame of hope that grew brighter as she worked out the details of their plan in her head.

"Did you actually sleep yesterday?" Zerina gave Telyn a quizzical look.

"Not really." Telyn admitted with a small smile.

"So you were plotting all day." Zerina sighed.

"You could say that." Telyn shrugged.

"Are we ready to go?" Colton asked with a yawn.

"I believe we are." Skylar walked into the room, tugging at the cuffs of her sleeves.

She was dressed in a pair of dark trousers, a loose tunic, and a pair of riding boots. Her wings formed a misshapen halo around her unkempt hair.

"Then let's get going," Cordelia said grimly.

Cordelia hadn't been with them long, but Telyn could feel the guilt gnawing at her. She felt like she'd stolen Cordelia's childhood. And now she was stuck on the front lines of a war.

The cold of the Winter Court didn't bother Telyn, she enjoyed the cool wind that pierced her feathers. Her court however, didn't feel the same.

Zerina, huddled in fur coats, was still shivering. And Cordelia clung to her legs. Colton was fighting to repress the tremors of cold, but every once and awhile, Telyn was able to spot one.

She shrugged out of her own jacket and tossed it to Colton.

Skylar glanced back at her. There was something unreadable in her eyes and Telyn found herself wishing she was as good at getting into Skylar's head as she was at getting into hers.

She flared her wings a little and let the air flow between her feathers.

Zerina shook her head with a wry smile.

It didn't take long for them to come to the edge of a dark forest. It made the sinisterness of Nym's forest look like a child's bedtime story.

The gnarled trees looked blackened and dead with a thick layer of snow on top of every branch. Telyn couldn't even see three feet into the gloom.

"It's not our prettiest forest," Skylar admitted. "In fact, most of us avoid it. It's high magickal intensity draws in some rather unpleasant guests."

Skylar grimaced.

"Should we send them back? I can go in alone, I don't mind it." Telyn suggested.

"We're not leaving you alone," Zerina objected immediately.

Telyn gave a pointed look at Cordelia.

Zerina sighed. "Alright. We'll sit this one out. But you have to sit it out too."

"Zerina, we can't just ignore the search. Princess Brea needs to be found," Telyn objected.

"I'll go with her." Skylar offered.

"I don't want the two of you going alone." Zerina frowned.

"It's nothing we haven't done before." Telyn scoffed.

"At your request, if I remember correctly." Skylar added.

"This forest is more dangerous." Zerina shifted on her feet.

"She can do it." Cordelia spoke up.

"The little one is right," Skylar said. "I'll have Portia sent over to aid you, Zerina."

Zerina locked her eyes on Skylar. "Don't ever let your guard down. My sister's safety comes first. She is your priority."

"She has been since the moment I met her."

Something about Skylar's words made Telyn shiver.

The raw honesty was unexpected. Skylar's eyes never left Zerina. Telyn didn't know how she knew Skylar meant it, but apparently Zerina could see it too. She softened a little, her hand dropped to the top of Cordelia's head.

"Don't make me regret entrusting her to you." There was a sense of finality in Zerina's words.

Skylar grinned. "I wouldn't dream of it."

Cordelia peeled away from Zerina's side and barreled into Telyn. She wrapped her small arms around Telyn's waist. "Please be careful."

"I will, I promise." Telyn smiled and picked up the little girl. "You know I'll always come back."

"Just remember, you can't help everyone else if you don't help yourself first," Colton said. He'd been fairly quiet the whole time, but he spoke now.

"I can handle myself. I'll be fine," Telyn promised.

"I trust you'll be able to find your way back?" Skylar asked.

"Yes, we'll be fine," Zerina replied.

"Good luck," Colton said.

"Hurry up and find that princess." Zerina picked up Cordelia and turned away.

"I'll try to hurry." Telyn grinned.

Zerina and Colton's footprints in the snow faded before they were even out of sight.

"She's homesick." Skylar said quietly.

"How can you tell?" Telyn asked.

"She wanted to stay with you because you've become familiar to her," He replied. "She misses that witch girlfriend of hers and she knows she won't be back in Alidain soon. So she's trying to keep as much of her home with her as she can."

"Maybe I should send them home. It's cruel to keep them here. It's dangerous. And though I trust my kingdom in Pip's hands, the people won't be happy about them taking my place." Telyn paced in front of the treeline.

"They'll always choose to stand by you. They know you need them. And they need you."

Telyn stared into the twisted trees, willing the knots in her stomach to smooth out.

"And you're fishing for time." Skylar noted.

"Aren't I always?" Her laugh was bitter.

"If you're afraid, you don't have to do it."

"No, I'll do it. I'll go. I have to. If I don't do this, if I'm not capable of even trying, how am I supposed to stop Carling?" Telyn paused and faced the forest.

"You keep looking at this like you have to do it all alone, but you don't." Skylar stepped in front of her and blocked her view of the trees.

"Yes I do!" Telyn gasped, trying to contain the torrent of emotions that flooded her mind. "If I depend on anyone else," She spoke around the lump in her throat. "Carling will take them away."

Skylar took Telyn's hand and placed it over her heart. The steady beat beneath Telyn's palm slowed her racing thoughts. "Listen to me," Skylar's voice was soft and gentle. "Carling can't take me away."

"You can't promise that." Her dread began to rise again. "You don't know how- you don't know what he's capable of."

"I do. I know he's horrible and cruel. But I made a deal with my own demon. He can't touch me." Skylar held onto her hand. "I'm not going anywhere. I'll stay by your side as long as you need me to be."

"Who-" Telyn paused and turned the information over in her head. "Seine."

"The one and only." Skylar smiled.

Telyn thought that there had only been two champions. So when had Skylar made her deal?

"So don't worry about him for now. Let's just worry about now and find Brea." She let go of Telyn's hand and it fell to her side.

"We can do this," Telyn said mostly to herself.

"Yes, we can," Skylar agreed.

She stepped out of Telyn's way and she stared into the dark forest once more.

"So let's do it." She took the first step into the trees.

Toxic Thoughts

> "The heart is an arrow.
> It demands aim to land true."
> -Leigh Bardugo, Six of Crows

If possible, the forest became even more imposing once Telyn stepped inside it's borders. The watery light from the winter wonderland behind them was cut off almost immediately. Telyn could sense Skylar as she moved beside her and she could feel the edges of her consciousness as it brushed against Telyn's mind.

The trees seemed to bend and warp further around them, impossibly making the pitch black forest even darker.

The noise did nothing to dispel Telyn's growing anxiety.

The snap of a twig, the rustling of feathers that weren't her own, and the screeching of an owl meshed together into an eerie song that sent uncontrolable shivers down her spine.

Branches snagged at her hair and clothes, and she stumbled over the roots that stuck out of the ground like grave markers.

A wolf howled in the distance and she let out a startled gasp.

She felt Skylar lightly take her hand. "The wolves here aren't dangerous." Skylar promised.

Neither were the wolves Telyn had met during her meditation, but something about it still felt off. It felt so dreadfully *wrong*.

Somewhere to their left a low moan floated through the trees and she suddenly felt light headed.

"Try to ground yourself. Don't let it's powers get to you." Skylar warned.

It was already too late.

Telyn could feel herself slipping away from the forest.

"*Turn back while you still can, child.*" A voice hissed in her ear.

"What do you mean?" Telyn fumbled around in the dark for any clue as to where she was.

"*This is no place for you,*" It hissed.

"Where am I?" She asked.

"*You're everywhere and nowhere. The answer you seek is one only you can provide.*"

"Must you be so cryptic?" Telyn fought to keep her head above the water that she felt rising around her, above the frustration and panic she could feel swirling inside of her.

Telyn!

Skylar's voice sounded muffled.

Where are you? Something was blocking her question.

Something was keeping her away from Skylar and she couldn't even see what it was.

Telyn remembered the last time she'd been in the dark. She trembled as the vivid accusations rang in her ears.

Telyn, don't give it what it wants, come back to me! Skylar's voice was frantic, but so far away.

Telyn fought against the water, trying to get closer to wherever she was calling to her from.

She stretched out her hand, fishing in the dark for some sort of line that would pull her back to Skylar. But nothing in the inky space surrounding her felt solid, it was all water. None of it felt real.

She could hear Kassian and Alexander's voices screaming at her that it was her fault. The sad blue eyes of a child flashed in her vision.

Finally, when she thought she couldn't hold on any longer, she brushed against something that felt vaguely human. The warmth that spread over her palm felt like an arm, and she clung to it with everything she had in her.

And just as suddenly as she'd been pulled under, she was yanked back into the forest. Into reality.

She was in Skylar's arms. Skylar was holding her up as she crouched close to the ground. Her face was covered in a light layer of sweat and blackish brown slime streaked above her brow and across her cheek.

"They shouldn't be out this early." Skylar swore under her breath and rubbed at her face, leaving more streaks of the strange substance.

"This place makes Nym's Forest look like a playground." Telyn groaned as she sat up.

"Something is wrong here. The mental manipulating monsters don't come out until daybreak. The fact that one is out now means that something scared it." Skylar helped Telyn to her feet.

"And we don't want to meet whatever it is." She guessed.

"Absolutely not." Skylar agreed.

"You're close to Brea, is there some tracking spell or something we can try?" She asked.

"There is, but it's a shadow magick thing. As far as natural talents go anyway."

So that's how Time had been able to find her.

It made her wonder how her mother had managed to keep them safe for so many years.

"Well," Telyn brought her hand up and their surroundings grew even darker. "That shouldn't be a problem."

"You never cease to amaze me." Telyn could only make out the glint of Skylar's grin in the gloom.

She let the wall of shadows fall.

"Give me your hand. It might work." She reached out for her.

She took Skylar's hand and watched as she closed her eyes.

Telyn felt a ripple of power go through her and her feet began to move on their own, taking her deeper into the forest. She pulled Sklyar along after her.

Before long, they came to a clearing. The circle of golden light that reflected off the snow contrasted the rest of the forest so much that it hurt Telyn's eyes.

When she could see around the glare, she found a small crumpled figure, half buried in the snow.

"Brea!" Skylar dropped Telyn's hand and she suddenly felt cold.

Skylar brushed matted blonde hair away from Brea's face and she stirred.

She pushed herself up onto her hands and knees and turned her face up to Skylar. Though partially hidden by the clumps of dirty hair that hung in her face, there was no mistaking the coal black that swallowed her eyes and stained the veins running from them.

Skylar gasped. *"Meus umbra..."*

"That's not Brea anymore." Telyn whispered.

Brea laughed, but the sound was broken and discordant. "You didn't truly think I would keep my shapeless form, did you?" Time's voice warbled out of the little girl and Telyn winced.

"Why won't you just stay dead?" Telyn asked as Skylar scrambled back.

"My plans are far too important." Brea's head shook.

"Who are you working for?" She demanded.

"You know him quite well. Figure it out yourself," Time purred.

"What kind of-"

Telyn wasn't able to finish her question. Brea, or rather Time in Brea's body, had disappeared faster than should have been possible.

"Come on, we're leaving." Skylar pulled Telyn back into the trees.

"But we had her!" She objected.

"She's possessed. That's not something I know how to fix. So we're going to go home and regroup." Skylar paused and let her think it over, let her make her own decision.

She didn't particularly want to stay out here with the monsters. "Let's go."

Telyn kept a tight grip on Skylar's hand as they wound through the trees once again.

The forest seemed determined to keep them trapped inside. More tree roots than Telyn thought was possible seemed to jump under their feet.

Her trousers were torn and bloodied from her scraped knees. Her palms stung from having to catch herself from falling so many times. The scent of dirt and decay shoved it's way into her senses and she fought off the urge to gag.

"This forest is going to be the death of me." Skylar groaned as she tripped for the umpteenth time.

The trees were too close together for them to fly out. Telyn felt stifled and weak not being able to fully extend her wings. She felt pinned down and small. She hated it.

"Is this another sentient forest?" She asked.

"Unfortunately." Telyn could hear Skylar brush herself off.

Telyn got the feeling that they were only getting even more hopelessly entangled in the forest. It was like a wooden cage.

Be quiet. Telyn froze as Skylar's whisper brushed against her mind. *Listen.*

She strained her ears, holding her breath as she waited for the sound that had driven them to silence.

The musky scent of smoke wafted through the trees. Then she heard it, the hungry crackling of a fire.

But there was still no light.

Where is it coming from? She asked.

I'm not sure.

She felt Skylar pull her off to one side and the smell of smoke grew stronger, but no flames leapt out at them.

Telyn was tense, ready to spring away from yet another invisible threat. She didn't particularly enjoy the fact that they would have to come back once they knew how to free Brea.

Follow me. She carefully stretched out the shadows, using them as extensions of herself to feel for the nearest exit.

She felt open air closest on their left, so she pulled Skylar along as she followed the trail of breadcrumbs she'd left herself.

Just as they came to an exit, hot blue flames leapt up in front of them.

Telyn stumbled back with a yelp and tripped over a tree root. She landed hard on the ground and sat frozen in shock.

Skylar pulled her to her feet and whistled. "I think we're going to be here awhile."

"No." She whispered. "We can't be stuck here."

The blue flames made Skylar's eyes look darker as they locked on her. "There's nothing to be afraid of." Her voice was gentle.

She shuddered as the flames spread across the forest floor. It reminded her of watching the Unseelie Court burn to the ground as Piran became it's king. It really went to show how destruction followed him wherever he went.

"Come here." Skylar motioned for her to come back into the trees, away from the line of fire.

She sat down on a fallen tree trunk and Telyn carefully perched beside her.

"This fire won't hurt you. It's meant to scare you, but it's not sentient like the forest. Nor is it capable of spreading far," She said.

"So we can just walk through it?" She asked.

"No, but I have an idea." Skylar watched the wall of fire carefully. "I can get us out of here. Do you mind?"

She'd come around behind Telyn and held out her arms. "You're going to have to stay close."

"Go ahead. If it'll get us out, do it." She nodded.

Skylar picked her up and held her tightly as a swirl of ice and snow enveloped them.

The world around them that had just been pitch black turned a brilliant white as the fire and forest were cut off from sight by the walls of ice that pressed in close around them.

Skylar quickly walked forward, the ice molded to her every move. It wasn't long before they met the resistance of the fire. Skylar gritted her teeth and pushed against it.

As soon as the resistance gave way, she set Telyn down and promptly face planted in the snow as her shield fell away.

"Skylar!" Telyn dropped to her knees beside the other girl.

Her breath clouded in the air in front of her. Her eyes were closed, her face smooshed in the snow.

"I'm fine." Skylar huffed and pushed herself into a sitting position.

"You don't look fine." Telyn's brow creased with worry.

"Just used too much energy." She slumped forward like a marionette with it's strings cut.

With an exasperated sigh, she hooked her arms under Skylar's and pulled her up. "Let's get you home."

She half carried, half dragged Skylar back to Ceris.

Zerina flew out of the front door, bundled in a heavy jacket. She completely ignored Skylar and immediately started to check Telyn over for injuries. "What in Noctem *happened* to you two?" She demanded.

"You're being quite rude to our host." Telyn noted. "I'm fine."

"She's not my sister." Zerina objected.

"Well, I would hope not." Telyn pulled Skylar around Zerina and into the house.

"Which way are your rooms?" Telyn asked.

Skylar mumbled vague directions as she leaned into Telyn.

She carried Skylar into her rooms and helped her into bed. "You're going to be alright, aren't you?" She asked, her hands clasped tightly in front of her.

"I'll be good as new after a bit of rest." Skylar promised.

"Good." She turned around to leave.

Skylar's hand closed around her wrist. "Stay?"

She looked so vulnerable at that moment. Her blue eyes were half closed, but focused on Telyn like she was the only thing in the world that mattered. No, not the world. The whole universe.

Skylar looked at her the way she'd so desperately wanted Alexander to look at her.

"Okay." She sat on the edge of the bed and Skylar's hand dropped to her side.

She watched Skylar for a moment. Her spontaneous and ragged breathing evened out and she heard her racing heart slow.

"Thank you for getting us out." Telyn brushed Skylar's hair out of her face. "But please, don't ever risk yourself like that again."

Telyn didn't remember when she fell asleep, but she woke to bright light streaming through the window. She was curled on her side, her legs hung off the bed, and her back popped when she sat up.

Skylar was still out cold beside her.

In her sleep, she didn't look as pained as she had been when Telyn had dragged her up to her rooms. She looked at peace. As if the past few days hadn't been able to rob her of anything yet.

It was like she was in a world where her best friend was still alive and Brea wasn't possessed. Telyn wished she could give her that world.

"Have you been awake this whole time?" Skylar yawned and sat up.

"No, I just woke up," Telyn admitted.

"We can sleep a while longer," Skylar said as she looked out the window.

She laid back down and folded a wing over herself to block out the sunlight. "I don't bite." She teased when Telyn didn't move.

Telyn sighed and crawled further onto the bed. She was exhausted and Skylar seemed to know it. Her wing covered Telyn as well. The dimness almost put her right back to sleep. It wasn't dark enough to cause her nightmares to resurface, but it wasn't light enough to keep her from sleep.

Skylar's feathers brushed against her shoulder and cheek and she shied away from the tickling touch.

Skylar's soft laugh rang in her ear as she scooted back and away from her feathers.

"Oh hush," She murmured as she closed her eyes.

Skylar's arm draped over her side, and to Telyn's surprise, she didn't feel as if she was being pinned down. Instead, she felt safe. Like this was where she belonged.

She realized that *home* was never just the Winter Court. It was Skylar.

That was why the ache in her chest dulled when she was with her. Why she didn't feel the urge to run north when she was near.

When she slipped out of consciousness, she was still thinking of her.

"Have you finally figured it out?" Nox's dark voice rumbled with amusement.

"Figured out what?" Telyn spotted the god of death sitting cross-legged in a field of roses.

"Your mate," Nox prompted.

"I don't-" Telyn started. *"What are you talking about?"*

"Everyone has a mate, it's typically easier for those with Silurian blood to find theirs." Nox plucked an orange rose from the ground and turned it over in his hands.

"Are you implying that-" Telyn paused. *"That Skylar is my mate?"*

"Darling, it was a little more than implied." Nox chuckled.

"How do you know?" She asked.

"The telepathic link. The constant pull that disappears when you're with her," Nox explained.

Telyn only stared at him.

"I had that once." Nox mused. *"Don't be foolish and lose her as I did."*

"I don't plan on it." Telyn's voice was quiet with shock.

"Does she know?"

"She's known for quite some time now."

"Why didn't she tell me?"

"Well I reckon, she didn't want to lose you."

Nox laid down the rose in his hands. "If you don't see how much that girl adores you, you are a blind fool."

Telyn opened her mouth, then closed it again. This was her business, not Nox's.

"I assume you brought me here for something other than discussing my love life?"

"Yes, actually. I come bearing a warning. The boy king grows impatient. He seems uncharacteristically bothered by his sister's disappearance." Nox stood up and brushed himself off.

"She's possessed. By none other than the evil spirit of my late uncle. We have to figure out how to fix that."

"There's a seer who can help you. Her name is Kallista." Nox began to wander around the field.

Where will we find her?" Telyn asked.

Nox continued to drift away, as if he hadn't even heard her question.

"Nox!" Telyn called out to him, but he remained unresponsive.

"If you were smart, you would walk away too." The voice sent a shudder up Telyn's spine.

"What are you doing here?"

"Negotiating our terms of war." Everywhere Carling stepped, the roses around him blackened and withered.

"There's nothing to negotiate." Telyn sneered.

"I just thought I'd give you a second chance to fix your allegiance." He dragged his foot through a row of roses and turned them to ash.

"You should have thought twice about altering Alexander if you wanted my loyalty." Telyn shook her head.

"I would rather risk not gaining you than losing my pawn." Carling gave a light laugh.

"You would also rather kill your sister's mate for sport than be a decent brother," Telyn sniped.

"He made the mistake of crossing me. The same mistake you are making now." Carling held his hands behind his back.

"You can forget it. You meddled where you didn't belong and involved me. In no universe would I take your side after that." The defiance in Telyn's voice would have made Zerina proud.

"Very well." Carling sighed.

"Just remember this is the path you chose." He reminded her.

"Oh trust me, I will." Telyn glared at him.

"Then I leave you with this. It is my promise to you." He presented her with a black rose that pressed itself into her hand.

Good For You

> "Hope is a powerful thing. Some say it's a different breed of magic altogether. Elusive, difficult to hold on to. But not much is needed."
> -Stephanie Garber, Caraval

Thorns pricked at Telyn's fingers when she woke up. It seemed Carling's sinister gift had come back to the waking world with her.

The god of war had meant the flower to be a threat. But death and loss weren't the only things a black rose symbolized. It also stood for new beginnings. The whole world would get a new beginning when she took him down.

"What's that?" Skylar's wing pulled back from around her, exposing her to the harsh sunlight.

"A threat." Telyn grimaced as she turned to face Skylar and the sun stung her eyes.

"From who?" When she sat up, she was far more alert than she had been moments earlier.

"Our favorite god of war." Telyn grimaced.

"How did he even find you here?" She asked.

"They have a habit of appearing in dreams when they're least welcome," She sighed and rolled the rose around in her fingers.

"What did he want?"

"To negotiate."

Skylar rolled her eyes and pushed herself to her feet. Her clothes were rumpled from sleeping in them, and her hair was a curled mess, but Telyn found it somewhat endearing.

"So, what are we going to do about it?"

"Do about what?" Telyn had zoned out for a moment.

"Carling." Skylar looked at her, something unreadable in her expression.

"We ignore him," She said it as if it was simple.

Skylar gaped at her.

"Nothing would anger him more than to know he's insignificant to our plans. If we act like we are not bothered by him, he'll try harder to make himself a problem. He'll get reckless, and then he'll make a mistake," She explained.

"He's a god. How can you be so sure he'll make a mistake?" Skylar asked.

"What are the gods if not flawed? He'll slip up eventually. And until then, we'll be on guard."

"Aren't you tired of walking around on eggshells with them? Aren't you tired of living around their whims?"

A flicker of something lit up behind her eyes. Hope maybe? "It's always been like this," Telyn's voice was soft.

Skylar was gentle as she took Telyn's hands in her own. "But it doesn't always have to be, we could forget about the war, let the gods handle their own problems. We could live our lives the way we want and not worry about any of this."

It *was* hope. And now that she was listening, there was more of it. "It'll only get worse if we ignore it all. Nox has already told us that if Carling has his way, Viridium as we know it will end."

Skylar hesitated.

Telyn knew it was because she wanted to argue that Siluria wasn't a part of Viridium.

But she knew Telyn had a responsibility to her kingdom. The same way she had a responsibility to the Winter Court. She couldn't leave them to the mercy of the war while she sat safely in another realm.

"I suppose the world can't wait forever." She sighed and raked a hand through her hair.

The two of them walked together to the dining hall, where a mix of familiar and new faces mingled.

"Portia, I wasn't aware you were bringing friends," Skylar said.

"I only brought one." The girl that answered had curled green hair that fell to her shoulders.

She motioned to the girl who sat beside her. This one had long, straight, lavender hair.

The other faces were far too familiar to Telyn. Alexander, Pip, and Lilith sat on the far side of the dining table. The moment Alexander's eyes landed on Telyn, his grin fell and his eyes hardened.

"Pip." Telyn smiled and pointedly ignored Alexander.

"We decided to come see how things are going." Lilith smiled. She was seated beside Zerina, who had an arm draped over her shoulders.

"We've run into some complications, but we're handling it," Telyn said.

"The King and Queen of Eralia died at *your* wedding, their princess is missing and you're *handling* it." Alexander scoffed.

"Yes, we're handling it." Telen glared at him.

"I fail to see how sleeping in is handling it." Alexander's voice was cold.

"That is enough." Skylar scowled.

"Her incompetence is far from my fault," Alexander said.

"You will not speak of your queen that way." Skylar's voice was angrier and colder than Alexander's had been.

"You have no authority over me."

The two were locked in a stare down.

"While you are in my court, you will learn to manage your tongue. Should you speak to *any* woman in an unbecoming manner, I will have it removed from your head."

Gone was the playful girl who'd pretended to fight Telyn to catch the attention of some guards. In her place stood the High Lady of the Winter Count. It was a side of her that Telyn had never seen before.

It both excited and terrified her. And it scared Alexander into silence.

"Am I understood?"

"Yes, ma'am. " Alexander refused to meet Skylar's eyes across the table.

The Lavender haired girl cleared her throat and glanced at Portia before she spoke, "Well now that our little dominance skirmish is over, we should discuss our plans for the rest of the day."

"Yes, Vespera. I've already gone over a few things with Zerina, but I was wondering when would be a good time to train both of you, Telyn." Portia locked eyes with Telyn.

"Not today... We've been tasked with finding a seer by the name of Kallista," Telyn said.

"No one has seen her in centuries "Portia frowned.

"But I'm sure Telyn knows exactly where to find her." Alexander's false optimism made Telyn's stomach twist. He was only there to watch her fail, and they both knew it.

Pip's intentions may have been good, but he had only tagged along to make Telyn's life miserable.

Telyn refused to allow him the pleasure of derailing her plans for the day.

"I believe we should be focusing on finding her because even if she has fallen off of the face of Siluria, she's got to be somewhere. And Nox thinks she can help us. He's never pointed me in the wrong direction before." He'd only withheld important information on several occasions.

"Telyn is at the head of this search. Whatever she needs, I'm going to comply with. The rest of you have the choice to disengage now, or help us fix this mess," Skylar said.

"Kallista was my friend," Vespera said with a soft voice. "If she is to be found, I would like to be present when it happens."

"Of course." Telyn smiled. "We probably can't accomplish this on our own anyway, so any help is most welcome." She was glad that Skylar's friends seemed so eager to help, no matter the situation. If they were less like, well fae, and a little more like Alexander, Telyn could see her task being immensely more difficult to manage.

"The best place to start would be her home." Portia suggested.

"Do you think Wes would be willing to help?" Skylar asked.

Vespera gave a short laugh. "The man has entirely too much time on his hands. He would help you catch a sphynx if you asked nicely enough."

"Don't speak for me, please and thank you." A voice came from the door.

Telyn hadn't noticed anyone else had arrived, but Skylar seemed unsurprised as the stranger came to perch on the arm of her chair.

"Thank you for joining us, Wes. I hope I didn't interrupt your nap." Skylar's smile was a bit wry as she shifted her gaze to the new man.

A mess of dirty blonde curls fell into his eyes as he leaned down to survey Skylar's plate of untouched food.

"Not at all. It was scheduled to end an hour ago. I simply enjoy taking my time to wake up."

Across the table Telyn heard a small giggle escaped Lillith's lips.

Wes was going to fit right into the group just fine.

"I should take my leave then." Pip cleared their throat and rose from their seat.

"Take the girls and Colton with you," Telyn said. "I don't want them here if things turn sour."

"There is no way in the twelve realms I'm leaving you here to deal with this alone. What if Piran changes his mind and comes for you?" Zerina demanded.

"I'll be fine."

"She has the aid of the Silurian Courts," Skylar said calmly. She'd been expecting the hesitance as much as Telyn had.

"She'll come to no harm while she's with us." Vespera promised.

Zerina looked at the fae women for a moment. Respect and worry warred behind her eyes, but eventually, she gave a terse nod and stood.

Lillith rose with her and gave her hand a small squeeze.

"She'll be okay." The whispered promise had Zerina striding out of the room.

Telyn hoped it was in search of Colton and Cordelia.

It didn't take long for the witches and Alexander to follow her out.

"This whole situation seems a bit fishy." Wes wrinkled his nose as if mentioning the smell had brought it into existence.

"Would you care to elaborate on that?" Vespera drawled.

"Think about it, the prince sets out to marry our Lady Morris."

Skylar cleared her throat, interrupting Wes' speal.

"Whatever." Wes rolled his eyes and continued. "She leaves him at the altar and the whole wedding hall goes down in dust. The only casualties being his parents, who happen to be the ruling monarchs of our kingdom, and his sister mysteriously vanishes. It just seems too perfect an elimination of the royal family to not be orchestrated."

"I'm sure some poor woman was outraged that someone dared to steal her poor prince's heart then wound his pride before the whole kingdom." Disdain tinged Vespera's voice.

"What human woman has that kind of power? We were all here, Siluria had a separate ceremony planned," Portia said.

"What?"

Four sets of eyes turned to Telyn.

"You didn't know that wasn't the official marriage ceremony?" Wes asked.

"If I had known it was a void ceremony, I wouldn't have caused such an uproar." Telyn shook her head in disbelief.

"She wasn't raised here." Skylar reminded the others.

She turned to Telyn. "That was the human ceremony, it was a show for Eralia to see. The true ceremony was to be held here. It was going to be a traditional Silurian wedding, and that's the one that would have bound you. Either way, it couldn't be prolonged. You got out at, likely, the last possible moment."

"Back to Kallista." Telyn shook her head again.

It was a lot to process, but they didn't have time to be distracted by such trivial matters.

"Her house, that's where we start. We search the place top to bottom for any clue as to where she might have gone," Telyn said. "And we go from there."

"Portia." Wes looked at her from across the table.

"The rest of you would truly be lost without me." Portia gave a small smile.

She closed her eyes and a second later, soft purple smoke swirled beside her.

Her portal was different from Skylar's. It seemed calmer and more stable.

"Ladies first." Wes grinned.

Vespera rolled her eyes before she squeezed Portia's shoulder and stepped into the inky darkness of the center of the portal.

Telyn followed the other woman's lead and she felt Skylar follow her as she made her way over to the portal and stepped in.

The other side of the portal was almost as dark as it's center. Dust coated everything, and the shadows were so thick, it was hard to tell where one surface ended and another began. Bookshelves were almost more dust than they were books, and the writing on the spines were illegible through it. Mounds sprung up from the floor, the objects creating them lost to imagination.

Portia stepped through the portal last and snapped her fingers. A small flame hovered in her palm and illuminated their surroundings.

"I haven't been in here since she left." Vespera whispered in awe.

"It looks like no one has." Skylar commented.

"Well, I'm not sure we'll find anything with all of this dust." Telyn was beginning to feel skeptikal. She'd known it had been centuries since this house had been inhabited, but somehow she'd expected the area to be more... preserved.

She hadn't accounted for dust obstructing her clues.

"Can't hurt to look around." Wes shrugged.

They all moved to different parts of the room and began dusting off shelves, books, and odd little trinkets.

It felt like hours before they'd made any progress. Telyn's fingers and legs ached from walking around and prying things apart. Eventually, she plopped down on the floor. The dust around her was riddled with footprints and skid marks from people stumbling and tripping over one another in the small space.

Telyn's arm fell against a slim leather bound book that felt different from the other books she'd found. It was rougher around the edges and looked like it had been used more than the others had.

She carefully pulled the cover back and examined the front page. Cramped handwriting filled the space. It was in Silurian, but Telyn's mind had no trouble understanding the words. They spilled all of the details of what Kallista's personal life used to be like. The woman had been miserable. The world around her had grown stagnant and there was no joy or discovery in her life any longer.

No wonder she'd left.

"Hey guys, I found something," Telyn said.

Skylar plopped down beside her and the others crowded around the two of them. "What is it?" Skylar peered over Telyn's shoulder.

"I think it is, it was her journal," Telyn answered.

She flipped through the pages, careful not to rip the fragile yellow pages until she came to the end of the entries.

'The day has finally arrived,
I'm going to leave this dreadful place!
I haven't told anyone where I'm going in case something goes wrong.

But, I believe I've figured out how to get to Nihiliara. They claim it to be the land of nothing, but I don't believe that. There has to be something out there, something that's just waiting to be discovered. All I have to do is be brave enough to go find it.'

"Well, we know where she is now," Wes said.

"Yes, but how do *we* get there?" Vespera asked.

It was a simple enough question. And Telyn thought it might have a simple answer. "We portal there," She said.

"How would we do that?" Portia asked. "I've never seen it, so there's no guarantee I can come up with a portal there."

"I've been there." Images of a sea of black inky blood flooded to the surface of Telyn's mind. "Not, in person, but it's all we've got."

"There's no harm in trying." Skylar shrugged.

"It could take us to some random place." Portia objected.

"And we have you, so we can get back home quickly if we do end up in the wrong place," Wes said.

"With all of us there, it can't be that dangerous," Vespera said.

"Very well." Portia sighed. "Give me your hand." She stretched a hand out to Telyn.

Telyn took Portia's hand and focused on the scenes from the dream she'd had when Nox had first revealed himself to her. Then she channeled those thoughts to Portia. She could feel the power flowing through her and into the other girl through their linked hands.

When she opened her eyes, a portal of pure darkness swirled before the group.

Telyn was the first to step through it.

It was exactly like it had been in her dream, though now she could tell that the agitated waters were not blood. It was just black water. It was thinner than it had felt in her dream, more like the consistency it was supposed to be. The grass was more vibrant too, now that it wasn't being projected through magick. It definitely wasn't nothing, but it still felt so empty.

The others filed through the portal, and Portia held it open after she crossed. She looked hesitant to venture out into such a strange place.

"This is it," Telyn said.

That did nothing to ease Portia's worried look.

"How about you three wait at the cabin. I can get back from here. I need to have a word with Skylar." Alone.

"If you find Kallista, bring her back immediately," Vespera said. She was holding onto Portia's hand, and the other girl was clutching it like a lifeline.

"Of course." Telyn smiled.

Wes winked at Skylar before he backed through the portal and vanished.

Portia and Vespera were next.

Once they were gone, the portal closed in on itself behind them.

"What did you need to talk about?" Sklyar asked as she eyed the inky water that lapped mere inches from her feet.

"Nox told me more than just to find Kallista," Telyn said.

"What else did he tell you?"

"Something you haven't."

Skylar looked nervous now. Her eyes fluttered to the grass beneath her feet as she swallowed.

"You could have told me we were mates."

"I didn't want to scare you." The admission was softer than the breeze that rustled the grass.

"It doesn't scare me. It answers questions I've had my entire life," Telyn said.

"Being mates doesn't ensure you won't leave me. All it means is that genetically, we are made of the same things. And we complete each other. It doesn't promise me your love, that is still your choice. And I didn't want to push a decision on you. I didn't want to move too fast and scare you. I know you're mourning for your fiancé. It was not my place to intervene."

"That was a lie."

"I was being completely honest!"

"No, not you. The fiancé story. I was never engaged. He was my best friend, and I loved him. When he died, I was heartbroken, but there was never anything official or long term between us. It was just stolen time to say words we'd left unspoken the first time."

"The first time?"

"Kassian died twice. Once protecting me from a guard acting off of the assumption I was a witch. And then again after my uncle died. Their lives must have been linked without my knowing." Telyn frowned.

"Well, I'm glad you have trusted me with this, but it doesn't change where I stand. I will wait. However long you need to process and mourn your losses. However long it takes you to figure out your feelings. It will be your decision."

"Thank you." She gave Skylar a soft smile.

"You aren't supposed to be here." A voice growled from behind them.

Skylar whirled and took a step in front of Telyn.

"We're looking for someone, a seer named Kallista." Telyn peered around Sklyar's shoulder.

A woman stood in a defensive pose. Her dark brown hair was twisted into a harsh braid that fell down her back and her brown eyes were cold. "I didn't want to be found."

"Nox sent us to find you. We need your help."

"Of course." Kallista raked a hand through the wisps of hair that framed her face. "What has he muddled in this time?"

"The princess has been possessed by a shadow demon. We need to know how to get rid of it," Skylar said.

"How far has our realm fallen that they must seek me for a simple exorcism?" Kallista sighed.

"You would be surprised how much changes when you're gone for centuries," Telyn said. "We just need to know how to do it, then we'll leave you to your solitude."

"You need fire and a few well spoken words." Kallista folded her arms across her chest.

"And those words are?" Skylar asked.

"*Protero inferī,*" Kallista said.

"Great, we'll be on our way then. Thank you for your help." Telyn smiled.

"Vespera says hello," Skylar said.

A moment of hesitation flickered across Kallista's features.

"I'll come with you. It's high time Siluria had a proper seer again." Her gruff demeanor was easy to see through. She missed her friend.

Skylar opened a portal back to the cabin they'd left behind. It didn't take long for the three of them to file through.

On the other side, Portia's fire still illuminated the room.

There was a moment of shocked silence when the three returned.

Vespera was the first to speak. "Welcome home, old friend."

"She really does exist," Wes said with an awed whisper.

"I'll let you guys catch up, but I need to go back to the Winter Court and figure out what our next move is," Telyn said.

"Come on, I'll take you home." Skylar held out her hand and Telyn took it.

Armor

> "Fight because you don't know how to die quietly.
> Win because you don't know how to lose."
> —— Nora Sakavic, The King's Men

The world outside was bright and green with crisp cool air. They were in spring. The season contrasted to the familiar comforts of winter so greatly that Telyn took a moment to pause and admire the scenery. Skylar gave her a soft smile.

"You know, you aren't confined to the Winter Court. The others like you, they wouldn't mind if you visited them every once and a while. Or stayed even," She said.

"I like winter, I've just never seen colors like these back on Viridium." It was the truth. Spring was pretty, but it didn't hold the comforts of home.

"Viridium isn't as connected with it's nature as Siluria is. Many of us rely on nature for our powers, and in turn, the world is nurtured when we use our powers. It's a balanced system that's sustained us for as long as any of us can remember. Many of the rulers in Viridium were always more concerned with gaining more power than they needed, they tool more than they gave, and it destroyed the balance."

The way Siluria worked was the way Telyn thought all of the realms should work. How all of the kingdoms should work.

They should work together for things that benefited them all. Instead they were practically at war with each other. They weren't just detroying each other, they were destroying everything little by little, and no one else seemed to be able to see it. It broke Telyn's heart that her people would never see anything as beautiful as they view in front of her now. They likely would never even try to restore the balance that had been broken long before she was born.

"Come on, we have work to do." Skylar's voice was gentle as she nudged Telyn forward.

She was right, she'd made a lot of progress today already, and there was time to do more. She just needed a plan.

Unfortunately, that plan would have to include returning to the forest. She fought back a shudder as she remembered what it felt like to be trapped in the inky darkness that she'd only found in there.

It was the last place Telyn wanted to go, but it needed to be done. So, she would do it.

Then she realized a slight detail she'd missed.

Kallista had said they would need fire to banish the shadow.

Telyn didn't know how to manipulate fire. It was one thing that Telyn had tried and failed.

And she'd sent Zerina away.

"We may have a slight problem," She said.

"What is it?"

"I can't manipulate fire. Not to the magnitude we're going to need it. I know what people have said about me and how I'm supposed to have control over all of it, but the flames have never responded to me the way they do to my sister and grandmother. I'm not who they need me to be."

"Portia will help us. I'm sure she'll be back tomorrow to gush about her reunion with Kallista. And you're all you need to be, don't forget that." Skylar smiled.

"You didn't want to stay and catch up?" Telyn had assumed Skylar would want to have some time with her friend as well.

"I never knew Kallista. She left long before I was born. The others are much older than I am, even if they don't look it." Skylar's smile took on a more playful twist.

"How old are you?" Telyn realized that she didn't know. She didn't even have a vague idea. Skylar was fae, she could easily be over a hundred years old.

"I'll be eighteen this month."

The answer surprised Telyn. She hadn't met another immortal so young, outside of her own siblings and cousin of course. Everyone seemed to be so old, and Skylar knew just as much as they did. She'd expected Skylar to be older.

Skylar laughed. "You weren't expecting that."

"You talk like them, I may have slightly misjudged your age." Telyn shrugged in an attempt to play off how wrong she had been.

"They practically raised me after my parents died. It was only natural for me to mimic them. They were my examples. They taught me how to lead my court." Skylar wore a fond smile as she talked about them.

She'd found her family the same way Telyn had found hers. And it seemed they both owed the discovery to coming into power. It was strange for her to see how close the people within the palace walls were. And it was strange to see how similar she was to Skylar despite being raised completely differently.

When she'd lived in Micaera, she'd seen all of it from the outside, and the royal family had always seemed so cold and disengaged. But now she wondered if they operated similarly to the way she did, the way Piran and his family had before they'd died. If they shared warm smiles and laughed over dinner together.

King Roland was the only ruler who seemed to be unaffected by the blooming war. That would change soon if Telyn didn't find a way to stop it before it spread.

When they reached Ceris, a familiar figure was arguing with the guards at the gate. "I demand you let me in. My *daughter* is in there!"

Nolan appeared to be absolutely livid. He jabbed a finger at one of the guards as he went on, an angry vein popped out of his forhead.

"Do you know him?" Skylar whispered, her brow was furrowed as she watched the situation that was spread out in front of them.

"Yes, he's looking for Cordelia, but I sent her back to Alidain." Telyn frowned.

Nolan turned at the sound of Telyn's voice, his demeanor relaxed and his face began to lose the unnatural amount of red it had been holding.

"Telyn, they've left Cordelia here! Alone! She's just a girl, she shouldn't be alone." Nolan walked over to Telyn as she and Skylar came closer to the estate.

"What do you mean? I sent them all back to the castle," Telyn said.

"They all came back without her." His hands flapped in a vauge direction away from them. He wasn't taking the situation well at all, but Telyn couldn't exactly blame him.

Telyn sighed. "Well, if she's been here, she's been in good hands. I'm sure they've taken care of her while we were away."

"Why don't you come in? We can find her and we'll all have dinner." Skylar nodded to the guards and they stepped away from the door to grant them access.

As soon as the three of them stepped inside, Cordelia came barreling down the hall in a blur of red, yellow, and green.

She crashed into Nolan and he wrapped his arms around her with a grin.

"Father! Everything here is so magickal! You can feel the magick, can't you?" She asked. She nearly vibrated with excitement, the green ribbon that had been tied neatly around the waist of her dress this morning was half undone and lopsided.

"Yes, I can feel it." Nolan laughed as he wrapped his arms around her. "I've missed you."

"When did this happen?" Telyn's voice was soft as she watched the pair.

"Well, it's not official, but I'm planning on adopting Cordelia once things have calmed down." Nolan flushed.

"That's wonderful." Telyn smiled.

"I believe this is cause for celebration," Skylar said.

"Dinner?" Cordelia sounded hopeful.

"Girly, we've been feeding you tarts all day, it's not as if you're starving." A maid chuckled as she passed and carefully fixed Cordelia's ribbon.

Nolan ruffled Cordelia's hair and wrapped an arm around her shoulders.

"Tarts or not, we're having dinner." Skylar smiled.

The table in the dining hall was piled with steaming hot plates of food. The smell of freshly roasted chicken made Telyn's mouth water. Mashed potatoes, green beans, flakey tarts, chocolate pudding, and more sat around the table, just waiting to be eaten.

"I'm here for dinner." Wes grinned from the doorway as the others settled into their seats.

Nolan was frozen in his seat, his eyes glued to Wes' ruffled form in the doorway.

Wes' blue eyes seemed pinned to Nolan as well.

"Do you two... know each other?" Skylar asked.

"Not yet." Wes grinned even wider as he strutted over to the table.

Telyn covered her mouth to muffle a laugh. She didn't know what was going on, but it sure was amusing.

"Who are the new humans?" Wes asked.

"This is Nolan, he's a member of Telyn's court." Skylar gestured to Nolan as he spoke. "And that's his daughter, Cordelia."

"Daughter?" Wes' grin faltered.

"Yeah! He adopted me!" Cordelia chimed in happily before she shovelled a forkful of green beans into her mouth.

"Well, I will be. Once things have calmed down a bit and Telyn has time to approve the papers."

"I'll sign them the moment you bring them to me, war or not." Telyn smiled.

"Thank you. It's much appreciated." Nolan smiled back.

Wes' grin was back and his eyes were still on Nolan.

Skylar smiled to herself and speared a piece of chicken with her fork.

That gesture was what made everything click in Telyn's head. She realized that Wes was looking at Nolan the same way Skylar looked at her.

Holy puddlefish...

You've picked up on it as well. It certainly took you long enough. Skylar's amused voice filled her head.

Does this mean they're mates?

I believe so. And Wes knows it. I think your friend is just stricken by how pretty Wes is.

Are you in love with him as well?

Telyn's eyes glittered as they met Skylar's across the table. She flushed at Telyn's teasing and gave a small shake of her head.

For me, no one can compete with you.

Telyn smiled. This was the closest thing she'd had to a family meal in what felt like forever. The gentle bickering between herself and Skylar, the looks shared between Wes and Nolan, Cordelia's childish obliviousness. They weren't worrying about saving the world. They were just enjoying each others' company and having fun. It felt like what having a family was supposed to feel like.

Telyn wanted to have more times like this.

It was the reason she fought.

She fought for a future for herself. She fought so Wes and Nolan could have a safe space to fall in love. Telyn fought so Cordelia could have a father, or perhaps two. She fought for her sister's happiness. She fought so Colton could seek his truth.

Telyn wasn't fighting for the world.

She was fighting for her family.

The world might need her, in whatever twisted sense Nox saw it as, but the world meant nothing to her if her family wasn't in it. Her family needed her more than anyone, even the people she was supposed to lead. To her, they came first. She wanted them to be able to have small intimate moments like this, where they could feel the peace, and simply be.

That was her reason for pushing against Piran and Carling, and everyone else who meant to harm them to get to her.

After dinner, Skylar showed Nolan to a guest room near Cordelia's.

Wes had decided to stay as well. He insisted he knew his way to a room he'd stayed in before. Telyn suspected he just wanted an excuse to spend some time with Nolan, uninterrupted.

Telyn and Skylar went back to Skylar's rooms, ending the night where they'd begun it.

Somewhere nearby, someone was playing soft piano music. The sound seemed so mournful and hopeful all at once. It reminded her of the music she used to play with her mother. It made Telyn want to dance.

When she turned to Skylar, she had a hand held out to Telyn. "May I have this dance?"

Telyn took Skylar's hand with a smile and she pulled her into her arms.

With one hand on Telyn's waist and the other in her hand, Skylar led her into a slow waltz. And she let the music lead her.

Telyn knew by the way that Skylar moved as she spun her around the room that their hearts were the same. Not only were they hearing the same music, but it spoke the same words to both of them.

The fear and grief of the past weeks, the worry, and anger, it was all there, in the notes of the song. Telyn felt like she knew herself better in the music, like it wasn't as hard to identify and address the things she was feeling. And something told her that Skylar felt the same.

She didn't have to think as her feet moved. They knew what to do on their own. They knew where Skylar would be.

She closed her eyes and listened to the music's voice.

It's alright to let go.

It's alright to love again.

You deserve every happiness life can afford you.

This time, it was not Skylar's voice that whispered in her head.

It was her own.

And she knew it spoke nothing but truth.

She did deserve to be happy.

And Skylar made her happy.

She didn't know what her future had in store, but she knew she wanted Skylar there with her every step of the way. She wanted her by her side as they dove into the darkness that surrounded their paths.

The last thing Telyn knew before she drifted into unconsciousness was that she was in Skylar's arms. She was happy, and she was safe.

The next evening, Skylar gently shook Telyn awake.

Moonlight was streaming through the window in the harsh way that the winter moon could. Telyn knew immediately that they'd been asleep for far too long. Something felt unbalanced, like the whole world was holding its breath. Everything was quiet and still. The only sound she could detect was the sound of hers and Skylar's breathing.

Something dangerous had come to Ceris in the day, and Telyn didn't know what it was.

She pushed herself to her feet and slowly walked towards the door. Skylar stopped her with a hand on her shoulder.

Are you sure we should go out there? Something's not right. Skylar's mind pulsed against hers, the sickening buzz of worry and uncertainty surrounded her thoughts.

We don't have a choice. I know it feels wrong, but if something has happened, we need to make sure everyone else is okay.

She took Skylar's hand from her shoulder and gave it a gentle squeeze. She didn't let go of it as she pushed the door open and stepped out into the hall.

Not a single maid or butler was in sight. The fire in the sconces burned feverishly low.

Whatever was here was affecting the magick that made Ceris come to life.

Everything felt wrong, and a sickening sense of dread grew stronger with every step Telyn took. It was too quiet. It felt like the life had been sucked out of the estate. Everything was more grey, it felt dead. And it felt like whatever had caused this was still there.

It felt like her and Skylar were the last living things there.

It was unsettling.

The instinct to run screamed at Telyn as she forced one foot ahead of the other. She knew these instincts were the ones meant to keep her alive, but she couldn't help it.

She had to get to the others, she had to know if they were alright.

She had to overcome the fear that gnawed at her bones with every breath.

The distance to Cordelia's room had never felt so big. A five minute walk on a normal day was taking forever to come to a close.

Now, it felt like they'd been walking for five hours already, and they weren't even halfway there.

The winding hallways seemed to lengthen and grow about six paces for every one Telyn took. They stretched further and further until Telyn felt like her eyes were playing tricks on her. Some of the sconces flickered down lower before they sprung back up to their original low level. It was a challenge to see much of anything in the dim light that lit their path.

She could have sworn she'd passed the specific crack on the wall that ran from under one sconce nearly to the floor at least once, probably twice.

Her mind was reeling with all of the horrible possibilities that could have fallen upon Nolan and Cordelia.

They could have been kidnapped, or mutilated and killed, left in their beds for Telyn to find as some sort of sick warning from Piran and Carling.

They had to be alive. There was no way they could have died without Telyn's knowledge.

But nothing in this place felt alive to her.

The only thing that reminded her that she herself wasn't dead was the warmth from Skylar's hand in hers as it seeped into her skin, and battled her fear.

She was likely the only reason Telyn was still moving.

She knew together they could end any threat to the estate, but that didn't eradicate the coursing fear in her veins and her pounding heart.

She couldn't help but think that maybe something much bigger than the two of them was roaming the halls of their home.

They finally reached the hallway that Cordelia's room was down.

The fires burned even lower, their fevered flames begging them to turn around and run from this horror while they still could. They knew something she didn't, and they were desperately trying to convey that the only way they knew how.

But Telyn couldn't leave her family.

She couldn't listen to their warnings when she was more concerned about their wellbeing.

She reached the little girl's door and peered inside.

When she saw what was inside, her blood turned to ice in her veins and she went still.

Fire and Ice

> "Why do people always assume
> volume will succeed when logic won't?"
> -L.J. Smith, The Return

Brea was in Cordelia's room. Her eyes were swallowed by shadows and she was even more emaciated than the last time Telyn had seen her. Her blonde hair was nearly brown with dirt and it hung in greasy matted clumps around her head. Her ribs stuck out in painful angles and her shredded clothes hung off of her thin frame. Cordelia herself was nowhere in sight.

The scene chilled Telyn to her core.

Brea turned her empty green eyes to Telyn and a wide, broken grin spread across her face. Her voice came out dark and warbled as she spoke. "I see you've come to play. The others were wise when they ran, but I feel this will be more fun."

Telyn shuddered and took a small step back. She knew she wasn't prepared to free Brea. She knew the words, but they were pointless if she spoke them without burning the shadow out of Brea's body.

And fire still refused to bend to Telyn's will.

That had been the task for the day, talk to Portia about learning fire magick. But that may be too late. *She* may be too late.

Telyn just hoped she would still be able to make it that far into the day.

Skylar kept close to Telyn's side as he stared down Brea. Telyn could see the heartbreak and pain in her eyes as she looked at the girl who had once been like a sister to her. It broke Telyn to see Skylar like that. Neither she nor Brea deserved the fate that had been pushed on them.

Telyn pushed the distracted thoughts from her mind and stared at Brea. She could do this. She *would* do this. For Skylar's sake.

She focused on the heat of her anger at the cruelty Skylar was forced to suffer through, the heat of how strongly she'd grown to love Skylar. The blazing fire that burned as she saw how poorly Brea had been treated in the time she'd been under Time's control. She concentrated all of that into the palm of her hand and willed it into existence, willed it to burn brighter than the fire that she felt burning inside of her.

A small spark flickered in her hand.

Then it fizzled out.

Brea roared with otherworldly laughter at the attempt. It sounded like shattering glass.

"You weren't strong enough to take me out the first time. I had to do it myself! What makes you think that you're capable of beating me now?" Brea took a slow step forward.

Telyn scowled as she summoned a more willing shield. Shadows snaked around her wrists, poised to strike as Brea paced closer. She didn't want to hurt Brea. She knew Time might not feel it, but she didn't see another way out of this. Skylar seemed to know it too, she stayed back, her hands clenched at her sides as she watched on helplessly.

Brea laughed again. "In time, you'll see the truth. Then you'll come crawling back to me, begging me to tell you how I've done it. Eventually you'll see that you and I are the same, the darkness that runs through my veins runs through yours, and it's impossible to escape it." Her voice was a hushed whisper. "You're weak while you cling to the light, but once the darkness consumes you, you'll be near unstoppable. You just won't be fighting for the same side anymore. You were born to play the part of the villain, darling."

"You don't know what you're talking about." Telyn's voice shook.

"I didn't spend thirty years in exile for nothing. I know far more than you ever will." Brea grinned. "Our little game is fun, but either way, you'll be the one losing everything in the end."

There was one thing that Telyn did know.

She didn't lose.

She wouldn't allow herself to lose. Not to Piran, not to her uncle, and not to Carling.

Too much had already been lost, but it wouldn't happen again.

This time the flames didn't spatter out. A small ball of fire hovered over her palm and she launched it at Brea and prayed to Nox that it would be enough.

"*Protero Inferi!*" She shouted.

Before Telyn could tell if it had worked, Brea was gone.

She'd just vanished.

There were no footprints or marks anywhere to hint at where she could have gone.

There were no scorch marks either.

Telyn didn't know what to do. She didn't even know what had happened.

"Did it work?" Telyn asked. Kallista hadn't said what would happen after she did it.

Skylar shook her head. "Brea would still be here if it had worked. He got away."

Telyn scanned the room again. There was no Brea, no Cordelia, no anyone.

Telyn backed out of the room and walked a few doors down to Nolan's room.

She didn't pause to knock as she barged into the room.

A vase shattered against the wall beside her head and she ducked away from the spray of broken glass. "It's me!" She shouted.

"Oh, Telyn." She could hear Nolan's relieved sigh from across the room.

"We thought you were the princess. Have you fixed her?" Wes asked. Judging by his posture and position in front of the others, he had been the one to throw the vase.

"No, but she is gone," Skylar said.

"What do you mean she's gone?" Cordelia asked.

"We tried to do the banishing spell Kallista taught us, but I must not have been strong enough because she just vanished," Telyn said.

Telyn could feel the disappointment in herself swell as she accepted the fact that they had failed because of her. Anger bubbled up into her throat and made it hard to breathe as fear and worry crashed over her like a wave. If she had trained a little harder, tried a little harder, been a little stronger, and a little less afraid, then Brea would be safe. And she would be out of Piran's line of fire. And Skylar wouldn't have to worry about Piran trying to hurt her or take her away because her debt would have been paid. Instead, the five of them sat huddled in a room that felt like Nox had visited it, cowering in fear from someone who was already dead.

And Telyn knew it was all her fault.

Slowly the staff began to emerge from their hiding places around the estate. Ceris slowly began to return to it's normal schedule. The nervous energy that surrounded everyone made it clear that they had been very shaken when their princess had turned up, not quite being herself.

Despite the disruption, they had lunch laid out in less than an hour.

The incident hadn't seemed to change Cordelia's appetite at all either. She was scarfing down her food like she'd never see a full plate again.

Telyn couldn't blame her. She didn't know how long Cordelia had been out in the streets and she really hadn't known when her next meal would be. Telyn just hoped the girl would be able to realize she wouldn't have to live like that anymore.

Telyn knew that Nolan would give Cordelia the best life he could provide for her.

He wanted to be the kind of parent to her that his mothers had never gotten the chance to be for him. She could see it in the way he looked at her and constantly checked in to make sure she was doing alright.

Nolan was another constant reminder of how badly Time had hurt people. His life was another mistake that Telyn would have to fix.

Skylar gently squeezed Telyn's shoulder. "You're doing great," She whispered.

She didn't feel like she was doing great. She felt like she was losing again and she hated it. She didn't have anything else she could lose. At least not survive losing.

She felt like she would finally break if they managed to take anything else from her.

"We need Portia here. I need to be stronger." Telyn's voice was quiet as she pushed food around on her plate with her fork. It was nothing but the truth. Both times she'd faced her uncle, she had been too weak to stop him. She needed to do better if she expected to protect the people in this room and beyond it.

"You're strong enough, you just need practice. You're capable, you just need to learn control. No one should have to learn how to handle a situation like this. I am already so proud of you for even trying. So don't beat yourself up over one mishap. There will be other chances," Skylar said. She put a reassuring hand on Telyn's shoulder.

Telyn didn't understand how Skylar could have so much faith in her when she could barely believe in herself. Skylar always said she knew Telyn was capable of whatever she set out to do. And in the past, she had been right. But this time it felt so much bigger. There was so much more at stake, so much more to lose if she couldn't pull through. Had the expectations come from anyone other than Skylar, Telyn felt like they might have suffocated her.

Skylar had seen Telyn at that prison, and then she'd seen her cower in the face of Piran. Yet she still thought that because she'd made it this far, they would make it. That was the kind of faith Telyn needed to have in herself, but she couldn't seem to find it.

Once again, she couldn't escape the feeling that her mother would have known what to do. She would have taken charge and cleared the whole situation up within a day. This would all be in the past already, and they would have been able to enjoy this lunch like nothing was wrong.

From the stories Telyn had heard, Maria had always been sensitive to the peoples' needs, and a problem never lasted long when she was working on it.

Telyn was a little disappointed she'd never gotten the chance to see that side of her mother. That Maria had never been able to teach Telyn how to do the same. Instead Telyn was left here scrambling without her.

The Maria Telyn had known was a meek seamstress who was unable, or perhaps unwilling, to stand up for herself when her clients tried to take advantage of her.

Telyn would have done almost anything to have the strong example of her mother Lune had talked about. But there was no getting that woman back now.

So Telyn would have to continue to learn to manage without her mother. Even though she so desperately needed her.

It was nearly sunrise by the time Vespera and Portia arrived. They immediately felt how off everything felt. Portia's brow wrinkled in worry and Vespera frowned. "What happened here?" Portia asked.

"Let's just say we weren't prepared for a showdown this evening," Skylar said.

"It appears as if everyone's escaped unscathed," Vespera said.

"Including Time using Brea's body as a puppet." Telyn stood behind Skylar as they met the couple at the entrance of the estate.

"Oh…" Portia squeezed Vespera's hand.

"We have some work to do," Vespera said. Her voice was about as grim as Telyn felt.

"Indeed." Telyn's expression was solemn as she fought to rein in all of her thoughts and emotions that continued to ripple beneath the surface.

Remember, you're doing great.

Skylar's gentle words in her head soothed the storm that had been raging all night.

"Teach me how to control it." Telyn turned to Portia. "The fire, that's what we need. Teach me to listen to it and learn from it."

"Let's get this lesson started then." Portia gave her a small smile.

Telyn and Portia stood out in the snow a good distance from Ceris.

"First thing's first. Show me what you can do," Portia said.

Telyn brought back the feelings she'd used that evening and felt the heat materialize in her palm. The ball of flames was small, but it generated enough heat that Telyn thought it might burn her if she held it long enough.

"Good, it's a start," Portia said. Telyn could hear the strain in her voice as she saw what Telyn already knew.

"It wasn't enough," Telyn said it for both of them. She knew it was what Portia was thinking.

"It just isn't used to answering to you. Fire is more similar to plants and animals than you might think. It needs to be nurtured, fed, and sheltered." Portia cupped her hands together and her own little ball of flames sparked. "When what you start it with isn't enough, give it more. Draw from more sources, draw from your surroundings. You're only limited by the depth of what you feel."

Telyn watched as Portia's fire grew to triple it's original size.

"I know that with all you've been through, there is a lot for you to draw from. The well of your power has untold depths. Not only can you manipulate three different elements, but you've shown great progress and mastery in the short time you've been able to utilize your gifts. Draw from your experiences and those who have wronged you. Use his actions against him."

Telyn reached for any warmth she could draw from the air around her, the warmth of hers and Portia's breath.

Slowly but surely, the small fire in her hands grew. As she fed it, it pulsed stronger, the flames burning hotter, but somehow leaving her hands unscathed. Telyn watched in amazement as she watched a visual representation of her own power grow. She filtered in some of the anger and fear she'd felt when her mother had died and the flame sparked brighter. She thought about Nolan wheb he had been thrown into her cell bloodied and nearly dead, about Zerina, having to work for Time for her own safety, about how he had hidden Kassian away and used him against her when she had finally found some hope in the dark existance she'd found herself in; all thanks to him.

The flames grew bigger and brighter until the ball of it contained in her hands was bigger than her head. She could feel her control over it start to slip.

Portia shielded her eyes. "Don't give it too much or else it will grow out of control." The warning was neccesary. Telyn had been prepared to feed it more, let it grow until there was nothing left in her to draw from.

Telyn cut back on the feelings she was putting into her flames and they died down a bit. She reeled in the emotions she'd let spill out into and as she took the last of it back, the flames fizzled and died out in the palm of her hand.

Though the flames were gone, she could still feel the remnants of the power she had felt while she held it, the heat that had threatened to singe her fingers and hands. She had done it. She could control it now. She could finally do what she'd tried to do so many times before.

This time she wouldn't fail. Not with the memory of that power so close and fresh on her mind.

"Just remember to let it flow, feed it, but not any more than you need," Portia said. "Wild fires are easy to start, but hard to stop. Don't let it gain its own control. If you completely lose control of it, you'll never be able to get it back. You'll have to put it out some other way, and with a fire that big and powerful, that's going to be hard to do."

"How will I know how much is enough?" Telyn asked. She could feel the constant shift in the ebb and flow of the magick that found an outlet in her hands. It pushed to be released again now that it knew that it could.

It wasn't like the whip-quick reaction of the shadows or the calm obedience of the water, it was a hungry consuming kind of magick. It felt like it would burn her up if she wasn't careful.

She knew it would.

Portia had just said as much.

It would burn everything up if it was given the chance. But all Telyn wanted to burn was Time, and Piran, and Carling; though that might be pushing the extent of her powers.

"You'll know." Portia smiled. She didn't know the doors she'd just opened by teaching Telyn how to use the power that had lain dormant inside of her. Telyn wasn't sure she fully knew them herself, but she knew they were there. The opportunities she had waited to surface so she could finally rid herself of the god and the king.

"I'll know." Telyn thought she was going to start hearing that a lot more often. She was the only one who could know, wasn't she? They were all relying on her far more than they should, but she knew she couldn't let them down. Not without giving it her everything.

"Let's go find the princess." Telyn returned Portia's smile.

The women walked back to the estate together. They knew it was time for the hunt to truly begin. This time they would not be betrayed by a lack of understanding in control. Telyn wouldn't hesitate. She wouldn't let her fear get the better of her. She wouldn't let Time get the best of her. It was time for him to leave once and for all. He had gotten a second chance he didn't deserve, and Telyn would make sure that didn't happen again.

He had chosen the rules last time, he had planned his death and rebirth.

Telyn wouldn't give him that liberty this time.

This time, when they found Brea, they would bring her back. She would kill Time herself and he would never haunt her again. They would free everyone from the promises and threats that held them hostage.

Monster Hunting

> "You don't forget the face of the person
> who was your last hope."
> -Suzanne Collins, Hunger Games

Telyn and Skylar were going back into the forest, but this time, they weren't going in alone. Wes, Vespera, and Portia were with them, all wrapped in thick winter clothes against the biting cold. Nolan had opted to stay with Cordelia in Ceris in case anything went wrong.

With their plan in place, nothing should go wrong, but if Telyn had learned anything in her time alive, it was that something could always go wrong.

Winter seemed colder now that Telyn knew what darkness was waiting for her once she breached the tree line. She shivered and pulled her coat tighter around herself as the group came closer to the forest. The normally comforting chill of the Winter Court had turned frigid and unwelcoming.

Vespera and Portia huddled together, a ball of flames suspended in Portia's palms at a safe distance from any flammable items, but close enough that they could still feel the heat that emanated from it.

Wes was wearing what looked like three different jackets, and Telyn could barely see his face through the fur of all of the hoods.

Skylar stayed by her side, dressed much lighter than the others, already used to the cold nature of her home, including the air that surrounded them now.

Telyn wondered how often Skylar had had to come to this forest. How many times she'd subjected herself to the horrors inside it.

A mixture of cold and anticipation set Telyn shivering harder the closer they got to the forest. It was almost like the trees were sucking all of the warmth out of the air that they could. Even Portia's fire didn't seem to be providing the heat it should anymore. It pulsed and flickered as it fought to remain burning. As hard as that little flame fought, it wasn't enough, but they both knew they couldn't expend too much of their energy on staying warm until after they freed Brea and could go home.

The forest looked just as dark and menacing as it had the first time Telyn had gone into it. The same menacing branches reached out for her, their withered bark appearing to be cringing away from the cold as they were thrust forward. There was no sign of leaves or greenery. Even the trees that had the rough bark of a pine tree were left bare in the frozen forest around them.

"Let's do this," Telyn said, her hands clenched into fists at her side.

As much as she wished for a weapon, she knew it would be no help in here. The only thing that could help them was the power they already held. No blade would be able to cut through this twisted path.

The group plunged into the forest, armed with bravery and determination.

Once again, it didn't take long for all of the light to be swallowed up by the thick canopy of branches that intertwined in a thick lattice above their heads. The light that Portia and Telyn provided only pierced the darkness by a few feet to allow minimal visibility.

The eerie sounds of a half dead forest filtered through the hushed silence that surrounded them like a pocket.

The forest *felt* dead. The same dread she'd felt when her mother and Kassian had died filled her with every step she took further into that forest.

Once again, Brea could be anywhere in here, and they would never know until they stumbled into her. But this time, they were prepared. Telyn was stronger, and even if she couldn't do it alone, Portia was with them as well.

They were more than capable of doing it together.

Telyn took Skylar's hand as the forest grew darker still.

You'll be fine. I won't let anything happen to you.

I know. I'm not worried, this place is just unnerving.

They continued in silence until the paths led them to a clearing.

An empty clearing.

Watery light fell into the clearing, the absence of tree branches allowed it to light up. The light pulled at Telyn, it was an invitation to step out of the dark and into safety, even if it was only for a moment.

Slowly they filtered into the clearing. They looked for anything that Brea might have been carrying with her.

If there was one thing Telyn knew, it was that this forest didn't ever do anything without a reason. So they needed to find it's reason for bringing them to this clearing.

The only thing was, the forest didn't seem too keen on revealing it's reasoning. At least not easily.

An alarm went off in the back of her head, the vaugue suspicion that the clearing was a trap.

They turned over piles of leaves, checked under rocks and tree roots, and looked in the lower branches of the trees that formed the clearing, but they came up empty handed from every place they searched.

"It wouldn't lead us here just to strand us. So what are we missing?" Wes asked as he raked a hand through his messy hair.

"Maybe it's a trap." Telyn voiced the thought that had been naggin at her.

"It could be."

Telyn felt the energy of the group shift as they took in this possibility.

"Perhaps it knew you had information I needed."

Telyn whirled as a husky feminine voice sounded from behind her.

"Who are you?" Vespera asked.

"That is of no relevance. I need her." The woman pointed to Telyn.

She was tall, her skin tinged an unnatural shade of pink. With jet black hair that fell down to her waist. Telyn couldn't see the color of her eyes, it was still too dark to tell, even in the watery light they were in.

"You can't have her," Skylar said. She stepped between Telyn and the woman, forming a physical barrier.

"I'm afraid it's not your choice to make." The woman gave Skylar a sickly sweet smile.

"What do you need from me?" Telyn asked. She got the sense that this woman would do what she deemed neccesary to get what she wanted. They needed to be smart about this.

"I need to know about my son." She said, "And I have reason to believe that he's close to you."

"Kinada?" Telyn's voice was barely above a whisper.

"How do you know my name?" The woman's voice grew cold.

She didn't appreciate the unexpected information in Telyn's possession.

"A woman named Senekah told me a thing or two." Telyn stepped around Skylar.

"That infernal woman doesn't know what she's talking about." She waved a dismissive hand.

She clearly held the same fondness for Senekah as Senekah held for her.

"That's funny. She said you were the infernal one," Telyn said. "You're an inferi."

"Yes, once again, it's of no importance. My son however; is." She was getting agitated. Telyn could see it in the way her eyes bounced between the members of their group and her feet as her balance shifted from one to the other.

"What do you want with him? It's been eighteen years, and you weren't there for any of it." Telyn couldn't understand the fierce protectiveness that she felt when she thought of her cousin at the hands of this woman. She might be his mother, but that didn't mean Telyn trusted her.

"My reasons for leaving are probably more than your fragile mind can comprehend." Kinada rolled her eyes. "But, if you must know; I left because of his father. The filthy scoundrel got himself into a grave he couldn't dig himself out of, and I refused to let him drag me down with him. I was never there of my own free will anyway."

"So you left your son with a psychopath? You couldn't take him with you?" Telyn demanded. Kinada didn't sound like much of a mother to her.

"Noctem is no place for a child with mixed blood. As an adult, he stands a chance, but if I had brought him there as a child, they would have torn him apart limb by limb for the blood that contaminates ours. I did the boy a favor by leaving him with that pathetic excuse for a father."

"He certainly doesn't think so." And neither did Telyn. There had to have been a better way to handle the situation.

"Then he's a fool, and quite possibly not my son."

"Colton is one of the smartest people I know. I also know he was very hurt by your abandonment. I will not lead you into his life only for you to leave him again."

"I don't plan on leaving him this time."

Telyn was still skeptical. She had left once, what was to stop her from doing it again?

"Why do you want to meet him now?"

"Because it seems the realms have need of his power. And I don't intend on letting my son get trampled over in the mad grab for power that seems to be ensuing."

"What do you mean?"

"It's none of your concern, faerie."

"First of all, I'm not one of the fae. I'm some sort of hybrid, and you will put some respect behind *whatever* you call me. Second, Colton is family, and if something affects him, I am to be involved. *Third*, you don't get to call the shots here. You lost that privilage a long time ago."

"Oh, you must be Senekah's prized little gem." Disdain dripped from Kinada's voice. "You didn't think your side of the family were the only ones gifted with power, did you?" She laughed. "Being an inferi comes with certain abilities. My blood runs through the boy's veins, so it's only reasonable to think that he shares some of my gifts."

"Would you care to explain?"

Telyn hadn't missed the fact that the others were giving her space to talk. They had been silent ever since she'd taken the lead. What she didn't know was if it was because they respected her or if it was because they were testing her.

"Various things, most of them linked to Noctem, but the ones that work here are more powerful in Noctem." She stretched her hand towards the ground and it began to tremble beneath their feet. Another gesture towards the trees and they were bending away from each other, opening a gap in the darkness for more light to shine through and fall into the clearing.

"So can you please bring me to my son?"

Do you think we'll find Brea in here? Telyn projected her question to Skylar.

If Colton's mother is here and looking for him, it's a possibility that Time may be looking for his son as well. If Colton is nearly as powerful as she is then he needs to be taught how to use it. If we help her, we may be able to convince her to help us win this war.

Everything always came down to politics.

Telyn took a moment to think over Skylar's words. She had a point. Kinada could be a turning point for them in this war.

"Fine, I'll take you to him," Telyn said. "Portia, a moment, please?"

Portia stepped off to the side with Telyn. "What do you need?"

"I don't want to go straight to the palace, I want Colton to have some time to prepare. If you can bring us near the border, I can send a bird ahead for him. Would you do that for me?"

"Of course, just channel the energy of the place you want to go through me and I'll take care of the rest." Portia smiled.

It didn't take long for the group to get out of the forest and to the border of Alidain and No Man's Land.

As soon as they were on the other side of the portal, Siren appeared. Telyn frowned. The little cat had disappeared again when Telyn had been preparing to leave for Eralia, but now, here she was. Nearly the second Telyn had returned to the country.

Siren peered up at Telyn with yellow-green eyes and meowed.

"What is it, little one?" Telyn crouched and scratched Siren behind her ears.

Siren meowed again and gave a strangely meaningful glance in Kinada's direction.

"You want to deliver the message?"

Another meow.

Telyn took the quick note she'd scribbled and tied it to Siren's collar with a piece of twine.

The cat licked Telyn's hand once when she was done, then turned around and went back the way Telyn assumed she had come. Skylar crouched to give Siren a brief pat before she left.

As strange as the encounter had been, Telyn doubted it would be the most strange thing she would see all day.

"Alright, I know where we are. The palace is about a day's walk from here," Telyn said.

"Why did you take us so far from our destination?" Kinada asked.

"There are wards around my land, this was as close as we could get." Telyn lied with a shrug. "You can never be too careful these days."

"We should start walking," Wes said.

And walk they did. The fresh grass of spring was beginning to poke through the winter haze. The further they got from the border, the warmer it would get.

It was so strange, walking in the dewy grass after having spent so much time in the snow.

Skylar seemed to think so as well. Though her face was a mask of neutral expressions, Telyn could see the curiosity glittering in her eyes as she hopped from one patch of dirt to another. In the blossoming spring of Viridium, and away from the responsibilities of her court, it was like Skylar became a little girl again.

Despite the lack of the vividness of spring in Siluria, she still seemed to find amusement in it.

Telyn admired the way she could find joy in such small mundane things.

She envied it a little bit as well.

But she didn't have to. Maybe Skylar could teach her to see the little miracles of life again.

Once things had settled down.

Once they won the war.

She knew they couldn't truly have a life together until after the gods agreed to leave their lives alone. And that wouldn't happen as long as this war was going on.

As long as Carling lived, he would fight to make Telyn's life miserable.

And as long as she was alive, she would fight to keep him from succeeding.

Right now, they were at a stalemate, both too unsure of their next steps and how their current situations would affect their decisions. Telyn knew it wouldn't last long, but she welcomed the reprieve.

She hoped it would last long enough for her to get a break after they returned Brea control over her body. Once her debt to Piran was paid, she was free.

And she wanted it to be a Carling free time when she did.

It brought her a small sense of satisfaction to know that she had at least temporarily confused the god of war. Him taking his time meant that she'd proven she was an opponent he needed to think about. She wasn't easy to take out. Even for him. He needed a strategy to take her down, one that required him to actually think about how he was going to do it. And that meant she was far stronger than she'd been giving herself credit for.

For now, all she could do was chip away at all of the tasks she'd been given. It might have helped if people would stop adding things to her list.

But if it would help them in the long run, Telyn couldn't turn the request down. Having allies couldn't hurt. The more people on her side, the better chance she stood at getting through the mess she'd found herself in.

She snuck a glance at Kinada as they walked. The woman's gaze was focused on the horizon before them, her steps long and confident. She knew what she wanted, and she knew how to get it now that she'd found Telyn.

Telyn still wondered why she'd chosen now of all times to seek out Colton. It seemed almost too coincidental, and too random all at the same time. Wanting to protect him from the wild power grab that was beginning to happen made sense. Or it would have if she had expressed any concern for any of the other dangerous situations Colton had been in. But she'd left him with Time, and she was no where to be found when he had died. It would have made more sense for Kinada to come as soon as Time had offed himself.

If she cared about her son that much, she should have been waiting for the moment she could go back to him.

But here she was, much later.

What had kept her away?

Senekah's warning rang in her head.

Kinada Yukio is not a woman you should want to find.

Technically, Kinada had been the one to find them, but it still unsettled Telyn. There seemed to be some sort of history between Colton's mother and their grandmother. Telyn doubted it was standard mother-in-law problems. They had both lived too long to be bothered by something so petty.

It was too mundane for a family like theirs. Amongst mixed bloodlines and strange powers that no one had seen or heard of before, social problems would be the least expected history between the two women. Though there were likely some disagreements, there had to have been something that one of them had done to cause such a strong distaste for each other. With the Ramirez family, nothing was straightforward. There were likely more twists and details to this story that Telyn hadn't been told. It was just another myster she would have to unravel herself.

Which begged the question: What had they fought over?

Family Reunion

> "Maybe it's better to have gotten it right
> and been happy for one day
> instead of living a lifetime of wrongs."
> -Adam Silvera, They Both Die at the End

By the time they reached the palace, Colton and Senekah were at the gates, waiting for them. Senekah wore a scowl that carved wrinkles into her normally smooth skin and her eyes tracked Kinada's every step as the group got closer. Colton looked more reserved, though Telyn could still see the excitement that shimmered in his eyes as he looked at his mother for the first time he could remember.

"You just couldn't leave my children alone, could you?" Senekah growled.

"They aren't yours. In fact, one of them is mine," Kinada said. "Hello, darling." She smiled at Colton. Telyn could tell the smile was forced. She couldn't tell if it was because Senekah was there or if some part of her managed to be disappointed in Colton already.

"Mother?" Colton looked as if he might cry.

Telyn watched as he took a tentative step towards them.

Kinada reached a hand out to her son and he ran into her arms.

Telyn hadn't expected any less from him. She was his mother after all. Even if she had abandoned him, he was still a child that had always yearned to feel his mother's love. He still loved her, that was inevidable. What surprised her was the gentle way that Kinada held him and stroked his hair. Telyn hadn't expected the woman to be so motherly. She'd been so cold and demanding with them that Telyn hadn't expected that to melt away when she met the son she'd abandoned so many years ago.

But she had completely transformed from the woman on a mission that Telyn had agreed to bring into her territory. She almost looked like a mother who had never left. Who had never *wanted* to leave.

"I thought you were dead," Colton whispered. Telyn could see the tears that streamed down his face from where she stood.

"I had to leave," Kinada said, "but I'm back now."

"Time said you'd died," Colton said, still clinging onto the miracle that stood in front of him.

"That's what I led him to believe. I couldn't have him trying to find me again. Even if I hadn't, that man was always nothing but a liar." Kinada smiled.

"Why didn't you bring me with you?" Tears began to pool and spill over Colton's cheeks faster than they had before.

"I couldn't keep you safe there, love. I knew you had a better chance at survival here. Even if that meant you had to stay with him."

"Where did you go? Where have you been all of these years?" Colton wiped at the tears that streaked down his face.

"I was in Noctem. I was home." Kinada hesitated. There was something more she wanted to say, but she was holding back.

"Tell him," Senekah said.

She had seen what Telyn saw. Kinada was here for something, but it wasn't her son.

"I was with my family." The inferi's voice was soft as she spoke, her eyes adverted to the ground.

"What do you mean? I'm your family…"

Telyn couldn't take the way Colton's voice broke.

"I didn't bring you here to break his heart," Telyn said. "If that's all you're going to do, you can leave."

Kinada turned to look at Telyn. "I told you before that I had a purpose in being here."

"Then get on with it." Telyn glared at her

"Could you not rush us?" Kinada glared right back.

"I apologize, but we're all under a bit of a time limit." Skylar stepped in to defend Telyn.

"So get on with it." Senekah sneered.

"That's a little hard to do when you've dragged us away from our mission." Wes snarled.

Being so far away from home was beginning to wear on him. It was starting to wear on all of them. Telyn feared it might have been a mistake to bring Kinada here. This wasn't at all how she'd expected the reunion to go.

The party moved into the palace as it grew darker outside.

Kinada was clearly not happy about being rushed, and Telyn was not happy about being slowed down. The world didn't revolve around either of them, but Kinada seemed to think otherwise.

When they got into the palace, Zerina, Lilith, Pip, Harley, and Lune rushed to Telyn's side and wrapped her in a big hug.

"You're back!" Zerina squealed.

"Not for long," Telyn said.

"We're just on a bit of a side quest at the moment," Skylar said.

"Why is *she* here?" Zerina glared at Skylar.

"Be nice. I want her here," Telyn said.

"You hurt my sister, and you're dead." Zerina wasn't going to let up on her protectiveness anytime soon. She had been there for the aftermath of Kassian's second death and Alexander's betrayal. Telyn knew Zerina was only looking out for her, but she was beginning to wish she would give Skylar a chance. She was the one who had introduced them after all.

"Hello," Wes said. He waved from behind Skylar.

"There's more of them!" Harley gasped, her baffled tone earned a laugh from Pip.

"Yes, there's more of us. Six total," Vespera said.

"One Lord, three Ladies, a queen, and an inferi," Portia said.

Potentially a fourth Lady? Or would it be a Lady Queen?

Telyn's head snapped up and she looked at Skylar.

She had the softest expression on her face.

Part of Telyn melted at the sincerity and the hope that she put into those two simple sentences. And part of her hesitated. She didn't know if she was ready for such a big commitment. She'd just escaped from one she didn't want. She'd only just gotten the ability to choose what she wanted. And she didn't know if she wanted to choose a commitment so big so soon.

Her only response was to gently take Skylar's hand.

She wasn't ready to give her an answer yet.

She didn't know if she would ever be ready to give her an answer, but she took comfort in the knowledge that she would wait for her. It wasn't something she had to ask for. Skylar would give Telyn what she needed, and right now that was time.

"Telyn?" Zerina was giving her a concerned look.

"Yes?" Telyn blinked and looked up at her sister.

"You zoned out for a minute, are you alright?"

"Yes, I'm fine." Telyn smiled.

"Alright, good. Wanna explain the pink princess in our home?" Zerina gestured to Kinada.

"That would be Kinada, Colton's mother," Telyn said.

Zerina's face went blank as she paused to process the information. "She's *what*?"

"Our aunt."

"And she chose now to come back into his life?" Zerina looked as skeptical as Telyn felt. There was something very off about their situation.

But when was there not when it came to their family?

"Unfortunately."

Zerina shook her head. "Well, let's see what she has to say for herself."

"I've already explained myself several times. I am growing tired of it, and I do not appreciate children second guessing my motives." They hadn't noticed Kinada as she crept up on them.

"Well we don't appreciate absentee mothers coming back after eighteen years," Zerina said. Though her tone was light, Telyn could taste the venom in her sister's words. Telyn had learned that she was quite good with insults, veiled and otherwise.

"And what of your mother?" Kinada sneered.

"She's dead, no thanks to your pathetic excuse for a husband," Zerina replied.

"I am not responsible for my captor's actions." Kinada huffed.

"Nor am I responsible for yours." Zerina shot back.

"Everything I did was to protect him."

"Then why didn't you come back sooner?" Colton cut in.

It was reasonable for him to want to know why he had been abandoned for eighteen years, only to return when Colton was old enough to move on from the trauma and start a family of his own if he so chose to.

"What?" Kinada was at a loss. As if the question hadn't been clear enough for her.

"Why didn't you come back sooner?" Colton repeated. "I'm twenty-one. Why wait so long to come back for me?"

"I had to find you." Kinada crossed her arms, but Telyn didn't miss the flicker of uncertainty in her eyes.

"It couldn't have been too hard. Time did it, several times over in fact," Telyn said. She hated to take advantage of the woman's insecurities, but she couldn't risk the safety of those in this room for her comfort.

If Kinada was here for something malicious, Telyn needed to know.

"I was a bit held up. You'll have to forgive me." Kinada glared at Telyn.

"You're my mother, and I love you. But I do not have to forgive you for things you refuse to explain. You have another family. You abandoned me to stay with them, and you come back for me now, when we're in the midst of a war. I would like to know why."

"Because you're my son." Kinada twisted her fingers together in front of herself.

"No, because if that were the reason, you would have come back the moment he left me. You would have come to take me with you or at least stay here with me so I didn't have to grow up alone. But I did. So what is it you really want?" Colton's expression had hardened.

Telyn was proud of him for standing up for himself and not allowing his mother to pretend the things she'd done hadn't happened.

"Have you noticed anything strange happening around you?" Kinada worried her bottom lip between her teeth.

"Puddlefish, Mother! We're in the middle of a war! Of course things are strange!" Colton gestured to the room around them. "Nothing is normal anymore!"

"I mean with you. Any unsettling feelings? Things being misplaced or burnt?" Kinada sighed.

Colton was silent.

Telyn didn't know about what Kinada was talking about, but she would consider rising from the dead pretty strange. Though it had happened several times by now.

"That's why I'm here. To teach you how to control it." Kinada stretched out a hand to Colton.

"I don't need your help." He turned away from her and ignored the hand she offered.

"Yes, you do. And your friends need yours. This power of ours, it could ensure we win this war." She was getting desperate.

She couldn't promise what she didn't know, but for some reason, she needed Colton. And she would say whatever she had to to get him to go with her.

"There is no we! This doesn't affect you! You just want me to learn either so you can brag about me or so you can use me, and you don't have the right to do either of those things. You lost that right when you left. Everything I am is because I taught myself how to survive. None of it is from you, and none of it is from Time. I was my own parent. That's not going to change now."

"Please..." Kinada turned back to her son. "Just let me help you."

"And just what does your *help* entail?" Colton asked.

"Teaching you how to use the powers you have to the best of your ability." Telyn could see tears brimming in Kinada's eyes, but she doubted they were real.

"And then staying in my life for the rest of yours?" Colton asked.

Kinada was silent. She refused to meet anyone's eyes.

"That's what I thought." Colton's tone almost sounded disgusted.

The thrill and excitement that he'd held onto moments ago had evaporated into distrust and betrayal. Telyn knew that Colton wasn't eager to let his mother leave him again.

After all he'd been through, he deserved better than a second abandonment from the woman. Everyone but his own mother could see that he wasn't going to just accept her half apology without a fight. He wanted a valid reason and a promise of a life with his mother. But that wasn't something Kinada was willing to offer.

"You said you wanted to come back into my life and help me. That requires you to stay. You can't fix what you left behind only to leave again," Colton said.

Telyn knew what it was like to place all of your trust in someone and then have them cruelly remove themselves from her life. She couldn't imagine how horrible she would have felt if it had been her mother that had done that.

Maria hadn't left of her own free will, and that might have been the only thing keeping Telyn from hating her mother from beyond the grave. The difference was in the choices. Kinada had made hers, where Maria's had been stripped from her.

"You don't understand," Kinada tried again. "I can help you."

"No, I don't think *you* understand," Colton said, "I will only allow you to help if you agree to stay. I am not obligated to let you build a relationship with me, just to abandon me again and ruin what little semblance of a family we regained. We fought for this, what we have here. You don't get a free pass because of how hard you've had it. News flash, we've all had it hard. None of our lives have been easy, and they certainly aren't now."

Kinada's shoulders fell and her breath came out in a huff. She knew she couldn't win this argument. At least not without giving up the one thing she seemed unwilling to sacrifice.

Colton's expression was shuttered. The hope and disappointment that had been on full display mere minutes ago was gone, replaced by a stony stare of cobalt eyes. "I think we're done here." Colton's voice was devoid of any warmth. "You can go *home*."

The way he said it made it sound like the word had personally offended him. And Telyn supposed that, in a way, it had.

"Very well." Kinada straightened as she turned. She knew she had lost.

It was like by even just turning her back on the thing she had already left behind once made her stronger. Like she thought her son made her weak. And that knowledge made it that much easier for her to leave him. She judged him for his blood the same way the people she'd claimed to be protecting him from did. She was no better than any of them, no matter how hard she pretended to be.

She was probably telling herself that her sorry attempt at trying had been enough. All she could do for her son. It wasn't.

She was no mother. Not one that deserved the second chance she'd been given.

The moment Kinada was gone, Colton's stony wall of indifference was gone. His blue eyes were watery as he fought back tears.

His mother had essentially just told him he wasn't important enough to her for her to stay. He hadn't asked for much, but she hadn't bothered to even try for him. If anyone had gotten the short end of the stick when it came to parents, it was Colton.

And that was another thing Telyn would have to eventually make up for.

Telyn wrapped him into a hug, hoping that the comfort she could provide him with would help at least a little as he processed what had just happened. She found it absolutely unacceptable that Kinada wasn't willing to compromise for him. Especially after everything she'd put him through. *Nothing* should have been more important than him, and yet she put her other family first. When they should have been equal, she hadn't prioratized them as such.

Telyn never should have brought her to Alidain.

She had had a hand in the disaster that had just happened. She was partly at fault for hurting Colton. She should have said no.

She was learning more and more that was a word that needed to be in her vocabulary.

A respected word at that.

"Well." Pip cleared their throat. "I hate to interrupt, but while you're here, you should update your people on what's going on. I've noticed a few have begun to get a bit bold in their ignorance." They had bags under their violet eyes and they were leaning heavily against the wall. They needed a break.

Telyn sighed and pulled away from Colton. "Very well."

She supposed it was only typical for the people here to think they knew how things should be. Even if they didn't know the whole situation. Their ignorance would be their downfall one of these days. Telyn wasn't sure she could save them from such a detrimental flaw.

She caught Sklyar's eye from her place beside Wes. Skylar looked like she was ready to go home. Her grey speckled wings shifted uncomfortably in the warm air and her arms were wrapped tightly around herself. There was something she needed to say, but Telyn couldn't quite read what it was, but she knew Skylar didn't want to voice it out loud.

What's wrong? Telyn sent the question down their bond.

Skylar looked at her, her blue eyes narrowed in concentration and worry.. Everything was silent for a moment before she finally replied.

The atmosphere just feels off. Something happened... Something is wrong.

It seemed to be bothering Skylar, so Telyn took a moment to just feel. She let the thoughts filter out of her head as she let herself check in with what was around her and what she was feeling.

She was right, something did feel off. It felt like something major that kept the world together had shifted or had been misplaced. Everything was just a little bit off center. Her body felt like it was coiled too tightly, and now that she was aware of it, she couldn't ignore it. She could feel the same chill she'd gotten when Time had come to Ceris.

"We need to go back," Telyn whispered. "It's Brea."

Whispers

"When everyone knows you're a monster,
you needn't waste time doing every monstrous thing."
-Leigh Bardugo, Six of Crows

Telyn hated to leave Pip in charge of handling the budding chaos in Alidain, especially when she knew they needed a break, but she could feel something much bigger happening in Siluria. The feeling of off-centeredness grew stronger the closer they got to being back home. Time or Piran had done something, to Brea, to Siluria, to something. Whatever it was wasn't anything good. It made Telyn feel sick with anxiety.

She fought to breathe and think around the fog in her head as her stomach tied itself into knots that twisted over and over. They couldn't get home soon enough.

Skylar squeezed Telyn's hand, her gentle blue eyes worried as she looked at her mate. Telyn knew she was feeling the same things. Siluria was Skylar's home too, and she was more connected to it than Telyn was. It couldn't be an easy thing to handle.

Something was wrong with their home. They'd left their mission and their home to help Colton, and not only had something gone wrong while they were gone, but they'd also failed Colton. If anything, Telyn thought they'd made the situation worse. The only thing Colton had gotten from his mother was possibly some closure.

Kinada's distraction had done nothing but slow them down and hurt people.

It had been a trap. Kinada had been a distraction, she had pulled them away long enough for whoever was orchestrating this mess to make things go so terribly wrong.

Telyn figured that was what she got for trying to help everyone.

You can't keep everyone happy. She reminded herself. *Just worry about yourself and Skylar. If you can get the two of you through this mess, you can get through anything.*

Skylar glanced at Telyn, her step faltered, and Telyn almost barreled into her.

"Sorry, I shouldn't have gotten distracted."

"Well, move it!" Wes snapped.

Telyn knew what was aggravating him. Nolan and Cordelia were still in Siluria. They were in Ceris, oblivious to the danger that had possibly already hit them. Nolan was Wes's mate. And by association, Cordelia meant just as much to him.

Telyn didn't know how she would be able to bear it if Skylar were the one trapped, and she was in Wes's shoes.

It didn't take long to find out what was wrong. The second Telyn walked through the threshold of Ceris, she *knew*. She could feel his presence, and that only made her feel more sick.

Piran sat in the modest throne room of Ceris, his legs thrown carelessly over one of the arms of Skylar's throne. Telyn felt her face twist into a snarl as Piran gazed at her, his eyes full of contempt. He had been what was wrong. He always was. She should have known.

"What are you doing here?" Skylar demanded.

As badly as Telyn longed to give Piran a piece of her mind, she knew it wasn't her place. This was Skylar's territory, and Skylar had a reputation to uphold. Telyn wouldn't undermine her by acting out of place.

"I decided to drop by and see how your mission was going," Piran said. "Any updates?"

"We've spotted her a few times. She appears to be possessed by a demon. We're working on retrieving her and ridding her of the creature." Skylar's eyes were molten ice as she glared at Piran, who made no move to get out of Skylar's throne. The blatant disrespect was marked by all of them. He didn't see Skylar as another leader, just as another pawn. And he was making sure everyone else knew that too.

Telyn watched Piran's face carefully as it morphed from contempt to contemplation. Telyn could almost swear that part of Piran was tempted to tell them to abandon the search, to let Time use Brea's body until she was nothing more than a corpse. Something told her that the reason he was searching for his sister wasn't for a joyful reunion. Something darker was lurking under the surface. And Telyn intended to find out what it was.

"Continue your search." Piran's tone was indifferent.

It bothered Telyn how seemingly unbothered he was by the fact that his younger sister's life was at risk.

"Very well. Now please leave." Skylar turned her back to the king and strode out of her throne room.

It took half a second of staring after her for Telyn to realize she wasn't coming back. The king had marked his disrespect, this was Skylar showing him she didn't respect him either, and that she wouldn't let him walk all over her.

The rich purple carpet of the throne room abruptly ended at the door and gave way to the dark wood that made up the floors of the rest of the estate. Telyn followed Skylar to the kitchens. There were no cooks or maids running around, so it was just the two of them in the darkened room.

"Why are we here?" Telyn settled onto one of the granite counters that circled the room.

"No one would think to look for us here. Primarily, it's to avoid the king. But it is also quiet," Skylar said. She leaned against the counter beside Telyn.

"That's fair." Telyn stared up at the vaulted ceiling that loomed above her. It had been a long day for all of them, and she was fairly certain they shared in her sentiment of wanting it to be over already.

She felt Skylar's arm brush against her thigh as she shifted closer.

"What do you think we would be doing if we didn't have to worry about all of this? The cruel king, the warring gods, the possessed princess." Telyn's eyes were still on the ceiling as she spoke. The dim light in the room cast eerie shadows on the wooden beams that supported the roof, but they didn't feel ominous. In fact, Telyn felt rather at home in the atmosphere of the room. Feeling Skylar's warmth beside her, the faint smell of the day's meals, the low light, and the quiet. It was the most peaceful Telyn had felt in awhile.

Skylar moved to stand in front of Telyn.

"Well we might be somewhere similar to this," She said. "A place of our own refuge, somewhere quiet and away from the rest of the world. Just the two of us." She took Telyn's hands in her own and Telyn looked down, her red eyes met Skylar's blue ones in the dark.

"Would we even have met without this?" Telyn's voice was quiet. She was mildly afraid of the answer.

She was a little too aware of the fact that she hadn't been able to hear Skylar's voice until after her mother had died. Was it a trade off? Losing her mother, her best friend, and her life as she knew it all to be where she was. And was it a decision she would make if she'd been given the choice?

"Love, no matter what, I would have found my way to you. Not even the gods could keep us apart because I've known for a long time that it was you I was meant to be with. I have known you for far longer than we have physically been acquainted. My soul knew you before we existed, and I fully believe that I would have done anything in my power to get the chance to see you just once."

Telyn leaned down, her forehead rested against Skylar's. "But I have been lucky enough to have you in my life as much as I have. I can only hope you'll choose to stay," Skylar said. Her hands were warm in Telyn's.

Telyn felt her heart melt a little and her eyes softened. "Darling, I will always choose to stay. There is no home for me without you."

Skylar's hand came up to cup Telyn's cheek.

"May I?" Skylar's warm breath brushed Telyn's mouth and neck. Her voice barely breached a whisper, almost as if she was afraid of the answer. Afraid Telyn might say no.

"Yes," Telyn whispered.

Skylar tilted her head back. Telyn felt her stomach flutter with anticipation as Skylar's lips met hers.

Skylar tasted like freshly fallen snow and Telyn loved it. She loved Skylar. She wrapped her arms around Skylar's neck and pulled her closer.

Skylar pulled back a little to breathe, her hands on Telyn's waist. Her pale skin was flushed and she wore a smile. "Thank you."

Telyn laughed and kissed her again. "I should be the one thanking you." She wondered why she had ever held so much distance between them. Why she had ever denied herself the luxury of feeling what she felt for Skylar. Why she had told herself she couldn't be happy until this was all over.

"I love you so much," Skylar whispered when they broke apart.

"I love you too." Telyn smiled.

Skylar clung to Telyn and Telyn clung to her right back. They sat for a long moment just holding each other, Skylar's face tucked into Telyn's shoulder, and Telyn's hand stroking absently at Skylar's short brown hair.

"We should be clear." Skylar sighed.

It was clear that she didn't feel like facing the world just yet.

"Maybe we should give our guest another five minutes to clear out." Telyn suggested.

"That sounds reasonable." Telyn felt Skylar's smile against her neck. "Skylar!" Wes yelled from somewhere down the halls.

Skylar groaned and reluctantly pulled herself away from Telyn.

"What is it, Wes?" She stepped out into the hallway, Telyn close behind her.

"Have you seen Nolan and Cordelia? I can't find them anywhere." Wes's eyes were wide and frantic as he peered around Skylar and Telyn into the dark kitchen.

"What do you-" Skylar started.

It hit her the same time it hit Telyn.

Piran had taken them.

He knew the rules, he knew he couldn't harm Skylar and Telyn, not in any way that would matter. So he'd taken the next best thing, the ones who had chosen to stay with Telyn in Ceris.

Four hours of searching revealed nothing but dread and confirmation of what Telyn feared. She hadn't provided results, so Piran had taken hostages. She wasn't sure how long he would keep them alive, but she hoped it was long enough for her to get Brea back.

Fury and disappointment swirled in her stomach. It was her fault this had happened. She knew it was her fault. And she didn't know how to fix it. No matter how much she fought to get ahead, Piran and Carling were always two steps in front of her. It was like there was no winning to them. There was no way to take back everything she'd lost, and there was no way to keep those she had left safe.

"We'll get them back," Skylar promised. She was leaning on the arm of a lounge chair in her office.

Telyn paced in circles around the chair. She didn't think she could get going again if she stopped now. She didn't want to find out either. So she kept herself moving.

"Even if we do get them back, how can we ensure he won't take anyone else?" Telyn gnawed on her nails, the torn pieces of them caught in the stray hairs that framed her face.

"We tighten security. He may be the king, but that isn't a free pass to wherever he wants. He provides a threat to my house, and so he will not be welcomed," Skylar said.

"But he is still the king." Wes raked a hand through his already messy hair.

The man looked completely undone. His shirt sleeves were rolled up and the top half of his shirt was unbuttoned. His face was pale and his eyes wild.

Telyn felt a pang of sympathy for him.

"War is coming." Telyn's voice was quiet.

"What?" Wes looked up at her.

"War is coming." She spoke louder.

Skylar met her eyes from the short distance between them.

"The gods are fighting each other, and they seem intent on dragging us into it. Before long we will be forced to choose sides. Skylar and I have chosen our side. My people are with me. Piran has chosen his side as well. Unfortunately it seems to be the side bent on the destruction of Viridium as we know it," Telyn said.

"How long do we have?" Wes asked.

"It's already begun," Skylar sighed. "Piran is growing bolder. He feels more entitled. We must stop him before it goes much farther." She plopped down into the chair she'd been leaning on.

"We need more people for that. He's the king of both courts of Siluria. There is nothing he won't do to ensure he gets his way," Telyn said.

"If we get in his way, he will kill us," Wes said.

"Unless we kill him first." Skylar's voice was colder than Telyn had ever heard it before.

She contemplated the idea. It wouldn't cut the head off of the snake, but it would slow it down. It would put part of their problem out of commission, which would allow them to focus on their much larger problem, Carling.

"Let's do it." Telyn settled onto the arm of Skylar's chair.

"How do you suppose we'll manage that?" Wes demanded.

"We have a plan." Skylar's voice was careful as she spoke. "We just need to adapt it a bit and put it into motion."

"Would you care to share this plan of yours?" Wes asked.

"The fewer people know, the better. Just trust us," Telyn said.

Wes raked a hand through his hair again. "I want to trust you, I really do, kid, but you don't understand."

"I understand perfectly well. He is your mate, and I am deeply sorry you have to go through this, but I know how I would feel if Skylar were in Nolan's place. I know how scary the thought is, and the reality must be unbearable, but I will get them back." Telyn took Skylar's hand.

"She's not your mate, you couldn't possibly understand." Wes rolled his eyes.

"She *is* my mate," Telyn said. She squeezed Skylar's hand.

Wes watched the pair of women closely for a moment. "My apologies, I've been too wrapped up in my own head."

"It is quite alright. You have every reason to be panicked right now. Just know that I understand and I will do everything in my power to get Nolan and Cordelia back," Telyn said.

Nolan and Cordelia were important to her too, even if Nolan wasn't Wes's mate, Telyn still would have done whatever it took to get them back to her safe and sound. They were the closest thing to family she'd been able to find in the shattered world that her life had taken residence in. There was no way she would leave them stranded.

She wasn't Kinada.

"So what's our first move?" Wes asked.

"We find Brea, and we get that demon out of her," Telyn said.

If only it was as easy to accomplish as it was to say...

"That narrows it down." Telyn chose to ignore the sarcasm in Wes's tone.

She knew what they needed to do. She just had to lure Time to her. He'd been setting traps and catching her off guard, and now it was her turn to make him come to her.

"I know what we need to do. Just follow my lead," Telyn said.

"You're expecting us to put a lot of trust in you."

"Trust she has more than earned," Skylar said. "Without her, Kallista would still be lost to us, we would be unaware of the danger brewing, of the tyrant that sits on our throne now. She has done nothing but aid us. So if she needs our trust, I will gladly give it to her."

"You would gladly give her anything she asked for." Wes narrowed his eyes at Skylar.

"I would, because she deserves nothing less."

"As sweet as these proclamations are, we have work to do. So please stop bickering." Telyn pushed herself to her feet.

Skylar smiled after her, nothing but pure adoration in her eyes.

"Let's go get them, love."

Wes rolled his eyes but followed the girls out of Skylar's office and into the halls.

The walls somehow seemed warmer, like they had found the same acceptance that Telyn had. She knew who she was, what cards she had to play, and exactly how to play them. And Ceris seemed to know it as well. It was almost as if the house was proud of her. In a way Telyn liked to imagine her mother would have been if she could see her now.

Telyn pushed the thought of Maria from her mind.

She couldn't go and get distracted now. She had a job to do, and she fully intended to see it through as soon as possible.

Once things were settled, she would make Piran pay. She would get her revenge for every time the man had crossed her. She would take his throne out from under him. She would rip him to pieces and make his life as miserable as he'd made her. And she would do it from inside his own palace walls.

A wicked grin spread across Telyn's face and more confidence powered her strides. She was done playing the losing side of the battle. It was high time the tables turned in her favor. If no one else was going to play fair, she didn't see why she should have to either. She could play just as dirty as Piran and her uncle. She could make her own rules and make everyone else play by them too. She had been denying her own power for far too long, and now she knew how to change that. If that meant she had to shake the playing field to even it, then so be it.

Remember That Night

"Every story has the potential for infinite endings."
-Stephanie Garber, Once Upon a Broken Heart

The trap was laid, and now, Telyn just had to wait for her prey to walk into it. She stood in the clearing in the forest, her hands folded loosely behind her back. She could feel Skylar's eyes on her from the bushes a few feet away. If she looked hard enough, she could make out the grey speckles on her wings from the powdery snow that concealed her.

"Come now, Uncle. I thought you enjoyed a good game." Telyn walked in loose circles, letting anyone watching believe that she was relaxed and calm.

The cold brushed against Telyn's skin like a blanket as the snow crunched under her feet. It felt like home. Like it finally welcomed her new mindset, her new approach to the problem.

"You called?"

It was scary how easily Telyn could recognize Time's voice. Even after his death. Even if it was coming from the mouth of a little girl, it was still *his* voice. His dying words rang in her ears like a bell, '*You're nothing but a failed experiment. Asteria will come for you.*'

"Indeed. It's been a moment since we last spoke." Telyn let her hands hang at her sides, the very image of complancency.

"You've changed."

Curiosity and confusion twisted Brea's haggard face.

"So have you."

Brea's clothes were even more dirty and torn than they had been the last time Telyn had seen them. She was thinner too. Time was letting her body waste away as he used it however he pleased. He wouldn't be able to use it much longer at this rate. He was growing weaker.

"Very funny." Brea's lips twisted into a smile. "Have you come to your senses and decided to change your role in our little game?"

"Something like that." Telyn mirrored the smile.

"What's that supposed to mean?" He took a step closer.

He was right where she wanted him.

She brought her hands up and rested them on her hips, and Skylar and Wes charged out from their places in the bushes, they used a thick rope to pin down Brea's arms and hold them in place.

Time fought, Brea's thin arms thrashed and pushed against the rope, but she wasn't strong enough to break through the bonds as Skylar and Wes held her.

The tears that brimmed Skylar's eyes broke Telyn's heart.

Skylar hated seeing Brea like this. She hated having to be the one to pin her down, even if it was for her own good.

And Telyn hated seeing Skylar hurt like this. She would have done anything to prevent the pain Skylar must have been feeling now from reaching her.

Portia was the next to emerge, and together, she and Telyn channeled a ball of flames, burning hot blue as they chanted *"Protero inferī,"* under their breath.

An inhuman shriek tore itself from Brea's throat and Telyn watched as the shadow that had been her uncle emerged from Brea's body and burnt to ashes. The white flakes that remained of him fell to the ground like snow.

And just like that, he was gone.

It seemed far too easy.

Skylar caught Brea's body as it crumpled and fell like a puppet whose strings had been cut. Skylar's eyes met Telyn's across the space between them. There was no masking the fear and worry that clouded those ice blue eyes.

Because they didn't know what happened next. They didn't know if this was supposed to happen. If she was supposed to wake up soon.

Or if she was supposed to wake up at all.

"Let's get her back to Ceris," Portia said.

Skylar gave a sharp nod and led the way through the forest, Brea cradled in her arms.

Part of Telyn was glad that they'd been able to recover Brea, but now she was afraid she wouldn't be the same Brea as before. She was left, once again, remembering that Kallista hadn't told them anything about what would happen afterwards.

Of course she wouldn't be the same. Her parents had died, and she'd been possessed by an evil shadow. There was no way she could be the same as she had before. Telyn knew she wouldn't because she knew she wasn't the same as the girl that used to sit at the harbor with her best friend and read stories. She wasn't the same as the girl who sometimes came home to baked treats from her mother's attempts to quell the grief. She wasn't even the same as the girl who came to Alidain, feeling completely alone and afraid.

She and Brea were both princesses who had lived through more trauma than they deserved, but at least they would both come out the other side stronger.

Or so Telyn hoped.

As soon as they got back to Ceris, Skylar was cleaning Brea up and getting her wrapped up in warm clothes and piles of fuzzy blankets, but still, the girl's eyes wouldn't open.

"We can't give her to him like this. He'll kill them." Wes groaned.

That earned a glare from Portia.

"We can not give her to him like this because it is not safe," Skylar growled. "For her or them."

"Who knows what he would do." Telyn agreed.

"To any of us," Portia said.

Piran was already unhinged, and no one could control him now, not after his parents had died. If they gave Brea to him in the comatose state she didn't appear to be coming out of, there was no telling if any of them would survive the encounter. It was clear that there was only one thing Piran cared about in the world, his own power. He could very well kill all of them if that's what he thought would give him the most power, but he knew that where Telyn was involved, it wouldn't be that easy.

She had defied him time and time again. And that had angered him. He wasn't used to being told no and kept from what he wanted.

He was too selfish for anyone's good.

But Telyn was thinking that maybe she needed to start being a bit more selfish. She wasn't after power after all. The only thing her selfishness would do was protect the ones she cared about. She didn't need the crown or her title, all she needed was for the people she cared about to be safe. That could only help people, right?

And that couldn't possibly be a bad thing.

Could it?

Telyn shook herself out of her thoughts.

"We won't be bringing the princess to Piran until she wakes up. At the least." She decided. She shot a pointed look at Wes.

Thank you. Appreciation and affection brushed against Telyn's mind as she met Skylar's eyes across the space between them.

Skylar was sitting beside the bed that Brea had been bundled onto, holding Brea's hand.

Telyn's stomach twisted as she took in the cracked, dirt plastered, broken nail beds at the ends of Brea's frail fingers. She was so thin, and any of her bones looked ready to snap at the slightest inconvenience.

But at least she was safe now.

And Telyn's uncle could never hurt anyone again. He was gone for good this time.

But there was still the problem of whoever he had been working for.

It worried Telyn that they still didn't know who was behind it all.

This invisible threat couldn't be fought as long as it remained unseen. And the longer it was left to fester, the more dangerous it would be when it emerged. They needed to solve this problem soon.

They had so many problems that they needed to solve.

And not nearly enough time to solve them.

Not all of them.

Not even most of them.

One problem at a time. Telyn told herself.

She closed her eyes.

She needed to figure out how to wake Brea up. Maybe the princess would know something about how her parents had died. She had fled for a reason, and that reason might save a lot of lives.

If only they could get her to talk about it.

Telyn took a breath and prepared to do something she'd hoped to never have to do again.

"What is it?" Telyn could feel Skylar's concern radiating off of her. She must have sensed Telyn's reluctance.

"I'm thinking that maybe if I can feel the cause of this problem, we might be able to wake her up." Telyn opened her eyes as she let her protective barriers fall.

The concern and fear that washed over her was nauseating and Telyn fought to keep her breakfast down. She carefully approached Brea's bed, letting herself grow accustomed to the emotions that were not her own. She gently placed a hand on Brea's shoulder, and started to strip away more of the barriers.

Slowly she started to feel what Brea was feeling. She was exhausted, and so painfully hungry. But she felt so stuck. She still wasn't in control of her body. She was still trying to fight her way to the surface of her consciousness, even if nobody was forcing her back anymore.

She hadn't been in control of herself for so long it was hard to remember how to do it. How to use her own body and live again.

It was a mental battle that Telyn had no way of helping. But she could try to help by making her body's physical demands less pressing.

She separated herself from everyone else's feelings and put her barriers back up.

When she felt fully herself, she shifted her gaze to Skylar.

"We need to get liquids into her. If that goes well, we can work on getting some food into her. This is something that only she can get herself out of. The only thing we can do is keep her physical needs met. Hopefully that will make it easier for her to take back control," Telyn said.

Immediately a maid scurried from the doorway.

She hadn't even had to check with Skylar for verification.

Telyn glanced at Skylar. She didn't know if it was okay for Skylar's staff to be taking orders from her.

"It's fine. You're as much in charge here as I am," Skylar said.

"I'm really not. You're the lady of this court. I'm a queen from a completely different world."

"But you're my mate, my girlfriend, and hopefully once this mess is done, you'll agree to become my wife. You are fully in authority here."

Telyn felt her cheeks color, and for once, she wasn't opposed to the thought of marriage. With Kassian it had been pushed to a problem for another day, with Piran it was a definite no, but with Skylar it was a future where Telyn thought she might actually be able to be happy.

A future that, with a little bit of fighting for, could actually exist.

It was a future that Telyn refused to let anyone take away from her, try as Piran might. This was something Telyn would fight for, and she would die before she let him take it from her.

"We can do this later." Wes raked a hand through his hair.

No one reprimanded him. Everyone knew he was stressed out beyond imagination. Even more than Telyn was.

The maid returned with a jug of water, and Telyn held her breath as she watched the girl carefully pour a bit of it into Brea's mouth. Within a few seconds, the maid tried again with a satisfied expression. So Brea was taking the water. That was good.

Skylar had decided to stay with Brea through the day to ensure she was going to be alright. So naturally, Telyn opted to stay with them both.

She could hear Wes pacing in the hallway beyond the door all morning. She wouldn't be surprised if she woke up to find that he'd worn ruts into the carpet.

She glanced over at Skylar, who had dragged in a pile of blankets and pillows for them to use on the floor.

Telyn sat on a pillow on the floor and started to create a little nest around herself for them.

Skylar was beginning to pace now. She knew that Brea would be alright, she knew that she was taking the water without any problems, and tomorrow they would try giving her some food. But Telyn knew that didn't ease the worry that Brea might be like this forever.

It was a vital part of the process that Kallista had left out.

Maybe not even Kallista knew. It was possible that Brea had been held under for far longer than others had. She had been so close to just withering away.

Telyn reminded herself to ask the seer about it later. With her back around Telyn was bound to bump into her somewhere. Especially with Skylar and Vespera being friends. Vespera had seemed to be the closest to Kallista.

Skylar stopped her pacing to come sit beside Telyn in the little nest she'd made for them.

Telyn wrapped her arms around Skylar's waist and Skylar leaned into her with a soft sigh.

"I know you're worried, but it'll be alright. I'll be with you every step of the way, and I'll do everything I can to help," Telyn said.

"Thank you, darling." Skylar pulled one of the blankets up around them.

The chill had never bothered either of them, but right now, the warmth was what brought comfort into the moment.

It didn't take long for Skylar to fall asleep in Telyn's arms.

Once Telyn could feel Skylar's even breathing against her, it was easier for her to let herself drift into unconsciousness.

Telyn knew she was dreaming before she even saw anything. She'd come to recognize the feeling of almost weightlessness that came with dream walking.

"Who's there?" Telyn asked as her surroundings faded into focus.

There were dead trees in every direction, burnt and withered as far as the eye could see. The grass was in a similar condition. She couldn't see anything else around. There was only death, dust, and the dread Telyn could feel as it bubbled up inside her. Besides Telyn, there was nothing truly living within sight. But she could feel the presence of something.

Though she couldn't place what it was.

"I see you've found me," A sickeningly familiar voice said.

"Carling." Telyn's voice turned to a growl. "What do you want?"

"To show you that you shouldn't be getting comfortable. Nothing you consider safe is safe from me," Carling said.

Skylar appeared beside Carling. Her dark hair was sleep mused and her half awake face was twisted in confusion.

"Don't..." Telyn warned.

"Stop me then." Carling's cold grin spread across his face as he wrapped a hand around Skylar's neck.

Telyn's mind flashed back to another man with his hand wrapped around another lover's neck.

"Let her go!" Telyn screamed.

She refused to let history repeat itself. Carling didn't control her, which meant she could save Skylar. She would be perfectly fine with never saving anyone again as long as she could save Skylar. This was one battle she would win out of sheer will. Carling would not *take anything else from her. She wouldn't let him.*

But as soon as she moved in for the rescue, Skylar's skin began to dessicate and flake away.

Telyn's jaw dropped in horror.

It took mere seconds for Carling to turn Skylar to ashes.

Telyn woke up screaming.

"What's wrong?" Telyn could feel the panic in the voice.

There were warm hands on Telyn's face, and icy blue eyes peering down into hers with creased eyebrows hovering uncertainly above them.

Telyn's heart still thundered in her heart at the memory of the nightmare, but it slowed as she realized Skylar was in front of her. Whole and unharmed.

"You're okay." Skylar whispered, her thumbs brushed over the tears that had stained Telyn's face while she slept. "It was just a nightmare. I've got you."

Telyn clung to Skylar, she didn't care if her tears stained Skylar's shirt, she was just relieved that she was still here. That she could touch Skylar without having to watch her crumble to dust before her eyes. Telyn took a shaky breath, letting the feeling of Skylar beneath her fingertips ground her in place.

This was what was real.

The warmth, and the love, that was real.

The nightmare wasn't real, and it never would be.

Telyn would make sure of that.

"Do you want to talk about it?" Skylar ran gentle hands through Telyn's hair.

"It was Carling." Telyn fought to even out her breathing and calm down.

"What did he do?"

"He killed you..."

"Love, he can't hurt me. Not with Siene being my patroness." Skylar promised.

"I know, but it felt so real." Telyn's lips trembled as she fought to reign in the terror that still surged through her.

Skylar was quiet. Her hands paused their tracks through Telyn's hair and shifted down to wrap around her waist.

"I'm here. I will always be here. Right next to you." Telyn could hear the sincerity in her voice, but she didn't need to. She knew Skylar wouldn't lie to her. Not about something as important as this.

"I know, I just couldn't handle having to see that." Telyn looked up at Skylar.

"I'm sorry he scared you like that," Skylar said, her voice low as she gently brushed hair out of Telyn's face. "Do you need anything from me?"

"Can you just hold me like this? Until I fall asleep?" Telyn asked.

She'd managed to slow her racing heart, but she still didn't want Skylar to let go of her. She needed to know that she was still there, even if she couldn't see her.

"Of course." Skylar shifted so they could lean against the pile of pillows behind them.

Telyn closed her eyes and let Skylar's warmth seep into her and lull her back to sleep.

COMATOSE

"Remember this feeling.
This is the moment you stop being the rabbit."
-Nora Sakavic, The Foxhole Court

The days that passed felt waterlogged. Everything stayed the same, endless mundane tasks that needed done took up most of Telyn's time. Her hands repeated the actions that needed to be done, and her brain was hardly a part of the equation. Her eyes glanced over pages and pages of work, not fully absorbing the words or what they meant. Her concentration had checked out hours ago. If not days. The hazy memory of time almost made it feel like she was the one in a coma instead of Brea.

Skylar had been scarce around Ceris, she'd had things to take care of in the Winter Court, people to reassure and aid. She was taking care of the responsibilities she'd been given.

Its what Telyn should have been doing in Alidain. Instead she was at Ceris, completing office work that Pip had left for her. They had been doing a good job of leading the kingdom while she was away. And keeping Alexander off of Telyn's hands. But she was sure the people thought their queen had abandoned them in favor of a vacation.

She knew it hadn't been wise to leave so soon after her coronation. The kingdom would be seen as undefended and vulnerable. The people would feel she was an unreliable queen. They might even just accept a mew one in her stead.

If the king of Micaera truly wished to undermine her, he had been given the perfect opportunity to take her kingdom from her. Even with Pip and the coven there to defend it alongside the guard, it would have been an easy thing to do. Especially if the people decided they wanted a true monarch to lead them.

But still, work and responsibility had found it into Telyn's hands, in the form of endless piles of parchment that sat on her desk in front of her.

Telyn did most of her work in Brea's room. Papers spread out across the mahogany desk that sat in the corner with a quill and well of ink. The wood was marred with scratches from nibs pressed on too hard and splotches of ink made by uncertain hands. A crumpled pile of papers had taken residence at Telyn's side, responses that had been started and restarted over and over again. All of it would need to be burned later.

There was a single torch lit on the wall above Telyn, lighting her work space as she stared blankly at a request from a group of Alidain's citizens. They wanted to open a community garden. An easy enough request to approve. It would be beneficial to the kingdom, it would provide food for those who didn't have enough. It would go perfectly with the shelter Telyn had had set up. But Telyn couldn't think of anything to say. Not in a way that would sound like a queen instead of a partner agreeing with a good idea.

She had an image that she needed to build and maintain, but she didn't know how to do it.

The rest of the room was dark, the only light spread from Telyn's torch.

The only sounds were the soft repetition of Brea's quiet breathing, and the crackle of fire burning through it's accelerant. They were sounds Telyn had grown uncomfortably aware of over the past hours.

It was still dark out when Telyn peered out the window, the stars winked down at her as she watched. She could see the faint pink outline of the sun beginning to rise on the horizon. That meant Skylar would be home soon. Which meant she could take a break from the seemingly endless pile of parchment in front of her.

Telyn waited for the ink on her half written paper to dry before she neatly tucked all of her papers away into a folder.

She wouldn't be able to finish it even if she tried.

Her brain was too muddled to make sense of much of it. She wasn't taught how to do these things as a child, and now that it was expected of her, she felt like she was grasping at straws. The projects that would have been quickly addressed by any other monarch would have to wait awhile longer before Telyn completed them. She knew she was still learning how this new world worked, but she still felt like she wasn't learning fast enough.

She missed Skylar. Being around her gave Telyn a sense of ability. Like she could do anything when she was by her side. Even the dreadfully boring task set before her now.

Perhaps it was the urge to impress her, but all the same, she knew she was capable of more when the two of them were together.

Skylar was Telyn's other half. Most of the time, that meant she knew about all of the court rules that Telyn didn't.

She had been more than grateful when Skylar had walked her through basic book keeping a few days ago. Telyn would have been completely lost if Skylar hadn't taken the time to sit down beside her and show her the way things were supposed to balance out.

Skylar knew more about travelling as well. She knew when certain ships should be back in harbor based off of when they left and where they were going. They were all things Telyn should have known herself, but she didn't.

She couldn't help but feel that maybe if she'd grown up in the palace as she was meant to, things would have come easier. She would have been trained to handle these things, and maybe they wouldn't have become quite so overwhelming.

They also might not have been so overwhelming if she hadn't let it pile up like scrap paper. But it was a bit too late for that now.

And She still had piles of it to get through.

But without Skylar's gentle guidance, she found it hard to grasp any sort of motivation.

Telyn watched as the sun crept over the horizon. It was like its climb was draining her energy.

Over her time in Siluria, her body had grown accustomed to the change of pace. She had always been more of a night owl anyway, so it had only taken a few nights for her to get used to sleeping through the day. It was one thing she was born for that came naturally to her. She didn't need to be taught when to sleep, it was something that had been ingrained in her. It was her blood. As was the throne. But that was not quite so simple.

The sound of the door creaking open pulled her from her thoughts.

"Welcome home," Telyn said. She turned to face the door.

Skylar looked as exhausted as Telyn felt as she stood in the doorway.

"Long day?" Telyn asked.

Skylar wordlessly plopped down on the floor beside Telyn's chair and dropped her head onto Telyn's legs. Her dark hair spanned out across Telyn's lap in short sweat soaked strands.

Telyn gently brushed Skylar's hair out of her face as Skylar's eyes slowly slid shut.

Telyn knew running a kingdom wasn't easy, and she was sure Skylar had much more to do than she did. Telyn had the luxury of delegating her responsibilities, but from what she'd seen, Skylar didn't have any help running the Winter Court. She had no advisors, no council.

The only help Telyn had seen Skylar get was the occasional guidance from one of the other lords or ladies of Siluria.

Whether that was by choice or design, Telyn didn't know. She did know that it didn't lighten the burden. No one person had ever been meant to rule alone.

Skylar gently tugged on one of Telyn's arms and Telyn carefully sank to the floor beside her.

Telyn pulled one of the blankets from their pile on the floor and wrapped it around them. "Sleep well, my love." Her voice was barely above a whisper as Skylar snuggled into her, burying them both deeper into the blanket.

The next evening, Ceris was bustling and full of life. Servants whisked through the halls, platters and streamers filled their arms. Rosy cheeks and wide grins flashed past everywhere Telyn looked.

"Are we doing something today?" Telyn questioned as she walked down the hall, hand in hand with Skylar.

"We're celebrating Kallista's return."

"That feels like so long ago now."

"It's barely been a week." Telyn could hear the exhausted tone that settled over Skylar's words.

"I know, but the nights have dragged on for so long." And they had, the stress had stretched the days until there was nothing more to gain from them.

Telyn watched as a girl strung up silver and black streamers. They lined the walls like late Yule decorations.

"When will the others be here?" Telyn asked.

She assumed that if it was for Kallista, then Vespera and Portia would show up, and Wes had never left. He was likely sitting with Nolan and Cordelia as they spoke.

It made her wonder how he managed to run his court.

"They're already here." Skylar scowled. "I should have remembered that they're always early to a party."

"Everyone?" Telyn raised an eyebrow.

"Including Kallista." Skylar raked a hand through her hair.

This celebration might become more of a stressor than a reliever...

"You think we should talk to her." It was more a statement than a question, but Skylar nodded anyway.

"Something went wrong when we tried to bring Brea back. Kallista is the only one who knows anything about this. Maybe she'll know how to wake Brea up," Skylar said. They both knew it was wishful thinking.

"That's a good idea." Telyn's teeth worried at her lower lip. She didn't know how Kallista would react. She might not have a solution to their current predicament. She might be old and wise, as well as a seer, but that didn't mean she had all of the answers.

Telyn didn't know what she would do if that were the case. Kallista was the last card they had to play right now. If she was a dead end, everything could end up unravelling around them. That wasn't something they couldn't afford; now or any time in the forseeable future.

It didn't take long for Telyn and Skylar to find Kallista, she was sitting on a balcony attached to the main dining hall, bundled up in what must have been at least five blankets and a heavy hooded cloak. A bottle of wine was cradled in her gloved hands, bundles of blankets wrapped around it as well.

"Child, I appreciate the sentiment, but couldn't we have done this in a warmer court?" Kallista's teeth chattered as she looked up at the other girls.

Skylar offered Kallista a small apologetic smile. "We can talk inside, it's a little warmer."

"Sounds good." Kallista bundled her blankets up around herself as she stood, her bottle of wine entirely hidden by the masses of fabric.

When they reached an empty room, Kallista shed three of her blankets and opted to sit on top of them on the floor.

"What did you children need to talk about?" She took a swig from her bottle.

"Well," Telyn started, "we were able to separate Brea and Nathaniel."

"But Brea has been in a coma since then," Skylar said, she was picking at her nailbeds.

"What do you mean?" Kallista's brow furrowed.

"She hasn't woken up." Telyn gently took Skylar's hand to keep her from destroying the skin around her nails.

"For how long?" Kallista took another sip and her frown deepened.

"Almost a week." Skylar's voice was quiet.

"Well, I can't help you." Kallista shrugged.

"What do you mean you can't help us? You're the only one who knows anything about this!" Telyn said. That couldn't be it. The nonchalance was what bothered Telyn most, it was like Kallista was hiding what she knew.

"I knew how to separate them. Usually they're fine afterwards. I've never seen anything like this before," Kallista said, her attention had almost entirely returned to the bottle that she turned in her hands.

"Can you at least look at her?" Skylar asked.

"You're better off asking Vespera. She's always been better at detection magick than I was."

No matter what they tried, Kallista wouldn't budge. She didn't want to help them. She was adamant about staying out of it, and Telyn didn't know why.

It confused her that Kallista would come back to Siluria, only to be more cold and distant than she was in Nihiliara. It was like there was something about the situation that scared her badly enough to fight to avoid it.

Telyn would have preferred the Kallista that had been rude but willing to help them to this barely attentive one. But it didn't seem like she would be getting a choice.

"Where's Vespera?" Telyn asked, not willing to waste anymore time on a battle she knew she wouldn't win.

"Off with Portia. They're sampling your wine."

Telyn glanced at the bottle of wine in Kallista's hands, then at Skylar.

They're not so different after all. There was no amusement in Skylar's comment, only the tired resignation of someone who didn't know what else to do.

It seemed some party crashing was in order. Luckily for them, they specialized in it.

They found Vespera exactly where Kallista had said they would. She was hiding out in the wine cellar with Portia under her arm, a bottle of wine sat open between their legs.

Telyn had never been down to the wine cellar before. The room was lined with dark wood shelves that held more bottles than Telyn could count. It felt strangely cozy for such a dimly lit room. She could understand why Portia and Vespera had come down there. It provided a little pocket that felt like it was far enough away from the rest of the world to have a break.

Portia glanced up at Skylar and Telyn as they walked into the room.

"Vespera, we could use your help if you're not too drunk," Skylar said.

The words should have been scathing, but Telyn could hear the hint of amusement in her tone. Skylar was only teasing Vespera, they were too close for Skylar to truly be angry at something so small.

"You know I don't get drunk, Sky." Vespera scowled, but she couldn't keep the corner of her lips from wavering into a smile. Her lavender hair curled slightly at the nape of her neck from the sweat that beaded there due to the heat of the cellar.

Despite the cold of the world outside, the cellar was even warmer than the other parts of Ceris.

"We need to know what's causing Brea's coma so we can get her out of it," Telyn said.

"What about Kallista?" Portia asked.

"She refuses to help us." Skylar sighed.

"And how do you expect me to help you figure that out?" Vespera pushed herself to her feet.

"Just try to detect any traces of magick or anything else that might be keeping her from waking up," Skylar said.

"I won't promise results," Vespera said, "but I'll do my best."

It didn't take long for them to reach the room where Brea had been staying.

It was just as quiet as it had been when Telyn left that evening. Brea's soft breaths were the only sound that filled the room. The fire had died down to embers. Skylar stoked the wood that burned, coaxing it back into a flame.

Vespera seemed hesitant as she approached the bed. It was like she could already sense something sinister that kept Brea just below her own consciousness.

Telyn watched as Vespera placed a trembling hand on Brea's forehead.

Vespera recoiled almost immediately.

"What's wrong?" Portia took Vespera's hand as she pulled away.

"There is dark *dark* magick keeping her under." Vespera frowned.

"How do we get it off of her?" Skylar asked.

"There is no getting it off of her. Not for us anyway. The only one capable of removing something so sinister is Sprin. You don't go to Sprin unless you have a death wish though. His help is never worth the price you pay, there is nothing we can do for her," Vespera said.

"Promise me you won't go," Portia said.

Skylar and Telyn glanced at each other.

We won't go."

They both knew they would go either way. Skylar would do anything for Brea. And Telyn would do anything for Skylar.

If Brea didn't wake up, the price would likely be much higher than anything Sprin could cook up.

Telyn knew it was foolish to make such an assumption when she knew nothing about Sprin, but Piran scared her far more.

With Carling backing him, he was their biggest threat. If he found out Brea wasn't waking up, Telyn didn't trust him to not make the call to put Brea out of her misery.

Portia however, seemed satisfied with their answer. She and Vespera headed for the door. Vespera glanced back at Brea nervously before she shut the door behind them.

Telyn suspected the girl might feel the need to get drunk after this. If that was even possible.

Once Skylar had deemed the others far enough away to not overhear, she turned to Telyn. "We have to go."

"I know." Telyn wouldn't try to argue. They both knew there was no other way. Telyn knew there would have to be sacrifices made, prices paid.

War was never easy. There were always complications, plans being ruined, and little set backs that needed to be fixed before another move way made.

And they were both willing to pay whatever price Sprin demanded. There was nothing they weren't willing to give up if it meant they could get past this little set back. If it meant they could get Brea to wake up.

"Where do we start?"

PART 2

Rebirth

"Yes. All men must die,
but we are not men."
-Game of Thrones

The Search For Sprin

> "You love her because she sings a song
> only you can understand."
> -L. J. Smith, Secret Vampire

Telyn shouldered her bag. She knew this would be the second big expedition she would be going on with Skylar, but this time it felt different. Things had changed between them; on top of that, the stakes had changed as well. It wasn't *just* her sister's friend helping her anymore.

Skylar was her mate. And more than that, she was her best friend. Somehow Telyn found herself with more to lose than before.

It made her even more afraid to find out what Sprin might ask for.

But there was still a chance it would be a milder demand than Piran, who never had enough. Piran kept taking more in his greed. Telyn hoped Sprin would be content with receiving the payment he asked for.

"Calm down." Skylar's voice was gentle as she laced her fingers through Telyn's. We don't have to agree to anything too outlandish. We have the choice to walk away from this."

"Are you sure? Lately, we haven't been able to walk away from anything. Not without someone getting hurt." Telyn hated to admit it, but she was afraid.

This was another person they would have to rely on.

Someone else who could stab them in the back.

"We'll be fine, love." Skylar gave her a soft smile. "I'll protect you."

Telyn didn't want to tell her that it wasn't her own protection she was worried about.

"How are we even supposed to find Sprin?" Telyn asked.

"We don't," Skylar said.

"What do you mean?"

"Nobody finds Sprin, Sprin finds you." Skylar grinned.

"Sounds like an adventure."

Despite the fear that begged Telyn to stay in the comfort of Ceris, she couldn't deny the thrill that thrummed through her veins.

She knew that adventure was a part of her. And it would never leave. In Micaera, she had only ever felt alive when she was being chased. The slow palace life of paperwork and people pleasing made her feel like she was slowly dying.

But when she had an adventure in her hands, that was when she felt like herself. That's when she was Telyn Ramirez, best friend of Kassian Tyre. Not Telyn Ramirez, Queen of Alidain.

"Are you ready?" Skylar asked.

"I'm always ready." Telyn grinned.

She knew it wouldn't be easy, but with Skylar by her side, she would be able to face anything that was thrown at her.

It didn't take long for the girls to pack a small bag with a few changes of clothes and toiletries.

The challenge would be getting food and water skins from the kitchen; and getting out. All without Portia and Vespera seeing them.

Telyn wrote out a quick note to Nolan, explaining her absence, and slid it under the door on her way to the kitchen.

By the time Telyn reached the kitchen, Skylar already had two water skins strapped cross her back, and she was shovelling dried food into a third bag.

Between them, it wouldn't be much to carry, but they would have to be careful about finding shelter. Bedrolls would have made it even more obvious they were planning on looking for Sprin of Portia spotted them.

Are we ready? Skylar glanced up at Telyn as she walked in the door.

As ready as we're going to be. Telyn took the now closed bag of food from Skylar's hands.

Then let's get sneaky.

Telyn rolled her shoulders back, tucking the bag of food out of sight between her wings, the strap covered by her hair.

They made it all of five steps before Portia rounded the corner, Vespera not far behind her.

"Where have you two been?" Portia asked, her hands on her hips.

A blush colored Skylar's pale cheeks as she glanced at the floor.

"Oh, honestly, Sky?" It's nearly sunrise, couldn't you wait?"

"Oh, wait, no!" Skylar became even more flustered.

"Well, your little date can wait. We're about to have dinner with Kallista. You know, the entire reason you had all of us over?" Portia shifted on her feet.

"Yes, of course. We just need to drop a few things off with Wes. We'll leave it in his room and be right there." Telyn smiled.

"Alright, but hurry." Portia huffed.

With that, she and Vespera turned back towards the dining hall, and Skylar and Telyn walked back to Cordelia's room.

"I've never seen you slip like that," Telyn said.

"Portia helped raise me. She knows all of my tells. She would have been suspicious if I'd tried to lie to her outright." Skylar shrugged.

"This is going to be harder than anticipated." Telyn sighed.

"We just have to wait until they go to their rooms after dinner, then we can leave," Skylar said.

"We could always go through our window," Telyn said.

"That's not a bad idea, but if we miss dinner, she'll know something is up and come looking for us. At least leaving after would give us some time before she realizes we're gone."

"Alright, at least we're not leaving on an empty stomach."

They stashed their bags under Brea's bed and headed for the dining hall.

When they arrived, everyone was already sitting around the table.

The two seats at the head of the table had been left empty for them, and as soon as they took their seats, the others dug into their food.

Quiet chatter filled the room. It got even brighter as the sun spilled over the horizon and it's light flooded the room.

Portia glanced at the window and Telyn watched as she stifled a small yawn.

"I think it's time we head to bed," Vespera said.

Everyone's plates were cleared. All that was left was the quiet chatter of old friends catching up, and the occasional refill of fairy wine.

Portia nodded in agreement and stood.

Skylar and Telyn watched as the two women left the dining hall.

Skylar sipped at her glass as she waited for the other girls to be out of ear shot.

"Telyn and I will be leaving for a while," Skylar said. Her voice was lowered as she glanced back towards the door.

"Where are you going?" Wes asked.

"To find someone who can help Brea," Telyn said.

"There's someone who can help her?" Wes asked.

"We think so. And if there's a chance, we'll follow it," Skylar said.

"Of course," Wes said. "What can we do to help?"

"Keep Portia and Vespera from noticing we're gone," Telyn said.

"Why?" Kallista's focus was on her wine glass as she spoke.

"They don't want us going, but all of our other options have been exhausted at this point." Skylar stood up and Telyn followed her lead.

"Just keep them from getting suspicious for as long as possible," Telyn said.

"Alright, just be safe." Wes's lips twisted into a frown.

Telyn could tell he didn't like the idea, but he wouldn't try to stop them.

"And if the king comes?" Kallista asked.

Telyn glanced over at Kallista and took a moment to think her words through before she answered. "He shouldn't, but if he does, tell him we'll be back soon."

With that, Telyn and Skylar made their way back to Brea's room to retrieve their bags.

"Want to have some fun?" Skylar glanced over at Telyn with a grin.

"Always."

Skylar swung open the window beside her and climbed out. She dropped a few feet before her wings caught her and she hovered beside the window. "How about a bit of flying?"

Telyn mirrored Skylar's grin and climbed out the window after her.

Skylar closed the window behind her as she caught herself.

"Where are we headed?" Telyn asked.

"Well, now is as good a time as any to show you the rest of the Winter Court."

For the first time, Telyn was flying with someone without having to carry them. It felt wonderful. Skylar flew a little above her so that their wings didn't crash into each other, but she was still close enough that they could talk as they flew through the crisp morning air.

Their backs were to the rising sun as they made their way deeper into Skylar's homeland.

Skylar's face was one of pure joy as she soared above it all. The wind ruffled her grey speckled wings as she dove to cross just above the tall pine trees that dotted the hilly land that surrounded them. She dragged her fingers through the clumps of snow that had formed on top of the pine needles and sent it spraying down to the ground.

Skylar's joy was infectious. Telyn found herself laughing along with her as they weaved around trees and birds. The tension of their quest eased as they let themselves be for a moment.

The chilly air and the snow dusted morning brought a thrill with it rather than exhaustion.

It made Telyn think that this might just be what life could be like once all of their problems were solved.

There will always be more problems to fix. More messes to clean up. A shadow brushed Telyn's mind and she faltered. She dropped a few feet before she regained her senses and climbed back up above the trees.

"Is everything alright?" Skylar asked.

"Nox is back..."

"Are you sure?"

Skylar knew as well as she did that the gods had gone silent again. The last either of them had heard from them was before they started looking for Kallista.

Telyn had hardly expected to hear from them again at all unless Nox needed something.

Carling was past making his threats. His message had been clear, and he knew that.

Telyn had supposed that she would be on her own until he came to tear her down. She wasn't sure she really appreciated these less than helpful comments from Nox out of the blue.

"It's not important. If it was, he would have said more than one blasted sentence."

Telyn shook her head and kept flying.

The glimmer of sunlight reflected off of glass on the horizon. They must have been getting close to a city. Telyn flew a bit closer to Skylar, taking her lead as they approached a city that looked like it was encased in ice.

"Is it normally like this?" Telyn asked, her brow furrowed in concern.

"Usually there's a bit of ice, but it's never been encased like this." Skylar frowned and started to descend faster. There was an urgency to her speed that kicked Telyn's heart into overdrive and spurred the adrenaline in her veins.

They landed beside the largest mound of ice. It blocked the door to the building, but they could see distorted light shining through the windows and the ice.

Telyn pressed her hand against the ice sealing the door and focused on Skylar's warmth beside her.

She could feel waves of it rolling off of Skylar from the exertion of flying and the work it took to stay warm in such a cold climate. Telyn channeled the heat into her hands and slowly, the ice began to melt.

As soon as it was thin enough, Telyn yanked open the door.

The five people inside startled when the door opened. There was an obvious look of relief on their faces when they saw Skylar. One woman sighed and rubbed her eyes as they began to water.

"What happened here?" Skylar asked. She examined the walls of the house to make sure none of the ice had wormed its way into the house to cause structural damage.

"We don't know. There was a snow storm, but those are common-place, so we didn't worry too much. But the next day, we were iced in. The snow wasn't even that high, but the ice encased the whole house," The woman said.

The man that sat to her left gave her a reassuring pat on the leg. "We were running low on rations and beginning to fear we would never make it out of here," He said.

Three small children peered curiously around their mother at Telyn and Skylar.

The smallest locked her large brown eyes onto Telyn's and smiled.

Telyn couldn't help but smile back.

The child toddled forward and her siblings followed.

Telyn crouched down as they approached her and Skylar continued to talk with their parents.

"Who are you?" The little boy asked. His eyes were brown like his little sister's but where she had a shock of blonde hair like their mother, his was a grey-ish blue.

"She came with High Lady Morris, so she's a friend." Confidence rang in the older sister's voice as she marched right up to Telyn.

Telyn wished she remembered what it felt like to be that fearless.

"She's my mate." Skylar answered from her place beside the parents.

The children's eyes widened.

As if they didn't already find Telyn interesting enough.

"Is that why you both have wings?" The little boy asked.

"Zaron." His mother scolded. "Mind your manners."

"Sorry, mother." He replied sheepishly.

"I'm glad you were able to have enough supplies to last this long, I think it's best we go release the rest of the city from their ice prisons." Though Skylar's tone was light, Telyn could tell that the whole situation was bothering her. This should not have happened, and yet it had.

"How long had they been holed up like that?" Telyn asked.

"A week."

It couldn't have been a coincidence could it?

The same time they had severed Time from his host, a whole city got blockaded in ice. But how would he even be capable of something like that? His powers lay in shadow manipulation, not ice.

Telyn spent what felt like hours melting ice and running around helping get everyone what they needed.

Some of the less prepared people weren't as fortunate as the first family she'd freed. Especially those that were older or lived alone.

Skylar kept a neutral expression, but the occasional small tremor that took over her hands betrayed her uneasiness. This shouldn't have happened, and she knew it.

And Telyn knew that she must be blaming herself in part.

It's not your fault. Telyn gently took Skylar's hand once the last of the people had been accounted for.

If I had been more attentive, this never would have happened.

You had your own problems to worry about. You can't be expected to do all of this alone.

Skylar didn't answer.

The people of the city were a bit rattled, but those who had survived seemed to be more at ease with their high lady present.

The trust they had in Skylar amazed Telyn. They had tried to help Telyn melt the ice after they had been freed themselves, but living in the winter court, a very rare few held the ability to do so, but the effort had been admirable. They had been willing to try just about anything to help their community.

It wasn't hard to see where they took their example from.

"Is that everyone?" Skylar glanced around the city again, hesitant to leave in case they had missed a home.

"We're all here," The father from the first house said.

His children were still watching Telyn.

"Alright." Skylar stretched her arms out in front of herself. "I suppose we'll leave you to it, if there isn't anything else you need."

"Oh, won't you stay?" The little girl's voice was mournful.

"Anastasia." Her mother warned. "The high lady is very busy."

Telyn glanced over at Skylar.

"We can stay for the day." All eyes turned to Telyn as she spoke.

The question hadn't been intended for her, but Skylar would have insisted on continuing on; despite the fact that she was in no condition to go on like this.

"We needed to find a place to settle for the day. Our journey can resume tonight." Telyn explained. If Skylar complained, Telyn would use her own exhaustion as an excuse.

Walking through the woods tonight wouldn't get them anywhere. Not with the dead look that haunted Skylar's eyes. She would be too distracted to keep herself safe. And Telyn didn't know the area as well as she did, didn't know if there was anything she needed to keep an eye, or an ear, out for.

"Very well, we'll stay." Skylar sighed.

"They can stay with us!" Zaron announced as he pulled on his mother's skirts.

His mother gave him a soft smile and nodded.

Telyn and Skylar followed the family back to their home.

The father showed them to the guest bedroom while the mother got the children cleaned up for bed.

"Thank you." Telyn smiled and he nodded.

Skylar was silent.

As soon as the man left them, Skylar slumped over into an armchair, her head in her hands. Telyn quietly sat on the floor beside her. "It's going to be alright. We'll make sure this doesn't happen again."

"These people are my responsibility, they depended on me, and I failed them."

"You didn't fail them, you still came. We got them out."

"Fourteen people died, and we don't even know how long ago. All because I was too preoccupied with my own problems. I should have been able to protect them."

"Skylar," Telyn's voice was quiet. "Kassian died because of me, twice. My mother died because I wasn't there. We can not change the past, so we shouldn't dwell on it. We just need to remember those we lost, and do our best to keep it from happening again. We owe it to them to at least try."

"You're right." Skylar took a deep breath and looked at Telyn for a moment. "What would I do without you?"

"Mope around all day." Telyn teased with a small smile.

Skylar laughed. "Well, you're not wrong there."

"We should get some rest. We've got a long way to go tomorrow night."

"Alright."

Telyn was relieved that Skylar's mood seemed to have lifted at least a bit. The dejected faithless person who had taken her place after they'd found the first of the dead had been so different and more distant than her usual self.

Telyn wanted to protect her from ever having to feel that way again.

The One

> "You don't forget the face
> of the person who was your last hope."
> -Suzanne Collins, Hunger Games

Skylar and Telyn only stayed for a brief breakfast when the moon rose. After that, they thanked the family for their hospitality and left.

Skylar wanted to check on the other cities to make sure nothing fatal had befallen them. This time, they walked. The crunch of the snow beneath their boots in the dark was a soothing repetitive sound. Telyn found herself zoning out more than once, her brain focusing on the soft padding of their footsteps.

"Are you alright?" Skylar asked.

Telyn pulled her attention away from the snow. "Yeah, I'm fine. Why?"

"You've just been quiet. Even your mind is silent."

"I just haven't been thinking." It sounded strange to say it out loud.

Telyn's mind had been such a busy place her entire life, it was unusual to feel like there was nothing to think about.

"How far is the next city?"

"If we're lucky, we may be able to make it by daybreak."

Telyn wasn't sure if she was relieved it was so close or disappointed that it was still so far. She was enjoying the solitude of just walking with Skylar, but at the same time, it felt like they would never reach their destination. With no physical destination in mind, they could be wandering around the Winter Court forever.

There was something strangely intimate about seeing the same things and understanding them without having to use words. Just being in the same space brought a sense of peace that Telyn never wanted to let go of.

They paused as a golden yellow unicorn filly pranced across their path. There was no sign of its mother, but it didn't seem bothered by the fact that it was alone with them.

Telyn watched it as it shook out it's mane and tail. She'd never seen one before, she hadn't even known they were real, but here it was, standing in front of her.

There was so much she had missed out on when she'd been hidden away in the human realm. There was so much of her own world that she had yet to explore. Some of it was dark, some of it beautiful, and she imagined some of it could be both.

The filly leapt into the bushes on the other side of the path and the girls continued down it, getting closer to their final destination for the night.

Luck seemed to be on their side. They walked into the outskirts of the next town just as the sun began to rise over the horizon.

However, these people only watched with vague curiosity as they walked through the streets. A few of them bowed, but not to Skylar. They were both surprised to see that the respect was directed towards Telyn. These people had no way of knowing who she was, it was baffling to see how they barely even gave Skylar a second glance, but focused on Telyn as if she was the rising sun.

"What's going on?" Telyn questioned.

"We've been waiting for you," One of the villagers said. "Please, this way before the sun rises and our day's rest is wasted."

"How did you know I was coming?" Skylar asked as they followed the girl to a cabin that was a comfortable distance away from the outskirts of the city.

The girl that was leading them faltered. "Who are you again?"

Telyn glanced at Skylar.

What did the girl mean? There was no way she would know Telyn and not Skylar.

"The High Lady of the Winter Court," Skylar said.

The girl seemed to think for a moment. "I can't recall ever meeting you."

Something was definitely going on, but Telyn was too tired to try and figure out what it was.

We can figure this out tonight. Telyn could almost hear the sigh in Skylar's voice.

She wasn't going to object. She couldn't imagine Skylar was any less tired than she was. They had been walking all night. Snow clung to their boots and clothes. It hadn't melted as they'd walked, if anything, it had solidified into ice in places. That didn't even touch on the layers of snow that had fallen on them as they'd walked. It stuck to their hair and their eyelashes, making everything seem much heavier than it should have been.

They did their best to knock off the snow before they went into the house, but the stubborn flakes refused to be dislodged. With a resigned sigh, Skylar set her boots just inside the door. Telyn followed her lead.

The girl gave Skylar a curious look but said nothing as she motioned for them to follow her into a back room.

The room didn't have any personal effects, which was a bit of a relief. Telyn didn't want to kick anyone out of their room for a night. Despite the lack of personalization, it was a nicely made up room. The walls were a cozy cream color that matched the drapes and the sheets. A dark oak writing desk sat in the corner and in the opposite corner was a heavily plushed chair next to a small shelf full of books.

Skylar plopped down on the chair and picked up one of the books lying on the shelf.

"You're not tired?" Telyn asked. "We could have gone further into the city if you wanted to."

"I'm getting there. Just need something to wind down a bit."

Telyn could tell Skylar was in her own head.

It was times like these she wished she could peek into Skylar's head as easily as Skylar looked into hers. She didn't like not being able to help her through the demons she had to be fighting.

Telyn knew she had her own to fight, but she wouldn't be able to do that without Skylar. It made her feel like she was taking more than she was giving, and it didn't sit right with her.

"I'm here for you, you know." Telyn's voice was gentle. "Whatever you need to talk about, whatever you need to fix, I'm here."

"I know." Skylar gave her a soft smile from across the room. "I just need to think some things through on my own first, but I promise if I need you, I'll come get you."

It wasn't what Telyn wanted, but she wouldn't push. Skylar was allowed to try and handle things herself, it was more her problem than Telyn's after all. She just didn't want to sit around and do nothing while Skylar needed help. At least this way, Skylar would come to her for help if she needed it.

Telyn felt restless as she watched the sun begin to rise. She knew she needed the sleep that she should have been getting at the moment, but something in her brain wouldn't slow down enough for rest to be an option. Her fingertips drummed against her legs as she tried to clear her mind.

Her racing thoughts refused to slow as she curled up on the bed.

It felt like they were so close to their goal, but at the same time, it all felt so far away.

She couldn't figure out *why* it felt like the finish line wasn't where they'd expected it to be.

She woke up the next night to find Skylar passed out in the chair she'd been sitting in the chair she'd been lounging in that morning.

The moon cast a faint glow over the planes of Skylar's face. Sometimes Telyn wondered if the horrors of reality couldn't quite reach Skylar when she slept.

The silence didn't last long.

A harsh clatter came from where Telyn assumed the kitchen was. The noise jolted Skylar from her sleep.

"I guess that means it's time for us to leave." Skylar pushed herself to her feet and brushed off her sleep wrinkled clothes.

"Before we leave, we should probably find out who they think I am. And why they don't know you." Telyn followed Skylar out into the hallway.

A maid was dusting flour off of her apron with a scowl painted across her face. That must have been the source of the clattering that had woken Skylar up.

"Oh, Miss!" The maid hurriedly folded her hands in front of her and dipped into a short curtsey. "Can I help you with anything?" Her eyes were focused on Telyn and she completely ignored Skylar.

That bothered Telyn.

She fought to keep a frown from twisting her face as she walked a little closer to the girl.

"Yes, actually." Telyn gave a small smile. "Who exactly do you think I am?"

"The Chosen Queen, of course. We've been awaiting your arrival since the dragon came." She gave a small shudder.

Telyn's stomach fluttered. A dragon? The last dragon she'd faced had been relatively easy to kill, but it had also killed Colton in the process. She would rather avoid repeating that.

"What do you mean by the 'Chosen Queen?'" Skylar asked. "You know there is no queen now. Much less a chosen one. Just the king."

"Oh no, not from Siluria, though she has our blood." The maid's tone of voice had changed, almost like she thought she was talking to a child. "She comes from the human realm. The prophecy said as much, but one day, she will be more revered than even our late queen."

Telyn rolled her shoulders back. "Skylar is not a child, she is your high lady, and you will treat her with respect. Regardless of if she is me or not."

Skylar shot a quick glance in Telyn's direction, but didn't correct her.

"Pardon?" The maid's brows furrowed in confusion. "What high lady?"

Their memories really were skewed if they didn't even remember having a high lady.

"We should just go, the sooner we take care of this, the better."

Skylar seemed strangely unaffected by the whole situation, it was almost like she was eager to leave.

"Are we going to find the dragon?"

Part of Telyn didn't want to try, but she knew she couldn't let these people down. Not if they needed her the way the maid said they did.

"Yes, I need to figure out why it's wreaking havoc and get it to stop." Skylar headed for the door.

Telyn followed her, but she had an odd feeling about the whole situation. Something about it wasn't quite right. Something other than the fact that these people couldn't seem to remember who they were supposed to answer to.

It didn't take long for them to freshen up and head back into the woods. Skylar followed a path Telyn couldn't see. Occasionally she could catch a glimpse of a tree with claw marks marring the bark or black dirt peeking out from under disturbed snow.

The further they went, the more tension got pent up inside of Telyn. Dragons were bound to be more powerful and intelligent here than they were in the human realm. Most everything was. So what would that mean for them? She didn't want to have to fight the beast. Not if they could avoid it.

"What are you going to do when you find it?" Telyn asked.

"Talk to it." Skylar made the answer sound obvious.

"They can talk?"

"Most of them. The younglings haven't quite mastered the Silurian tongue yet, but they can communicate amongst themselves in their own language."

Telyn found that Siluria had a surprise hidden around just about every corner. There was so much for her to learn here and she couldn't wait until she had the time to discover it all.

For now, they had a dragon to find.

They found the dragon hovering over a small lake. Telyn could see something shimmer, trapped beneath the ice. As she watched, the dragon blasted the ice with flame and it melted, allowing it to scoop up a glimmering piece of armor before the ice began to freeze over again. Water dripped from the breastplate in its talons to the ice below it. And its glowing red eyes narrowed on Telyn and Skylar.

"What are you doing here, so close to the city?" Skylar asked.

The dragon seemed to consider its words before it spoke. "I am not here for them, I am here for you." Her voice was a deep rumble.

"What do you mean?" Telyn asked.

The dragon turned away from them and started walking deeper into the forest.

It didn't make any sense.

She expects us to follow her. Skylar seemed almost hesitant as she shifted her weight forward as if to follow, but then back like she'd thought better of it.

Should we follow her?

Do we have much of a choice?

Skylar shook off whatever unease she'd been experiencing and followed the dragon into the depths of the woods.

The dragon didn't even look back as she walked. It was like she knew the girls had no choice but to follow her.

She took them to another clearing, this one had no lake at it's center, rather a dark cave at its edge. Telyn couldn't see what was inside it, but she did see the occasional glimmer of something that reflected the moonlight.

The dragon stopped in front of it, blocking Telyn's view before she could determine what was inside.

"I assume you have us where you want us," Skylar said, "Now what do you want?"

"I want many things, faeling." There was a small smirk set into the dragon's scaled face as she eyes the girls. She was enjoying being vague.

Or she was stalling for time.

Telyn couldn't tell which.

"I am not the one who wanted to see you. Someone has found your search for them rather meddlesome."

Was she talking about Sprin?

She had to be, that was the only person they had been looking for until they'd taken the time to find this dragon.

Though it seemed the dragon had let herself be found.

Telyn watched as Skylar's jaw worked but she didn't speak. She was waiting.

"You two better have a good reason for coming after me. I'm hard to find for a reason." A new voice drifted into the clearing. It sounded like it was coming from around the dragon, but Telyn couldn't see anything.

"Reason is relative. You must have thought it was worth it if you sought us out," Skylar said.

A small figure walked out from behind one of the dragon's legs. "I do think it's worth it, but my help will not come without a price." Sprin couldn't have been more than a foot tall, and his grey skin was wrinkled in several places, but he walked as if he knew he could take up all the space in the clearing if he wanted to.

"We didn't expect any less from you," Telyn said.

"Good."

Telyn could already tell she wasn't going to like Sprin very much. The smirk on his face was too manipulative for her tastes.

She was beginning to wonder if he truly was a better option than Piran.

It was hard to tell, but since he was willing to help, she was going to have to give him a chance.

"What do you want in exchange for Princess Brea to be able to come back?" Telyn asked.

"I'm afraid this process isn't so simple." Telyn didn't like the way his smile deepened. "First, I need to be sure you are worthy of my help. If you don't have what I charge, then there's no point in proceeding with negotiations."

"Well, if you don't tell us what you want, we can't know whether or not we have it."

"You'll find out soon enough."

"How?"

"Through a test."

Telyn felt like her entire life was just a series of tests. The first of which had been living in Micaera, then losing Kassian, then her mother, then Azriel, then everything that had followed. And now here she was, faced with yet another test. When would they end?

When would she find out if she had been good enough or not?

"What test do we need to accomplish?" Skylar asked.

"Not both of you, just her." Sprin's eyes were pinned on Telyn.

"No, this is more my task than hers. If any of us is doing it, it will be me," Skylar said.

"The king sent her out for this, did he not?" Sprin asked.

Sprin didn't stick to a single side, but he would use the sides against each other. That much was clear.

"Besides, you don't have what I need." He waved a dismissive hand at Skylar.

"Either way, we need to know what this test is," Telyn said.

She was growing impatient with these word games. She needed Sprin to say exactly what he needed from her so they could get on with it and rescue Brea.

"Well it's all a game, really."

"Do not waste my time with games. Some of us have things to do." Telyn's voice was cold, her impatience taking over.

"Fine." Sprin's grin fell.

"You must spend a full day, locked inside the dragon's den. With her." Sprin seemed rather proud of himself for this truly creative idea.

"Fine." Telyn could handle a day in a dragon's den. She'd suffered worse.

"No," Skylar said.

"Why? It's not like it's hard," Telyn said.

This drew a laugh from Sprin.

"You might change your mind once you see how protective she is over her young. If I were you, I would watch where I step."

So that was the catch.

Sprin would help them because he didn't expect Telyn to survive.

And if she did, even that wouldn't be enough for him.

He still wanted more from them, even though he was already putting Telyn's life in danger.

He was just like Piran.

The only difference was, he didn't hide behind the pretense of kindness. He might want more than he deserved, but at least he didn't outright lie to people about what he was dragging them into.

Dragons

"Stories can make someone immortal
as long as someone else is willing to listen."
-Adam Silvera, They Both Die At The End

I'm going to do it. I'm sorry you don't like it, but this is our only choice. Telyn directed her thoughts to Skylar.

She watched as Skylar's ice blue eyes narrowed at Sprin.

"If she dies, you will find I am not an enjoyable person at all."

Sprin only grinned through the threat. "Whether she lives or not is not up to me."

The sun was beginning to rise on the horizon. It had felt like it had gone down mere hours ago, but here it was.

"Time to go." Sprin dipped into a bow and gestured to the cave.

The dragon had already gone inside. Her lithe scaly body was curled around her pile of treasures.

And as Telyn got closer, she realized that pile of treasure included five writhing baby dragons, teetering on the edges of the shells that they had hatched out of. If she had to guess, they'd hatched the day before or sooner.

Which meant they were at their most vulnerable right now, and their mother knew it.

And Telyn was about to spend the day locked in with them.

In all the stories Telyn had read, dragons were notoriously protective of two things, their hoard, and their young.

This was off to an excellent start.

The dragon glared at Telyn as she took a step into the dark cave. Her thick tail wove around sharp-looking stalactites as she coiled around her belongings more tightly.

As soon as Telyn was inside the cave walls, another wall rose to block the exit.

And with the dark came the memories.

Telyn flinched as faces flashed through her mind, their angry voices filling her ears. Then a flash of green vanquished the nightmarish memories. The dragon's eyes were pinned on her, and they glowed in the dark, emitting a faint green glow into the darkness of the cave.

"What's your name?" Telyn tried for a light and friendly tone.

"Sevina." Her voice was a hiss.

"Well, it's nice to meet you." Telyn sat in a corner by where the entrance had been moments ago in an attempt to make it clear that she wasn't there to steal from Sevina.

Telyn could hear chittering noises coming from the baby dragons. They were too awake to sleep through the day. Something Telyn was sure Sevina didn't appreciate at all.

"When did they hatch?" Telyn asked.

Sevina's eyes narrowed, and the glow of them dimmed, leaking more darkness into the area.

When Telyn didn't say anything else, Sevina answered, "Last night."

So this was their first day in the world.

It was oddly refreshing to know that the little dragons didn't know the rules yet and that no harm would come to them even if they didn't. Because their mother was there to protect them.

And right now, Sevina viewed Telyn as the threat.

It was going to be a long day, but Telyn didn't feel like she was in danger. She knew that if she didn't do anything to put the baby dragons in danger, their mother would have no reason to snap her in half.

When Telyn woke, she was sore all over.

She'd fallen asleep curled up in the corner of the cave. She wasn't quite sure how long she had been out, but the days in the Winter Court were brief, and the nights were long. So sooner or later, the wall at her side would vanish.

Unless Sprin had lied.

He could be planning to keep her in here until Sevina decided to feed Telyn to her young.

The thought sent a shiver of panic down her spine.

It's almost nightfall. Skylar's voice was a soothing thought in the back of Telyn's mind.

Telyn knew Skylar wouldn't let Sprin leave her trapped in here. Not without a fight. It eased some of the panic that had begun to creep up on her.

That's when she noticed the silence.

She tried to make out the shape of Sevina's body in the dark, but she couldn't. The dragon must have fallen asleep. That would explain the lack of light.

And now that Telyn had noticed it, the dark was suffocating.

The voices were starting to come back. Shouted accusations and screams of outrage filled her head as she squeezed her eyes shut against the torrent of memories. But then their faces burned into the back of her eyelids. Her mother, her father, Kassian, Colton, Alexander, and that little girl.

That little girl had been lurking in the back of her mind ever since she'd seen her in that dungeon.

Telyn still didn't know who she was, much less how she'd gotten the poor girl killed.

Maybe it hadn't happened yet, which meant there was still time for Telyn to save her. If she ever found out who she was.

The wall beside her shimmered faintly then faded, it was enough to snap Telyn out of the spiral she'd begun to go down.

The moonlight was like a lantern, leading Telyn slowly back to the reality of where she was.

She was safe, she wasn't trapped, she wasn't going to die.

She had to remind herself of it frequently.

She would never be down in that dungeon again.

Nathaniel was dead.

He couldn't hurt her.

Skylar rushed over and knelt beside Telyn, checking her over for injuries.

"You're not hurt?" She demanded, holding Telyn's face between her hands.

"I told you it would be easy." Telyn mustered a smile.

Where was Sprin?

She glanced around Skylar in an attempt to locate the little monster.

He stepped out from around Skylar and gave Telyn a once-over.

"Not even a scratch." He mused.

Skylar glared. "So, you did expect her to die."

Sprin shrugged.

"Will you give us what we need now?" Telyn asked.

The little girl's face was still burning in the back of her mind, but she would have to deal with that later. Right now, Brea needed her to seal this deal.

"Not quite yet. I haven't received my payment yet." Sprin's contempt grin was back.

Telyn hated it.

"What do you want from us?" Skylar asked.

"Again, not you, her." Sprin was still watching Telyn.

"Well get on with it, we've already wasted a day." Telyn's patience was wearing thin.

"I want a fraction of your magick. Just a tiny sliver. You won't even notice it's gone." His expression didn't falter.

"Fine."

Skylar looked skeptical, but Telyn was ready to get this over with.

"Take it."

Sprin reached for Telyn's arm and she let him take it.

She felt something like a thread being pulled from her. Though she couldn't see it, she could feel that threat pulling at the well of magick she had stored inside of her. It was just uncomfortable enough to make her squirm.

Skylar snatched Telyn's arm away from Sprin. "That's enough." Skylar's voice had been rough but her hands had been gentle on Telyn.

Sprin frowned, but he didn't reach for Telyn's arm again.

Something about his expression seemed almost disappointed. Like he hadn't quite gotten everything he'd wanted.

"The cure?" Skylar prompted.

Telyn worried for a moment that he wouldn't give it to them. He hadn't gotten what he'd wanted, so why would he give them what they wanted.

But the expression cleared from Sprin's face, replaced by his insufferable grin. "Of course. Just make the girl drink this, and she should be up within the hour." He held out a tiny vial of glowing purple liquid.

The thing looked toxic and fragile, but it was the only thing they had. The vial spun in different shades of violet and purple depending on how it hit the light. Sprin had gotten what he wanted. At least enough of it to get him to uphold his end of the deal.

Telyn took the vial with gentle hands and tucked it into one of the inside pockets of her cloak.

"Thank you, but we should be getting back." There was nothing polite about Skylar's tone.

The girls stood in the mouth of the cave for another moment before heading out into the forest.

There was a small chitter of despair from behind them and Telyn paused.

A little green dragon scampered out of the cave and away from the reach of Sevina, and right up to Telyn.

Telyn glanced at Sevina as the little dragon scampered up to perch on her shoulder.

The red dragon just gave a brief nod before she turned her gaze back to her other younglings.

The dragon on Telyn's shoulder chirped and nestled itself into her hair. Its scales were warm against her skin as it cuddled right up to her.

Sprin was nowhere in sight.

"It looks like someone has taken a liking to you," Skylar said as they continued to walk.

"I thought dragons were more protective of their young." Telyn frowned. None of it made sense. The day before, Sevina hadn't wanted her anywhere near the babies, now she was letting one of them leave with her.

"It is rare someone wins the favor of a dragon, but occasionally, the young know where they're meant to be, and the dragons have no choice but to let them go."

"They're not all that different from us."

The little dragon on her shoulder chirped in agreement.

They had gotten what they needed, now it was time to head back. But Telyn couldn't get that one town out of her head. The one where no one seemed to remember anything other than her. She wondered if they were back to normal now if Sprin and Sevina had had something to do with their muddled memories. "We should go check on those people from before."

"That's what I was thinking. We'll need a place to stop in the morning, so what's the harm in going back?"

The town seemed calmer when they reached it that morning. It made sense, they no longer had a dragon calling for their blood. There was no need to panic when there was nothing wrong. More people were roaming around in the streets, children included. Telyn hadn't seen any children the last time they had been there. They had likely been hiding inside, where it was safer.

There was no sign of the girl who had taken them in previously."

No one acknowledged them as they wound their way through the streets.

In a way, it was even more strange to go completely unnoticed.

It was almost like the people were afraid to address them in the snowy haze.

Like something else had gone wrong after they'd left.

Even the day before, they had recognized Telyn at least. They'd tasked her with rescuing them from Sevina. But now, it was like they couldn't even remember that.

Telyn still didn't understand how they could forget Skylar so completely. Even before Telyn had known who she was, she had been unforgettable. She'd thought about her often after her little trip into Eralia.

The Skylar that they knew might not be the same Skylar Telyn had grown used to, but her personality couldn't change so much when she was High Lady that no one remembered her. Telyn refused to believe that was the case.

She could see that it bothered Skylar.

Skylar's fingers tapped against themselves and her thigh, playing along to a silent rhythmic beat Telyn couldn't hear and she held herself stiffer than she usually did. It was like she was forcing her High Lady persona to the front.

They didn't see the cause of the odd silence until they reached the center of town, where a man stood, giving orders to what appeared to be feathered salamanders.

They were odd little creatures, parts of their feathers were coated in the slime that covered their bodies, leaving Telyn to wonder what the purpose of the feathers was.

Telyn glanced at Skylar.

She didn't seem to recognize the man, but that didn't stop the anger that smoldered in her eyes.

"What exactly do you think you're doing?" Skylar marched forward, planting herself right in front of him.

"I wasn't aware I was intimidating enough to draw the High Lady from her palace." His smirk was full of poison. "But it's all the same. Makes things easier for me."

Telyn didn't like the direction this confrontation was headed.

She stepped up beside Skylar.

"And who's this?"

"We'll be the ones asking questions around here," Telyn said.

To her surprise, he laughed.

It was a deep boisterous thing, and it was completely genuine. He was amused that they'd come to stop him. Telyn scowled. She knew he felt he could take them on with his little army of stranger creatures.

Who did he think he was?

She would show him.

No one got to mess with Skylar, and Telyn was prepared to make an example out of this man.

"What are you doing here?" Skylar seemed to be unbothered by the situation, but Telyn could feel the rage that was boiling under her calm facade.

"I'm taking over, darling."

It was Telyn's turn to laugh. The shadows gathered around her as she did so.

The glee on his face faded as he saw what he was up against.

Telyn could feel the brush of darkness that pushed her forward, urged her to take everything from him. To protect what was hers. It was the small, cruel part of her that relished in the fear that glinted in the man's eyes as his face began to fall.

His grin changed to a snarl and the feathered salamanders returned.

They snapped surprisingly vicious-looking teeth at the girls.

A tendril of shadows lashed out at one of the little monsters and it whimpered in pain.

Then the man reached a hand out to his side and they all attacked.

They weren't terribly terrifying, but there were masses of them that surged up to bring Telyn and Skylar down.

The little green dragon let out an outraged squeak before it sprayed a thin stream of fire at the salamanders.

Skylar's wind fed the flames as they covered the feathers and Telyn's shadows whipped them back.

It didn't take long for the tormented creatures to flee from their master's side.

The man was left alone, the last one standing on his make-shift battlefield.

And when the magick was turned on him, he fled too.

All his anger and bravado had bought him nothing but a bruised ego. Telyn wanted to chase after him, ensure he knew not to bother them again. She imagined this must have been a bit like what her uncle had experienced, Which would explain why he'd been driven to madness by a thirst for power. Telyn tried to push the thought away.

When the adrenaline faded, and Telyn's heart slowed to a normal pace, she felt the power slip from her.

She felt herself sag as energy seeped from her like blood from a gaping wound.

Skylar's arm wrapped around her waist to keep her from falling. "Are you alright?" Telyn couldn't stand the worry on her face as she looked down at her. It felt too much like pity.

"I'm fine." They both knew it was a lie as soon as the words had left Telyn's mouth.

But Telyn couldn't afford to be weak, especially not now.

There was too much on the line for her to be anything less than perfect. Brea, her friends, her family.

Skylar.

Skylar, who was now carrying her into the nearest building, demanding a room be cleared for them.

"I can walk, put me down," Telyn said.

"Don't be ridiculous." Skylar kicked the door shut behind them, leaving a group of gaping on-lookers in their wake.

Light was spilling into the room from a single window as the sun crept above the horizon.

Skylar set Telyn on the bed and drew the heavy black-out curtains over the window, leaving them in complete darkness.

Telyn could barely make out the glowing blue of Skylar's eyes, but she could sense the worry radiating off of her.

"I'll be fine." Telyn propped herself up on her elbows. She had to fight the dizziness that threatened to knock her back down. She closed her eyes for a moment, allowing her head the time to stop spinning.

"Do you even know what happened?" Skylar's pacing footsteps echoed in the small room.

"No..." She wished she did. It wouldn't have felt so scary if she understood it.

"Most fae, like Sprin, have a limit to their power. Their well runs dry if they use too much. The Silurian have a much larger well, so much so that it seems limitless. Sprin took too much of your power, more than you agreed to give."

The pacing stopped.

"This is fine, the fae have survived this long, I'm sure I can too," Telyn said. She knew she might have been taking an optimistic stance, but it wouldn't do them any good to worry over something that had already been done.

"You're used to having access to more power. You've already over-exerted yourself."

"It'll come back. I'm sure I just need some rest."

"You can't be sure of that. Do you know what happens to the fae that push too far?"

Telyn couldn't miss the fear in Skylar's trembling voice. "They burn up and they die. With no well to pull from, the magick begins to pull energy from the host."

The reality of just how much she'd given up hit Telyn like an arrow to the chest.

She'd traded away her ability to protect the people she cared about and earned herself a new threat.

And if Skylar hadn't stopped Sprin when she had, he would have taken more.

And Telyn, likely, would have been dead.

Surely this would all resolve itself.

She just needed to rest.

And by nightfall, everything would be back to normal.

Telyn felt the mattress dip as Skylar sat down on the side of the bed. She reached for her hand in the dark. "We'll get through this."

"I hope you're right," Skylar sighed.

The Cure

"Fear is a phoenix.
You can watch it burn a thousand times
and still it will return."
-Leigh Bardugo, Crooked Kingdom

Telyn's powers hadn't made a reappearance by the time they reached Ceris. And they hadn't discussed it any further. The rest of their journey had been blissfully peaceful.

The only thing Telyn had to fight was the silence that hung heavy over them. Skylar's fear and paranoia was nearly tangible in the air between them, and it was rubbing off on Telyn.

Every snap of a twig had her tensing up. Whether it was to run or fight, she couldn't tell.

Telyn hated feeling so afraid.

Even away from Piran, she had still found a way to get herself trapped.

There had to be an out somewhere that she wasn't seeing. She couldn't sink any further than she already had. She had to find a way back up.

Ceris felt so alive and real after the strange behavior in the cities. There was no danger. No muddled brains. Just, now, solvable problems. Telyn's fingers curled around the vial in her pocket. It would solve at least half of their problems. With the princess awake, the king would leave them alone.

Which only left Carling, who was still biding his time.

Telyn got the unnerving feeling that the god of war would make his move soon. The air held more tension, it felt like it was inclined to snap at any moment, and Telyn wasn't sure she would be prepared to counter it.

"Shall we?" Skylar's fingers twisted around themselves as she spoke. Telyn could feel her uncertainty as she reached for the doorknob to Brea's door.

"Are we sure this is worth it? I mean, your powers-" Skylar let her hand drop away from the door.

"What's done is done," Telyn said. "So let's make the best out of what we have." She reached around Skylar and opened the door.

Brea hadn't so much as moved since they'd left. Her head was in the exact same spot on the pillow, her blonde hair fanned out over it in tangled knots. Her green eyes were shut, but they flickered in a frenzied manner beneath her eyelids.

Telyn took the vial from her pocket. The purple glow it gave off was barely enough to illuminate her fingertips. It didn't look like it was enough to do anything. There was barely a swallow of liquid in the thing, but it was all they had.

Telyn uncorked the vial and gently tilted the contents into Brea's mouth.

Almost as soon as it was down her throat, Brea's eyes fluttered open and she lashed out, her hand swung for anything within reach.

Telyn ducked out of the way.

"Calm down, little bee." Skylar sank to the floor beside Brea and smoothed her matted blonde hair from her forehead. "You're safe."

Brea didn't say a thing. Her eyes were wide and hazy as she stared at Skylar.

Slowly, the terror slipped from Brea's expression and was replaced by something softer.

But still, no words spilled from her mouth.

It seemed Sprin's cure had loosed her soul, but not her tongue.

And she was the only one who knew what had happened after Telyn fled the wedding.

"Brea?" Skylar's voice was soft and hopeful.

But Brea only looked at her.

Telyn sank to the floor.

Piran would blame her for this. Accuse her of using magick to tie up his sister's tongue, and he would use that to drag her back to Eralia with him.

They couldn't hand the princess over, not yet.

Telyn knew she couldn't keep him away forever. She was running out of excuses. She needed another plan. One that would buy her more time.

She wasn't going to go with Piran unless it was absolutely necessary. And it wasn't. Not until all of her cards had been played.

And she still had a few up her sleeve.

She just needed time.

"What do we do?" Skylar turned to Telyn.

"We wait." Telyn looked up to Skylar.

She hated to see her so disappointed and worried.

And it hurt to know that she was partly the cause of it.

"We wait."

Days had passed and Brea still hadn't said a word.

Skylar was pacing around their rooms, her bare feet barely made a sound against the stone.

"Telyn, I-"

She cut herself off with a shake of her head.

"What is it?" Telyn looked up from the letters she was reading at the desk.

"It's nothing."

"It's something." The letters settled onto the desk with a soft rustle of paper as Telyn stood.

"It's foolish."

"It is not foolish if it is bothering you. Speak your mind, love." Skylar's pacing stopped as Telyn took her hands.

"The wedding. The explosion. Someone planned that," Skylar said.

"Of course. It wasn't an accident. What are you getting at?"

"Who is the only one benefitting from this? The king and queen are dead, Brea was missing, the people are terrified."

"Piran is king." Telyn couldn't keep the bitterness from her voice.

"Piran is king." Skylar agreed. "He is the only one benefitting from this chaos."

"You think he caused the explosion."

Telyn thought of Piran's hand wrapped around Alexander's throat in Nym's Forest as he threatened them all.

Telyn couldn't say she didn't think him capable of such violence.

Not with the image of the Unseelie Court in flames, Piran with King Rhode's head in his hand, burning in her mind.

Piran was more than capable of murder if it got him what he wanted.

And he wanted power.

Power that could easily be gained from inheriting the crown in the event of his parents' deaths.

With no witnesses to say what he'd done, he got exactly what he wanted.

"I think you're right."

They had no proof, it was purely circumstantial, but it made sense. More sense than any of the other theories that had been circling.

"We don't have any proof, but it might cause enough suspicion to undermine his authority," Telyn said.

"He's the king, we can't just drag his name through the mud, he'll have us executed," Skylar said.

"I'm a queen," Telyn said, "I can extend my protection to you and your people. An act against you is a declaration of war as far as I'm concerned."

It was time to stop reacting to the things happening. Telyn needed to find a proactive approach. One that would force Piran and Carling to react to her.

She was a queen, she should never have spent so much time playing as a pawn.

Ceris seemed to slow down. Now that Brea was awake, everyone was less frantic.

Brea joined them for meals in the dining hall, but, that was the extent of her interaction with the others.

Skylar had been keeping a close eye on her. Brea was the closest thing she had to a sister, and her over protectiveness proved it.

It was rare Telyn caught Skylar outside of Brea's room. She came out with Brea for meals, but aside from that, they were both bundled up in the room.

With Skylar at Brea's side, Telyn was left to deal with their unwelcome visitor.

"My Lady, the king is here." One of the maids fidgeted nervously and refused to meet Telyn's eyes. "I couldn't keep him out, I'm sorry."

"It's not your fault," Telyn sighed.

She'd known that Piran would come to collect eventually. It was only a matter of time before his patience wore out and he demanded results. That was the only thing that hadn't changed throughout the mess of a year Telyn was having.

Now, she just had to get him to give Cordelia and Nolan back and go away again. At least until they could get Brea to talk again.

Telyn took a slow breath before she made her way to the drawing room to meet Piran.

She would not be afraid of him.

She would not allow herself to be weak.

She would face him, and she would get what she wanted.

When Telyn entered the drawing room, Piran was lounging on one of the chairs, staring at a painting on the wall. There were books on the table beside him, but he didn't seem to have any interest in them.

Cordelia and Nolan were standing behind the chair he was in. Their posture was rigid as they kept their glazed eyes on the wall.

Piran's eyes fell on her from across the room and a contempt smile spread across his face. "You're not hiding from me after all."

Telyn scowled. "I do not wish to be here, some of us don't have the luxury of escaping that which annoys us."

"Where's my sister?"

"Hand over the members of my court and go find her yourself."

Piran sat up, his smile replaced with a snarl. "If I wanted to find her myself, I wouldn't have set you on the mission."

"Even if you're king, you're going to have to learn to do things yourself," Telyn said.

Cordelia and Nolan flinched.

She knew that was not something he wanted to hear, but she was tired of lying through her teeth and bending over backwards to comply with his every whim. She had told herself she would stop reacting and start acting, now was the perfect time to start.

"We are not your babysitters, nor hers, for that matter." Telyn crossed her arms and held herself up straighter. "I put in the work to find my family, you should be doing the same for yours."

Piran's rage was palpable.

Fear began to creep up Telyn's spine. Perhaps she had been too bold...

No.

She deserved to be here just as much as he did, if not more. She was not a pawn he could dance around a board however he pleased. She wasn't under his control at all.

But she was still mildly afraid of him.

He was capable of terrible things, she'd witnessed them first-hand. They had to end. And if she wasn't the one to stop him, he would continue to terrorize the people of both realms the way he had her. No one else would stop him. So it had to be her.

Telyn took a breath to steady herself and met the king's eyes.

"You may be king, but you demonstrate a horrible lack of initiative. You delegate everything and laze about in your palace. The people will begin to think you're weak." There was no tremor to Telyn's voice, only cold calculation.

The people weren't the only ones she could begin to stir doubt in.

"Then I will show them that there is no weakness to be found," Piran said.

"How?"

"I will kill any who dare suggest it."

His response was painfully on brand for the person she'd come to see him as.

Nothing mattered to him but his own power.

"You have no one," Telyn whispered. "How long will it be before you tire of this existence?"

"With the world in my hand, I won't need anyone."

"The world is not so easily tamed, there will always be opposition to your rule, especially if you continue on such a tyrannical path."

Telyn expected yelling, maybe a raised hand, or threats at the least.

But Piran turned on his heel and walked out, leaving Cordelia and Nolan behind.

Telyn didn't move until she heard the door to the estate slam shut.

She had stood up for herself and she was safe. Completely unharmed, a little shaken, but safe. She had done it by herself too, no one had been with her to boost her confidence.

This was her small victory, and hers alone.

It gave her hope for the future. The more she stood up to him, the better at it she would get.

If nothing else, it told her she was capable of more than she'd thought she was.

It was a step in the right direction.

She sighed and approached the others. They had relaxed a bit without Piran in the room, but it was evident that he hadn't been kind to them in the time they'd spent together.

"Are you two alright?" She asked.

"We will be." Nolan mustered a smile.

"As soon as we've bathed." Cordelia sighed and slumped against the back of the chair Piran had been sitting in. "We'll just give him a few more minutes to get out of here before he changes his mind."

"Of course, just let me know if you need anything." Telyn smiled to herself as she left the drawing room.

Dinner was quiet that evening. Brea hadn't wanted to come out, and Skylar refused to go without her. Telyn was left with Nolan, Cordelia, and Wes for company, and it seemed they didn't have much to say.

The silence made it hard for Telyn to comfortably sit still. She felt like she should be doing other things.

Her skin crawled with the need to feel like she was doing something meaningful. She forced herself to remain seated and work her way through her dinner.

"Telyn?" Cordelia shifted in her seat beside Nolan. "You're quiet."

"There's just not much to talk about, little heart." Telyn smiled.

She didn't want to worry the girl. She was beginning to regret dragging her into it all. It was too dangerous, but it was too late to let her go now. Too many people knew she was a part of the court, if she was left alone, she would be in even more danger. It was better if she was here, where Telyn knew she could protect her.

Or at least try to.

She'd slowly been testing her powers to see if anything had changed, but every time she tried, it was like she was draining her energy. No matter how little magick she used, it was always the same.

She was hoping it would change with more time. She knew enough about fighting to be able to stand her own for a bit, but she was far more useful with her magick.

She hadn't noticed when everyone else left the table. Or when Skylar walked into the dining hall.

Telyn glanced up as Skylar approached her. "You're out. Is everything okay?"

"Everything's fine, I just needed to stretch my legs." Skylar offered a small smile.

There were shadows under her sunken in eyes. She seemed more restrained than usual. It was like she was trying to keep herself from falling apart.

Telyn wondered when the last time she'd slept was.

"Let me take care of her for awhile," Telyn said.

"She hardly knows you, I'm not sure she would feel safe." Skylar yawned.

"You need to sleep. She'll trust me if you're the one who leaves her with me." Telyn stood up and pushed her chair under the table.

Skylar seemed to consider it for a moment.

"Has she said anything yet?"

"No. Something is keeping her quiet, but I don't know if it's physical or mental."

"There's no way to know until she finds a way to communicate it with us."

They stood in silence for a moment.

"You need sleep. You're practically a walking zombie," Telyn said.

"You'll protect her?"

"You know I will. I won't let anything happen to her."

"Alright, come on."

Skylar led Telyn back to Brea's room. When they opened the door, Brea was sitting on the bed, facing the open window.

"I'm back, little bee."

Brea turned at the sound of Skylar's voice and gave a small smile, but remained silent.

"This is Telyn." Skylar gestured Telyn ahead of her into the room. "She helped me wake you up. She's going to stay with you for a little bit, I promise I'll be back soon."

Brea nodded and turned back towards the window.

It was going to be a long day, but if Skylar got some sleep, it would be worth it.

Telyn plopped down in the chair beside the bed and gave Skylar the signal to leave.

The door clicked shut behind Skylar as she left and Telyn was left in silence once again.

Brea was facing away from Telyn, her eyes on the window once again. It was almost like she expected something to come through it.

Telyn could see the pale pink of the sun staining the horizon as day break began. Brea didn't move to close the curtains. She didn't move at all.

She just sat and watched as more color spilled into the sky. It was something that Telyn had taken for granted for so long. The beauty of sunrise was breathtaking, but for so long, it was just what was expected.

But Brea hadn't been able to see a sunrise since before the wedding, and even then, with the way time worked in Siluria, Telyn wasn't sure the girl had ever been able to see one. It made her realize how lucky she was to have something so beautiful to represent a fresh start.

A new day, another chance.

"We should get you to bed too." Telyn stood to close the window, but Brea shook her head.

"You don't want to sleep yet?"

Brea pointed a single finger to the window.

She was waiting for the sun. Telyn watched her as her eyes followed the movement of the sun as it slowly crawled higher into the sky and broke through the trees.

Seemingly satisfied by its progress, Brea closed the curtains, and left the room in darkness before she settled back onto the bed and curled up under her blanket.

Telyn thought she understood why Brea had wanted to watch it.

It was like proof that the good in things would break through eventually. The same way the sun fought to rise in the sky and clear the darkness of light. It was just as much a symbol of hope for her as it was for Telyn.

As different as Siluria was from Vesteria, it seemed they still had their similarities.

The people here, they were just as much her people as the ones in Alidain were. Not by way of authority, but through kinship. They had struggled through what life had thrown at them, and they found hope in the same things. They were all just people. People who hadn't asked to be brought into this world full of hatred and power thirsty leaders. Not a single one of them deserved to be subjected to what Piran would put them through if things went his way.

Telyn wasn't just fighting for the people she cared about, she was fighting for the people like Brea, who had no one else to fight for them. It was a lot more responsibility than she had originally bargained for, but she didn't see a way out of it now.

It was getting harder to keep up with all of her responsibilities, but she couldn't just drop them. Not when so many people depended on her.

Visitors

"Every good story needs a villain."
-Stephanie Garber, Legendary

The next evening, Ceris had some interesting visitors. Telyn hadn't expected to see Sorcha again. She had been the original plan of escape, one that Telyn had deemed unneeded once Skylar had rescued her.

But the captain stood scanning the shelves when Telyn entered the drawing room.

With Skylar still reluctant to leave Brea's side, Telyn had taken over seeing to the visitors that occasionally wandered into the estate. This one in particular gave her an odd sense of excitement.

There was something different about the way Sorcha held herself. She'd held an air of confidence the first time Telyn had met her, but something about it was now more self assured.

Like a facade had slipped and now she was more herself.

Sorcha turned when she noticed Telyn hovering by the door.

"What a surprise." Sorcha grinned. "It's nice to see you here, Telyn."

Telyn found herself smiling right back. "The same to you. What brings you around?"

"I decided to pay home a visit. I'm sure you know things are getting dicey around here. I wanted to see everyone one last time before things got too bad." Sorcha pulled herself away from the shelves and plopped down on one of the chairs.

"I didn't realize you were from the Winter Court. I hope your people are doing well." Telyn sat across from Sorcha. Her eyes caught on the window behind her for a moment before she returned her attention to the captain.

"Yes, our High Lady takes good care of them." Telyn could feel the pride for Skylar in Sorcha's voice. "My baby brother works here. He's been doing well from what I can tell. He was never much one for talking though."

"That's good. Do you know where you're headed next?"

Sorcha hesitated for a moment. "Listen, I'm only telling you this because I trust you'll end up on the right side of this war. You're a lot of things, and stupid isn't one of them. The pirates are gathering together to stand against the king. Ezra and his system have got the beginnings of a plan. I'm going with them. If I'm to die in this war, it's going to be fighting for my family and the folks in the mainland, not like some dog who slipped in obedience classes."

Telyn let the information sink in for a moment. "Good luck. I'll be standing with you when the time comes."

There was no need for her voice to be such a hushed whisper, everyone in Ceris was on the same page about the war, but it still felt wrong to speak of it any louder.

"Thank you. I best be getting off, they won't be at the same port for much longer. If you need help, just ask for a Captain Ezra. They'll find you." Sorcha stood and brushed off her trousers.

As soon as the door clicked shut behind Sorcha, Telyn moved towards the window.

There had been something out there when she'd sat down, and something told her it would still be there.

She scanned the ground outside, and hidden in the reflections of the stars bouncing off of the snow, stood a figure in a black cloak.

Telyn frowned. There was no reason for anyone to be sneaking around. And it certainly wasn't a good idea to be doing so when the people of this realm were most active.

Telyn pried the window open and jumped.

She let her wings slow her fall. She coasted to the ground and landed right in front of the figure, who didn't look at all surprised to find her there.

"Who are you?" Telyn demanded.

"You didn't recognize me, child? I'm disappointed." Telyn recognized the voice as a small smile crept over the figure's face and he removed his hood.

Anger boiled up inside Telyn.

"All this time, you've been silent, and *now* you show up?"

Nox stood in front of her. Strands of his shoulder length black hair were braided around the grey horns that stuck up through them.

Telyn was a bit surprised. Their time had always been limited and kept to dreams. He'd never physically appeared to her. But here he stood.

What had changed?

"You don't seem happy to see me in the slightest." He frowned.

"Why would I be? You practically abandoned me when I needed you the most." Telyn folded her arms across her chest.

"You know I couldn't interfere with that," He sighed.

"You are a god. You can do whatever you want." Telyn scoffed.

"Yes, but we have rules. You have to understand that though I was capable of it, I was not allowed to do so. It would have created more problems."

"Yes, because your brother is so good at following those rules."

"His ignorance of those rules is what got us here in the first place. Had I followed in his footsteps, there would be even more fractures between my siblings and I, and this war would be much worse."

The last time Telyn had seen him, it had been in a field filled with rose bushes. It was so strange to see him here in the stark frozen landscape of the Winter Court.

"Would it have made a difference for us? Will our realms even survive this war?"

She knew it was a possibility. Things got destroyed when the gods fought. Her home could very well be one of them, along with everyone living there.

"As it is, there is a chance you and your people can survive." There was something restrained about his voice, like he wasn't telling her everything.

"But it's a very slim chance, isn't it. You don't think we'll make it."

"I can not say whether or not you will, but I will try to do my best to ensure that outcome."

"You can do more than you're doing now?" Telyn didn't believe he would, even if he could.

"Not as things are. You would need to become a Handmaiden, and that is no easy feat. But if you were to accomplish the tasks, I would be able to be more direct in my approaches."

"How do I do that?"

"You're not ready." Nox shook his head.

"How will I know when I am?" She hated being told that what she wasn't enough. Especially when doing this could make the difference between saving the people she cared about or not.

"I'll come for you when you are, trust me. There are a few more trials you're meant to go through as you are now."

If Telyn didn't know any better, she would have thought the god was sad about what he'd just said.

But that was impossible.

She was nothing but a pawn to him.

"How are you here physically? Before, you'd always just come during dreams."

"Things are growing more tense, Carling is gaining power, because of that, people are dying, and I'm getting more power."

"Then why are you trying so hard to stop him if it's benefitting you?"

"Because I don't need power, nor do I want it. My loyalty is to Siene. What Carling did to her was wrong, and as her older brother, it is my place to ensure he pays for what he's done."

"Even though he's your family too?"

"Especially so."

Telyn thought about the way her family worked and determined it wasn't much different. There was a mix of them, there was her and Zerina, then there was Colton, and Sabina, and Nathaniel had done them all wrong. He wasn't much different than Carling in that way.

It was strange to think that even the gods had to deal with things like that.

"Any more questions before I leave?" Nox glanced behind him, like he thought something else might emerge from the woods.

"Why did you chose me?"

Nox seemed to contemplate the question as he looked at her. "You reminded me of myself. You were broken and in need of a way to fix yourself. You had the drive to mend what had been torn apart in your own life, and now it has extended to the rest of the world. You were the only person capable of being who I needed you to be."

With that, Nox vanished.

One second he was there with a soft smile, the next, Telyn stood alone in the snow. There wasn't even an indent in the snow to indicate he'd ever been there.

Telyn looked up at the window she'd left open and quietly made her way back into Ceris.

Telyn ran over the conversation in her head over and over again. She'd known that no one else would take her place if she stepped down, but she hadn't known that no one could, even if they wanted to.

There was too much she didn't understand.

Nathaniel had become Time because he had valued his power more than he had valued his family. But Carling was a god. What more could he want?

"Telyn?" Cordelia tugged on Telyn's sleeve.

"Yes?" Telyn looked down at the little girl.

She'd grown since they'd taken her in. She was nearly as tall as Telyn now.

"Brea is going to be alright, isn't she?"

"Of course. She's already doing much better. She just needs time to realize she's safe now." Telyn patted the top of Cordelia's head with a soft smile.

"I hope she'll be able to talk again. She was really nice before..."

"You've talked to her before?" Telyn hadn't realized the girls even knew each other.

"A little, before the wedding. Well, I suppose the not wedding. But she was very nice. She seemed a bit weirded out by the whole situation. I think she knew what was going to happen." Cordelia twisted a section of her red hair around her fist.

There was no way Brea would have been able to know what was going to happen.

"What makes you say that?" Telyn's full attention was on Cordelia now.

"Well she was really nervous during the ceremony, she kept saying something about hoping her brother wouldn't get mad." Her hair was tight around her fist now. It bothered the little girl as much as it was bothering Telyn.

It seemed Brea knew more about her brother than they'd originally thought.

"He won't be able to hurt her anymore." Telyn promised.

"But you're giving her back." Telyn didn't miss the disapproval in Cordelia's voice as she glared at Telyn.

Telyn was silent for a moment. "She will be safe. We won't let her get hurt. I promise you that."

Brea meant a lot to Skylar, Telyn had already been planning on protecting her, but if there was ever any question about it, there wasn't now. Cordelia needed friends her age, and she seemed to have found one in the princess. So Telyn would do everything in her power to keep that bond safe.

Cordelia needed more than just the adults around the castle. She had Nolan, and now Wes, and she had the rest of the Alidainian Court, but she needed people her age to relate to.

Friendships would be a hard thing to maintain during the war. Especially as a child, but Telyn intended to do everything in her power to keep Cordelia not only alive, but content as well. If that meant keeping her with Brea, then so be it.

She was fairly certain Skylar would think it was a good idea for Brea to have a friend too. Telyn and Skylar wouldn't be able to be around to keep the girls company all the time. There were too many responsibilities for them to take care of to play babysitter for Piran and Nolan.

However, they would have to keep Brea from Piran.

Telyn couldn't shake what Skylar had said.

It was possible that Piran would just kill Brea once he got his hands on her. So it was best to keep her protected. Especially from him.

"Do you need to talk to me about something else?" Cordelia hadn't left Telyn's side yet.

Cordelia glanced at her hands for a moment before she shook her head. "No, there's nothing else."

"You know you can talk to me about what happened after he took you. I'm here for you too."

Cordelia gave a small smile and a nod before she scampered off.

Telyn had expected the occasional bought of odd behavior from the girl, but something about this felt different. It wasn't just the antics of a child getting used to not having to fend for herself.

There was something else going on with Cordelia, and Telyn wished she would tell her what it was.

Maybe Nolan would know something about it.

Before Telyn could leave to go look for Nolan, Wes barged into the drawing room.

"Have you been hiding in here this entire time?" He demanded.

"I wasn't exactly hiding, but I was here, yes." Telyn was taken aback by his tone. "What's happened?"

"That captain of yours," Wes hissed. "Either get him on a leash or fire him. He's here and he's acting like he owns the place!"

Telyn fought back a groan. Why would Alexander be at Ceris out of all the places he could be, it had to be the one place where she was.

"Where is he?"

"Down in the main hall. I don't know what or who he's looking for, but it's making Brea uneasy. She can hear him yelling." Wes shook his head and muttered something under his breath that Telyn couldn't quite catch.

"I'll get him somewhere where he won't bother her and figure this out." Telyn turned to leave the room but Wes caught her wrist.

"Do you need any help?"

Wes didn't know everything, but he knew enough to think that Alexander might hurt her.

And she hated to admit that he was probably right. With Carling's spell still held over him, he was unpredictable.

"I'll be fine."

She didn't give herself time to change her mind before she left the room.

As promised, Alexander was pacing around the main hall, yelling for her.

"I'm here, stop yelling!" Telyn snapped as she came to a stop directly in front of him.

"I will yell as much as I want." He glared down at her.

"What did you come here for? You clearly have something you want to take up with me. How about we handle it like the civilized adults we are?" Telyn crossed her arms and glared right back up at him.

"Fine."

Telyn started walking. She didn't look behind her to see if he was following. She didn't need to.

His heavy footsteps echoed against the stone floors as they made their way to the other side of the estate.

"Now, what do you want?" Telyn closed the door behind them and turned to face him.

"I want to know what you did to me." The fire that burned in his eyes was familiar.

"I didn't do anything to you."

"You did *something*!" He was raising his voice now, getting louder with every word.

"No, Carling did something."

"Stop lying to me! I should *hate* you! I do hate you! But for some reason, I'm always getting drawn back in. So what was it?" His fists were clenched.

Telyn took a step back.

"You were never meant to hate me. You *loved* me for the gods' sake. He's the one who made you hate me." Telyn fought to keep her voice even.

"You're lying! Just because you're a queen doesn't mean that everything you say is the truth!"

"Maybe not, but it's clear that you can't trust me even when I do. If you can't put your personal feelings aside to do your job, I will have you replaced. You will be stripped of your title and dishonorably discharged. Am I clear?"

Telyn tried to muster the confidence she'd heard Skylar use so many times before.

Alexander didn't respond.

"Am I clear?" She repeated.

"Yes ma'am."

"You step out of line one more time, and you're out."

He nodded.

"Now go back home, and do your job. Pip needs you."

"Pip isn't the one that needs me."

He turned and he left the room.

When he was gone Telyn sighed and raked a hand through her hair.

Carling's hold on Alexander was slipping, that meant he was focused on something else. Which in turn meant, he was likely preparing to make his next move.

Things were getting to complicated. There was too little that made sense. If Telyn could just get answers, she could fix the colossal mess that Carling had created.

Which left the question: why was she cleaning up after a god?

He was perfectly capable of managing himself, or at least he should have been. And if he had refused to keep himself in check, his siblings should have been able to do the job for him.

There was no logical reason for Telyn or any other lesser being to be involved in all of this. Yet here they were.

Why?

What was the reasoning for all of this?

Telyn found herself pacing, a habit that had undoubtedly been picked up from Skylar. In fact, she could see little worn paths in the carpet she was pacing over, remnants from another worry Telyn's partner had likely had in the past.

The pacing didn't help her think any better, her mind was still muddled with questions that didn't have any apparent answers, but it made her feel better to be moving. To be doing something with herself instead of just sitting still.

There had to be an answer to all of it somewhere.

She just wasn't looking hard enough.

But where would she even begin to look for answers about beings that most people didn't even believe existed?

The red book would have been a useful tool, but it was still missing.

Something told her that Piran had taken it. And the only way to get it back from him would be to get close enough to steal it.

She couldn't risk something like that right now.

There had to be something else that just wasn't clicking yet. Something she wasn't quite seeing.

Haunted

"Who said 'please'
that made you hate the word so much?"
-Nora Sakavic, The King's Men

The only place Telyn could think of to start her search, was the library. The library in Alidain hadn't proved to be much help, but the libraries were much older in Siluria than they were in Vesteria. The books and people were older too. So it stood to reason that there would be more information about the old gods in a place that was closer to their times.

There was a chance that people like Kallista may have even met them. The trick would be finding those people and getting them to talk to her.

The library in Ceris might have been bigger than the Alidainian palace as a whole. Telyn had never seen such a large space. At least not one that bore the touch of humanity. That sort of space was reserved for forests and lakes and mountains.

But the only forest in that room was the one made of books. They rose in shelves that reached the ceiling, covered the walls, and stuck out in rows in between.

Telyn had thought that the library would be the easiest place to start, but she didn't know where to start *in* the library. It was so big that she couldn't even begin to imagine where anything could be.

The lanterns were already lit along the walls, they made it easy to find some sort of navigation amongst the labyrinth.

The words on some of the spines of the books *felt* strange. It was almost like she was trying to read the red book again. The longer she looked at them, the more familiar they felt. It was like they were the words to a story she'd been told once, and couldn't quite remember.

She pulled one of the older looking tomes from the shelf and let it fall open in her hands.

It was nothing more than a history book, telling about the time when Siluria was nothing more than a world overrun by nature.

Telyn's eyes lingered on the pages, telling her of how the Silurians were placed here along with their fae mother and they learned to wield nature's magick and bend it to their own will.

The longer she read, the more the world in the pages began to resemble the Siluria that Telyn had come to call home.

She also noticed the corruption that slowly crept into it.

Piran wasn't the only monarch who wanted more than they were supposed to have.

Carling had been working his claws into this realm, and others for a long time.

Despite the calm calculated front the former king had presented when Telyn proposed an alliance, his hands weren't the cleanest when it came to bloodshed.

Though Telyn did notice that after he'd married Queen Tara, the atrocities had dwindled, and eventually ceased all together.

He had been amongst the lucky ones.

Others chose to pursue their power over being happy with what they had. And they never won. They ended up overthrown and executed, assassinated, and tortured.

It gave Telyn a bit of hope.

If the people that had lived in the realm then could stand up against their tyrannical leaders, there was no reason the current people couldn't do the same now.

She thought back to Nox telling her that Carling was growing stronger.

That was what had changed.

If Nox was strong enough to come to Ceris, Carling must have paid a visit to Piran as well.

And Siene might have visited Skylar.

She might know more than Nox did.

Telyn tucked the book under her arm and left the library. There would be more time to explore the rest of it later. For now, she needed to know if the other gods had contacted their champions as well.

Telyn checked for Skylar in Brea's room, but neither of the girls were there. The room was empty, the blankets on the bed ruffled, and the curtains flapped in the wind from the open window behind them.

Telyn dropped her book onto the bed and reached for the curtains. She pulled them open and peered into the darkness below her.

Skylar and Brea were sitting in piles of snow.

Telyn could hear the faint sound of their laughter as it drifted up on the wind. They threw clumps of snow at each other and traced pictures into the mounds of it that surrounded them.

"What are you two doing down there?" Telyn called down with a smile.

The girls glanced up and Skylar beckoned Telyn over with a wave.

Telyn climbed through the window and let herself drop to the ground, sending a spray of snow over the other girls.

"We were just playing. I thought it was about time Brea got out of the house," Skylar said.

"That's great." Telyn watched as Brea began to build something in front of herself.

"What have you been up to?" Skylar leaned back and her elbows sank into the snow.

"Just a bit of research. I wanted to talk to you about something."

"Go ahead."

"Well, we've had a few visitors. Nox was one of them. I was curious as to whether or not Siene had visited you." Telyn sat down beside Skylar.

Skylar's face went blank for a moment before she answered. "She has. She was here not too long ago. What did Nox have to say?"

"Nothing helpful. Just that I wasn't ready."

"Ready for what?"

"If I become a Handmaiden, I can get him to help us more. He says it's against the rules otherwise."

"But he won't let you do that yet."

"That about sums it up. What did Siene have to say?"

Snow clung to Skylar's sleeves as she sat up and studied the structure Brea was working on.

"She said that this war was going to require hard decisions to be made, sacrifices as well. She hates that this is what it's come to, but if they don't stop Carling now, he'll only get more powerful and arrogant."

"Well, that explains why he chose Piran to be his champion," Telyn said.

"They choose those like them," Skylar agreed.

"I wonder if that's how any of them became the gods that they are now." Telyn's voice was quiet.

Skylar's focus was on Brea. Something about her had shifted at the mention of her brother.

Her hands had stilled in the snow as she stared past it into something much darker than the night around them.

"Brea?" Skylar gently took the girl's hand. "What's going on?"

With a trembling hand, Brea traced words into the snow.

He killed them.

"Who killed who?" Telyn puzzled as she stared at the wobbly lettering.

Piran.

And with that, the pieces began to fall in line.

"He killed your parents," Telyn said. "And he tried to kill you too, but you ran."

Brea nodded.

"So he really was behind that explosion," Skylar whispered.

It was one thing to theorize about who had been heartless enough to risk the lives of thousands of people.

It was another thing to know that that theory had been correct.

And the man behind the trigger was the king.

"Brea, did he try to kill you too?" Skylar's voice was gentle, but Telyn could hear the edge behind it.

Brea nodded.

"He can't be allowed to get away with this." Telyn knew she wasn't the only one thinking it. Someone willing to kill their own family for a throne wasn't someone who deserved to have one.

If he cared so little for his own family, there was no guarantee that he would care for his people any more.

He didn't want what was best for Eralia and Siluria, he wanted to be in control. He didn't care who it hurt.

"How are we going to stop the one person that outranks us?" Skylar asked.

"He doesn't outrank *me*." Telyn stood up. "He has no real control over me. If we can get the people to realize how horrible he is, they'll stand beside us. He can't do much without an army. We just have to be the example, show them that they're not the only ones who disagree with him."

"Where would we even start?" Skylar pulled Brea into her arms.

"We don't have to. Someone else already has."

"What do you mean?"

"Sorcha was telling me about a group of pirates. They're getting ready to stand against Piran. We just have to show that we're with them, they're not standing alone."

Everything felt so much more urgent now that their suspicions had been confirmed. Piran had been two steps ahead of them this entire time.

"Will it be enough?"

There was no way to know the answer to that.

"It's going to have to be. At least for now."

"Say we do join these pirates, what next? Would we be under their command? Would they listen to what we have to say? Are we going to progress at all or are we just signing ourselves off to another tyrant?" Skylar raked a hand through her hair.

"We can talk to them. I'm sure they're smart enough to realize what Piran is doing is wrong. If their goal is to be like him they won't get very far. But if they truly care about liberating Siluria, they'll agree to an alliance of sorts. Neither of us work under the other, we'll work together, and when Piran is gone, we go our separate ways."

Skylar seemed to think this over for a moment. "Where do we start?"

"The docks. We're looking for a Captain Ezra. Sorcha said we would find him if we asked for him."

Skylar glanced over at Brea. "We can't leave her here alone. It's too dangerous."

"Even with Wes and Nolan here?"

"I suppose they'll take care of her." Skylar sighed. "Do you want to go stay with Uncle Wes?"

Brea nodded.

"It's settled then. Let's go find this Captain Ezra." Skylar pushed herself to her feet and offered a hand to Brea.

Once the girls were on their feet, they made their way to Nolan's room, where they unsurprisingly found not only Nolan, but Cordelia and Wes as well.

"Wes, can you watch her for a bit?" Skylar asked.

Brea didn't wait for a response, she slipped into the room and took a seat beside Cordelia who smiled when she saw the princess.

"Sure, we've got her. Have fun." Wes waved Skylar off.

"We'll try." Skylar rolled her eyes and shut the door behind herself.

Telyn followed Skylar out of Ceris and into the cold of the Winter Court.

The walk to the docks didn't take long. Ice slushed up the water that sluggishly moved through the harbor as boats came and left. The docks were full of sailors and aids, moving boxes and barrels, and preparing ships to sail. Amongst the obviously pointed ears and tinged skin of the fae and Silurians, there also appeared to be some humans in the crowd, which sparked Telyn's curiosity. The only humans she'd seen in Siluria so far were the ones she had brough with her.

Skylar pulled one of the sailors aside. He had a shock of black hair tucked under his cap and Telyn could see a bolt of grey going through it.

"Can I help you?" He glanced between the girls.

"We're looking for a Captain Ezra." Skylar glanced over the sailor's shoulder like she could summon the captain just by saying his name.

The sailor chuckled. "That's an easy one, but who's asking?"

"What's your name?"

Telyn could tell Skylar's patience was wearing thin as she scanned over the sailor with narrowed eyes.

"Well, I'm Wren, but lucky for you, I'm a close friend of Ezra's." The sailor's lopsided grin shifted to a frown and his eyes narrowed.

"What do you want?" The sailor's voice had changed, his accent was more heavily accented and more suited to being out at sea.

"Captain Ezra?" Telyn tried.

"Yes, I'm here, and I'm not very patient."

"You're Ezra too?" Skylar asked.

"I'm a lot of people." Ezra shrugged.

"We were told you were making a stand against King Piran. We wanted to tell you you have the support of Alidain and the Winter Court." Telyn nudged Skylar, who nodded in response.

Ezra's eyes widened. "Well that was certainly unexpected." He cleared his throat.

"What do you need us to do?" Skylar asked.

"Just extending your support is enough, really."

"No, we want to be an active part of this. He's done things to hurt us too, we don't want to sit back and watch while others go down fighting for a cause we believe in," Telyn said.

Ezra looked her over for a moment, his face had gone a little pale, but he was smiling. "You're Corbin Ramirez's daughter, aren't you?"

"How did you know?" Telyn frowned.

"You sound just like he did. Follow me."

Ezra led them onto one of the ships and into a room below deck.

The atmosphere made Telyn jittery, but she pushed through the discomfort. It was the least of their concerns at the moment.

The room was small and completely wooden, the only thing that stood out was a map that was pinned to the table in the center of the room with a gold hilted dagger. There were several figures sitting on top of the map, most of them ships of varying sizes and colors.

"These are our people and their positions." Ezra gestured to the map. "We're cutting off trade routes and supplies to the palace, but maintaining the ones that feed the citizens. We want to minimize the harm caused to everyone, but we need to cut him off."

Skylar nodded. "That's a good plan, but how are you ensuring the innocents in the palace are getting food? What about the prisoners?"

"We have runners into the palace, they ensure the servants and the prisoners get what they need. We have people on both sides of those bars." Ezra's tone had shifted, like it pained him to talk about it.

Telyn wasn't surprised they had people in the prisons, they were pirates after all, and no matter how much good you did, the title held a negative connotation.

There were likely many people in those cells who didn't deserve to be there. If there weren't before, Telyn didn't doubt that there was now. Piran had a habit of getting rid of inconveniences, no matter how small. The ones that were in the cells were the lucky ones.

She didn't want to think about how many people he had already killed between his parents, and now. There were probably too many.

"So what do you need us to do?" Telyn asked.

"You're closer to him than we are. He's required to work with the two of you as fellow leaders. What does he want? What can we keep away from him that will help us beat him?"

"All he cares about is power. He's the one who killed the previous king and queen, and he tried to kill the princess too," Skylar said.

"How do you know that?" Ezra asked.

"The princess told us," Telyn said.

"She's with you?"

"We've had her for awhile. She's not really talking, but she's communicating when she wants to," Skylar explained.

"We've had people looking for her since she went missing. We figured she was the only one who knew what had really happened the day the king and queen died, and we were right." Ezra shook his head and sighed. "To think, this entire time she was safe, with you."

"We're keeping her away from him, we'll continue to do so. I don't want him killing her too," Skylar said.

"That's not a problem, we've got what we needed from her. So please do keep her safe. Once Piran is out, we'll need another leader, and it would be an easier transition if it was another member of the royal family." Ezra leaned against the table.

"She's too young to have to handle that responsibility," Skylar said.

"She'll have help. I doubt she'll follow in her brother's footsteps, she's too much like her mother, but we'll have people guiding her just in case."

"So, really, you'll be the one leading the country." Skylar frowned.

"No, we'll only be making suggestions, Brea is free to make her own decisions based off of which suggestion she finds to be best."

"She's too young to be making those kinds of decisions."

"As much as I hate to say it, it may be years before it's necessary. We don't know how long this war will last," Ezra said.

"It won't, either it ends, or we'll be dead by the end of the year." Skylar didn't sound bitter, she just sounded tired.

This must have been part of what Siene had told her.

That meant things were much worse than Telyn had previously thought.

If even the goddess helming this thought there was no hope if this dragged out, then was there any way they could actually win?

"Either way, we have to try. We fight for as long as we can. If we die, at least we die standing for our freedom and not cowering under some spoilt brat who calls himself king."

Telyn glanced at Skylar.

He's right.

I know.

"Well then it's settled, we fight until there's nothing left," Telyn said.

Telyn didn't have much to defend, just a handful of people and the kingdom she had never wanted to begin with. It wasn't much but it was enough to give her a reason to fight. It was enough to keep her from saying it wasn't her problem. they made it her problem because this war affected them. And as their queen, it was her job to protect them from the fallout.

For now, they would have to keep working on a plan, build their defenses, and find Piran and Carling's weak points.

Which under normal circumstances would be easy, but how was anyone supposed to beat the god of war at war?

Tide's Change

"Evil will never find peace."
-L.J. Smith, The Awakening

The walk back to Ceris somehow felt longer. The girls didn't need words to communicate. They both knew they were in a bad situation, with limited cards to play. There was only one way to go though, they would fight and claw their way to the top and overcome all it eventually.

Eventually was the important part there.

Telyn knew she wasn't patient, she knew that no matter how hard she fought things wouldn't change overnight. All she would achieve by rushing into things was messing things up because she had rushed into things.

Alidain wasn't safe, and neither was Ceris. They were both safer than most places, but they had been places where bad things had happened. But with everyone spread between the two places, it made it harder for Telyn to protect them all.

She couldn't bring the entirety of Alidain to Ceris, so she would have to go back.

As much as she hated the idea of leaving Skylar and their home, she knew that there were going to be sacrifices she would have to make.

And she had responsibilities. She couldn't just put them off forever.

Pip had been doing Telyn's job for long enough. It wasn't fair of her to ask them to do it for longer than necessary, they had their own problems to handle.

But leaving meant bringing Nolan and Cordelia with her, and Wes and Brea wouldn't be too happy with that.

There was no clean cut solution to having them all separated.

Brea needed someone, Skylar needed to be able to run her court.

And Wes. He was just stubborn.

Telyn wasn't sure she would be able to get Nolan away from him if she tried. Not after Piran had taken him. Wes had lost him once, and she doubted he was willing to again. Even if it was just to Alidain.

So even with the best planning, they would all remain divided.

She needed to find a way for them all to be safe even while they were apart. On one hand, that meant she wouldn't have to leave Skylar; it also meant things were likely going to get more complicated.

It would be much easier if she could just put everyone in a bubble and face whatever came for them without risking their lives.

But life didn't conveniently provide saftey bubbles, even if some people deserved them. If Telyn couldn't be defensive, she would need to take a more offencive stance. One that could protect everyone without trapping them in the confines of where she could watch them.

Just as they reached Ceris, something clicked into place.

History had a habit of repeating itself.

The monarchs before Piran and his father had all been overthrown in some way. By the people. The people had rallied together to over throw a king that was against them. The trick was getting all of these people together.

Captain Ezra and Sorscha had begun with their group of pirates, but they would need more than that.

They would need the support of the other courts and Eralia.

But what would be strong enough to pull the people away from a victimized king?

He'd done a good job at painting himself the victim. Left at the altar on his wedding day, his parents killed, and his sister kidnapped on the same day. To them, what had befallen him was nothing short of a tragedy.

But the truth; that would turn heads.

If Telyn revealed *why* she had left, and that Piran was the hand behind his parents' murders, then most, if not all, of his subjects would turn their backs to him. They had families of their own, and most of them probably wouldn't ever imagine being able to do something so horrible to the people they loved. He would no longer be the victim, he would be exposed as the villian he was.

And as they'd seen time and time again, history would repeat. Piran would fall, and with him, Carling would lose his pawn.

And as easy as that, it could be over.

Telyn could regain some semblance of normalcy in her life.

Things would always be different, she didn't see any way of ridding herself of her responsibilities as queen, but they would be the mundane tasks and challenges of a monarch. Not fighting to stay above all of the drama and danger that came with being associated with Piran and the gods.

In a stange sort of way, she imagined it would almost feel boring.

"Are you alright over there?" Skylar asked.

She had been just as quiet as Telyn during their walk.

"Yes, I'm just thinking," Telyn said

"About what?"

"Ways to bring the rest of the people to our side. I know I have the support of my kingdom, but it's going be hard to sway Eralia to support the woman who broke their king's heart."

"What heart?" Skylar scoffed.

"The one he's convinced them he has. We may know that it's a rotten dead thing inside his chest, but they don't. That's what we have to show them."

"Well, if anyone can figure it out, it'll be you."

Skylar was wearing a soft smile when Telyn looked over at her.

Telyn knew Skylar believed in her more than Telyn believed in herself. It was a comfort knowing that no matter how bad things might get, Skylar trusted her to be alright in the end, and she was there to help when it was needed.

But she also gave Telyn the space she needed to figure things out on her own. It was nice having someone to bounce ideas off of, but there were some things Telyn needed to handle herself.

And she was grateful that Skylar gave her that space.

Cordelia and Brea were sitting on the floor of the foyer, waiting for Telyn and Skylar. They were playing with what looked like paper dolls. Dolls that were quickly abandoned as soon as they saw Telyn and Skylar.

"You're back!" Cordelia launched herself into Telyn's arms.

"Did anything interesting happen while we were gone?" Telyn asked, she smiled as she watched Brea hug Skylar with more reserved enthusiasm.

But the little girls' smiles fell.

"Her brother came back," Cordelia said.

Skylar and Telyn exchanged a look.

He had been waiting for them to leave. He was planning something.

When is he not? Skylar echoed Telyn's own thoughts.

We can't leave them alone like that again.

"Where are Wes and Nolan?" Skylar asked.

They had been the ones who were supposed to watch the girls after all. The ones who were supposed to keep things like Piran arriving unannounced from happening.

"They told the mean prince to go away. We didn't see them after that." Cordelia shrugged.

Telyn felt ice shoot through her veins.

They would have gone back to the girls once Piran was gone, right? He had to have taken them. That was the only explanation, and it was scarily on brand for his character.

He wouldn't try taking people again, would he? Not after last time. Telyn pulled her eyes away from Skylar and forced a smile. He couldn't be *that* stupid.

I wouldn't put it past him. He's proven he's not above anything at this point.

She was right. Every time Telyn thought Piran couldn't sink any lower, he did something to prove her wrong. He did something to show her that not only was he the monster she knew him to be, but he was much worse than that.

She couldn't believe she'd been naïve enough to trust him before she really knew who he was.

Truth be told, if it hadn't been for Skylar's comments on his behavior, Telyn might have been in a lot more trouble than she already was. She couldn't count the number of times Skylar had saved her life already. Even before she knew she was more than just a voice in her head.

Far more than she should have had to.

That was for certain.

Telyn would have to find a way to make it up to her.

For now, though, they needed to make sure Nolan and Wes were safe.

Telyn reached for Cordelia's hand as she made her way through the foyer and into the heart of Ceris.

We should check their rooms first. Skylar's voice rang in Telyn's head as her footsteps echoed behind her.

It didn't take long for Telyn to reach the door to Nolan's room. She pulled it open to find...

Nothing.

It was empty.

Telyn fought to tamp down on the sense of dread threatening to drown her.

They still hadn't checked Wes's room. They could be completely fine in there, or anywhere else in the estate. She just needed to find them to be sure. She needed to know she didn't need to run a kidnapping rescue again.

Skylar took the lead as they moved down the hall towards Wes's room.

Cordelia squeezed Telyn's hand. She knew something was wrong, Cordelia had always been more in touch with everything going on around them than she should have needed to be, but in a way, Telyn was glad she was so sensitive to these things. It meant she was less likely to get into trouble and get hurt. She knew what was and wasn't safe, she knew what to avoid.

Telyn had no doubt that that sense of caution and worry would keep both her and Brea safe as things unfolded.

Piran had made it clear that he wasn't done with them yet.

As exhausting as it was to deal with him, something inside Telyn got almost excited to see how much it would take to break him. How far she would have to go before he realized he'd lost.

Because he would lose. Telyn had never been more sure of anything in her life.

This man had manipulated her, abused her friends, killed his own parents, and likely would have killed his sister too. He had pushed her to her breaking point, but all that had done was make her more adamant about ruining his life worse than he'd ruined hers.

So, no, she didn't feel any guilt about the things she was going to do. If there was anyone so deserving of the most painful and cruel death, it was Piran.

As long as her friends and family were safe, she would do anything it took to keep him out of the picture. If that meant killing him, she promised herself she wouldn't hesitate this time.

Piran was not her uncle. He wouldn't end it for her. Time may have come back, but Piran wasn't stupid enough to put himself in such a vulnerable position. He wouldn't make it easy for her. She had no doubt that she would experience his manipulation once again, but she wouldn't hesitate. This wasn't just about her anymore.

If she got the chance to end the storm that was brewing, she would take it.

After what felt like entirely too long, Skylar opened the door to Wes's room.

Telyn let out a sigh as she saw the boys sprawled out over the bed, limbs stretched out and crossing over each other, and books in hand as they looked up at the people standing in the doorway.

"Is everything alright?" Wes asked as he closed the book he had been reading, his thumb held his spot.

"We were just making sure you hadn't been kidnapped," Skylar said. "The girls said they hadn't seen you after you told Piran to go away."

"I told you we should have gone back to check on them." Nolan nudged Wes with his elbow.

"I said they would be fine, and they are." Wes shrugged. "They were just worried about us."

"It's better to be safe than sorry," Skylar said. "Piran is unpredictable. We need to stay vigilant."

"Do you have any sort of a plan yet?" Nolan asked.

"A bit of one." Telyn offered a small smile. She knew where she wanted this to end, and how, she had a few steps to get there, all that was left was to tie it all together.

"What is it?" Wes asked.

"You'll just have to wait and see."

Telyn knew that the second she put herself in front of Piran's people they would see her as the villain. To them, she had already ruined Piran's life. They hadn't seen all he'd done. Their immediate reaction would be to run her out, or worse.

But she had a plan. The people of Siluria would be the easy part, she'd already met several that had their suspicions and problems with their leader. It was the humans in Eralia that would be hard to convince. They saw everything through the lens Piran had given them. They only knew what he wanted them to know.

It was Telyn's job to make sure they could see the truth.

But getting them to believe her, that might prove to be difficult.

She could talk as much as she liked, but that didn't mean they would believe her.

But she had to try.

They could do this without the humans, but it would be helpful if they weren't in their way either.

She couldn't rely on Nox anymore. He hadn't been much help up until this point, and she didn't have time to wait for him to decide she was ready to be a handmaiden. The longer they waited, the harder it was going to be to do this, the more time Piran would have to sink his claws into his people.

The sooner they knew the truth, the better.

Siene hadn't seemed to be much help either. She'd told Skylar that this war was going to require a sacrifice from everyone. But they already knew that. They themselves had already sacrificed so much to get this far. And they'd come too far to fail now.

Telyn knew that if the favor of the gods was going to be any help, she had to prove she was ready to take on the responsibility that came with that help. She needed to prove she was ready to be a handmaiden, what better way to do that than taking initiative and starting a revolution? And if it still wasn't enough for him, she would have to do it on her own. She knew she was more than capable of handling this herself now that she had a plan. And a backup plan. She was prepared to do whatever it took to end this, and end it in a way that ensured the people she cared about would stay safe. When she did finally end it, she would be free. And she would relish in the fact that she had taken down her enemies on her own. That the last thing Piran would see of his crumbling control over this realm was her face as she stared down at him and watched the life drain from his eyes.

Telyn shook herself from her thoughts as the door opened and Skylar came in with an undone tie hanging around her neck.

"I didn't think you would want to come with," Telyn said.

"Of course I want to come with, where you go, I go." Skylar was fiddling with the tie and tried to get it right as she stared in the mirror at the back of the room.

"Well alright then." Telyn watched as Skylar continued to struggle with her tie.

"Have you considered what would happen if this goes the complete wrong direction and they fully turn against us instead?" Skylar frowned at the knotted fabric in her hands.

"You don't have to come with. No one would know you're involved," Telyn slipped between Skylar and the mirror, took the ends of the tie from Skylar's hands, and fixed it for her. "I don't have anything to lose here, but you do. So, I'll understand if you'd rather stay here and not worry about the fall out."

"I'm not letting you do this alone. I know full well that you can protect yourself, but I don't want them thinking you're vulnerable and trying anything. I don't care about any fall out; I care about you. Yes, those people are my responsibility, but there's only so much I can do if they can't see what's happening around them."

"I'll be fine." Telyn leaned up on her toes and gave Skylar a quick kiss. "It's your decision though."

"Even so, I'd like to be the one to officially show you around." Skylar smiled.

With everything going on, there hadn't been much time for sightseeing, and there was a lot of the Winter Court that Telyn hadn't gotten to see. She'd been able to see a few of the outlying towns, but the city at the heart of it all was still a mystery to her. As was much of the rest of it. She knew she would get to it eventually, when things had calmed down.

Which could take anywhere from a few weeks to a few years.

As much as Telyn would have loved to conclude this mess as soon as possible, she knew there was going to be a certain finesse required to end it in their favor. And she was willing to play the long game if that meant she got her revenge.

"Whatever happens, whatever they say, don't let it get to you." Skylar took Telyn's hands and gave them a gentle squeeze.

"They're entitled to their own thoughts and opinions, Sky," Telyn said.

"I know, and what you're saying is going to reach the right people, but there's always going to be people that disagree. There's always going to be people who side with him. Don't let them get under your skin if they start saying things that aren't true."

"Everything is going to be alright. I can handle myself." Telyn smiled.

"Of course it is, you're amazing." Skylar smiled back.

"Well thank you, but if we keep standing around, we're going to be late." Telyn pulled away and made her way towards the door.

"Very well, I suppose we can't be late to this." Skylar followed her and shut the door behind them.

People's Choice

*"It takes ten times as long to put yourself back together
as it does to fall apart."*
-Suzzane Collins, Mockingjay

Telyn had to give Skylar's people some credit. Despite knowing nothing about what was going on, they all waited attentively in a square at the very center of the Winter Court. Women were shushing children and soothing babies so they would be able to hear what was going to be said. What would likely anger at least most of them

For the first time in a long time, Telyn felt a surge of anxiety as she stood in front of all of those people. She didn't think she'd ever done something so important.

Not a word was uttered as they waited for her to speak.

Skylar squeezed Telyn's hand, a gentle reassurance that she didn't have to do this alone.

"It has come to our attention, that your king is not who you thought he was," Telyn said.

There was a small collective gasp, but no one shouted out. They waited for her to finish.

"As you all know, there was an incident at the wedding that resulted in the death of the late king and queen, as well as the disappearance of Princess Brea. After an arduous and long search, we were able to find her. Once we were able to get her to communicate with us, she revealed that it was your new king that was responsible for the events that took place."

Hushed whispers swept across the square.

Telyn waited until the noise died down before she continued. It gave her time to fight to breath around the tightness in her chest.

"This may come as a shock to you, but Piran has been hiding things from his people for quite some time now. The only reason that wedding was being held in the first place was because he wants access to Alidain's throne. He did this by threatening the lives of my court members, the people who are close to me. And he didn't stop there. He wanted power so badly that he was willing to eliminate his own family to get there. If that's how he treats his own, how do you think he'll protect your families?"

The whispers evolved into debates that broke out in groups across the crowded square.

Telyn had known that not everyone would believe her, that there would be people who called her a liar, and remained loyally at their king's side. What she didn't expect was to cause outright discourse among the people in front of her.

They were flat out arguing, and there were clear lines of who stood where.

Most of the women were arguing in Telyn's defense, they claimed it was typical of a king to try and take advantage of a woman who ruled alone. There were a few men that agreed with this as well, but most of the men, a majority of which appeared to be wearing nicer clothes and bore fancy titles, argued that *she* was the one trying to take Piran's throne.

They thought she was relying on the sympathy of soft-hearted women like their wives to overthrow the king and take his place.

That couldn't be further from the truth.

Telyn didn't even want the throne she already had. She just didn't want to see people suffering and slaughtered because they'd put their trust in the wrong man.

Because that would be what happened if Piran was allowed to continue down this path he'd carved out of bone.

Thousands, if not millions, of these innocent people would die, simply because he'd deemed them an inconvenience.

"Let us hear it from the princess!" A shout rang out through the chaos that was unfolding.

"Yeah! You said you'd found her, let us see her!"

Other men joined in the shouting, demanding to see the princess.

Skylar stepped in to interrupt. "I don't believe that is a good idea at the time. Princess Brea is still recovering from the time she spent trapped in the Enchanted Forest."

That got them to quiet down again.

"Rest assured that when the princess is ready to address you, she will. Until then, we ask that you remain patient while she recovers," Skylar said. "For now, you are dismissed. Take some time to process the information that has been shared."

Skylar took a few steps back, pulling Telyn with her.

You did well, darling. Skylar squeezed Telyn's hand.

They didn't take it too well. Telyn squeezed back.

We can't control how they take it or what opinions they make, we can only control the delivery, and you did amazing.

As usual, Skylar's quiet support made it easier for Telyn to breathe.

She hadn't completely failed this entire public speaking thing.

It might not have gone as well as she had wanted, but it had done as well as it could go. Which was honestly better than she had expected. There wasn't as much back lash as she'd expected, but there was plenty of justified hesitation.

This war wasn't going to be won in a moment, or with a single speech. It would take time, and Telyn knew that. The waiting just got hard sometimes. Especially when it seemed like every minute spent in this semblance of freedom felt like a stolen one.

She felt like she was running off of stolen time, and it was a feeling that she hated.

She shouldn't need permission to live her own life.

And yet here she was, clinging to her peace and hope until Piran made another move meant to scare her into submission.

By agreeing to marry him, she had set a precedent. He knew that he could bend her until she broke if he pushed the right buttons. She had shown him that it was possible to manipulate her, and now he would never stop doing it. Not without the proper motivation to do so.

Telyn didn't intend to stop at giving him that motivation. She didn't trust him enough to let him live after all of this.

The war would end one way or another; with his head on a spike, or hers.

If Telyn had her way, it would be his.

She knew there was the possibility that it wouldn't work out in her favor, but she would rather go down fighting than being silent and complacent.

Her mother had been the one to remain silent, and it had resulted in her murder. Telyn loved her mother, but refused to condemn herself to the same fate.

She didn't know much about her father, but she had been told that he fought when things got rough. He had fought with his people and for them. That was the kind of leader Telyn wanted to be. She wanted to be right there with them, fighting until the end. She would much rather have that than run and hide like her mother had.

The way she saw it, was she had already spent most of her life running and hiding from people, from who she was, but that had to end.

She wouldn't get very far in life if she allowed others to control anything about her. From her self expression, to the way she ran her kingdom, and who she married.

So, she had to pave her own way, make her own rules.

And by accepting Skylar for who she was, and by accepting herself, she had taken the first step in reclaiming her life.

That was what had led her there, to declaring her truth to whoever would listen.

She never would have made it out of that wedding hall without Skylar's help, and she never would have had the courage to face all of these people without her support.

Even before Telyn knew who she was, all Skylar had done was look out for her.

She should have listened to that voice in her head more often.

No.

She should have been more sure in herself. She should have been capable of better judgement. It wasn't Skylar's responsibility to keep her out of messes, it wasn't anyone's responsibility but her own.

If she had learned nothing else from this, she had at least learned that trust needed to be earned. If you blindly gave it away to people, they would use it against you.

No one in this world was purely good or evil. Life wasn't so black and white. Everyone had motivations, reasons for being the way they were. But that also meant that everyone had a little bit of bad in them, some more so than others. And if she wasn't careful, she would end up giving her trust to the wrong person again. Someone with just a little too much evil in their heart to be any good to anyone.

She didn't think she would ever meet anyone other than Carling that could be worse than Piran, but she didn't want to find out either.

Two people.

That was all she really had to manage.

Two very dangerous, very blood thirsty people.

If she could keep Carling and Piran in check, everyone else would be able to take care of themselves. Granted, keeping those two in check wasn't exactly an easy task, certainly not one meant to be done by a single person, but Telyn would do what she had to do.

She only saw one path out of this mess, and she was determined to keep it as clear as possible.

She knew it would be messy and things would go wrong, they always did, but if she was smart enough, she could get around it and find a way to make it work for her.

~~~~~

Telyn had to admit that it soothed her nerves to walk around the heart of the Winter Court, Skylar's hand in hers as Skylar pointed out different shops and landmarks along their path.

It held the vague sense of normalcy in the hurricane that had taken over her life. Despite her wild accusations of their king, the people continued their days, shopping, chatting, living.

Living without the pressure of their entire kingdom resting on their shoulders.

Even after all of this was over, Telyn knew she couldn't have that. With Piran dead and Carling subdued, Telyn would still be the queen of Alidain. She would still be responsible for running that kingdom and making sure its people stayed safe. Her job would never end.

In a way, it was more restraining than even Piran.

At least he could die.

The only way Telyn could get away from her responsibilities would be convincing Zerina to take her place. And Zerina had made it abundantly clear that she didn't want to do that.

That was the funny thing about responsibilities, often, they weren't wanted; and usually, they weren't avoidable.

Telyn would have to figure out a way to spend time with Skylar and run her kingdom. Maybe they could try six months in Alidain, actively ruling, and six months spent with Skylar in the Winter Court.

No matter what ended up happening, Telyn couldn't imagine it would be more difficult than what she was facing now.

She couldn't stop thinking about how her revelation had been received.

She knew how these things went. In the end, the woman was always blamed. It was *her* actions that had provoked a man to treat her the way he did. And if it wasn't that, she had to be lying.

Telyn had seen it happen time and time again. And the story always ended the exact same way.

All she could do was hope that things were different in SIluria.

After all, humans were the worst monsters, right?

"Hey." Skylar nudged Telyn with her elbow and pulled her out of her thoughts. "What's going on up there?"

Telyn knew full well that Skylar knew exactly what was going through her head. Skylar was giving her the chance to talk about it, and the chance to keep it to herself if that was what she wanted.

"I desperately want to believe that the people here are different, but I can't help but feel that they won't be. People of any race are far too similar to make a big enough impact on what's normal," Telyn said.

"Give them a chance, darling. They'll show you what they're capable of."

Skylar knew her people better than Telyn probably ever would. And she trusted Skylar.

It was possible that things truly were different in Siluria. All she had to do was wait and see.

Even if they weren't, Telyn was going to give them the chance to be.

For now, she just needed to relax and let it run its course. She would see the results of her words when the time was right.

Telyn allowed Skylar to pull her into a quaint little bakery, the walls painted a pale pink, colorful winter plants sprung from planters in the window sills, and the smell of mouth wateringly delicious pastries wafted out the door.

The people that drifted around in the building didn't give Telyn any of the strange looks she was accustomed to. They simply existed, in a way that allowed her to exist with them. Like it was somewhere she could belong.

The bakery was full of light laughter and sugar-coated finger-tips. It felt warm and welcoming.

"I thought you would like it here." Skylar smiled.

She always knew just what Telyn needed.

And right now, that was the warmth that filled her chest as people passed her with smiles instead of the scowls or pitying frowns that surrounded her in Viridium.

She had needed to know that things were different here, and they were.

The only place that felt more like home was Ceris.

But with Skylar at her side, and the peace that filled the area around her, she felt like this could be home too.

The Winter Court was *home*.

Telyn wasn't sure she would have the strength to ever leave it.

Skylar walked up to the counter and ordered a few things, leaving Telyn to look around in wonder at the little shop so full of love. Shelves lined the walls, tiny little glass animals arranged along them like a miniature zoo. Some of them moved slightly, some of them made noises, and some of them were simply strange colors. Telyn had never seen anything like it.

When Skylar came back, she had a large brown bag filled to the brim with the sweet-smelling pastries that sat behind the glass of the counter.

"Let's sit down for a minute." She gestured to one of the booths along the wall beneath the shelves.

Telyn slid into the seat across from Skylar, who began to take the pastries out of the bag. "You have been stressed out for months." She handed Telyn a sugar-coated bun with strawberry cream smeared inside of it.

"We all have been." Telyn took the treat and took a small bite.

"You more so than any of us. You deserve a break. Just take the day to relax, alright?" Skylar took a bite out of her own pastry.

"I can agree to that," Telyn said.

As much as she hated to leave work to be done later, she knew Skylar was right. She did need a break, and if she didn't take one while she had the chance, her body would force her to do it when she couldn't afford to.

So, she stayed in that booth for what felt like hours, munching on the delicious pastries on the table in front of her and watching the people that filtered in and out of the shop with bright smiles and kind words.

"Are you ready to go?" Skylar asked when the last of their very unhealthy lunch was finished.

Telyn picked up the bag of their trash and dropped it into the garbage can by the door. "What's next?"

That earned her another smile.

Telyn thought that if she couldn't do anything else in her lifetime, if she could just keep making Skylar smile, it would all be worth it. That was all she needed through all the chaos and the madness.

Skylar took Telyn's hand and led her out of the bakery, back into the familiar chill of the Winter Court.

Telyn flared her wings and let the cool air slip between her feathers.

Once again, she was amazed at the lack of dirty looks aimed her way. The freedom she was afforded in a place like this was so terribly new that she couldn't help the surge of anxiety that bubbled in her stomach. The fear that somehow, the home of her powers would shun her the way Viridium had.

She was finally able to live with what once would have gotten her killed, and almost did.

She still had a hard time figuring out if she had been lucky to escape death that day, or if she'd just signed her life away to a nightmare ever since.

The only solace she found was in the knowledge that all nightmares came to an end. And so would hers. Eventually.

Telyn couldn't tell what the next building contained as they approached it. The walls were black brick and the sign outside only read: *Sophie's*.

There weren't any windows she could see through; they were all painted the same black as the bricks. It was like whatever was inside wasn't meant to be seen by everyone.

"What's this?" Telyn asked as she eyed the bright red door in front of them.

"You'll see." Skylar grinned as she pushed open the door that led inside. There was a rush of warm air and a barrier of light that further supported Telyn's theory that this shop wasn't meant for everyone. Whatever was contained in this building was special, and likely not very accepted by most people. It was exactly the kind of shop Telyn expected Skylar to enjoy, full of mystery and anticipation.

At first, Telyn couldn't see anything beyond the wall of multi-colored lights that threatened to blind her. Reds, blues, greens, and purples swirled in her vision for a moment before her eyes adjusted enough to take in the room.

Sophie

*"Memories: some can be sucker punching;
others carry you forward."*
-Adam Silvera, More Happy Than Not

Telyn was greeted by shelves upon shelves of curiosities. There were more glass animals alongside those made of bent and warped clockwork that ticked as they shuffled and hopped around their shelves.

The place looked like an enchanted second-hand store. Each of the items that lined these walls and shelves felt uniquely off and looked very old.

Telyn was even more surprised to see Siren in the shop. The little black cat wound around Telyn's ankles a few times before she jumped up onto the counter in the center of the shop.

In another blinding flash of light, Siren was no longer sitting on the counter. In her place sat a woman with deep olive skin, long black hair, and piercing yellow eyes.

"Hello, Sophie." Skylar offered the woman a warm smile.

"I knew you would bring her to me eventually." Sophie crossed her legs and propped herself up with one of her hands.

"What happened to Siren?" Telyn asked.

She had always wondered where the little cat disappeared to when she wasn't guiding Telyn.

"Well," Sophie examined the long pointed nails of her free hand. "Even around here, people get suspicious of a name like Siren. So, I tweaked it a bit. A few of the same letters, some left out, and a few new ones as well."

It appeared that Telyn's mother was friends with more interesting people than she'd realized.

"Which do you prefer?" Telyn asked.

"Honestly, I prefer Sophie. It's more disarming to the people that are worth tricking. No one expects to be conned by a woman named Sophie." She smiled, revealing two sharply pointed canine teeth. "They think I'm too innocent and naive to know when I'm being undersold, but the joke's on them."

"Is that what you do here?" Telyn asked with a small smile.

"On occasion." Sophie admitted. "Only the nasty men who come in thinking they can take more than they can afford."

Telyn didn't know what she'd expected her feline friend to enjoy, but it certainly wasn't this.

"For my more agreeable customers," Sophie gestured to Skylar. "We skip the tricks."

"Straight into the good stuff." Skylar agreed with a soft smile.

"So, what brings you here today?" Sophie asked.

"I'm just showing Telyn a few of my favorite places so she can have a day to relax." Skylar shrugged.

"Is it working?" Sophie turned her yellow eyes on Telyn. There were secrets held in those eyes. Secrets that Telyn found herself wishing she knew.

"For the most part. It's hard to relax at a time like this, but this is the most peaceful I've felt in a long time," Telyn said. It was the truth, she felt the most at peace with Skylar, she always did.

"That's good. Would you like to take a look around?" Sophie slid off of the counter, the hem of the slinky black dress that wrapped aaround her body pooled on the ground and dragged behind her as she walked.

Telyn wanted to ask Sophie a million different questions, but today was her day off.

Her questions could wait. No badly how badly she wanted them, the answers wouldn't change if she asked tomorrow.

"Sure."

Telyn followed Sophie around the shop at a casual pace as she outlined the separate sections of the store and pointed out the more dangerous areas.

Dangerous magickal objects, illusion mirrors and brushes, transmutation wands, and all sorts of other things filled out the shelves of the shop. Things that could be used for anything from children's pranks to assassination.

What caught Telyn's attention was the shelves in a corner, stacked to the brim with books and scrolls that looked as if they would fall apart at the slightest touch.

"What are those?" Telyn asked.

Sophie's expression darkened. "No one wants to mess with those."

"Why?" Telyn glanced over at Sophie.

"People fear what they don't understand, but they would rather blindly follow their gods than understand what they really are," Sophie said.

Telyn remembered hearing Pip say something similar when they'd discovered she was working with Nox.

"Can I look at them?" Telyn asked.

"Go right ahead, take a few if you feel so inclined," Sophie said.

"Thank you."

Skylar followed Telyn over to the books.

They looked older than any of the books that had been in Alidain's library.

Judging by Sophie's words, they contained more information as well. The Red Book had helped them piece together enough of the story to get them where they were, but there were still a lot of blanks left unfilled.

There were still a lot of things that Nox hadn't told her.

Maybe these books held some answers.

"It's your day off." Skylar reminded as Telyn pulled a scroll off of the shelf.

"I know, but this isn't the first time someone has said that the gods aren't what they seem. Since we're working with them, I think we deserve to know the truth," Telyn said.

"Alright, what can I do to help?" Skylar asked.

"Just look for anything we didn't know before," Telyn said.

"Well, that's a broad area." Skylar started picking through the scrolls on the shelf behind them as Telyn started to read through the titles in front of her.

She could tell just by looking at them that they weren't in the common language. It had to have been Old Silurian.

"Do you want to take these back to Ceris?" When Telyn turned around, Skylar had an armful of yellowed scrolls.

"It might be more comfortable," Telyn said.

"I can always bring you more when you need them. These things have just been taking up space for centuries." Sophie emerged from the shelves.

"That would be great." Telyn smiled.

Her mother had been right in thinking that the cat that had found them on the day of her death would be a guide. Telyn only wondered if her mother had known it was Sophie.

The way she saw it, she could never have too much knowledge. Knowledge was power, and this kind of knowledge, the one Sophie had shown her, might give them a leg up in the war.

They had been relying on the gods to provide information for far too long. If they wanted to stand any sort of chance against Carling, they needed to know the truth. All of it.

It didn't take them long to get back to Ceris.

The relaxation time had been nice, but it was time to get back to work.

Skylar had tea sent up to the study as they gathered Wes, Nolan, Brea, and Cordelia.

Skylar passed pencils and paper out to everyone as they sat down. Telyn passed out the scrolls. "Write down anything you've never heard of before or anything unusual. We can share as we finish," Skylar said.

The next few hours were filled with the sound of paper crinkling, cups clinking against their glass saucers, and the occasional whispered exchange at the door.

The six of them were sprawled out across the study, some spread out over chairs, others laying on the floor.

Telyn had never expected her life to involve so much reading, much less require it.

But here she was, not for the first time, scouring page after page for answers.

When Telyn looked up, everyone was watching her. It seemed she was the last to finish.

She felt a rush of relief as she saw that everyone's papers were covered in scrawled notes.

"Should we start with Telyn?" Wes asked.

"I don't mind going first." Telyn straightened out her paper and looked at the bullet points she'd put down.

"Go ahead."

"Well, our dear friend Nox has been hiding quite a bit," Telyn said.

"Anything relative to our situation?" Nolan asked.

"A motive." Telyn smiled. "Nox used to kill everything he touched. He couldn't control his powers. Siene is the one who taught him to do that. He fell in love with a human woman. When he found out Cygnus was the reason for Nerissa's death, his control slipped, and he killed his wife. From the darkness of his grief, he created Calla."

"But he's a god. How could he not control his own powers?" Cordelia asked.

"I don't know," Telyn said.

"I've got some information on Nerissa's death." Brea offered quietly.

"Go ahead, honey." Skylar gave her an encouraging smile.

"The scroll I was reading through said she didn't really die. She just went dormant as a part of the sea. It also said that one day she would reemerge."

"Well, it would be nice if she could do that now and get a handle on her children," Wes muttered.

"It might not be something she can control. I'm sure there's some sort of external factor to it," Skylar said.

"Yes, there's supposed to be two people that hold the key to waking her. One of her handmaids and a sailor," Cordelia said. "That was in mine."

"All I got was how Carling and Asteria had always been close and worked together to create several wars and other disasters," Skylar said.

Wes and Nolan shared a look.

"Out with it, you two," Skylar said.

"We were able to piece together a bit of a legend." Nolan said.

"All of the gods could have champions, but only Nox had handmaidens like his mother did. They acted as a sort of omen of death,' Wes said.

"If you saw her, a lot of people were about to die." Nolan agreed.

"She was said to reap the souls of the wicked. She carried around this big sword." Wes showed them a drawing of a very intricately designed great sword.

"Did she have a name?" Telyn asked.

"Kylin Eris." Nolan held out the scroll he had read. "They had a lot to say about her."

Telyn scanned over the paper. The handmaiden's most identifiable features had been her purple eyes and dark hair. Many had feared her, but many had loved her as well.

"There were others. After she died," Wes said. "There's not much about them, but there's one thing they all had in common."

"What's that?" Skylar asked.

"They all went mad. They became the evil they were supposed to destroy," Nolan said.

And that was what Nox wanted Telyn to be.

The fate he would condemn her to as a price for his help.

He didn't want her to be a handmaiden, likely to avoid this fate, but he also refused to help her unless she was one. It was like the illusion of free choice.

Because there was no choice. If it came down to needing Nox's help, they all knew what would happen. There was no choice to be made. It was a matter of survival.

Nox could just as easily help anyway, after all, it was his brother causing problems. Instead, he insisted on following some unknown set of rules.

Rules that he could easily change because he was a god. He could do whatever he wanted.

Perhaps it was just that he didn't want to help them. Maybe he wanted to watch the worlds burn at Carling's hand.

"Maybe choosing to work with them was a mistake." Skylar's voice was soft as she contemplated the new information.

"No, the deals we have now keep Carling from directly harming you. That is nothing but a blessing," Telyn said.

"We can't let Nox make you a handmaiden though," Skylar said.

"We may not have a choice." Telyn leaned forward on her elbows. "Whether we like it or not, we might need the help."

"There has to be a better option," Nolan said.

"There may be, but this is our last resort. If nothing else is working, then we know what I have to do," Telyn said.

Did she want to sacrifice her sanity and her life?

No.

But this was bigger than her.

If she had to sacrifice herself to keep Skylar and the others safe, she would.

And everyone in that study knew it.

There was silence as the information sunk in. As everyone realized what this could mean for them.

Telyn especially.

She had spent so much of her life waiting to be able to be the one in charge of her own future. Only to reach a point where she'd begun to realize she might never get that.

No matter which path she took, there would always be someone who tried to control her. It didn't matter if she was a queen or even if she was some preordained warrior, destined to save them all, someone would always want to use her for the power she held.

It was a lesson she was sure Sklyar had learned as well, though perhaps a bit sooner.

I can't let you throw away your life like that. Skylar was looking at Telyn from across the room.

You've done so much to help me. If this is what I give in return, I'll do it gladly.

Telyn had a lot of things to make up for. If this was how she did it, she wouldn't hesitate.

At least they would survive.

And so would she, even if she wasn't fully herself.

Being alive was the goal.

Anything more was luxury.

"There's nothing left to discuss here unless someone has more information," Telyn said.

"Not yet, but there's a lot more material to work through." Cordelia gestured to the stack of scrolls they hadn't even touched yet.

"And there's a lot more where those come from," Skylar said.

"This is a start. We know more than we did before," Telyn said.

"It's not much, but it's a start." Nolan agreed.

Telyn would argue that it was quite a lot, especially considering how little information they were given, but they had other things to worry about.

But there was little more to do than wait for the time being.

Telyn reached for another scroll.

"The sun is starting to come up," Skylar said. "I think we have enough for now. Get some sleep, this can continue tomorrow night."

Telyn's fingers stuck to the parchment as she reluctantly let it drop back onto the table. She knew nothing would change if she waited, but she also knew she would have trouble sleeping.

There was too much on her mind. In a way, there was always too much on her mind. Most days she was able to quiet the thoughts that ran on an endless track through her head.

Now though, those thoughts weren't quieting down. If anything, they were getting louder. They demanded her attention in full, not just in passing as she tried to sleep.

She tried to be as still as possible to avoid waking Skylar, but she could tell it wasn't working. She could feel Skylar's breaths beside her. They weren't the long even breaths of sleep; they were the quick and even ones of the still conscious.

"You can't sleep either?" Skylar asked.

"Not at all." Telyn rolled over to face Skylar.

"You're going to be alright; I won't let them hurt you." Skylar brushed some hair away from Telyn's face.

"That's not what I'm worried about." Telyn smiled. "You've already done so much for me, and protected me from the worst of monsters, it's my turn to protect you, darling. And we'll still both be alright."

"Because we have each other," Skylar said. Her finger tips were soft and gentle against Telyn's face.

"Exactly."

The thoughts that had been racing through Telyn's mind began to slow.

Nox was manipulating her the same way Piran was. The gods had more secrets than perhaps anyone, but those were all problems she could solve later.

After Telyn had gotten some sleep.

She knew her head would never be completely silent, but it was quiet enough that the steady rhythm of Skylar's heartbeat was able to lull her to sleep.

The sun sank well below the horizon as Telyn opened her eyes.

She could already tell it was going to be one of those nights where she didn't want to get out of bed. Skylar shifted beside her and she closed her eyes with a soft sigh before she forced herself to sit up.

"You're awake already?" Skylar murmured.

"I don't want to be." Telyn rubbed her eyelids with the backs of her hands.

"There's no harm in sleeping in a while longer," Skylar said.

But there were things that needed to be done.

Things that shouldn't be put off.

Telyn swung her legs off of the side of the bed. She knew if she stayed in the warmth of the blankets any longer, she would never be able to get up.

Skylar was close behind her as she padded to their door and swung it open.

"It seems you've already given the night a purpose," Skylar said.

"Yes, I put it off yesterday, but there's no sense in doing it any longer. I need to speak with Sophie."

"Darling." Skylar smiled.

"Yes?" Telyn turned back to Skylar.

"You're still in your night clothes."

Telyn could feel the light amusement and laughter through their bond as Skylar fought to keep it from making a physical appearance.

Telyn felt her cheeks warm as she glanced down at herself and realized Skylar was right. She might have been a little too anxious to get her questions answered.

"Perhaps the conversation is best left for after breakfast." She moved to her pile of clean clothes that sat on top of the nearly empty vanity table in the room.

After a quickly assembled meal of fruits and yogurt, Sklyar and Telyn flew back inti the Heart of the Winter Court. From there, they made their way to *Sophie's* on foot.

When they walked through the door, they were once again met by a wall of multicolored light, but this time, Telyn was ready for it.

Sophie didn't bother with theatrics when she saw Telyn, she immediately shifted into her human form. Her black painted claws curled around her biceps as she crossed her arms. "You're back so soon."

Forget Me Not

"We are all someone's monster."
-Leigh Bardugo, Six of Crows

"Yesterday was supposed to be my day off, so I held my tongue, but you knew my mother," Telyn said. "Did she know you as Sophie?"

"Yes. Your mother was a very interesting individual. It's a shame that ended after White Haven." Sophie frowned.

"The Maria Ramirez everyone else seemed to know isn't the mother I knew. I want to know what she was like before," Telyn said.

"Well," Sophie smirked. "I knew your mother before she married your father, so you've come to the right place."

Sophie led Skylar and Telyn to a set of chairs she had on display.

"Are these safe?" Skylar asked.

"Just very old." Sophie assured.

They sat down, and Telyn mentally prepared for the conversation ahead. Knowing was always better, right?

"To start, how did you know my mother?" Telyn asked.

"We grew up together, here in Siluria. I suppose you could say we were lovers for a time as well. We both knew it wouldn't last, but it's better to have loved and lost than to have never loved at all, isn't it?" Sophie's self-satisfied smirk had taken on a softer look.

Telyn was a little surprised. She didn't think anyone expected their parents to be attracted to the same gender, especially not if they were married to the oppilate, and happily so.

Her mother herself had said she'd been smitten by Telyn's father.

"What was she like?" Telyn asked.

"She was wild as everything in that wood. She was more familiar with the rough bark under her fingertips and the dirt and leaves beneath her bare feet than anything she found in Viridium. But she loved your father. Everything she did was for him, and for you and your sister." Sophie played with her hands in her lap.

"You wanted it to be you," Telyn said, her voice soft. "You wanted to have that life with her, but she chose him."

Sophie's eyes darkened. "As I said, I knew it wouldn't last. Maria was never meant to be mine. All that matters is that she was happy with your father, and she was. Up until your uncle started scheming anyway."

"Did she change?" Telyn asked. "When she went to Viridium."

"Yes, she was no longer the wild woman I had loved. She became more mature with her new title and role. Though her kindness never changed, It was harder for her to maintain after White Haven. The trauma grew to be too much some days," Sophie said.

"I'm well aware." Telyn sighed.

It wasn't hard to recall the bad days. Often, Telyn found it easier to remember the bad things about her mother. That was part of why she wanted to know more about her, in hopes she could learn more good about her, even if it was from a time she couldn't remember.

As time went on, it got harder and harder to remember the good parts of anything in the past. It was overwhelmed by all of the negative things that never seemed to end.

She needed more good to hold onto, to hope for.

"Where was it?"

"Where was what?" Sophie gave Telyn a curious look.

"My mother said she'd lived in an ancient Silurian wood. Where was it?" Telyn asked.

"Where *is* it would be the better question." Sophie's eyebrows lowered and she bit her lip. "I believe you've already been."

"That's ridiculous, I would know if I had." Telyn scoffed.

"Our home was the Enchanted Forest," Sophie said.

"But it's so..."

"Dead?" Sophie offered with a sad smile. "It wasn't always like that. Before your mother left, the Enchanted Forest was known by a different name, Lithiara. It was beautiful and alive. There's a reason it has the strongest magickal pull of our world. It was the heart of Siluria.

The monsters that are now feared were once gentle giants, loyal to your mother. The twisted dead trees used to live in full evergreen bloom.

But fifty years ago, the forest started to die."

"Because my mother left?" Telyn asked.

"In part, but we never blamed her for that. None of us knew she was tied to it in the way she was, but I believe our mourning her loss is what truly changed it. It fed off of how we felt, then became something worse," Sophie said.

"The others have mentioned that the Enchanted Forest wasn't always such a dreadful place, but this is the only version of it I've ever known," Skylar said.

"It makes me wonder just how much of a change *you'll* bring to our world." Sophie levelled her gaze on Telyn. "Your mother was never one to cause a scene, but you've already proven you refuse to remain silent."

"I can't think of a situation where I should have to be," Telyn said.

"I am not saying you're wrong. I am simply saying: be careful." Sophie smiled. "These old folk need to be rattled every century or so."

"I'll try to remember to keep them on their toes." Telyn returned the smile.

The Enchanted Forest...

Lithiara.

Telyn almost didn't believe that it used to be her mother's beautifully magickal home. But if the dead twisted wood hadn't been dead before, maybe there was a way to restore it.

No. They needed to focus.

And Telyn never wanted to step foot in that dreadful place again.

She needed to assess how her announcement was fairing. She was a bit surprised Piran hadn't shown up to do any damage control.

Though if he was bent on ruling through fear, a bit of a bad reputation would only help him in his eyes.

He hadn't seen what large groups of people were capable of. What these very people had done to his ancestors.

His ignorance would be his fall.

And Telyn would see to it.

Her arsenal was far from empty.

She was beginning to think there wasn't anything she wouldn't do to be able to watch the king's demise.

She wanted to watch Piran and everything he'd built burn to the ground. And she would be the one to strike the match.

But there were a few steps she needed to take before she could get there. Once everything was in order at Ceris, they could assess how the news had spread.

The world hadn't deigned to stop while this whole mess went on. There were still things that needed to be done outside of Telyn's vengeance plan.

While Skylar was busy running the estate, Telyn took the time to read more scrolls.

By now she'd realized she should have listened to Pip the first time they'd told her she didn't know what she was getting into.

The gods had been complex beings to begin with; their origins shrouded in mystery.

Even after Nox had begun to communicate with Telyn, there were so many questions left unanswered, but now, she was beginning to think all of her answers were in the scrolls she held in her lap.

They had already provided so much more information than the god had. And they'd revealed just how little Nox cared for her. He would sacrifice anything to stop his brother.

But wouldn't she do so as well?

There were a few she wasn't willing to sacrifice, but the rest of the world was fair game.

Telyn didn't want to catch everyone in the crossfire, but she didn't see another way.

This wasn't just a matter of state. Where the gods were involved, everyone was affected. There was no escaping it. Some were just luckier than others.

Not even the scrolls had a solution for that. Amongst the endless rolls of paper that contained everything from the origin of the second-generation gods to tales of handmaidens gone mad, there was no mention of how to escape their wrath.

All that was said was they were dangerous.

But there was one scroll that caught Telyn's eye, one that said something a bit different.

The edges of the scroll crumbled in Telyn's hands as she read it, but the words were left unmarred.

It claimed the gods were once people too. A different kind of people, but not so far outside of the idea of normal. Nerissa and Cygnus had been no more than refugees from another war.

They only reason they, and their children, were gods was because they had wiped out the small population that had already lived in the realms.

Where other texts said there had been nothing there, this one said there had been genocide before the beginning.

As wild as it was, there was no one left to confirm or deny the claim.

Nerissa and Cygnus were gone.

Telyn could always ask Nox, but that didn't guarantee a truthful answer. It was easier to believe the worst, especially when the gods had been so adamant about their secrecy.

But if what the scroll said was true, that meant the gods could be killed like any other man. It might be more difficult to pull off, but they weren't invulnerable. They could be killed like anyone else.

Perhaps Telyn didn't need Nox's help. If she could find Carling's weakness, or even Piran's, she could kill them herself.

She didn't need the help of a god if the only thing special about them was the genocide their parents committed.

Come to think of it, the only power that greatly deviated from those of the Fae and the Silurians was that of Renelleph. His power of creation and life was the only power Telyn hadn't seen a similarity to in her own people.

She had seen invasive plants wither at the fingers of one of the Fae, darkness and disaster had fallen in the Unseelie Court when Piran had murdered its king for his crown, war had been waged by men, fortunes had been told by mere humans. Telyn herself could manipulate the waters of the world, music and light had still been created from the hands of her Silurian brothers and sisters, love and luck had been manifested and given.

The twelve realms had been founded on the mystic powers they believed only the gods could hold.

This entire time, they had been blind to the power they wielded themselves.

Everything the gods represented could still exist without them. They had made the mistake of passing their traits to the people they had repopulated their stolen universe with.

These people didn't need the gods.

Telyn didn't need the gods.

She only needed herself.

She had been told she was the one who would save them all, the one blessed by the gods with all of their powers. She could already manage the shadows, water, and fire, there wasn't much more for her to master.

Once she was done, only all of the gods working together would be enough to stop her.

All she needed was to trust in herself and her powers.

Part of which Sprin had taken from her...

Her plan would have been flawless had it not been for that little slip.

Her willingness to save Brea's life might cost her the ability to save the rest of the realms.

It was possible that no matter how hard she tried, she would never be able to master everything, because Sprin had taken too much.

She should have known better than to give him full access to her untapped power. He'd taken more than she'd promised, and had Skylar not been there, he likely would have taken more.

But she had to at least try,

She would never be able to forgive herself if she didn't try everything at her disposal.

If she was going to go down, she was going to go down swinging, and she would bring all of her enemies down with her.

If she had to hunt down Sprin and find a way to get her stolen power back, she would.

She owed it to everyone to at least try.

She was the savior that had been promised. If she couldn't save them, no one could. And she refused to lose.

There was nothing else she could lose without losing everything. So her solution was to destroy everything that got in her way.

Carling and Nox would be dead by the time she was done with them. Piran as well, and anyone else who stood in the way of her protecting her family.

She didn't want the power to be able to rule the twelve realms. She couldn't care less about ruling. The war needed to end. That was what she cared about.

Time and time again she had been torn down and told she was nothing, that she was nothing but a tool in a man's game, but she wasn't.

She was so much more than a tool, more than a pawn to be danced around the board. She was a queen with a kingdom to defend.

They were playing by her rules now, and there was nothing the king could do to stop her.

He could run and fight as much as he wanted, but he would always be right where he wanted her. And he would stay that way until she decided it was time to make the killing move.

And once the king was out of the way, the gods were next.

As a child she would have called anyone who wanted to fight the gods mad, but now she understood.

They had never been there for the people. They had never tried to protect them. The people of the realms were nothing more than toys for the gods. The gods had never done anything to save the people from the terrors and traumas that filled their lives.

Why should the people pray to them anymore?

All they had done was cause the problems that hurt so many people.

Over the years, the prayers Telyn heard had dwindled. And so had the ones she'd said herself. They had gone unanswered for so long, she'd given up.

Then Nox had walked into her life and given her false hope. She had thought he wanted to help, but all he was using her for was entertainment. And when she was no longer entertaining, he would discard her. The same way he had all the other girls he'd turned into handmaidens.

But she would make him pay for all of the lies he'd spoon-fed her. She would make him pay for the false hope he had given her. He had done nothing but use her for his own amusement.

Well, she would ensure he was thoroughly entertained until his very end.

As for his brother, she would force him to endure the same pain he'd put her through. She would rip everything he loved from him and watch the light drain from his eyes as he realized he had lost at his own game, and she ensured he would never threaten her or her family again.

Piran wanted to rule through fear because he knew no other way. He knew no mercy, had no heart or regard for human life.

Telyn would rule through fear to ensure her people remained safe. Those who threatened their safety would be severely punished. And Piran and the gods would be made examples. Visual and historical reminders of what would happen should anyone threaten the people Telyn loved.

She could not be seen as soft, or weak and complacent.

If she was going to make this work, she was going to have to become almost as bad as the people she was trying to fight, but once it was all over, she wanted nothing to do with it.

She didn't want a crown or the title of savior. She only wanted her life to be her own. She wanted to be able to choose Skylar and live a long happy life with the woman she loved.

But she could not do that until Piran and Carling were dead.

Nox was negotiable, she might allow him to beg his way out of death, but ultimately, his life was in her hands.

He had hurt her, he had withheld his help without an acceptable reason, he would pay for those offences.

You were born to play the part of the villain, darling.

Her uncle's voice rang in her ears.

He might be right on this account, but was she was truly a villain if her motives were good.

She didn't seek to destroy people with no reason. She didn't do it out of sheer jealousy as he had. She was doing it to protect the ones she loved.

She was getting her revenge. Revenge that she had been owed since she was three years old and Carling's corruption had driven Nathaniel Ramirez to murder her father. But she had already killed him. It was time to move to the next rung on the ladder.

Her uncle may not have been working directly under Carling, but Piran was, and she was certain the king had been involved with her uncle's insurrection.

She had killed her uncle, and with him the vilest parts of the Ramirez legacy.

Next, she would kill the king.

Oh, she would take her time and enjoy every moment she deceived him and regained his trust. It was what he wanted after all. All she had to do was make him think that was what he was getting, unfiltered access to her powers.

But before another man was able to take what belonged only to her, when the time was right, she would kill him, and he would join Nathaniel in Noctem.

And from there, with no mortals standing in her way, she would begin her fight with the gods. She would take them down one by one, starting with Carling, until they accepted that the realms no longer belonged to them. The realms belonged to the people, and if Telyn had to kill every single one of the gods to make it so, she would.

They didn't deserve the worlds their parents had founded on bloodshed. It was time the people took back control.

PART 3

Dawn of a Matriarchy

"Winter is coming."
-Game of Thrones

Hell Hath No Fury

> "I used to love the idea of something so tremendous
> it was worth dying for."
> -Stephanie Garber, Finale

The next time Telyn went out with Skylar, she was greeted with warm words of support. It would seem the people had decided to take her for her word. They believed her, but that did not mean they would fight for her. She had to continue to build the bond of trust between herself and Skylar's people. Vespera, Portia, and Wes had said that word of Piran's misdeeds had spread to their courts as well.

The king himself had yet to come forward in response to Telyn's accusations. She could only assume that meant he thought the people feared him, but she could see the anger in their eyes.

They weren't afraid of what he'd done, they were angry they'd been deceived. The prince they had grown to love had turned into a king with no morals. A man who believed himself better than any group that would rise against him. They would show him they weren't to be trifled with.

They may not outright defy him at first, but there would be small things, little stands of disapproval. Then, as he grew crueler, they would grow bolder, angrier. Until eventually, they would be fighting on the same side of the war as Telyn.

She couldn't offer to protect them all. That wasn't within her abilities, but she wouldn't kill them. Not without being deserving of it, and that was more than Piran was offering them.

The man's preconceived notions about his people would be his downfall.

If Telyn was lucky enough, she wouldn't have to do much work to when it came to ending him. He would do most of the work himself.

"My Lady." A woman reached out for Telyn, but thought better of it.

"Yes?" Telyn watched as the woman retracted her hand.

Though the title was rightfully Skylar's, the woman's eyes were on Telyn.

"I just wanted to let you know that the Heart is with you. We will be your hands as you fight this injustice. The boy is no king to us." Her eyes flicked to Skylar, then the ground.

"Thank you." Telyn smiled. "What is your name?"

"Rheana, My Lady." She dipped her head into a bow.

Rheana's words were treason, she knew it just as well as Telyn did, but in the face of her high lady, she did not cower as she spoke them. If they were wrong, she did not want to be right. Even if that meant death.

"I'm honored to have your support, Rheana," Telyn said.

Rheana smiled.

Telyn had begun to win the peoples' favor.

Unlike Piran, she understood that their allegiance would be what made or broke this war. The number of soldiers helped, but there wasn't much a king could do without the loyalty of his people. And the more people he killed, the more people he manipulated, the less loyalty he had.

And Telyn didn't need them to love her. She just needed them to loathe him.

He was perfectly capable of doing it himself, she'd only needed to reveal who he really was. That hadn't been hard to do either.

As long as the people believed her, they would hate him.

If she could get them to witness what he did, that would be even better, but Piran was too smart to let his evil doings be broadcast. If she wanted to have that much ammunition, she would have to be clever about getting it. She would have to not only devise a trap capable of luring in the king, but she would have to subject herself to his cruelty once again.

If she went into the viper's den, she would be prepared.

She wouldn't walk back in as the same girl that had been bullied and manipulated into submission. That girl had been weak, and now she was dead. Telyn refused to be that girl ever again.

"Telyn." Skylar called, her voice gentle.

She was a few feet away, her hand outstretched. Rheana was nowhere to be seen.

Telyn caught up to Skylar, she hadn't realized she'd spaced out.

"If you are willing, I may have a plan." Skylar kept her voice low as she waked with Telyn.

Telyn took Skylar's arm in her own. "What is it?"

"How do you feel about mithridatism?" Skylar asked.

"Micro dosing poison to build immunity?" Telyn glanced up at Skylar.

"Yes. It would be an easy way to protect yourself, as well as kill Piran. But if you're not comfortable with it, we can find another way." Skylar kept her eyes on the path ahead of them.

"I'm not opposed to it, what did you have in mind?" Telyn asked.

"One of the hardier plants we have in the Autumn Court is belladonna. It doesn't take much to kill someone. We can make a tea of sorts using just a single berry to start. This would keep you safe if he planned on using it on you once he has what he wants, but it wouldn't keep him safe." Skylar explained.

"How would I go about administering it?" Telyn asked.

"I trust you to be creative. This is your revenge after all, darling." Skylar smiled.

Wes greeted them when they arrived at the Autumn Court, Skylar showed Telyn how to identify belladonna so she could collect it when she needed more. Ten of the little, black, round berries, that was all it took to kill a full-grown man. They could all fit in the palm of her hand.

Telyn popped one into her mouth.

She knew that she would feel a little off, maybe a little sick until her body adjusted to taking in the poison, but it was a price she could pay.

One of the few that required little thought. It was a small price for a big pay off, and it only hurt her a little.

She would stick to one berry every day for a while, then increase the amount as her body adjusted to what it was taking in. It would require patience and care, but as long as she didn't up the count too quickly, she would be perfectly fine.

Skylar already had people working on finding a way to concentrate the juice of ten of them into something that would be able to go unnoticed if it was to be added to a drink or some other thing.

Telyn pocketed a handful of the berries to bring back to Ceris. She could freeze them for safekeeping until they were needed.

"Are you sure about this?" Wes asked. "It's dangerous."

"I'm sure, I'll be careful. This process is going to be a long one, but if it does its job, it will have been worth it," Telyn said.

"You're allowed to back out any time you'd like," Skylar said.

"I won't need to." Telyn's fingers were lightly stained with purple splotches from the berries.

"Keep some charcoal on hand, just to be safe." Wes glanced over at the bush full of ripe berries.

"We will," Skylar said.

The berries were meant to kill. Telyn knew assassins were fond of them, and in a way, she was becoming a lot more like her older sister.

She wondered if Sabina would be proud of her. If not for being brave enough to even consider this path of action, then for planning to kill the man who had harmed her, time and time again.

There was no way for Telyn to ask her. Not immediately.

Perhaps by the time this was all over, all of the Ramirez siblings would have a plethora of stories to share with each other. Perhaps Sabina would finally decide to be a part of the family once she saw how easily they all could have lost each other.

Telyn knew it was wishful thinking, but that was all she had sometimes, and it had gotten her this far.

"Are you ready to go home?" Skylar asked.

"Yes, we have work to do."

There were still plenty of scrolls to read through. Where there was more truth to be learned, especially concerning the gods, Telyn wanted to be involved.

She had been stupid to sell her service away without knowing the man she was selling it to. She should have done more research then, before she'd agreed.

But she had been desperate.

She didn't think she'd be able to save her people herself. She hadn't realized how much power she had back then.

If she had, none of this would have happened. Her mother would still be alive, and she would be none the wiser to the dangers that raged around her.

But she also wouldn't have met Skylar, or her sister.

As painful as it had been to lose her mother, she knew now that it had happened for a reason. There were still days where she missed her terribly and wished she was there to tell her what to do. To tell her that everything would be alright.

But Telyn had needed to come into her power.

And that never would have happened in a place like Micaera, where her powers were seen as treason. Where her very existence was seen as treason.

She had needed to leave, and she wouldn't have done it on her own.

One day she would see her mother again, in Noctem, where the dead went to rest, but for now, she had a job to do.

The realms needed saving, and it looked like she was the only one who could do that.

The sun was beginning to rise over the horizon as Skylar and Telyn walked into Ceris and knocked the snow from their boots. Nolan was waiting for the foyer. He had Cordelia and Brea leaning against him and a book laid in his lap.

"Help me with these two, would you?" Nolan gestured to the girls with his head.

Skylar gently pulled Brea up into her arms and headed for her room. Nolan stood with Cordelia in his arms and followed.

Once the girls were carefully tucked into bed, Telyn and Skylar headed for the study while Nolan stayed with the girls.

The closer Telyn got to the study, the stronger the smell of smoke became.

There was always the underlying scent of it with all the fires that burned in the estate to keep it warm through the winter, but it shouldn't be as strong as it was.

Something was burning, more than the wood that was meant to be burning.

Telyn sped her pace to a jog and threw the door open when she reached it.

She was greeted by the smoldering ashes of her pile of scrolls and the contempt face of the king.

"Why are you here?" Telyn's fists trembled as she fought to control her rage.

Piran had snuck in while they were gone and burnt centuries worth of valuable information. Information that no one would ever get to read again because of his reckless stupidity.

"To teach you a lesson," He said. He used the tip of a dagger to clean dirt from beneath his pristine fingernails.

His hands had never seen a day of hardship. He took what he wanted, when he wanted, and the dagger wouldn't be able to clean the blood from his hands for him.

"I was under the impression I had helped you. You wanted to rule through fear, did you not?" Telyn glared at him over the pile of white ash on the table between them.

"I did, but those people do not fear me. They hate me. Hate does not garner respect; it stirs the heart of rebellion." Piran's knuckles were white as his fingers gripped each other, his elbows propped up on the table, sleeves covered in ashes.

"Then maybe you shouldn't have killed your parents." Telyn's voice was quiet and lethal.

Piran was silent for a moment.

"So, you don't deny it." Telyn folded her arms across her chest.

"I've killed others to get what I want. You know that. And I would do it again," Piran said. "That is what monarchs do, Telyn."

"It is what conquerors do. Killing King Rhode was one thing, but Tara and Bran were your blood. They were your parents," Telyn said.

"You stand here calling me a monster when you've murdered your own blood as well? I know what you did to your uncle." Piran scoffed.

"I only killed my uncle because he was trying to kill us. I did not kill him for a throne," Telyn said.

The smile that crawled across Piran's face said he'd won.

"So, you admit you killed him?" He asked.

"If you must know, he ended himself. He did it so he could come back as that *thing*." Telyn was growing impatient with this game. Piran had done what he had come for. Why was he still there?

"You didn't kill him then."

"No."

"Then you are weak. You had an enemy of your kingdom within reach, you had the opportunity to kill him, but you couldn't bring yourself to do it." Piran stood. "You have the soft heart of a woman."

He walked past them to the door, his hands folded behind his back, "That is why women should not rule. They are all weak." Without another word, he left.

Skylar followed him to make sure he didn't seek out any hostages to take with him.

Telyn knelt in front of the table covered in ash.

She dragged her finger through the dust.

Centuries of information that could have helped her, gone. Those scrolls had been teaching her how to save the realms on her own, and ow their information was gone. No one would ever know all the secrets they contained. There were no copies.

All they had were the notes they had taken the first time they'd sat down to read through the scrolls. Six half written pieces of paper. That was all that remained of them. Telyn had stored them in her desk with other important documents.

She should have thought to put up the rest of the scrolls as well.

She picked up a handful of ash, the particles fell through her fingers like sand and left a dusty grey coating over her hand. The warmth lingered. It wasn't hot enough to burn, but it fought off the chill that had begun to creep into the room.

There was no spell that could restore what she'd lost. What Piran had destroyed.

He was continuing to take from her. He always would until she buckled and broke. Until she did what he wanted her to.

Telyn was all too aware of the belladonna berries in her pocket.

She ought to shove them down the king's throat while he was still here, end the war between them already. But she knew she couldn't win in a fight of force. If she tried to overpower him, she would lose. She would have to get creative like Skylar had suggested.

And she would make it personal.

The only intimate moment she wanted with the king was the one where she watched the life drain from his eyes as he realized she'd finally beat him. That he had lost to the woman he had declared weak.

Telyn focused on calming herself as she carefully swept the ashes into her hand and transferred them to the hearth.

The coals in it were cold. The only warmth Piran needed had come from his petty revenge.

Telyn was silent as she worked. Even when Skylar came back into the room, announcing that the king truly was gone, and he'd taken no hostages this time. When she realized Telyn wasn't going to say anything in response, she crouched beside her to help clean the table.

When most of the ashes were removed, a maid came in with a bucket of heated water and a rag. She moved to wiped down the table, but Telyn held out a hand for the damp rag. The maid handed Telyn the rag and left in silence as Telyn removed the last of the ash from the table.

"In time, he will pay for his crimes," Skylar said as Telyn placed the dirty rag into the bucket of murky water.

"I know," Telyn said. "I'm going to be the one delivering his sentence and he'll see just how weak I am."

"Your patience is admirable. I had half a mind to slit his throat as he walked away, but it is not my revenge to take." Skylar smiled.

"I thought about it, I have the berries, enough to end him. It wouldn't have worked though, he would have over powered me, then it truly wouldn't have worked. If we want him to take the poison willingly, we have to get him to trust me again. We have to make him think I'm his." Telyn let her hands rest on the edge of the bucket.

"We knew you would have to go back eventually, even if we both don't like the idea." Skylar sighed.

"It's just a matter of when." Telyn nodded.

"I think he'll ask. If he doesn't just take you. You're too important to what he wants for him to leave you alone. Right now, he's antagonizing you in hopes you'll return on your own to get him to stop. When he grows tired of that, he'll try something different." Skylar stood and held out a hand for Telyn.

"I can't leave now; we have to warn Sophie before anything. We have to protect the girls, and the scrolls, and work with Captain Ezra." Telyn wrung the rag out in her hands, needing something to do with them.

"You will be helping by infiltrating the viper's nest. I can take care of things here. When he asks you to go with him, do it. Make it hard, don't agree right away, he'll get suspicious, but ultimately, go with him," Skylar said.

"Are you sure?" Telyn asked.

Skylar nodded. "The best way to kill the king is by his side in his own castle. When he won't see it coming."

Lessons

> "I am a bad person
> trying very hard to be a good person."
> -Nora Sakavic, The Raven King

Telyn's dragon preferred to stay in the warmest depths of Ceris. She often went weeks without seeing a single green scale from the little thing. Telyn supposed dragons weren't much suited for Winter. They preferred the searing heat of summer fire. Which left Telyn to wonder why Sevina had strayed so far from summer.

Telyn wandered through the halls of Ceris, following the warmer paths until she came across her dragon curled into a tight ball in the dungeons. Bones of small animals littered the ground around her; some of them still had charred flesh clinging to them.

When Telyn had brought the dragon home, she had been no bigger than a mouse, now she was the size of a house cat.

The little thing would need a name before long.

When she saw Telyn, she stretched out her wings and ambled over to her. Telyn reached out a hand and the little dragon rubbed her head against her hand.

"What do you think of Calynn?" Telyn asked as she scratched behind the dragon's ears and around her horns.

The dragon chirped and pressed her head against Telyn's hand once again.

Calynn it was.

"Are you ready to come out with me?" Telyn asked.

Calynn was far from big enough to ride, but she was big enough to prove a threat. Telyn could feel the fire that churned in her stomach through her scales. She was already a force to be reckon with. Once she was full grown, Telyn could imagine she would be unstoppable.

Piran had no dragons.

But it would be years before Calynn would be full grown.

Telyn didn't have years. She was sure Calynn would be a great help as she was if she chose to be. Telyn wasn't quite sure just how loyal the little dragon was to her. Calynn had chosen Telyn, just as the people had, but she didn't understand why.

What could a dragon possibly want with her?

"She can sense your power, the same way we can." Skylar was standing in the doorway, watching Calynn and Telyn.

Calynn flapped her strong leathery wings until she was high enough up to perch on Telyn's shoulder.

"I reckon her mother sensed it as well. It might be what saved you the day you spent with them." Skylar came close enough to pet Calynn.

"How could everyone tell but me? I thought I was normal until I fought my uncle and the shadows revealed themselves. Then everything happened so quickly. I wasn't prepared for it," Telyn said.

"We too often don't recognize our own power. Even if it is manifest in a more mundane way than magick. Great leaders don't recognize their own prowess until they have been tested. They can have dreams and ambitions, but nothing is sure until they have been tried." Skylar stroked the top of Calynn's head.

"If I had known sooner, we could have avoided a lot of this mess." Telyn sighed.

"You may avoid the brunt of it yet. Her mother and siblings may choose to side with you in the war for her sake," Skylar said.

"Her name is Calynn." Telyn offered.

"It suits her." Skylar smiled.

"I can't rely on her family though. I can't even rely on her. I'm not sure she'd be willing to fight, she seems to prefer it down here in the dark," Telyn said.

"She chose you. She will fight for you. There wouldn't be a dragon in my dungeon if she hadn't made that decision before she followed you here." Skylar pulled back her hand. "Let's go back upstairs."

When Telyn left the dungeon, Calynn didn't leave her shoulder. For the first time since she'd come home with them, the dragon stayed with Telyn as she left her den.

Cordelia and Brea were delighted to see Calynn when they got to the more travelled halls of the estate.

"She's so big now!" Cordelia clapped.

Brea was quiet as she reached up to pet the scales of Calynn's long tail. "She's going to get even bigger, isn't she?"

"She's going to be huge, but we've got years before that happens. For now she'll stay fairly small." Telyn smiled as Calynn chirped and stretched her wings.

"How big do you reckon she'll be by the end of the year?" Cordelia asked.

"I'm not sure." Telyn glanced at Skylar.

"I'd guess maybe the size of a horse." Skylar shrugged.

There wasn't much that was known about dragons or their development. Not many people were brave enough to get close enough to study them.

Maybe Sophie would have information. If she didn't, Telyn might have to start recording it herself. Dragons had been misunderstood for as long as anyone could remember, perhaps it would be good to shed some light on them.

They could be big dangerous animals, but as Sevina and Calynn had proven, they could also be intelligent and kind creatures.

Telyn had spent a day locked in a cave with a mother dragon and her children and emerged unscathed.

The entirety of Ceris had been living with one for weeks. Granted, a reclusive and small one, but the only harm that had befallen anyone was the rodents that Calynn had hunted. Those rodents could infect their food with the diseases they carried if they got into it, Calynn had been helping them by preventing it.

Telyn knew a house cat could accomplish the same thing, but that didn't change the fact that it showed how beneficial dragons could be.

Telyn knew how it felt to be misunderstood. Many of the preconceived notions people had about dragons were the same ones the people of Micaera had held against Telyn in the time she'd spent there. She had almost been put down for what she was, the same way many dragons had been slain simply for existing.

Before Telyn had come to Siluria, she'd thought the beasts extinct.

Now that she knew they weren't, she would do her part to keep it that way.

"Did you hear about what happened in Heart?" Brea asked, she turned her attention to Skylar.

"No, what happened?" Skylar frowned.

"Yesterday morning, Piran strung up three people and burned them alive." Brea's face was a bit paler than usual. She was still occupying her fingers with Calynn's scales and spikes.

"He wanted to teach them a lesson too." Skylar's expression darkened.

The ultimate decision on those peoples' punishments should have been Skylar's, but Skylar was a woman, and Piran was the king. They didn't have to wonder why he hadn't included her in the decision, not with the comments he'd made the night before.

He held no respect for her. Which shouldn't have been surprising, considering he hadn't respected his own mother.

It wouldn't be long before he was doing the same in Summer and Spring, where Portia and Vespera were supposed to rule. The only court that might be safe was Autumn, solely because they were ruled by a man.

But Piran would only listen to Wes as long as he didn't oppose him. If Wes disagreed and tried to protect his people, he might be the one to get punished in their stead.

Piran was ruthless.

The sooner they were rid of him, the better.

Patience.

Telyn could feel the anger rippling through Skylar, but she knew as well as Telyn did that this was not something they could rush. If they were hasty, they would make a mistake. And in this game, a mistake could cost thousands of lives.

The king and queen hadn't been the only ones to fall in the explosion. There had been hundreds of fatalities. Innocents who had come to support their prince and been repaid with their deaths. Piran didn't care how many lives he took so long as he got what he wanted.

Telyn had been keeping that from him long enough for him to take measures like this. She needed to end it before there was nothing left for him to destroy; he would not stop on his own. Not even when there was nothing left. He would scream and beat at the pieces he'd left behind until they were ash.

Just as he had done with the scrolls.

He knew no limits.

How soon do you think we'll be able to do it? Telyn asked.

Safely? At least a month. You can't rush your immunity. Skylar shifted her attention fully to Telyn and gave a small shake of her head.

They both wanted him dead, but Skylar wasn't willing to risk Telyn the way she was willing to risk herself.

The patience was the hardest part. Telyn felt like she couldn't do anything. She was useless until she wasn't, and there was nothing she could do about it. Or anything at the time.

And while they waited, Piran continued to have a free reign of terror over his people. It wasn't fair to anyone, but there was nothing to be done. Not until they had a surefire way of killing him. They couldn't do that with force, they had to be smart about it.

Being smart meant patience.

For now, all they could do was extend their condolences to the families and hope they had time to act before it happened again.

Telyn followed Skylar outside the gates of Ceris.

The walk was a slow and silent one as they both thought of what they could possibly say to make the situation any better for those who had lost people they loved.

They would want justice, the same way Telyn did. She just hoped they didn't do anything foolish. As much as they might feel they wanted to, they were no good to anyone if they joined their loved ones beyond the grave. And that would be the only result to come of facing Piran with no other plan than blind vengeance.

She hoped she could offer them some sort of solace. A promise of what would happen if they could only take their time to grieve before they acted.

That's all she needed to do.

Buy time.

Piran might get suspicious if he caught her bringing nightshade berries with her to the palace. So, she would need to have a reason to stay in Ceris for at least a month. She would have preferred to never leave. Not in a way like she was going to have to, but it was her duty.

She had been chosen to save the people.

Her comforts couldn't limit her options in that.

A month, that was all she needed to buy.

Time had never really been on her side before, she hoped he would make an exception now.

"We knew the risks." A woman sat with a damp white handkerchief crumpled up in her hands. She was Rheana's mother.

Rheana had been one of the three people killed.

"She was so brave. She believed you the second you stood up there and told us what that monster had done." The woman sniffed. "She told me that she wanted to help you, more than anything. Those friends of hers were slower to believe you, but once they'd thought about it, they wanted the same thing. None of us want to be ruled by a cruel tyrant. The gods were cruel in not making him more like his mother."

"Indeed," Skylar said.

"I promise you; she was a great help to us. Just knowing we had her support was enough. And when the time comes, the king will pay for his crimes. I will see to it personally," Telyn said.

"Thank you." The woman smiled. Her eyes were still filled with tears, but there was a fierce light in them. She hadn't given up the fight yet.

She must have been the source of Rheana's courageous heart.

And for that, Telyn would forever be grateful for her.

Telyn couldn't bring Rheana back from the dead, but she could kill the man who'd killed her. She knew it wouldn't ease the grief, but it might make them feel safer.

She was sure Piran wouldn't take too kindly to people grieving traitors.

But they were only seen as traitors by Piran. To Telyn and Skylar, they were friends, and allies. They had had families that loved them.

Though Piran didn't seem to care about families. He'd murdered his own, why should he feel bad for someone else's?

"If there is anything else we can do to support you through this, please let us know." Telyn grasped the woman's hands tightly in her own.

Telyn saw that spark flash in the woman's eyes as she stared right into Telyn's eyes. "Just make sure you kill him when the time comes. Show no mercy to those who don't know the meaning."

The realm was ready for war.

They knew it was coming because none of them deserved to be treated the way Piran was treating them. They were ready to go to war for their freedom.

Telyn wasn't so sure they were ready to deal with the consequences that come from war. They would lose a lot more people than the three that had already been lost.

War did not discriminate between the sinners and the saints.

Carling did not discriminate between the sinners and the saints.

He would take whomever he saw fit.

Telyn was surprised he had waited this long before claiming the first lives of the conflict.

He was beginning to stir once more.

That meant Telyn was running out of time. She knew she couldn't handle both Carling and Piran at the same time. One of them had to go. And soon.

"Winter stands with you, My Lady." The woman dipped her head in Skylar's direction.

It always had.

And Skylar had known it. She knew the loyalty of her people. They were loyal to her because she was kind to them and treated them as people rather than subjects.

Telyn had been the one to doubt them; she saw now that her fears were unfounded.

These people wanted what was best for their communities, and by now, they all knew that wasn't the king.

That woman's words were the only things Telyn could think about on the trek home.

For the first time in her life, Telyn was beginning to understand the support she had.

She'd always stood on shaky ground with other people. She was never quite able to trust them.

For as long as she could remember, it had always only been her mother. There had been Kassian, briefly, but it hadn't been much of a support system.

Even with Alidain at her disposal, she had never felt she could truly trust anyone outside of her little circle. The kingdom's loyalty had lain with her parents, and with King Azriel, monarchs who had proven themselves capable of leading. They had had respect for Telyn, yes, but respect only went so far.

The people of Winter were loyal to Skylar, and somehow, Telyn had earned that loyalty as well.

She had people who supported her in what she was aiming to do, encouraged it even.

It was no longer just her revenge, it was revenge for Rheana's mother, and the others who had lost family and friends to Piran's violence. It was revenge for Brea, who almost died to get away from her brother. Telyn was fighting to avenge the king and queen who had been too blinded by love to see what a monster their son had become, those who had dared voice their opinions about the man who kept their realm bound in chains.

This revenge was no longer just for her. It had transcended from a personal vendetta to justice.

Even if Piran killed Telyn before she could kill him, there would be others that would try. Her death would signal the start of an open hunting season, and Piran could not survive it if he stood alone. Even with the god of death at his back, he would fall to the billions of people he had wronged to get his crown.

Carling could not save him from the harm he had sown for himself. Not even a god could reverse the consequences of his actions. He had brought his fate upon himself. He had signed his life away to this war the second he became a pawn to its god. He had no say in what happened to him now. He would die, one way or another.

"If we had any chance at all of choosing whether or not we went through with this before, we don't now," Skylar said. Her warm breath steamed in the cold air.

"For me, it was never a choice; it was a matter of survival." Telyn's voice was soft, but it bore the same effects on the air.

"It never should have been like that. I should have known he would turn out to be good for nothing." Skylar scowled.

"It would have truly been treason then. We have no way of predicting the future. He could have been alright. If he had never met Carling he might have been more like his mother," Telyn said.

"There are too many 'what ifs' to consider them all. What's happened has happened, but we should have been able to see the signs." Skylar shook her head.

"There are too many 'should haves' as well. You can't blame yourself for this. It was no one's fault but his own. He chose this path. He *enjoys* hurting people and killing them. That's not something you could fix, even if you'd seen it before it got this bad." Telyn took Skylar's hand. "We have done all we can for now, but the time will come for us to fix this. For *me* to fix this, and I will."

Of that, Telyn could be certain.

She would fix the mess Piran had made if it was the last thing she did.

It was far better than letting him continue on his path of carnage and destruction.

Rebellion

"You know, you've never really cared about anyone...
...But one day you will, and it's going to hurt."
-L.J. Smith, Seret Vampire.

"Only fools fear knowledge." Sophie shook her head, her red lips drawn into a tight line.

Skylar and Telyn were helping her move the remaining scrolls from the dusty shelves they'd been on for centuries into a clever little room hidden beneath a trap door behind Sophie's desk.

"I think we can all agree that if he is nothing else, the king is a fool. For many reasons." Telyn sighed as she tucked the last of the parchment into a dark corner and climbed back up to ground level.

Skylar helped Telyn up and once everyone was clear of the door, it was securely set back into place. Calynn turned in circles before she curled up on top of the door, a puff of smoke rose from her nostrils. The scrolls should be safe from Piran's flames of wrath as long as they stayed there.

The rest of the realm was not so lucky.

Twelve more murders.

Piran had slaughtered three more people in Autumn, five in Summer, and four in Spring.

They were all expecting more as the nights dragged on and the heart of the rebellion grew.

Telyn didn't think he knew he was only feeding the flames of the rebellion. With every burnt corpse he left behind, more of his people joined the rebellion.

He wanted to rule through fear, but these people did not fear him; they only hated him. That hatred grew more and more with every passing night.

"Portia, Vespera, Wes, and the captain are waiting for us," Skylar said.

Telyn brushed dust from her trousers and glanced at Sophie. "Be careful, he grows bolder by the minute."

"I haven't lived this long to be offed by a boy king with anger issues." Sophie smiled.

"He may be a boy, but he is dangerous." Telyn frowned.

"This shop is safer than anywhere else in the realm. I'll be fine here with all the dust and magick." Sophie gave the warped desk beside her a gentle pat and it arched up into her touch.

"If you need anything, send a bird." Skylar looked over at Sophie from the door. "We'll be here."

Telyn followed Skylar out into the cold of Heart, Calynn on her heels, leaving the lights of *Sophie's* behind.

Telyn couldn't say she'd ever sat on an official war council before. She wasn't sure King Azriel had one, and when she came into power, there wasn't enough time to assemble one before everything fell apart; but war council was where she was headed.

They all knew that things wouldn't end with Piran's death. The council knew that Carling was behind it all and would find another way to destroy the realms.

This meeting was to determine how they were going to handle the fall out of Piran's death. Siluria and Eralia would need a new king; quickly, before Carling had time to destroy too much. They would need armies in place, people ready to face their deaths to keep the rest of the realm alive.

"They've started to destroy his statues and burn what's left," Portia said. "They've taken down three so far."

"Can you blame them?" Captain Ezra scoffed.

"He's going to retaliate again, more of them are going to die," Skylar said.

"They know that," Vespera said.

Spring and Summer might as well be the same court, Vespera and Portia shared everything with each other, and they knew the other's people as well as their own.

"In fact, they're counting on more people dying," Portia said.

"The more people that die, the more loved ones that are taking up arms to make a change." Wes's arms were propped up on the table in front of him.

The bags under his eyes and his unkempt hair made him look older.

Telyn was sure she must have looked the same. The war had barely started, and yet it was already taking its toll on them.

"Who's to take the king's place once we've killed him?" Ezra asked.

"He has no heirs himself, the crown would pass to his sister," Skylar said.

"She's not old enough to bear such a responsibility." Vespera shook her head.

"Then one of you will act as regent until she comes of age," Telyn said.

"Why one of us and not you?" Wes asked.

"I'm not even fit to rule my own kingdom, I should not be advising another queen on how to rule hers." Telyn sighed.

Every time she thought of Alidain and the people she'd left there, all she felt was guilt. She had failed them. She had done her best, but she was never raised to be a queen.

"She trusts us." Portia's words were slow. "Instead of a single regent, we could act as a council for her, that way each of the courts are having their needs met and there are more heads being put together on how Eralia is managed."

"A council would be best for any form of ruling," Ezra said. "Would it be better to be rid of the kings and queens of this place while we have the chance?"

"That would be Brea's decision to make," Skylar said.

"Why isn't she in here?" Telyn asked.

"She doesn't need to be concerned with all of this," Wes said. "She's been through enough these past months; we can handle this until she is better suited to it."

"Very well, but the decision is hers to make." Telyn folded her hands in front of her on top of the table. "Whether it be a regent, a council, or a complete abolishment of the monarchy, it is her call to make."

"On that much we can agree," Vespera said.

The sentiment was echoed around the table.

"I expected to have to prepare these people more. I expected them to be afraid, but it looks like they already know the stakes, and are willing to pay in blood," Ezra said.

"These people have been around for a very long time, give them credit where it is due," Portia said.

"Age doesn't bring bravery like that. It's either bred or learned." Ezra shook his head. "They're ready for war. They may be fools for it, but they are ready."

"They have never faced anything like this before, they are not ready." Skylar shook her head.

"I want you to look at the determination in their eyes, little one, and then tell me they are not ready." Ezra leaned forward to look at Skylar.

The captain had a point. These people might not know the gritty details of war, but they knew that many of them would die, and they had deemed that risk worth it. So long as Piran went down with their dead.

Telyn only hated that so many of them had died already. She could barely stomach that that number would rise into the thousands before the war was done.

With the meeting declared over, they split apart, the ones who weren't already home started to head that way.

Telyn and Skylar made their way to their room. Telyn had letters to send off to Alidain, and Skylar was content to just be near her as she worked.

Calynn woke when they opened the door. She let out an excited spurt of flames when she saw Telyn.

"Good morning, little one." Telyn smiled and scratched her scaled chin.

Telyn pulled her wax melting supplied from a drawer and set them up on the desk. "Let's try something new today." She suggested. "*Pyris.*"

Calynn tilted her head to the side.

"*Pyris.*" Telyn repeated and pointed to the wick of the wax warmer.

Calynn chirped and flames spewed from her tiny mouth, lighting the wick in front of her.

"Thank you." Telyn rewarded the behavior with more scratches.

"It'll be useful, having her do that on command," Skylar said.

"I figured it would be." Telyn nodded. "She can't come with me when I leave; he'll kill her." She held a rose-colored stick of wax in the warmer and watched the end of it disappear as it melted.

"We'll take care of her here. She'll be safe." Skylar promised.

"I know. She's fully capable of caring for herself down in those dungeons. I just don't know if she'll come looking for me if I've been gone too long." Telyn pulled the wax stick from the warmer and poured the melted wax onto the parchment she had rolled up in her free hand. She set the warmer down and pressed her seal into the hot wax, sealing the message.

"She might, but by the time she reaches you, I would hope the danger is past," Skylar said.

Telyn was silent as she repeated the process for her remaining letters.

Skylar could hope all she wanted to, but Telyn couldn't promise the job would be quick. The timing needed to be right.

When she was done, she gathered the rolled-up letters in her arms and walked out into the courtyard.

There were caged ravens waiting to be given their assignments.

Telyn fastened each letter to a different bird's leg and let them go. She watched as they got smaller and smaller in the sky until they eventually disappeared.

Most of them would fly to Alidain as official responses to the many requests that had been filed since the transition of power. The others were personal letters for some of her court members.

Telyn needed to see how Pip was faring, if they needed any extra support. She wanted to check on Zerina, and Colton.

The last time she had seen them, it hadn't been under the best circumstances. She hadn't left in the best way either, and she missed them.

The only family she had left was in Alidain, but Alidain wasn't home.

She hoped there would never be a day where she had to choose between them and Winter. She wasn't sure it was a choice she could bring herself to make. At least not without forever feeling guilty for the one she didn't choose. Telyn needed to find a time to go see them again, not everything could be conveyed through a letter, but she couldn't spare the time.

Not when things were just beginning to close in.

Telyn didn't know what Carling's plan was, and she didn't know if Piran's murder sprees were a part of it, but she knew she had to be at least two steps ahead if she expected to survive this.

Piran wanted control over the realms, Carling wanted the realms destroyed. Which would inevitably happen if Piran ruled them all.

Asteria hadn't been mentioned. Which was strange. In everything Telyn had heard or read, Asteria had been Carling's partner in crime. Her disasters led to his wars, but she hadn't taken much part in this one.

It was possible that the city frozen in ice had been her doing, but that wasn't enough to fuel a war.

So, what was she doing?

She was supposed to be on Carling's side, but it didn't look like she was supporting him in his most recent endeavor. They hadn't suffered any major disasters; she hadn't chosen a champion as some of the other more involved players had.

It was strange.

But as long as she stayed out of it, the war might be manageable. If she sided with Piran for this, Telyn wasn't sure she would be able to take them both down.

Despite the prophecy and the support of the people, she knew her own capabilities. And killing the two gods who had invented war and strife wasn't one of them. She wasn't even sure she could handle the one, but only time would tell.

She had other enemies to end before she was anywhere near ready to take on the god. He would know she was coming, which would make it harder, but if she survived long enough to face him, she would use every last drop of the power she held to make sure he never got what he wanted.

Just as Telyn was about to turn to go back inside, a raven landed on Skylar's shoulder, a roll of parchment tied to its talon.

As soon as the message was in Skylar's hands, the raven flew off.

Skylar popped the seal and read the message.

She was silent for a moment.

"There was another riot, this one was in Summer," Skylar said.

"What did they do?" Telyn asked.

"They set fire to the king's vacation home and tore down all of the statues of him." Skylar rolled the paper back up and handed it to Telyn. "Burn it, if he finds this we'll be in more trouble."

Telyn took the paper and let a small flame ignite in the palm of her hand. The flames turned the paper to ash, then it was gone.

The people of the realm were beginning to actively reject their king.

Piran wouldn't take to that too kindly.

Thinking about what he would do to punish these offenses made Telyn's stomach churn.

His anger was too often left unchecked, and there was no one to stop him from killing whoever he wanted.

No one except Telyn, but she wasn't ready.

She hated that she required so much preparation to do the one thing that needed to be done as soon as possible. All of the petty bickering in Alidain, all of the royalty stuff, it could wait, but Piran was a problem that needed to be resolved immediately.

And yet it was the one thing she couldn't do when everyone needed it most.

This process should have started months ago. Telyn should have been poisoning herself from the moment she realized who Piran truly was.

But back then she hadn't realized just how firmly enemies had to be dealt with.

She had wanted to kill Time because he had killed her mother, but Piran hadn't done anything that extreme.

He had only forced her into an engagement she didn't want so he could use her for her power, and threatened the lives of everyone she cared about. He hadn't actually killed any of them.

Had she been smart enough to catch how sinister it had all been while it was happening, so much would have been different. People wouldn't have been suffering on her behalf, but it was too late now.

"How many do you think he'll kill this time?" Telyn asked.

"It's possible he'll take the entire city for something this big." Skylar sighed.

Hundreds of lives…

It was too soon for such a high number on the fatality rates.

They should have had months before they were seeing numbers like they were about to.

But it had been months, hadn't it?

It *had* been months since Piran had almost killed Alexander. Since Carling had turned Alexander against her. This war had started a long time ago, even if they were only now beginning to fight back.

They had been trying to break her down for longer than she'd realized.

She was the one who had waited far too long to fight back.

"Is there a way we can stop him?" Telyn looked at the sky as it began to grow light, the sun rising on the horizon.

"Short of killing him? No. We'll have to deal with the fall out of this tomorrow night." Skylar closed her eyes.

Telyn imagined she was fighting back tears as well.

She could feel the deep ache of hopelessness settle in.

They might not be able to see the walls that barred them from living the way they deserved to, but they were still caged.

Everyone on the realm was caged, and they would stay that way until Piran set them free.

They were beginning to push back and fight for their freedom, but it was just that; a beginning.

They still had a long way to go before they were free.

When Telyn went back to her room, she popped two nightshade berries into her mouth, the sweet taste almost burned like acid on her tongue.

They didn't have the time to spare on being patient.

If Telyn could increase her tolerance quicker, it would be ideal for everyone.

It didn't take long for the queasiness to set in.

Telyn had to lay in bed with a glass of water on the table beside her. Whenever she could muster the strength, she would take a few sips to help with her dry mouth and calm her roiling stomach.

She hadn't expected the fatigue to come with everything else.

The dry mouth had been a common symptom since she began, she had expected the nausea, but the outright tired ache in her bones was new, and it was very unpleasant.

She knew she hadn't taken enough to kill her, but that didn't stop her from feeling miserable, but she had done it to herself.

And if suffering through it meant she got to kill Piran quicker, she was willing to do it a thousand times over.

Telyn closed her eyes for a moment, willing herself to block out the pain. She thought if she was lucky, she might even slip into unconsciousness until the symptoms had faded.

But Telyn had never been very lucky.

After a few moments, she opened her eyes, but she wasn't in her room anymore.

Trees rose up around her in a beautiful, lush, green forest. The canopy of intertwined branches overhead provided a warm dappled light that led the way down a long winding path that curved around tree roots and bushes. Flowers sprung up where they could amongst the foliage, bright pinks and blues, dotted with the occasional purple or red. It was beautiful.

It almost reminded Telyn of Spring, but something about if felt older, and far more sacred.

This forest had been here long before any gods or Silurians had touched its ground.

Telyn didn't know how she knew that, but the truth of it rang true in her chest as she started down the path ahead of her.

GHOSTS OF THE PAST

"Destroying things is much easier than making them."
-Suzzane Collins, The Hunger Games

Telyn found herself in a huge woodland community. People walked down the paths below the trees, while the trees themselves held homes that were half hidden by their leaves.

"You're back early, Storm." A dark-skinned woman grinned at Telyn. She was carrying a wooden bucket full of water.

Kijana.

The name came to Telyn as if she'd recalled it from her own memory. The words that came from her mouth felt natural, but she knew they weren't hers either.

"Yes, not everything went according to plan, and I had overstayed my welcome." Telyn felt a slight smile pull at her lips.

"Well, it's a good thing you're home. We have some visitors. They arrived last night, claiming to be refugees from a war in another galaxy." Kijana laughed. "They sound crazy to me, but maybe you can help them."

Telyn frowned.

She knew how this story would end, but that didn't explain why she was in it.

Still, she followed Kijana through the winding paths under the trees until they reached a home built into the hollowed-out base of a tree that sat in the center of the village.

Inside, a woman with dark hair was wrapped in blue silks in all the shades of the sea. Next to her was a man with blond hair. There was nothing extremely remarkable about him, he was simply there.

"You must be the woman we've been waiting for." As the woman turned, Telyn could see the swell of her pregnant belly.

"I'm under the same impression. How may I help you?" Telyn could feel her stomach twist in knots as she tried to tell herself to run, but her feet remained firmly in place, and not a sound of protest left her mouth.

"I'm Nerissa, and this is my husband, Cygnus. We've come a very long way to escape a war that's tearing our home apart." She explained.

Telyn knew there were no wars going on in her world. They had been living peacefully for centuries, trading and helping one another as needed, it was how they survived.

But that was all about to fall apart.

"I'm sorry for your troubles, we would be happy to help you in any way we can." The smile that spread across Telyn's face felt like it was going to split her open. She wanted to eat the words spilling out of her mouth, prevent them from surfacing, and prevent the pending disaster that loomed ahead.

"Thank you." Telyn could see the poison in Nerissa's smiled, but she knew the owner of the body she was looking through couldn't.

Nerissa and Cygnus stood, Telyn held the door open for them. "Kijana, show them to their new home, make sure it's one that has a nursery in it. Two cribs."

Telyn could feel them now, the life and death that pulsed in Nerissa's womb.

Half of it was the same chill Telyn got when Nox visited her, the other half was unfamiliar, but she could assume his twin, Renelleph, shared the space.

She was doing all of this for them.

All of the peaceful innocent people of this community would die so she could have a clean slate for her children.

Children that would go on to try and destroy everything they had built for them.

Genocide must have run in the family.

The days passed in a blur. Despite Nerissa being decently far along in her pregnancy, she still helped the other women of the village as they gathered water and food. Cygnus hunted and built with the men. They were being helpful, and slowly but surely, they won over the people of the community. They earned their trust.

Telyn could see it in the way they greeted them over the days. At first, everyone had been wary of the newcomers, but by the end of the week, the couple was greeted with warm smiles, hugs, and handshakes.

They didn't know how badly they were about to be betrayed.

But Telyn waited for it.

Though she was doing and saying what Storm must have at the time, she knew that Nerissa and Cygnus were not who they pretended to be.

Months passed, and there was no change.

Nerissa and Cygnus still wore the masks they'd presented when they arrived. They still helped, in turn, their nursery and home had been decorated with gifts meant to bless them with good health and prosperity.

As Telyn observed them, there were no warning signs.

No flicker or falter in their presentation.

They genuinely seemed happy to be safe and welcomed.

Telyn saw Nerissa kneeling beside Kijana, dirt coating both of their hands and under their nails as they tended to the community garden, tomatoes, peppers, and corn rose up around them. The bright reds and greens, and the yellow of the corn silk stuck out in the browns of the forest around them. Kijana laughed at something Nerissa said and the two continued, gently placing new plants into the ground.

Nerissa had immediately taken to growing the seeds in her home until it was time for them to go into the ground. She had truly become a valuable member of their community.

Telyn still didn't know why she was there. Why she was living someone else's memories. She didn't know how she was doing it either; it didn't make any sense. What was she meant to do if she couldn't change what had happened?

But the moment the flames spread from tree top to tree top, Telyn knew who had started it.

Telyn ran out into the middle of the village, looking for anything to do to stop it from spreading further. She could hear the screams of Storm's people as they tried to escape the fire, but it was almost like the flames chased them.

When she reached the center of the village, she saw why.

Cygnus stood with his arms raised. The flames answered his beck and call, chasing anyone who was running, swallowing up the precious wood they had all called home.

Though Telyn was familiar with the magick, she knew Storm had never seen anything like it. She could feel the shock and fear that wasn't hers as it coursed through her.

But despite that fear, Telyn's feet found themselves walking towards Cygnus.

"What are you doing?" She demanded. She could feel the tears brimming her eyes from the combination of the smoke and the betrayal.

"Our sons deserve a clean slate." Nerissa smiled as she emerged from behind Cygnus, a bundled-up infant in each arm. "That's what we're giving them. When they are old enough, they will fill this place with the people they create, and they will rule over them all."

"You would have had so much support here." Telyn's voice cracked.

"We would have." Nerissa admitted. "But it is not support that we want. We want a clean slate, and we cannot have that while the old people of this realm live."

The acceptance and aid hadn't been enough for them. Telyn had known that when Storm hadn't, but it didn't keep her from feeling the betrayal and anger that Storm did.

"You won't get away with this." Telyn's voice trembled.

Storm believed the other villages would come to their aid as they had in the past.

And they would, but they wouldn't survive it any better than Storm and Kijana would.

Some of the screams had stopped, ended with the lives of those who had drawn the breath for them. Men, women, children, they had all been slaughtered by two they had called friend and welcomed into their homes.

Telyn screamed as she charged Cygnus, but Storm's body wasn't conditioned to fight. Her movements were slow and choppy. Her anger would only get her so far, but still, she tried.

She beat and tore at his arms in an attempt to sever the hold he had over the flames.

She fought, but nothing worked.

Nerissa threw Telyn to the ground and stood over her. Soot stained Nerissa's beautiful cold face.

"You didn't have to do this." Telyn sobbed. "You can still stop it."

"You're right." Nerissa smiled. "We can, but I don't want to." She carefully placed a foot on Telyn's chest and leaned forward on it.

Telyn struggled to breathe around the pressure on her lungs.

"Say hello to your gods for me when you see them. Tell them they're being displaced." Nerissa's foot slid up to Telyn's neck.

In moments, Telyn was gone.

"Telyn!"

Someone was yelling her name. She was too disoriented to tell who it was.

She blinked as flamed flashed before her ears; the sound of Kijana's laughter tickled her ears.

"Where were you, darling?" Skylar's face came into focus in front of Telyn.

"I don't know. Some sort of memory." Telyn mumbled and rubbed her eyes. "It wasn't mine though."

"Who's was it?" Skylar frowned.

"I don't know. It was from before, or rather during Nerissa and Cygnus's massacre." Telyn pressed her fingers to her temples. She could feel a headache beginning to throb behind her eyes.

"So, you saw it happen?" Skylar asked.

"Yes, well, the beginning of it." Telyn knew that more must have happened. Storm had died with the rest of her village, and eventually, the other villages had fallen as well.

Even with seeing it herself, Telyn still had so many questions. Like how had those people let such vile people into their home without knowing what they were?

They had been too trusting.

Just as Telyn had been.

It was a bit late for her to learn that lesson though.

"Why do you think you saw it?" Skylar asked, her voice had grown softer.

"I think I needed to see it to learn something, but I haven't figure out what that is yet," Telyn said.

She tried to remember what she'd seen, but it only came in flashes. Fire, a garden, laughter, and screams. There was nothing wholly solid for her to pull from. No clues as to what she was supposed to learn.

"The magick," Telyn said, grasping for whatever she could. "It wasn't here before they were. Nerissa and Cygnus brought the magick with them."

"Maybe that's why they were able to wipe out entire civilizations so easily. There wasn't much opposition if no one else had magick." Skylar frowned. "That just seems cruel though."

"It is cruel. *They* were cruel. They knew their plan before they'd walked into that village, and they still betrayed the people who had welcomed and helped them." Telyn felt a fresh wave of frustration.

It was the same thing Piran had done.

History was repeating itself, and she was powerless to stop it.

"So, if they didn't have magick then, the playing field has evened. We have a chance against them because we have what their last enemies didn't," Skylar said.

"In theory." Telyn thought about it for a moment. "It is a possibility, but I also didn't see the extent of their magick. The gods may still be far more powerful than we are. We only have part of their blood after all."

"That may be true, but there are a lot more of us than there are of them. We outnumber them, and we certainly outnumber Piran," Skylar said.

So, even if Telyn's plan failed, they still had a backup plan. They still had a chance. They might not have more power alone against any of their enemies, but the numbers were on their side. At least with Piran.

Sophie had been right about the gods though; people would rather languish in ignorance than truly face what they were.

Which meant Telyn might not have an army willing to go against them.

When they got to that point, she may truly be alone.

That was a possibility she would have to prepare for, but until then, they almost completely had a victory.

"We could take the citizens of Siluria and march on him now," Telyn said.

"We can't demand that of them yet." Skylar shook her head.

"They're ready," Telyn said.

"They *think* they're ready. They may be loyal to us now, but if we fling them into battle at the first inconvenience, I doubt they will take it well," Skylar said.

"They're already fighting battles on their own, and they're dying for it. If they help kill him, they can live." Telyn pointed out.

"But at what cost? How many of them will he slaughter in open battle before we can finally get to him?" Skylar asked.

"So, we stick to the plan," Telyn said.

"We stick to the plan." Skylar agreed. "And *if* that plan fails, then we can consider sending them in. They are civilians, not warriors. We can't forget that."

"They are going to have to become warriors if they want to survive this war."

Everyone was going to have to become things they weren't during the war: warriors, killers, and strategists.

If they were going to survive, they were going to have to do a lot of things they didn't like.

Telyn had already started down that road, and she knew she was far from the end of it.

Taking too much nightshade, and seeing that memory as a result of it, had been one of those things. She could still feel the tight roiling in her stomach. It had subsided while she was inside the memory, but now it was a constant ache.

But she couldn't tell Skylar she'd tried to rush things along. Skylar would insist on being the one to poison the king instead.

But Telyn knew it had to be her.

He wouldn't trust anyone else to let them get close enough to try. If Skylar requested an audience, he would get suspicious.

Plus, it would set them behind.

Telyn had been taking nightshade for about a week now, and they would have to start the process all over if Skylar had to do it.

So, Skylar would never know what Telyn did to get into that memory.

"What are you thinking?" Skylar whispered as she brushed hair away from Telyn's face.

Her cool fingers felt good against Telyn's hot skin.

"I just want it to be over," Telyn said.

We all do. Skylar's gentle voice filled Telyn's head. *You're getting better at hiding those thoughts of yours, little raven.*

I have to be able to surprise you on occasion. I can't do that if you go around reading my mind all day. Telyn smiled.

The surprises can wait until we've won the war. We'll have plenty of time for them then. Skylar brushed a soft kiss against Telyn's forehead.

I would rather make the war wait.

War was supposed to be a last resort, and Telyn supposed it was. Her job as queen, and Skylar's as high lady, was to keep peace and protect her people.

That was hard to do when Piran seemed content to slaughter them at the slightest inconvenience,

So, war it was.

They were playing right into what Piran and Carling wanted, but they had no other choice.

The best they could do was hope they could get a few steps ahead and hold that advantage.

It wouldn't be easy; nothing could ever be easy, not where Telyn was involved, but it would be manageable.

So long as they had enough backup plans.

One step ahead.

That was all they needed.

And they had it. They just had to be patient and let the plan work. Let the poison run its course through Telyn without harm so it could eventually kill him.

Telyn wanted to watch it happen. She wanted to watch him realize who had condemned him to death. She wanted to watch the life drain from his eyes, and that was how she decided she would do it.

The kiss of a dagger would have been preferrable, but she would never be able to overpower him on her own.

No, a normal kiss would have to do.

But either way, it would be one of death.

Piran wanted power, which meant he would want heirs. He would want to lull her into a sense of security enough to do that.

It would never happen, but she could pretend enough for their plan to work.

And that was all she needed.

Poison in his glass was too cliché.

Skylar had said to get creative.

It was both creative and intimate enough that Piran would die, and she would have the satisfaction of watching it happen before her eyes.

And then she would be free.

You're already free, darling. Skylar's voice had taken on a sleepy murmur. Telyn hadn't realized how close to dawn it had grown.

His cage may not be a physical one, but while he is alive, I will never be truly free.'

She would be trapped by fear and anger until he was gone. Living a life in fear and regret was no living a free life. It was not the life she wanted.

If Nerissa could justify slaughtering an entire realm for her children, Telyn couldn't bring herself to feel bad about wanting to kill one man so she could live out her life peacefully and unmanipulated.

There would always be those that tried, but Piran had taught her what to look for. People like him would always leave the same bitter taste in her mouth.

He might have manipulated her and threatened those she loved, but he had taught her one good thing that she would carry with her for the rest of her life: Never trust a man with no motivation.

No one was ever kind out of the goodness of their heart. They always wanted something. It may not be a drastic as her power and throne, but it would always be something. And Telyn couldn't allow herself to set a precedent of giving those people what they wanted.

She would make an example of the king. Those who tried to manipulate her would always end up dead if they were persistent enough.

THE BOY KING

"Time doesn't heal all wounds."
-Adam Silvera, History Is All You Left Me

Telyn woke to wailing and banging on the door.

Skylar shot out of bed and was at the door in moments. "What happened?" She demanded.

"He's back, he's slaughtering people in Heart." One of the maids must have been on the other side of the door. Telyn could hear the strain of tears in her voice.

Skylar yanked her jacket off of a chair and left the room.

Telyn scrambled to follow, only pausing to slip into her shoes.

The flight was quick through the biting cold. The wind tore at Telyn's clothes and hair, but she didn't dare ask to slow down.

She knew their timing was imperative. If they didn't get there soon enough, Piran could very well slaughter the entire city.

They needed to get there before that could happen.

Telyn could smell the vaguely sweet scent of the bodies before she landed. She could see the corpses littering the ground. Piran stood in front of a group of children, his hands ablaze. The children were screaming and crying.

Ice crackled across the ground and swallowed the flames.

With a growl, Piran shook ice shards from his hands, and turned on Skylar and Telyn.

"These people have done nothing to you. I suggest you go home, princeling," Skylar said.

Piran's face turned red. "They have disrespected me, and now they will pay the price."

"I don't know if you've suddenly become blind, but those are children!" Skylar stalked forward, ice cracked and shifted under her with every step she took.

"They will pay the same price their parents have. Traitors breed traitors." Piran gestured to the burnt corpses around him.

"No." Skylar's voice was ice cold. "You will leave the Winter Court and never return. Your ban is effective immediately."

"You can't ban me!" Piran roared. "I am the king!"

"You are no king of mine." Skylar spat at his feet.

Flames rushed for Skylar, but they were doused by ice and water.

Piran drew his sword and charged instead, and this time he was met with shadows.

"You will leave now and alive, or we can send your body back with your sister when she becomes queen," Telyn said.

"Only if you come with me." Piran fought to free his swords from the web of shadows that held it in place.

"Why would I ever do that?" Telyn scoffed.

"Because they're brainwashing you here. You know your place isn't here, but in Viridium," Piran said.

Telyn's shadows clenched tighter around the blade. "You truly do know nothing. My place is here, and yours is in the grave, but if you cooperate, you don't have to end up there just yet."

"One day, you'll see I was right all along. These people don't care about you the way I do," Piran said. He released his sword, leaving it to be suspended in Telyn's extended grasp, and in a burst of flames, he was gone.

He would be back, they all knew that, but hopefully when that happened, they would be ready.

Skylar gathered the trembling children around her. "Just wait here, we have more people coming to help you. I have to-" Skylar's voice faltered. "I have to take care of them."

The children sniffled and nodded, still huddled together.

Telyn helped Skylar carry the bodies into neat rows.

They did the best they could to keep them together and close to who they had been before, but they were unrecognizable. Pieces of their skin stuck to the cobblestone beneath them and to Telyn and Skylar's hands.

Slowly, the people who had come from Ceris on foot filtered into the city. Their faces paled in horror at all of the destruction, but they didn't dwell on it. Some maids tended to the children. Healers sought out the few that had survived the massacre, and soldiers helped clear rubble and relocate bodies.

By the time it was all over, there were two hundred people wrapped in bloodied white sheets.

With the ground frozen over, they would have to burn them again.

That was the way funerals were held in Winter.

It felt wrong burning those who had fallen to the flames, but they didn't have another option.

Those who had survived gathered around the destroyed square, standing in the remains of buildings that had once stood proudly. Most of the children had found their families, but a few stood sullenly, watching the wrapped bodies on the ground as one by one, Skylar lit them on fire again.

"These people didn't deserve this," Skylar said. Telyn could hear the tremble in her voice. "They were slaughtered without warning. This is the result of the Eralian king losing his temper. From this moment forward, the Winter Court no longer allies itself with Piran, King of the Unseelie Court, Ruler of Eralia. He is an enemy to the Court, and he is no longer welcome here."

There were soft murmurs of agreement, but with the dead still burning, these people weren't ready to move forward just yet.

Skylar wiped tears from her face as she turned away from the living, and dwelt with the dead for a while.

Telyn took Skylar's hand and watched everything burn.

Piran was no different than the gods. He took what he wanted, destroyed what he wanted, simply because he wanted it. He held no regard for life, at least none other than his own.

He had burnt down Heart and its people just as Cygnus and Nerissa had burnt that village.

Telyn was beginning to regret her decision to let Piran leave with his life. She could have killed him, they both knew she was capable of it, but Skylar had wanted to stick to the plan.

If her thoughts on that had changed, she wouldn't have stopped attacking Piran, she would have ended him as Telyn's shadows held his blade.

But she hadn't.

Telyn didn't know why, but she wouldn't question it. Now wasn't the time.

Skylar and the others needed the time to mourn.

The two children who had been staring at the bodies now clung to each other. Tears streaked down their faces. Both shared the same dark hair and drawn features. Already this war had produced orphans.

Those children would need to be cared for. Without parents to clothe and feed them, they would need to depend on someone else for that.

The rest of these people would need help rebuilding, they would need food, and shelter until their homes and shops could be rebuilt.

Wars were meant to be fought out in battle fields, army against army, with only the soldiers falling. It wasn't supposed to spill into the cities where innocent people lived. Those people weren't supposed to lose their lives because they lived on the wrong side of a boarder.

War was meant to be a clean scheduled event. Like a duel.

Not this messy monstrosity Piran had brought down on them.

None of it was right.

Nothing had been right since her mother had died.

Everything had devolved into chaos and manipulation.

Her mother would have known what to do. Her mother would have killed Piran where he stood, no matter what anyone else's opinion on the matter was.

But Telyn wasn't her mother.

Once again, when faced with an enemy that deserved death, she had hesitated.

She had let him go.

Even when she looked at all of the destruction and death he had wrought, she let him go.

He would do it again. As long as she defied him, and even after she stopped, he would continue to kill others for what she had done.

And she could do nothing about it until she was immune to some stupid poisonous berries.

At this rate, these people didn't have a month. Telyn needed a better option.

She could add a berry a day until she got to nine, then she would do nine until she could handle it without severe ill effects, and once she got to ten, she would be ready to go. It couldn't take more than a week or two, could it?

That would give Piran less time to come back and slaughter the rest of the Winter Court.

Telyn knew Skylar didn't want her to rush it, but she didn't feel like she had any other choice.

Either Eralia would fall or Siluria would.

Telyn couldn't let it be Siluria.

She was the one that was supposed to save them. She couldn't let them all die.

Telyn and Skylar brought the children back with them to Ceris. There, they would at least have Brea and Cordelia as company until Telyn could figure out what she was supposed to do with them.

They were twins, like her and Zerina. One girl, one boy; Catelyn and Caspien.

That was all the information they'd given Telyn on the long walk back to Ceris.

She couldn't blame them for not wanting to talk. Telyn hadn't wanted to talk when her mother had died either.

When her mother had been murdered.

Maria and these children's parents had been murdered by men who wanted more than they deserved.

Men who had turned a child's entire world on its head.

Men who, soon, would both be dead.

Telyn owed it to herself to kill Piran. And now she owed it to every person inside of Heart to do it too.

There was a gentle tug on Telyn's skirt and she looked down. Catelyn had a fistful of fabric as she stared up at Telyn. She couldn't have been older than five or six.

"What is it, little one?" Telyn scooped the girl up into her arms.

"I want the scary man to die." The little girl's voice was cold. She knew what had been done to her mother, and she wanted the same thing Telyn did.

"He will." Telyn promised.

"How do you know?" Catelyn asked.

"Because I'm going to be the one to kill him," Telyn said.

"Good." Catelyn pressed a gentle kiss to Telyn's forehead.

It felt more reassuring than any blessing of the gods.

Catelyn and Caspien might not fully understand why Telyn was doing it, but they understood that part of her reasoning was them. She was doing it for all of those people who had lost family at the hands of a mad king,

They understood that they were safe with her.

Telyn hadn't been able to protect her mother or theirs, but she refused to not be there to protect those two little lives.

They weren't her children, but they were her responsibility. And she would do her best to get them where they needed to be so they could lead happy safe lives.

They deserved that much.

Cordelia had found Nolan, and then Wes. She had a new family.

Maybe Telyn could help these twins find the same.

They needed people in their lives that could act as parent figures.

If Telyn could have provided that for them, she wouldn't hesitate to keep them herself, where she could keep a close eye on them.

But Telyn was in no position to be a mother.

For them, this war would end with Piran's death, but for her it went on, and became even more dangerous. She couldn't put them in a position like that. She couldn't risk Carling using them against her the same way he had used Alexander.

They wouldn't be safe with her.

She couldn't justify dragging them into the mess she was in.

They were far too young.

Cordelia and Brea were far too young, but they were still a part of it. Brea hadn't had a choice. Telyn had brought Cordelia into it, and she thought she might regret it for the rest of her life.

Every moment Cordelia was with anyone who associated with Telyn, she was in danger.

That was something Telyn had done to her, she couldn't do that to anyone else. Especially not more children.

But those little faces and soft voices reminded her of another mystery she had to solve.

The little girl that she'd seen in the dungeon.

She had been about their age.

Telyn still didn't know who she was or where she'd come from.

She didn't know if she'd ever find out.

After all, she had accused Telyn of never giving her the chance to live.

Which she didn't understand at all.

Telyn had known for a long time if she was ever to have children, they would have to be adopted, the same way Nolan was adopting Cordelia.

She had no desire to know a man intimately enough to have a child with him.

She never had.

She had loved Kassian, wanted a family with him even, but she didn't desire him in that way that most women desired men.

She was content to live out her life that way, it was preferrable as well.

She couldn't afford to be slowed down by a pregnancy and the time it took to recover from one. And with her preferences, there was no risk of one.

She was still capable of loving people. She had loved Kassian, she loved Skylar.

It was just a different kind of romance than most talked about.

Kassian had understood her, and respected what she wanted. He had never pushed her to do something she didn't want to do.

Telyn thought that might, in part, be why she liked Skylar so much. Despite how much she had wanted Telyn, she'd let Telyn choose their pace. Skylar didn't push or beg. She had expressed her intentions and then offered to wait for as long as Telyn needed.

Telyn had always needed that kind of patience, and Skylar gave it to her.

Skylar let her be herself without judgement. She loved Telyn unconditionally, something Telyn hadn't even gotten from her own mother.

Some might say it was just the attention that Telyn liked, but she truly cared for Skylar.

If Telyn had to set the world ablaze to make sure Skylar was safe, she would do it in a heartbeat.

She would kill Piran because it would keep Skylar safe.

It would keep everyone safe.

Telyn loved Catelyn and Caspien, but it was different from the way she loved Zerina and the rest of her family, and even that was different from the love she held for Skylar. She even had a touch of affection for the kingdom she was supposed to be ruling, but she held no love for Piran. She held no love for the gods.

They had taken too much from her to be forgiven.

They had taken a lot from a lot of people. Telyn could still feel bits of Storm from the memory she had relived.

It was like Storm was a living breathing part of her now.

Telyn couldn't remember what it was like before, but the flashes of memory that kept replaying in her mind, the lingering feeling of betrayal, it was all Storm,

Telyn didn't know if she would ever be completely herself again.

She still felt like the memory, Storm's memory, had been there to teach her something. Something important that she should have known, but she still couldn't find whatever it was.

It simply lingered in the back of her mind, reminding her that she was supposed to be looking for something.

If she could find it, she imagined it would be able to help them, but until then, she would just have to keep searching.

Say hello to your gods for me when you see them. Tell them they're being displaced.

That felt important.

It was natural to assume that the people of the ancient realm had had gods. Everyone believed in something, and those people had seemed to primarily work with gods of nature, but what had happened to them? And where had they been when Nerissa and Cygnus were burning their realm to the ground?

If they had been real, they were supposed to defend their people, but they hadn't.

And now all of their people were gone, but what had happened to them?

Had they vanished with the last of their believers? Or were they simply dormant somewhere, like Nerissa was?

Telyn shuddered at the thought of someone actually waking the goddess.

After meeting her once, Telyn wasn't too keen on doing it again.

But that hadn't answered her questions.

They couldn't have just disappeared, could they?

Maybe they had never existed in the first place.

Nerissa, Cygnus, and their children had just been people after all. Perhaps it had been a similar situation with the ancient gods. They had only been men who were esteemed above the others.

But that answer didn't satisfy Telyn.

She needed to know for sure.

They hadn't been willing to help back then, and she doubted they would return to help now, but they felt important.

What Nerissa had said nagged at Telyn.

Nerissa had known of the ancient gods, but Telyn couldn't tell if she had been genuine or if she was making a mockery of her victims' beliefs.

Nothing made sense and it was frustrating.

No matter how hard she dwelled on the subject, no answers ever surfaced, only more questions.

There was no new information for her to glean. There was only what she had seen in the memory.

Which in itself had its own questions.

Why had Telyn seen Storm's memory? Why had it come to her in such a moment of desperation?

Yes, it was possible that there was something she needed to learn from it, but Telyn didn't know who Storm was. Much less on a personal enough level to be able to live through her memories. It shouldn't have been possible, and yet it had happened.

Storm had to be connected to it all somehow.

Connected to Telyn in the least.

But how?

Telyn thought that she would remember something like that if she had been there. She clearly hadn't though, she was alive, and everyone that had lived then was dead.

So why did Telyn know what she knew?

Why had she seen what she had seen?

Sanctuary

"The water hears and understands.
The ice does not forgive."
-Leigh Bardugo, Six of Crows

Ceris was packed with people. Catelyn and Caspien hadn't been the only ones who needed somewhere to stay. Many had lost homes that would take time to rebuild. Already, there were people working on clearing out the rubble to make room for the materials they needed to repair the homes and shops, but that still left hundreds of women and children in Ceris during the day. The women that didn't have children to look after helped the best they could.

Telyn thought they just needed something to do to keep their minds off of what had happened. She couldn't say she blamed them, she wanted to be doing the same, but she had been unable to find anything capable of distracting her for long these days.

For now, she did her rounds. She stayed at Skylar's side and made sure that everyone under their roof was warm and fed.

She didn't think she would get used to the chorus of children wailing to go home.

There was constant chatter in the main halls. Telyn couldn't even hear her own thoughts over it, nor could she make out the words of any one conversation. They all meshed together into an incomprehensible melody.

Once everyone had been taken care of, she returned to the quiet of her rooms.

Four berries. That's what she was up to, but it wasn't enough.

The days felt like they were crawling by.

This wasn't what Telyn had meant when she'd asked for more time.

Six more days and she would be living out her worst nightmare and her greatest desire.

Piran would finally fall to her hands, but to get there, she would have to endure living with him long enough for him to let his guard down. She would have to talk to him as if she didn't despise him for everything he'd done to her.

She would pray to the gods that she wouldn't have to sleep with him, but she didn't think they would answer. Even if they did, she doubted it would be in her favor.

They would likely relish in her discomfort. She could almost hear them laughing at her from wherever they sat.

If she wanted anything done correctly, she had to do it herself.

These gods had failed their realms just as the ones before them had. What was the point in having them if they didn't do any good?

All of the prayers, the candles, the open worshipping in churches, it was all for nothing. Because the gods weren't really gods at all. They didn't care about the welfare of those they ruled, they only cared about the power the people thought they held.

They were nothing but usurpers who had won their thrones through the blood of innocents.

The ones that lived now might not have been directly responsible for the massacres, but they had done nothing to change their parents' ways. Not even when they had been abandoned by them.

Telyn would have hated Nerrissa and Cygnus for what they'd done if they had been her parents.

At least her parents hadn't left her willingly. They had been taken from her too early by an agent of the gods.

That was the only explanation Telyn could find.

She knew that her uncle had worked for someone, but *who* exactly, had never been clear. It could have only been Carling. The god of war had to have had his claws in Nathaniel, just as he had them in Piran.

The two men she hated most, led by the god she hated most.

Carling had something against Telyn.

She hadn't needed to guess that; he had said so himself.

She was a threat to him.

But how early on had he realized that?

Had Ennel given him a prophecy and he had decided to torture a child because of it?

In doing so, the fool had signed the papers to his own demise,

Had he left her family alone, her uncle untouched by his darkness, both of her parents would still be alive. She would have no reason to be involved in the war.

She might not have even known about it at all.

But then that would have left a second prophecy unfulfilled.

The one that named her savior of the realms.

But letting that happen would have been too easy. It wouldn't have entertained the gods. And so, they made Telyn and everyone around her pay the blood price for their entertainment.

Telyn felt whiney, even to herself, as she thought for the millionth time; it wasn't fair.

She should have learned early on that nothing in life was fair.

If she hadn't learned it from living with her mother, then it should have been when Kassian had died the first time, or the second time, or even after that, when Alexander turned on her while under Carling's influence.

There had been plenty of opportunities for her to learn that valuable lesson, and yet some small part of her still hoped that things would change. That when she finally accomplished what she was meant to do, there would be some sort of justice instilled to the realms.

Realistically, she knew that would never happen, but still, that small part of her still yearned for it. As if hoping for it hard enough would make it true.

She was being ridiculous.

She needed to focus on the tasks at hand.

The people would need fed again soon. There would be progress updates on the rebuilding of Heart, and tomorrow, she would be half way through her pre-infiltration phase.

It wouldn't be long, but it still felt like it was taking ages.

She just hoped that Piran would at least give Winter time to rebuild before he swooped in to destroy it again.

He couldn't be stupid enough to kill all of his magickly inclined subjects, could he? He knew the humans were useless to what he wanted.

He couldn't rule the way King Roland did, not when he himself had the blood of a traitor in Roland's eyes.

Piran knew that their abilities were what put them at an advantage. If he wanted to take Micaera, he would need them. They were no use to him dead.

That hadn't stopped him from killing hundreds when he wanted to make an example of them though. He would do it again, but Telyn wasn't sure how many more 'examples' the realm could take without losing their hope.

Or their minds.

One way or another, they would break.

That would either work in Piran's favor, and they would submit to him the way he hoped they would.

Or when they snapped, all of the anger and grief he had caused them would come to haunt him.

Those people would make him pay for what he had done to their loved ones. As much as Telyn hated to deny them of that revenge, he had hurt her first, those people were her responsibility, and she fully intended to avenge them.

With or without the help of the gods.

If she had to end him herself, with her own abilities, she would do so gladly. And she would enjoy every minute of it.

She had learned that she was stronger than she'd realized after her mother's death.

Someone who could go through a loss like that, then manage so many unexpected responsibilities and threats had to be strong. Which meant Telyn was strong.

She still would have done almost anything to have her mother back, but living without her had taught Telyn how to stand on her own two feet, and how to protect herself.

Because sometimes, there would be no one else who could protect her.

She still couldn't escape the feeling that her mother would have known what to do.

Maria may have run when White Haven had fallen, but things were different now. There was nowhere to run to. She would have figured out what they needed to do, and the most efficient way to do it.

Maybe the key to everything was where her mother's life had been her own the most.

But Lithiara didn't exist anymore.

Not in the way it had before.

There were no more remnants of her mother to be found in the Enchanted Forest. They had all been lost to time.

Storm's memories were supposed to be lost to time as well though.

Maybe there was a chance some of her mother had survived in the forest.

No, she needed to focus on rebuilding Heart with the others.

She didn't have time to go off on her own adventure.

War was no time for soul searching.

She could hear the dinner bell ringing down the hall.

It was time to face the masses once again.

She plastered a smile onto her face and went back out.

Platters of food were dumped into her arms and she carried them around, making sure everyone was fed. Others came out with glasses of water and napkins wrapped around silverware.

When everyone else had been served, Telyn sat beside Skylar at the head of the room with her own plate.

"We need to get those farms up and running soon. Ceris can't keep up with all of this for much longer." Skylar's voice was low as she spoke.

Even if they rebuilt the garden beds first and planted seeds, it would be months before they produced food. They were going to have to make do with what they had.

"Were all of the plots destroyed?" Telyn asked.

"The main ones, yes. There are a few smaller ones further out than where it happened, but not enough to sustain everyone," Skylar said.

"Do they have livestock as well?" Telyn asked.

"Yes, most of them survived, surprisingly." Skylar took a bite of the steamed carrots on her plate.

"Then we'll rely on those until we can get the produce back on track. Just be sure that those that can be bred are bred so we don't run out before the produce is up." Telyn pushed her carrots and peas around on her plate. "If it comes down to it, some of the other Courts may be able to help. Spring should have a variety of different plants, both food and medicinal."

"I can't ask them for that." Skylar shook her head.

"There's no shame in asking for help," Telyn said.

"They have their own problems to worry about." Skylar stabbed at a piece of lamb with her fork.

"Yes, but they're not having to rebuild half of their capital city. If we don't learn to rely on each other, we're never going to survive this war." Telyn finally took a bite of her own food.

Skylar sighed. "I've already depended on them so much. I'm not a child anymore, I can't continue to expect them to rescue me from all of these messes."

"Love, they are your family, they are always going to be there for you. They don't fault you for this," Telyn said.

"If they offer, we will accept, but I can't ask them." Skylar returned her attention to her food.

Telyn did the same, sensing that the conversation was over.

Asking for help was easier for some people than others, and it seemed Skylar was the type to want to do it alone.

There wasn't anything Telyn could do to change that, it would have to be a lesson Skylar learned on her own. Until then, Telyn could only offer her advice, which she knew wouldn't always be taken.

"What are our plans for tomorrow?" Telyn asked.

"The same as today, they won't need our help in Heart until later this week." Skylar answered.

"I want to go to the Enchanted Forest," Telyn said.

Skylar's fork froze, halfway to her mouth. "Why would you want to do that?"

"I can't help but feel that there's still parts of my mother there, and if I could just find them, I might have a better grasp on what we need to do. She would know what to do." Telyn went back to pushing her food around her plate

"The Enchanted Forest isn't the same place your mother lived in. It's changed since she left," Skylar said.

"And so have I, but I'm still me." Telyn pointed out.

"Do you want me to come with you?" Skylar asked.

"No, we didn't find anything last time we were in there together. I think this is something I have to do alone," Telyn said.

"Last time we weren't looking for your mother." Skylar popped a piece of potato in her mouth.

"I still feel like I need to do this alone," Telyn said.

"Very well, just be careful. You know how dangerous it can be," Skylar said.

Telyn nodded and turned her attention to the rest of the hall.

The room was crammed full of tables and chairs to accommodate the extra people. Groups of them huddled together, children hid and played in their mothers' skirts. Despite the misfortune that had befallen them, they had found ways to smile and laugh.

Even Catelyn and Caspien had friends to play with.

During their time there, they had found a kind woman who had taken to them.

Skylar had told Telyn that that woman had lost her own children to pox many years ago. After her children had died, her husband left her. No one quite knew where he went. But she had never remarried.

Though it looked like she was ready to care for more children.

She had lost just as much as the twins had, and Telyn was glad her heart was warm enough to let Catelyn and Caspien into her life in their time of need.

Perhaps they would get some happy stories out of this war yet.

And that was what mattered.

It was easy to see all of the misery and destruction, all one had to do was look. It was everywhere, but the joy, the little moments of peace, those were harder to find. You had to dig deep to find a reason to smile at a time like this, yet these people had all found one at one point or another.

Though they had lost more than anyone else in the war, they hadn't let it break them.

They wouldn't give Piran the satisfaction of having them bend under his cruel punishments. They would rebuild their lives and their happiness, just as they were rebuilding their homes and businesses.

It gave Telyn hope.

If these people had faith that everything would be alright after their world had been flipped upside down, then everything would be alright.

Though, they still believed in the gods that wanted them destroyed. That might prove to be problematic in the future, but for now, all would be right.

Which meant that Telyn could take the time she needed to explore the Enchanted Forest. These people were fed and safe as long as they were under the roof of Ceris, and they were happy. Telyn didn't need to feel bad about leaving them for a day to search for some peace herself.

After all, time was all they had now.

At least until she left with Piran.

That would still be at least a few days wait.

If they were lucky, Piran wouldn't return until then.

If not, Telyn would just have to threaten him into leaving again. If that ended up too much, she would have to break out her acting skills and beg him to take her back. As much as it would wound her pride, if it needed to be done, she would do it.

Her pride was a small price to pay in exchange for the honor of being the one to take Prian's privileges of life.

She would likely lose more than that by the time this war was over. She would be lucky if she didn't, and luck had never been a friend of hers.

Especially not in the recent years.

Just as the gods were not her friends now, Telyn doubted luck would become her friend anytime soon. Those that held themselves above everyone else often didn't make very good friends anyway.

She hadn't found one in King Roland, and she certainly hadn't found one in Piran.

Skylar was different, she didn't think she was any different than the people she cared for. She loved them like they were the family she had lost.

Telyn desperately wanted to lead the way Skylar did, but she couldn't help but feel she was too broken to do so. She wasn't as kind and selfless as Skylar.

She feared that as the days went on, she became less and less of the person she wanted to be. She could feel the urge for revenge grow stronger, but even that may not be strong enough to satiate the hunger for death that growled inside her.

Killing Piran wouldn't be enough. She wasn't even sure killing Carling and Nox would be enough.

She wasn't foolish enough to believe she could take on all of the gods, but she feared that was what it would take to quiet the lion in her that roared for blood. Once she began the slaughter, she wasn't confident she could stop it before they were all dead.

Telyn was all too aware of the fact that she was becoming a woman she couldn't recognize. When she looked in the mirror, she no longer saw the softness of her youth. The naivety and hope. It had been replaced by the cold calculating gaze of a predator. The kindness she had once held had thinned to a shadow of what it once was. The things she was willing to do to get what she wanted, that had changed as well.

Before she would have faltered at the thought of killing a man. She *had* faltered. It had been a moment she would have come to regret either way.

Now, she was prepared to murder at least three.

LITHIARA

"Heroes don't get happy endings.
They give them to other people."
-Stephanie Garber, Once Upon A Broken Heart

It was quiet when Telyn left for the Enchanted Forest. The sun was high in the sky as she walked through the snow. Everyone in Ceris was likely asleep. Telyn hadn't been able to sleep herself, and had decided to start her investigation early. The forest wasn't as scary in the harsh light of day. The sun had managed to pierce the thick canopy of dead branches. It almost looked like any other forest. Completely normal, save for the lack of life.

From what Skylar had said the first time they'd come in, Telyn knew that the beasts that roamed the Enchanted Forest were more active during the day. She would have to be careful, even if the, now sunny, forest looked safe. She'd felt the monsters that lurked in the shadows far before Sophie had told her they were there.

Brittle twigs snapped with every step Telyn took into the forest. Any leaves that would have been left behind had decomposed long ago and joined the soil beneath the snow.

Everything was quiet. Where there had been howls and the whispers of ghosts long gone the last few times, there was nothing but the twigs shattering beneath Telyn's heel. The crisp smell of freshly fallen snow burned the tip of her nose with every slow drawn inhale.

She had expected it to be scarier out in the woods by herself, but it was just as peaceful as the woods in Alidain had been. At least before they'd started screaming.

That did not mean she could let her guard down.

To her surprise, she had been walking for a good ten minutes, at least, before she started to hear the whispers.

"*We know what you did.*" She could feel the wind slither around her in an attempt to intimidate her.

"I know who you are," She said.

She paused her progression through the forest, waiting. They needed to know she wasn't afraid of them. Not now that she knew why they were the way they were.

"I know my mother left, and that hurt you, but if you can show me anything that's left of her in here, I can help you heal." She didn't know how she knew the forest and its cursed residents wanted to be healed. She was sure some would rather stay in their ghastly state of power, but this forest wanted to be healed.

And Telyn knew that with her mother's blood flowing through her veins, she was capable of giving them that.

The forest around her seemed to pause, the whispers went silent, as if they were considering her offer.

"You are blood of Maria Forestborn." It wasn't a question. And it wasn't a whisper.

The words that came to Telyn felt more corporeal.

"Yes, I am." Telyn watched as a tall lithe figure emerged from the trees. She realized why she hadn't seen it before, its body was made of twisted oak wood, branches extended as arms and legs, its head was wreathed in a crown of thorns.

"She abandoned us to chase love amongst the humans." The wood of its face creaked as it spoke.

"My love has led me here, perhaps I can fix her mistakes," Telyn said.

The creature grunted; its charcoal eyes studied her.

"What is your name?" Telyn asked.

"It is Callum, My Lady." His eyes were still on her, like he was trying to figure out if she was some trick of the forest.

"If we bring you to the things your mother left behind, you'll help us?" He asked.

"I will do everything in my power to reverse what she has caused." Telyn nodded.

"The sins of a mother are not a child's to atone for, but we will bring you. Follow me." He turned and beckoned for her to follow with the twisted twigs that made up his fingers.

It seemed Telyn's mother's departure had affected these people far more than she'd thought it had.

But they were not all monsters. In fact, if Callum was any example, they were quite civil.

Telyn followed him further into the forest. The longer they walked, the darker it became. The sun was beginning to sink under the horizon. Telyn wondered if the forest would become as scary as it had before. If it would still terrify her even after she'd seen it in the light.

"How can one so afraid of the dark live so far away from the light?" Callum rumbled.

"What do you mean?" Telyn asked.

"The dark, you fear it. I can feel it creeping into you as the sun sinks. Yet you live in a world where night is seen as day." He ducked under a limb that stood in his path.

Telyn walked right under it. "I only fear it from bad experiences. When I'm out there, with the people I love, it's not so scary."

"And the people you love are not here." He observed.

"No." She agreed. "I felt I needed to do this alone."

"You were right, we would not have heeded you had you brought companions not of this wood." Callum's pace had slowed.

"How many of you are there?" Telyn asked as she noted the change in pace.

"Half as many as there had been when your mother ruled. Many left, others died, but most stayed." He explained. "Lithiara is home. You don't leave your home."

"Not unless you have to." Telyn agreed.

"We have survived. In a cursed form, yes, but we are still alive." Callum nodded.

"How do I help you?" She asked.

"Your mother's life source is what fed Lithiara. As did her mother's before her, and so will yours. But first, what you asked for."

Callum pulled dead vines away from the entrance to a clearing where a small village sat. Telyn could tell just from looking at it that no one had lived in it for decades.

"The first hut here. That is all your mother left behind."

Callum let Telyn enter the clearing alone. He seemed content to wait for her where he was.

Dust crumbled off of the hut's door and the hinges groaned as she pushed it open.

It was hard to make out anything other than shadows in the growing dark. Telyn let a small flame burn low in her palm. It didn't take much to illuminate the small one room home. There was a delicately carved box in one corner. That was all that was left aside from the dust covered furniture. There was a dusty wooden bed frame and a mattress with long since decayed hay filling it, a few chairs, and a small table.

But the box looked untouched by time.

The grey that covered everything else was nowhere to be found on it.

The only sound Telyn could hear was that of her muffled footsteps as she crossed the room to get to the box.

The latch came off easily, as if it had recently been oiled. It didn't make a sound as she slid it out of place and opened the box.

Inside, there must have been a thousand letters, and all of them were written in the same two handwritings.

Telyn pulled the first one out to read it.

It was addressed to her mother, from Sophie.

As Telyn read through the letters, she could see the events described with a scary clarity. She could hear the echo of her mother's laughter at a joke. She could even smell the burnt sage and cedar of the bonfires they had held every fortnight.

The details were occasionally a little more than Telyn needed to know, especially about her mother, but she couldn't stop reading.

These letters had been written by her mother or for her mother. It shed light on the life she'd had that Telyn had never gotten to see. And Maria had been happy in Lithiara. She'd said so, countless times in her letters.

So, why had she left?

The letters ended the day her mother had left.

She'd written one last letter to Sophie, thanking her for the time they'd shared and the love they'd held for each other. But even as Telyn read it, she knew her mother didn't feel bad about leaving.

Telyn thought it might have been a bit like her and Micaera. It was the only home she'd ever had; it just hadn't ever felt like home. Telyn had always wanted to leave and find somewhere she belonged. Her mother had wanted the same thing, and she thought she'd found it in the handsome prince who had come to take her away.

Telyn reached for another letter, another response, but found nothing but the bottom of the box.

A bottom that bulged oddly in the center.

Telyn poked and pulled at the wood of the bottom until it came loose and revealed it hadn't been the bottom at all.

It had been a false bottom. Not a very good one, but it had been an attempt.

Beneath it was one last letter, but this one was in different handwriting. It was addressed to her mother as well.

'Dear Lady Forestborn,

It has been an honor to spend time with you and learn more about you.

It would be an even further honor if you would accompany me to Alidain, where

we can formally announce our courtship.

I look forward to seeing you come nightfall.

-Love,

Prince Corbin.

It was short, and somewhat formal, but Telyn could sense the excitement and love coming off of it.

Her father had been smitten far before her mother was.

That wasn't the way she had told it, but he had rarely been mentioned in her letters, and the two had shared everything.

That was no exaggeration.

So, the fact that her father hadn't been constantly brought up before that final letter meant she had fallen for him later. Something else had pulled her away from Lithiara. It might have developed into love, but that wasn't what it was at the start.

Telyn noticed a glint of black beneath where the letter from her father had been.

She held her hand above the box to see what it was.

A dagger.

Its blade was forged of black steel, and its hilt was black gold. A fine weapon, probably more decoration than it had been useful. Telyn was willing to bet the thing had opened more letters than it had seen battles.

She picked it up and caught a glimpse of an inscription on the blade.

It had certainly been ornamental then.

The words were in Ancient Silurian. It read: *'Oath Breakers and Cup Bearers.'*

An odd inscription for a blade.

She knew her mother must have owned it, but she hadn't forged it or carved it herself. Her mother had despised smith work. So, where had she gotten it from?

Telyn turned the blade over in her hands once before she pressed her finger against its edge.

It was still sharp enough to draw blood. She pressed her finger to her skirts to stop the bleeding.

She would have to find answers to her other questions later. She wouldn't find them at the bottom of an empty box anyway.

Telyn stuck the blade through her belt and carefully packed the letters back into the box.

If Sophie hadn't brought them with her when she'd left, Telyn doubted she'd want them to resurface now.

Once Telyn shut the box, she slowly slid the latch into place. Where it would likely sit for a few more decades, centuries even maybe.

With the black dagger at her hip, and her mother's letters behind her, she shut the door to the dusty little hut. It hadn't given her any of the answers she'd hoped to find, only more questions, but she had promised Callum she'd help his people. The ones her mother had hurt. She wasn't the oath breaker the dagger mentioned. It was time for her to go back out and do what she'd promised to do.

Callum was waiting for her, right where she'd left him. She must have spent hours in there, pouring over the letters of a dead woman. Yet it didn't appear as though he'd moved.

"Are you ready?" He asked.

"Just tell me what I need to do." Telyn nodded.

Callum led her further into the abandoned village. Doors creaked on their hinges as they swayed in the wind, left open, or raided long ago.

Telyn felt a chill go down her spine. Her discomfort ruffled her feathers and she tucked her wings tighter around herself. The village no longer felt simply abandoned, it felt haunted.

Callum had said that people had died when others had fled. Maybe the dead had never truly left.

As they came up to what Telyn assumed to be the center of the village, something strange came into view.

The entire forest was dead and twisted, but the tree that rose up in front of her was shriveled and burnt.

"My mother did this?" Telyn asked.

Callum shook his head. "It was part of the curse. This is the heart of Lithiara. That tree is what gave it life. It is true that it weakened when your mother left, but the people that lived here, they were the ones that went mad and burnt our tree. It killed them, and the rest of our forest."

Her mother's absence had driven these people to madness.

It was a little scary to think they had become so dependent on her that they'd lost themselves when she left. Maybe it had something to do with the nature of her leaving, but it still didn't sit right with Telyn.

But she had promised to help.

"What do I do?" She asked.

Callum gestured to the tree. "You put your hands on it. After that, I do not know. Just focus on your energy and pray to the old gods that it works."

Interesting. He had specified the old gods, and Telyn wondered why. She pressed her hands to the shriveled, burnt bark of the tree and closed her eyes.

As soon as she touched it, it felt like a string had hooked to her palms, it needed her to give it what it needed, but it wouldn't take anything she didn't give.

Telyn focused on channeling her energy into the tree.

It felt similar to when Sprin had taken some of her power, but it was gentler, unwilling to take more than she wanted to give. But even so, she could feel herself starting to slow.

If she didn't stop soon, she would end up spending the day in the forest, and she wasn't sure she was quite ready for that.

Telyn pulled her hands away from the tree and opened her eyes.

The wood in front of her was no longer shrunken and burnt, it was healthy and strong. The tree stretched up above her with fresh green leaves. Uncommon in Winter, but from the letters she'd read, that was how Lithiara had always been. The area around the tree had been revitalized as well. The new growth stretched for several yards, but beyond that was the same dead forest Telyn had walked into.

She looked back at Callum.

He surveyed the area around them and dipped his head. "It will take time. She has been dead for many years. Give when you can, we will not ask for more than that."

Before Telyn could answer, Callum was gone, leaving her to find her own way out of the forest.

That was, if the forest would even let her out.

If she wanted to heal it, fighting it would be rather counterproductive.

"Show me the way out." She whispered. Dead trees groaned as they shifted, clearing a path in front of her.

She just hoped it led her out instead of wherever it thought she needed to be in the moment.

She wandered around the forest, following paths for what felt like hours. Giving herself to the tree had drained her energy, but now she was downright exhausted. She wasn't sure she would make it to sunrise without collapsing.

Or even out of the forest. She still couldn't see the end of the skeletal trees, but they were still clearing the way for her, so, she forced one foot in front of the other, and kept walking.

If she wasn't back soon, Skylar would come looking for her, and Telyn knew the forest wouldn't treat Skylar as kindly as it had treated her.

The monsters that had come for them their first venture into the woods would come back, and Telyn didn't have enough strength to fight them. It would be better for them all if she made it out on her own. Sooner, rather than later.

Eventually, she could see the reflection of the moon on exposed snow. She could see where the trees ended and the fields of Ceris began.

Telyn pushed forward, urging herself to move faster.

The sooner she was out, the sooner she could see Skylar.

The sooner she would be able to sleep.

She would have no trouble finding it, that was for sure. She could bother everyone about the dagger later. For now, all she needed was to be back in Ceris.

Then the trees were behind her, and she was at the front gates.

She stumbled into the foyer, knocking the snow from her boots with the grace of a lame horse.

"You're back." Skylar leaned against the banister that led upstairs.

"How did you know?" Telyn's voice betrayed her exhaustion, and she knew it.

"I always know." Skylar smiled. "For now, let's get you to bed. You look exhausted."

Skylar scooped Telyn up in her arms and carried her up the stairs to their rooms. She didn't ask Telyn for any details, and for that Telyn was grateful. She needed time to process all of it herself before she attempted to tell someone else. When she woke up, she would explain everything.

Dragon Bone

"Ninety percent of the time
the very sight of you makes me want to commit murder."
-Nora Sakavic, The King's Men

Telyn didn't know how long she'd slept, but it didn't feel like it was long enough. She felt just as exhausted as she had been when she stumbled into Ceris.

Skylar was with her when she woke. That made her smile.

"Good evening." Skylar smiled back when she saw Telyn.

"What are our plans for today?" Telyn asked.

"The same as they have been." Skylar sat up with a sigh. "Do you want to tell me about yesterday?"

"Yes." Telyn sat up and slid her feet into slippers. "It was a lot. I found a bunch of letters between Sophie and my mother."

"Did you read them?" Skylar asked, not bothering to hide her curiosity.

"Of course, I wanted answers from my mother." Telyn laughed.

"Did you find any?" Skylar came around to the other side of the bed to sit beside Telyn.

"No, but I found more questions. A letter from my father to my mother, and-"

"This dagger?" Skylar reached over to pull the black dagger off of the nightstand.

"Yes. That dagger." Telyn nodded. "Do you know what it's supposed to be for?"

"No idea." Skylar shook her head as she studied the inscription. "But there's someone who might."

"Sophie?" Telyn asked.

"She's the closest person to this. If your mother had it, she might know why." Skylar nodded.

"Sounds like it's time to pay Sophie another visit," Telyn said.

"Do you think she ever gets bored of us?" Skylar asked.

"I think she was bored before she met us." Telyn smiled. "We make her life interesting."

Because nothing was ever dull when Telyn was around.

On the way to Sophie's Telyn got to see the reconstruction, and how far it had come in such a short amount of time.

The wood they were using looked so new in contrast to the old beams that had been up for longer than Telyn knew, and were covered in soot.

Some of the houses looked like they were nearly ready for people to move back in.

But it would take a long time for the whole city to be rebuilt. The shops were low priority. Once everyone was back in their homes, they would work on the shops. Skylar would help provide for the family's needs until they were able to get back to life as it had been before.

That could take months.

Telyn hoped to have the king dead by then. And she was so close to being able to do it. Just a few more days and she would be ready to infiltrate Eralia.

This time, when Telyn entered Sophie's there was no flash of light. It seemed she had toned it down temporarily.

"I was wondering when my favorite younglings would pay me a visit." Sophie smiled.

Her shop had been rearranged, chairs, tables, tea pots, and other home goods had been pushed to the front of the store, her more curious wares had taken the back shelves.

"It looks different in here." Telyn noted.

"I figured I would do my due diligence in helping the city. These are for the families that lost their own to the boy king." Sophie shrugged. "Enough about that though, what brings you here?"

Telyn pulled the black dagger out of her belt and laid it on the counter. "This black steel blade. It belonged to my mother; I want to know how she got it."

Sophie's face paled and she took a moment to school her expression into a calm one. "Well, to start, child; that is not black steel."

"What is it then?" Telyn asked.

"It is bone." Sophie flicked the blade, and the sound that came from it didn't sound like metal.

"What kind of creature has black bones?" Telyn studied the blade once more, trying to figure out why it shone like metal.

"Dragons." Sophie's claws traced the inscription of the blade.

"That doesn't explain why my mother would have it," Telyn said.

"Your mother was quite the adventurous little thing." Sophie pulled her hand away from the dagger and focused her attention somewhere else. "She would explore the woods often, bringing home bits of bone or metal. The day she met your father, before she'd met him, she found this. Simply lying in a pile of leaves. We have no idea where it might have come from, who it belonged to. It was there, then it was hers. Hours later she met your father, and not many days after that, she was gone."

"So, we don't know what it might have been for. Dragon bone blades aren't exactly common." Telyn picked it up and turned it over in her hands.

"No, but you've read the inscription, my guess is it was an executioner's blade." Sophie shrugged.

"Something this fine, wasted on criminals?" Skylar asked.

"They had odd habits back in the day. I wouldn't know what else this could be used for." Sophie shook her head.

"Executioner would make sense for the oath breaker part, but it doesn't for the cup bearers," Telyn said.

"It's possible your mother stumbled upon something she shouldn't have, but I wouldn't know what it was," Sophie said. "All I can tell you is that it is very old. From before the rise of the gods. No one now would be brave enough to slay a dragon."

Telyn could believe that. Everyone had been so afraid of Sevina when she had been waiting for Skylar and Telyn. Not a single one of them had tried to slay the dragon themselves, or confront her at all.

But then again, they had killed one in Alidain. They'd lost Colton to it for a time, but they had killed it.

More out of necessity than anything else. It would have destroyed the palace, and it didn't seem keen on leaving.

Slaying dragons certainly wasn't a common occurrence, which made carving weapons from their bones even more rare.

Which meant the dagger in Telyn's hands could very well be the oldest thing to exist.

Nerissa and Cygnus had razed everything to the ground. That much Telyn knew.

So, how had this little dagger managed to survive when so much had been lost?

"Hold onto it, it might come in handy one of these days. You never know," Sophie said.

I can't bring it with me to Eralia, he'll take it. Telyn projected her thoughts to Skylar.

I'll hold onto it while you're gone. Skylar answered.

Telyn trusted Sophie, but the fewer people who knew their plan, the better. They didn't need anyone warning Piran.

Most of the people had sided with Telyn, but that didn't mean that all of them would.

There would always be people who sided with the king. Whether it be out of true loyalty or fear. They would run to him the moment they knew of anything, and if they were lucky, they would live.

"Well, thank you. For everything. Try to stay safe," Telyn said.

"You as well." Sophie smiled.

It seemed not even the scrolls would help them with the dagger.

Those only went as far back as the new gods. There wouldn't be anything from before. Telyn was sure Nerissa would have had anything that might have held information like that destroyed.

They had done a good job of covering up their genocide. For a very long time people had believed them the creators of the realms. Even Telyn had believed that there had been nothing there when they settled.

As it turned out, everyone had been wrong.

The gods were far more self-serving than Telyn had originally thought. Which was a hard thought to wrap her head around.

People were still working as Telyn and Skylar walked back through the town, even as the sun was beginning to come up over the horizon.

If the past days had given any indication, they would work a few hours after sunrise before they went home, or to Ceris, to rest.

Those that were already at Ceris would be settling into bed by now.

And though she had woken not that long ago, Telyn felt ready to go back to sleep.

Helping the forest had taken more out of her than she'd expected, but she would do it again. Once she was well enough. She had promised to help them, and she would. At least until it was back to the way it was before her mother had left.

By then, she hoped she would be able to remain in Ceris, close enough to give the forest a boost when it needed one.

Perhaps it wouldn't be so dangerous once it was back to itself.

It had been, and still was, the strongest point of magick in Siluria. Those that held it should be able to visit the forest to learn more about themselves. The people like Sophie, who had left, should have the opportunity to return to their home without it driving them mad or killing them.

That was what Telyn hoped to achieve by restoring Lithiara to its former glory.

She wished she could do the same with all the realms.

Fix what the gods had broken.

But she knew she wasn't capable of something like that. She couldn't bring back what had died thousands of years ago.

Storm, Kijana, and all the others who had lived before were all long gone. They didn't even have descendants to remember them. Telyn was the only one they survived through now, and she was still trying to figure out why that was.

She had no connection to them, yet they only lived on in her memory, or rather Storm's memory, that Telyn somehow possessed.

It didn't make sense, but either way, Telyn would make sure they were not forgotten again. She would find a way to bring the truth to the people that blindly worshipped gods that used them for nothing more than their own entertainment.

They had the right to choose, just as Telyn had.

She didn't know how Pip had learned the truth. Sophie must have read the scrolls, but they had both learned the truth and decided to stay away.

The rest of the people deserved to make that choice as well.

But Sophie's words rang in her ears; People fear what they don't understand, but they would rather blindly follow their gods than understand what they really are.

Some of them would choose ignorance.

There would always be the ones that did, but that was their choice to make.

If they needed something to believe in that badly, who was Telyn to take it away from them?

All she would do was give them the opportunity to choose for themselves who they would serve. Their realm and community, or the gods that destroyed everything they came in contact with.

For Telyn, it was an easy choice to make.

It wouldn't be for many others, but that was okay. It wasn't her responsibility to force people into conformity, nor did she want it to be.

That was the beautiful thing about life. They could choose, they could be different.

It was something that even Telyn had taken for granted for far too long. Especially when she believed her choices had been taken from her.

She had always had the choice. She'd just been too afraid to fight before. Now, she wasn't.

Part of her would always regret not fighting sooner, but there was no changing the past.

She could only control what she did with her future, and for now, she would fight for the opportunities she wanted.

If no one else would fight for it, then she would.

That was the choice she was making.

Everyone else could make their own.

Ceris was quiet when they returned. Most had gone off to bed. There was the occasional shushing of a mother as she tried to calm a crying baby or a rambunctious child, but that was all.

Those people seemed just as tired as Telyn felt. They all had problems they were pushing back to another day.

They only needed to take it one day at a time.

Sometimes, Telyn needed to be reminded of that.

There was still so much she didn't know, and she had nothing but time for the next few days. As much as she wished she could speed up the process, she knew It wasn't safe. She'd already risked too much the first time she'd tried.

Which Skylar still didn't know about.

Telyn felt a little guilty about not telling her, but they'd had other things they'd needed to do.

She was alive. That was the important part.

They still had a few days before she would be ready.

Until then, she would do what she could to help around Ceris. They weren't wanted in Heart until later that week.

That meant Telyn had a lot of time on her hands.

She would still be slowed down for a few days until she had the energy she'd given to Lithiara back. She would have to do it again before she left for Eralia.

She didn't want the forest to regress while she was away.

The little bit she'd healed wasn't much, but she could tell it had meant a lot to Callum.

That was the most life the Enchanted Forest had seen in decades.

Callum could have berated her for not doing enough, but he'd understood it would take time to repair the damage her mother had left behind.

The forest was sentient as well. It would be slow to trust after it had been betrayed once before.

In a way, it was reassuring.

The forest depending on her for its life only reaffirmed her belief that Ceris was where she belonged.

It was where her mother had belonged as well, and Telyn still wanted to know what had managed to pull her from it.

Because it certainly hadn't been her father.

It had been something else. Something Maria hadn't even told Sophie about. Which meant it was something big.

Everyone else thought Maria Forestborn had left for love. Or to become queen.

But it wasn't either. She had barely tolerated Corbin when they left.

And if she wanted to be queen, she wouldn't have left Alidain with King Azriel.

Which raised another question: why hadn't she brought Telyn back to Siluria?

She had hated Micaera. It didn't make sense for her to willingly live out the rest of her life there.

There were so many things Telyn wanted to ask her mother. But she knew she would never be able to, no matter how badly she wanted it.

The dead wouldn't be coming back.

Not anymore.

If she was going to come back, it would have happened already. Before Colton and Kassian had.

She would have been the first.

But...

If Telyn succeeded in killing the god of death, she might be able to bring her mother back.

Nox wasn't truly a god after all.

He was only a little more powerful than her at best.

Because they had the same blood.

Once Nox was gone, someone else would have to watch the gate. Otherwise, the lines between life and death would no longer exist.

And Telyn had far too many enemies to let that happen.

But she couldn't guard the gate and heal Lithiara at the same time.

That was something she would have to figure out when the time came.

There were a lot of things she would have to figure out, but they all had their own times.

The only one she needed to worry about now was how she was going to get into Eralia at the king's side.

Telyn counted the nightshade berries as she popped them into her mouth.

One, two, three, four, five, six.

It wouldn't be long.

Her goal was crawling closer and closer with each passing day. She'd grown accustomed to the slight sting that came with the sweetness of the berries.

She imagined that if they weren't so deadly, they would be somewhat of a delicacy.

Good for deserts, especially tarts.

She supposed if she really wanted to, she could make them herself now. She would be the only one able to eat them, but she could still enjoy them. So long as she had a way to make sure others didn't eat them.

She wouldn't want to accidentally poison someone.

Though it could become a useful tool. As the queen or lady or whatever she ended up being, she was sure there would always be people who wanted to hurt her.

A delicious justice it would be if the sweetness on their tongue was the very thing that killed them.

If she was lucky, it wouldn't even be traced back to her.

Though she supposed if she was a queen, it wouldn't really matter whether it was or not.

But that wasn't what she wanted.

She had never wanted to rule Alidain. That had not changed in the months she'd spent away from it. She still didn't wish to rule. She wasn't even qualified to rule.

The role was better suited to someone who knew the ways of the courts. Someone who knew how to navigate the waters of trickery and betrayal better than she did.

At that point, she thought that might be just about anyone in the twelve realms.

She might have been born into this life, but she certainly hadn't been raised in it.

And she didn't think she would ever be able to get the hang of it.

It wasn't who she was, though it may be in her blood.

She would never be the queen her mother had been, and she wasn't capable of being half the leader her father had been.

People like Skylar were the ones meant to lead.

Not the ones like Telyn and Piran.

Though they were far apart on the spectrum of people who shouldn't lead. She was too soft, her hand wasn't firm enough. And he was too harsh, too blinded by his own thirst for power to care for his people.

Nightshade

"I fell in love with you.
I didn't do it on purpose."
-L.J. Smith, The Hunter

People were beginning to return home. Several of the homes with less damage had been repaired, even a few with more extensive damage were now livable. It was all thanks to the dedicated men of the community. They had refused to let the women and children help until it was lighter work. They were still holding to that. They worked, even as Skylar and Telyn led the first group of people home.

It was a long walk from Ceris, especially with the children occasionally deciding to skip off.

Telyn couldn't blame them, if she had been on their position, she would have been excited to go home too.

The town looked a lot better than it had the last time Skylar and Telyn had been through it. Most of the ash from the buildings and the bodies had been scrubbed away, leaving the cobblestone paths pristine.

As if nothing had ever happened.

The only signs of destruction that were left were the quickly diminishing holes that had been burnt out of the sides of some of the buildings. Before long, those would be gone too, and with them, any reminders of the terror Piran had caused these people.

But they would never forget.

The snow never forgets.

Water had memory. That was one of the few things Telyn had actually learned during her formal lessons. And snow was only frozen water. Not only did it remember, but it avenged.

Telyn would make sure that happened.

Even with the dark thoughts of murder and revenge floating around in her head, she put on a smile.

"The reconstruction is coming along much quicker than I thought it would." Telyn could hear the relief in Skylar's voice.

They still didn't have enough resources for a celebratory feast, but at least they knew they wouldn't have to starve their people to stretch until the reconstruction was complete.

"The best part is, I have another surprise for you when we get home," Telyn said.

"Do you now?" Skylar laughed.

The people were slowly filtering out of the squares, returning to homes they hadn't seen since the fire, It was almost like they were afraid they wouldn't recognize what they would find.

There was a sense of familiarity and safety in home.

Telyn hoped that hadn't been taken away from them. They'd already lost enough.

Catelyn and Caspien were the last ones left in the square.

"Where's the woman who's been taking care of you?" Telyn crouched down beside the twins.

"She's not our mother." Catelyn's lip trembled as the words spilled out of her mouth.

"She won't take us home." Caspien agreed,

"I know it's different and scary, but you'll be safe." Telyn promised. "I know she won't be able to replace your mother, or your home, but she'll take care of you."

"If she doesn't, you can always come stay with us again." Skylar added.

Catelyn looked like she was ready to cry but she nodded.

"Catelyn!" They could hear the woman calling out as she looked for the twins. Telyn could hear the tinge of panic in her voice. She'd taken to the kids; they would be just fine with her.

"Caspien?" The woman's hands were cupped around her mouth as she came around the corner, yelling for the twins.

"They're right here." Telyn smiled.

"Oh, thank the gods." The woman sighed. Her cheeks were flushed from the cold. "Let's get you two home."

Catelyn and Caspien clung to her skirts and she wrapped her arms around their shoulders as she led them back down the street.

"They'll be alright," Skylar said.

"I know." Telyn smiled. "She's a good woman. She loves them like her own."

"How can you tell?" Skylar asked.

"I've been watching her. I wouldn't let them go with just anyone," Telyn said.

"You like looking out for kids like them. That's how you ended up with Cordelia, isn't it?" Skylar smiled.

"It is, I do. I know what it's like to not have a family to turn to. No one deserves to struggle with that, especially not children that young. I would take them all in if I could." Telyn turned her back to the rebuilt homes and started the long walk back to Ceris.

Skylar matched her step for step. "Maybe once this is all over you can take in one or two. Whenever you're ready to."

"We'll have to see what happens. There are a lot of factors that weigh into whether or not I'm able to care for a child," Telyn said.

"If it is what you want, it will work out." Skylar took her hand. "The world owes you that much, and they'll owe you much more by the time this has all died down."

"Even if they do, I'll be happy to simply settle down for a change. I never expected my life to get quite so chaotic," Telyn said.

"What was it like before?" Skylar asked.

"Before my mother died?" Telyn glanced over at Skylar.

Skylar nodded.

"It was quiet, predictable. I knew what was going to happen and I could plan accordingly. Some days were bad. Those are the easiest to remember, the days when my mother screamed at me and cried because I reminded her of my father. But for the most part, it was peaceful. We had each other, and that was all we needed. Then she died, I was almost executed, and then I became queen. Which has led me here," Telyn said.

"You would have been content living a life like that?" Skylar asked.

Telyn paused, mulling over her words before she answered. "No. I always wanted to leave. I used to dream of the day I could cross the waters of the bay and find where I belonged. Turns out where I belong is here, even if it's taken a war to be able to find it. I don't think I ever would have been able to leave my mother though. I was all she had left."

"I promise you made her life better. She loved you. She wouldn't have brought you with her if she didn't," Skylar said.

"There never is anything quite like the love you hold for your first-born child." Telyn mused. "Though I was a twin, so I'm not sure it counts."

Skylar laughed. "So, what is this surprise you have for me?"

"Well, follow me, and you'll see." Telyn smiled.

They got back to Ceris a lot quicker with less people to worry about.

Telyn led Skylar up the stairs and into their rooms, where she kept the nightshade berries.

She placed ten of them on her desk.

Skylar sucked in a breath, but didn't move to stop Telyn as one by one, she popped the berries in her mouth.

By the time she was done, her lips were stained crimson from the juice.

"And you're alright?" Skylar asked.

"Immune to at least this much." Telyn smiled.

A grin split across Skylar's face and she laughed. "You're ready."

"I am. Have the chemists fulfilled their part in this?" Telyn asked.

"Let's go find out, shall we?" Skylar held out a hand and Telyn took it.

Skylar led her down into one of the darker corners of the dungeon. One where Calynn tended to take up residence. The evidence was in the bones that littered the ground around a makeshift lab that had been set up.

The bones grew bigger as Calynn did, they were now the size of smaller house cats and rabbits.

But Telyn's attention was snagged by the bubbling crimson liquid that boiled above a flame then flowed through tubes and a strainer before it fell into a vial the size of Telyn's little finger.

There was a man hunched over the setup, watching as it progressed. He wore no cloak; it was warm enough down there that he didn't need one.

Skylar cleared her throat and he looked up with a startled expression.

"My Lady." He dipped into a low bow.

"How is it coming along, Theodore?" Skylar asked as she approached the table.

"I believe it is almost finished," Theodore said.

There was the scraping of scales against stone as Calynn emerged from the shadows.

"Your little friend here has been very helpful with this flame." Theodore gestured to Calynn as he watched the last of the crimson liquid drain through the strainer.

"I'm glad she's made herself useful down here." Telyn smiled.

Theodore removed the vial from its place with a pair of tongs and placed it in an empty spot on the table. "Once it cools, I'll be able to cork it and it will be ready, My Lady."

Telyn knew the results wouldn't be immediate, she would need to choose her timing wisely, but they were so much closer than they had been before.

Even if it wasn't enough to kill him, it would slow him down enough to sink a dagger into his heart.

When the time was right, Piran would die, one way or another.

"I can leave as soon as it's ready," Telyn said.

"How do you plan on getting there?" Skylar asked.

"I can send a raven begging him to rescue me if I need to, but he's too proud to not return to see the destruction he caused," Telyn said.

"He won't find much left," Skylar said.

"Yes, but he doesn't know that. He has a tendency to underestimate anything that breathes and isn't him." Telyn crouched down to pet Calynn as the little dragon came closer.

Her green scales were growing darker as she grew bigger. Telyn wondered if they would completely change colors by the time she was full grown. She was once again reminded of just how little she knew about her fire breathing companion.

"He'll learn his mistakes soon enough," Skylar said.

"Indeed, he will." Telyn smiled.

"Don't try to rush it." Skylar warned. "You'll know when the time is right, don't act before then. He'll get suspicious if you move too quickly."

"I know. I learned everything I know about manipulation from him. I'd say I've had a pretty good teacher, as unfortunate as that is," Telyn said.

However twisted it may be, she knew it would feel gratifying to use his own tricks against him. In more ways than one, he would be the cause of his own downfall.

Telyn might be the one who would hold the knife, but all of Winter, if not all of Siluria was behind her.

She had stopped being alone in her mission the moment Piran had decided to murder three innocent people.

He had only further sealed his fate when he tried to burn the capital of Winter to the ground.

Piran might have shared in Cygnus's power, but he wouldn't have the same success.

At least Cygnus was still alive to the peoples' knowledge.

Piran would be very dead by the end of it all.

"Be careful. That's all I'm going to ask of you," Skylar said.

"Aren't I always?" Telyn smiled.

They both knew she wasn't, but there was too much at stake for her to be careless with this mission. She would be careful, and she would come home. She just hoped that would be sooner rather than later

Telyn didn't want to be away from home for long in the first place, but she also didn't know how long she could be away without the Enchanted Forest regressing.

It had taken a lot to get it where it was, and she would give it more before she left. She didn't want to lose that progress, and she doubted Callum and his people wanted that either.

She would go back before the sun came up, and if Piran didn't come the following night, she would send for him.

"It's ready."

Telyn watched as Theodore pressed a cork into the vial before he handed it to her.

"Keep it somewhere safe." Skylar winked.

Telyn smiled. "It will be very safe." She promised. "I have some business to attend to before it grows too late."

"The woods?" Skylar asked.

Telyn nodded. "I need to heal them a little bit more before I go."

"Does this mean it will go back to the way it was before?" Skylar asked.

"That's what we're hoping for. I don't want to be gone so long that death begins to reclaim what I've healed," Telyn said.

"Well, I suppose you should go then." Skylar smiled.

The path back to the Enchanted Forest was familiar now. Though the snow had covered any trodden paths that might have existed, she knew the way without having to look.

By now, it just felt like an extension of Ceris.

Ceris was her home, Lithiara had been her mother's.

It almost felt like they had merged since Telyn had started helping it. She knew she would always be welcome in the forest because she was helping it. She was fixing past mistakes, and the forest was grateful.

She would be safe as long as she was in there.

The only problem was, she was the only one who was.

She couldn't bring her family in to hide, or Skylar, or anyone else because the forest didn't recognize them. It didn't know they wouldn't hurt it.

If she wanted to, she could hide in the woods and be safe from everything going on outside, but she would have to abandon the people she loved, and she wasn't willing to do that.

She hadn't been willing to before, and she hoped she never would be.

As soon as she stepped into the forest, her path cleared. The dead trees twisted out of her way, they knew where she needed to be, and they were more than willing to show her the way. It still took a while to get there.

Telyn passed the time by noticing the little things around her. Like how tree roots snaked over puddles to provide her with a dry path or how an odd bird or two would flit by in the trees.

Most of them had the dark feathers of ravens, but she spotted a set or two of mockingbird wings.

It seemed as though the life was starting to spread on its own. It would still need her help in staying alive, but what lived now wouldn't be contained.

She hoped that those that still lived in the forest saw them and held on to a little bit of hope.

To Telyn's surprise, not only were there flowers springing up from the snow in the healed patch of land, but there was a small group of people that surrounded the life tree.

They parted for her as she walked up to it. She could feel their hands on her clothes, not grabbing or pulling, but simply touching. It looked like they had been decorating the base of the tree with the flowers that had sprung up in abundance around the village. The stems of the flowers twined through the tree's roots that stuck out of the ground. The blossoms ranged in color from white as snow to red as blood with every color in between.

It almost reminded Telyn of Spring.

She planted both of her hands on the tree and closed her eyes, drawing on the feelings she'd had the first time she'd fed it.

This time it pulled the energy from her slower, and it spread farther. She could feel it without even looking.

What had taken the most from her last time was simply bringing life into a place where there was none. Now that there was existing life, it was much easier to expand it.

Telyn didn't know how long she stood there to push energy into the tree, but when her hands fell away from its bark and she opened her eyes, she could no longer see the death that had surrounded her little patch of light.

The people stared at her with wide eyes that glistened with tears as they murmured their thanks.

"I want you to know that I must go for a while." Telyn sat with the people around the tree. "But I will come back to continue to heal your home. There is some other work I must do though."

"Lithiara will return in your time, Your Grace," One of the women said.

"We thank you for trying at all." Another person in the small crowd agreed.

"It will." Telyn smiled. "I will do my best to bring it back as soon as I am able. For now, tell Callum I will return again when all is settled outside the forest."

When she rose, the people returned to the tree, twisting more flowers into the tree roots and working their way up into the branches that had begun to blossom with flowers of their own.

This time it was easier to walk back through the forest to Ceris, she wasn't nearly as exhausted as she had been last time, and she imagined it would only get easier the more often she did it.

And the forest would only take what it was given. It knew it needed healing, but it wasn't greedy. It only took what Telyn could give it. And the more the forest healed, the less it would need.

Telyn only hoped that it wouldn't all be lost when she returned. She didn't want to have to start the healing all over again, but she would if she had to.

Her mother owed it to these people, but Maria wasn't there to fix her mistake, so it had become Telyn's responsibility.

It seemed as time went on, it revealed more and more responsibilities Telyn's mother had left for her. Maybe she would be able to share the load and make it more manageable.

Zerina would have gladly shared the burden if Telyn asked, but Telyn wouldn't ask until it was safe.

Not until Piran and the gods were dead.

Only then would it be safe.

Telyn wouldn't risk losing her sister to their jealousy as well.

Return to Eralia

"Stupid people are dangerous."
-Suzzane Collins, The Hunger Games

The sun was starting to come up once again as Telyn reached the gates of Ceris, and she knew it was going to be a sleepless day. She would be surprised if she could get ant rest at all before she went to Eralia, or during for that matter.

Instead of going to her rooms, she walked down the steps and into the dungeons. Torches were lit in their sconces along the walls.

Telyn found herself wondering if Theodore was still set up in his corner of the dungeon.

It didn't appear as if anyone else occupied it.

Aside from Calynn.

Almost as if the dragon had heard Telyn thinking her name, Calynn scampered around the corner. Her tail whipped from side to side and beat against the wall, causing a dull thud every time it hit.

Calynn had grown to be the size of a small goat, but she was just as excited for pets as she always had been.

Telyn crouched down to pet her.

She knew this could very well be the last time she saw Calynn for a while.

Telyn would have been safer in Eralia with a dragon at her side, but Calynn was still young, and Telyn didn't trust Piran not to kill her the first chance he got. She knew Calynn would be safe in Winter.

Oddly enough, the thought of spending the day in the dungeons didn't bother Telyn. She didn't know if it was because she needed to be alone or if it was because Calynn helped to calm her, but she didn't think she would be surfacing before nightfall.

She spent her time wandering the halls of the dungeons, Calynn at her side.

She didn't see a single other living thing down there besides them. Every cell was empty.

Which was a good thing, but it made the dungeons feel almost haunted.

The scorched bones from Calynn's meals didn't help the atmosphere, but Telyn knew Calynn was the scariest thing down here. They were both safe.

It didn't take long for Telyn to find Theodore's little lab, tucked away in the same corner it had been in last time she'd seen it.

This time, there was no crimson liquid flowing through the tubing, or any liquid at all. The machinery was still there, but it wasn't active. There were no flames, no chemicals, only papers.

At first glance, they only looked like notes on the nightshade project, but a few looked out of place. They were notes pertaining to different projects. A few of them looked far more dangerous than simply nightshade.

There were plans for weapons, both obvious and hidden. A hairpin meant to double as a poison releasing dagger, gloves with razors hidden in the fingertips. They were meant for defense, specifically women's defense. Telyn wondered if Skylar had instructed him to make these as well.

She hoped they were for Brea and Cordelia. The girls were far from warriors, but they needed to be able to defend themselves. Especially in the kind of world they were living in now.

Things wouldn't be changing for a while. Even if Piran was gone, Carling would find other men to wage his wars. It was high time it became common for a lady to pick up a blade.

Telyn wouldn't see the two little girls hurt or killed because the rest of the world refused to keep up with the times.

She didn't have anyone to teach them, or her for that matter. She only hoped Nolan had thought ahead enough to ensure his daughter could keep herself safe.

Telyn knew he was at least a half-way decent teacher. Kassian hadn't known his was around a blade before he'd been trained by Nolan, but she'd seen them training, and knew he had been good before he had gone for good.

If Cordelia could fight like that after lessons with Nolan, Telyn hoped they would have nothing to fear.

There were lots of weapons a woman could use for lots of different things, but knowing how to use a blade would be more prevalent as time went on.

The old ways wouldn't always be enough.

Times were changing, and the people needed to change with them, or else they would be left behind.

And those left behind in this world didn't often make it.

Telyn had seen it when people had been born a little different, a little defect, not picking up on things as quickly as other children, there were lots of things people had been kicked to the streets for, especially in Micaera. None of them had lasted long, that was one thing that wouldn't change.

People who were left behind and forgotten died.

When Telyn returned to her room, she signed one final document.

The official adoption certificate for Cordelia, signed by the queen. Skylar would give it to Nolan after she left, as a sort of parting gift.

And in case she didn't return.

The sun had sunk under the horizon and Ceris had begun to wake.

It wouldn't be much longer before things would be in motion.

Telyn sat in the dining hall, Calynn curled up at her feet. There were still far too many people in there. Far too many homes that needed rebuilt.

But if things went according to plan, Telyn wouldn't be around long enough to be able to help. She could very well be gone before sunrise.

"Keep an eye on Theodore," Telyn said. She kept her voice low so only Skylar could hear. "I don't know what you've instructed him to do, but he has a lot of good ideas."

"What do you mean?" Skylar asked.

"His lab was still set up in the dungeons this morning. He'd left plans behind for a few projects I assume he's going to work on. There were a lot of good ideas for concealed weapons, especially for girls like Brea and Cordelia," Telyn said. She poked at the poached egg in front of her.

She wasn't very hungry, but it was important to keep up appearances.

"That could be very useful in coming days." Skylar nodded.

Telyn took a bite of her egg, but it tasted like rubber in her mouth.

No, she wasn't hungry after all.

Instead of continuing to play with food she had no interest in eating, she folded her hands on top of the table.

"I'm going to be gone for at least a month, likely more," Telyn said. "Calynn will need checked on, I would like for the twins to be checked in on, someone will need to respond to Pip's letters for me."

"I know." Skylar smiled. "I've got everything covered. We'll be fine, just do what you need to do."

Telyn hated that she worried so much. She'd grown so used to the responsibilities that had been dumped on her, she didn't know what it would feel like to live without them. She only had one responsibility now.

She needed a break, they were important, but she wouldn't exactly consider what she was going to do a break.

It would certainly be far more stressful than what she had been dealing with.

Living with the enemy, and not just passively.

She would have to pretend she was in love with Piran. She wasn't so sure she was all that great at acting, and even if she was, she didn't know if it would hold up after prolonged exposure to the man she hated. Her skills of manipulation had only been learned passively.

In a way, fooling the king would be her big test. The apprentice would become the master, and the master would become the fool.

In truth, Piran had already been a fool. He'd become one when he decided to use Telyn for his own benefit. When he had charged for kindness she had not asked for.

It would have been kinder to let her freeze in the snow of No Man's Land than to treat her as he had. She would have chosen the cold over the king any day. She just hadn't been given that choice.

Breakfast passed without any major discourse.

Telyn helped clear the dishes and bring them into the kitchen. She needed something to keep her busy until it was time.

After the dishes were scrubbed and left out to dry, she walked around the gardens with Calynn at her heels.

There wasn't much to see. There wasn't much that grew in the frigid winter months, but a few sparse flowers managed to push their way towards the watery light that had been offered to them.

The garden would never be as grand as any of the ones in Alidain or the other courts, but it served its own purpose.

It proved that where life had a will, there was a way for it to survive. Perhaps it didn't thrive, but being alive was better than nothing.

It meant that though Eralia would make Telyn want to die, she would survive it. And one day she would go back home, where she belonged, where she could thrive.

All things came to an end.

Not all of those ends were death.

In this case it would be, but at least it wouldn't be hers.

Telyn knew that she would lose her dignity, and possibly more, but she would not lose her spirit. She knew who she fought for. She knew why Piran deserved the fate she was going to serve him on a silver platter.

Revenge was always best served cold, and there was nothing colder than the citizens of Winter.

And Telyn was one of them.

They weren't savages like those who dwelled in the Unseelie court, or like their king.

But they knew their way around revenge.

Telyn had learned a lot from the people and their community.

They may not all be blood related, but they were a family, and they looked out for each other. They were like Telyn and her court.

But when Telyn had decided to accept Skylar, those people had become her people too.

She had not been raised with them, but they taught her valuable lessons nonetheless.

She would suffer through living with her enemy not only for herself, but the family that had taken her in and made her feel like she belonged when no one else did.

Telyn would bear the burden of having someone's blood on her hands so that she could be free to right her mother's wrongs.

The people of Alidain needed her.

The people of Winter needed her.

Skylar needed her.

She wouldn't let them down. Most days they were all that kept her going, especially Skylar. This small part of her life could be sacrificed to keep them safe. She wouldn't mind it.

Zerina, Colton, Pip, Lilith, Harley, Nolan, Cordelia, Skylar.

They were her family, at least the one she had chosen.

They were all she had left.

Telyn had never met her father, but she knew for a certainty that he would have gone to war for them if he was in her position. He would have gone to war for Telyn had he still been alive.

Corbin Ramirez had loved fast, and he had loved hard.

Maybe that's what Maria had seen in him.

She hadn't loved him when they left, but perhaps she had seen that in him and gone anyway.

Perhaps that was where Telyn got it from.

Her father would have gone to war for the people he loved.

Her mother would have been smart enough to calculate the risks and then take them.

And what was Telyn if not the sum of her parents?

She had doubted herself for far too long. She had let people bully and manipulate her because she'd thought herself deserving of nothing more, but she knew better now.

She knew she was capable of doing the things that needed to be done, defending her family, her people.

Herself.

She was a queen. Queens did not survive by being passive and doing nothing.

Queens held kingdoms together and tore them apart.

As did kings.

But the king she was about to face had been foolish enough to cross the wrong queen.

It wasn't that Telyn had nothing left to lose that made her so dangerous.

It was the fact that she had so much to lose.

She had a family that loved her, people that respected her.

It was her duty as queen to protect those that had been placed in her care.

As Skylar's mate, and the future High Lady of Winter, that duty had been extended to the people of Winter.

She had failed them when Piran had attacked them the first two times.

It would not happen a third time and it would not go unpunished.

Telyn couldn't sacrifice her life for this mission. There were too many people depending on her to come home. And they would need her for the war that had yet to come.

But she wouldn't have to sacrifice her life.

She was far stronger than anyone had given her credit for, including herself.

She was smart, and brave, and that was all she would need to best Piran at the twisted game he had created.

They always had said that poison was a woman's weapon.

Telyn would be happy to claim that so long as it got the job done.

She didn't want to rely on her powers to best him.

She knew she could, but she wanted to save that for the gods.

Piran would die like a mortal, at the hand of poison.

He may be king of the Unseelie court and Eralia, but he was not a god.

Not even the gods were gods.

Telyn would not give him the honor of dying like someone who posed a real threat. He would die as he was, a disgusting piece of filth that didn't deserve the honors that had been given to him.

He did not deserve either of the crowns he held.

He did not deserve Brea.

Nor his parents.

Telyn was avenging them too, the king and queen who had been too kind to see their son's wickedness. She hoped that when Piran crossed he would see them again and feel some sort of remorse for what he'd done.

It might not be possible for a man like him, but she hoped he had to live with the guilt in death if he wouldn't in life.

Piran had tormented Telyn and the people she loved for far too long. She would be the first to admit that she should have seen it in the way he'd treated the people around her. Her life had been flipped upside down, but that was no excuse.

In the beginning it may have been her allowance that led him on, but as she learned who he really was and told him she was no longer his toy, it had turned on him.

He had made the decisions that had led them both to where they were now.

His death would be no one's but his own.

Telyn had been dreaming of this since she'd watched him nearly drain the life out of Alexander, just for her hand in marriage. He had believed that if he couldn't have her, no one could. But he had been so very wrong, and all the things he had done to control her, they had only made her vendetta against him stronger.

One of them would not be leaving Eralia alive.

And Telyn refused to be the one who didn't come home.

She would survive off of sheer will if she had to, but she would be the one that lived.

She didn't want his crowns; she didn't want his money.

Telyn only wanted her revenge.

It was a simple enough thing really, even a child could understand the concept.

Piran had crossed too many lines, and now he would pay for every single one of them.

She was looking forward to seeing the regret in his eyes when she killed him. It wouldn't be long now.

Telyn didn't have to wait much longer for Piran to return. As she had predicted, he came back that night, as she had expected him to. He had returned to Heart, and was quite displeased with how quickly repairs were coming along. His long pale face was twisted by a frown as he surveyed the town.

Flames danced in the king's palms by the time Skylar and Telyn reached him.

"You weren't supposed to fix everything so quickly." Piran tossed the ball of flames from one hand to the other. It danced threateningly close to wood that had just been put up to repair one of the shops.

"We couldn't keep our people out in the cold," Skylar said.

Telyn could feel the anger coming off of her in waves, but Skylar kept her distance. She knew what needed to happen. Telyn knew that Skylar was a leader who truly cared for her people, that was why it was so hard for her to understand how Piran could be so cruel. Telyn wasn't even that close to her people and she still struggled to understand it.

She supposed some people were just born heartless.

"I suppose I could destroy it again, that might be some fun." Piran mused. Once again, his flame ventured just a bit too close to the wood. The board singed a little where it made contact.

"Don't." Telyn took a few steps forward.

Skylar watched as Telyn walked away from her.

Telyn glanced behind her once to see Skylar one last time before she lowered her voice. "Just take me with you before she knows what's happening."

"What?" Telyn could see the flicker of confusion that crossed his face.

"She's trapped me here, and I want to leave." Telyn whispered.

Piran glanced over Telyn's shoulder at Skylar.

Telyn couldn't see what Skylar was doing, but she knew it wouldn't be anything that could give them away.

She watched as the king puzzled out her request, then before Telyn could react or change her mind, Piran grabbed her around the waist, and as a dizzying mist swirled around her, she heard Skylar's voice in her mind.

Be careful, darling.

Epilogue

You've come so far.

Things have been changing around here. The hold the mist has on us is weakening.

Your mother is here.

She sees everything you're doing; I don't think you'll ever know how sorry she is.

For leaving behind this mess you're having to clean up.

She has the answers you're looking for, she just doesn't have a way to tell you.

They won't even consider letting her out because of what she knows.

They know what you're planning too, and they are not happy. You were never supposed to know the truth.

They say you're becoming too bold, you're forgetting what you're supposed to be.

I think they've forgotten what you really are.

They're afraid because they know the more aware you grow, the more dangerous you become.

They thought you were Nerissa, a ghost of their mother come to haunt them, but they couldn't have been more wrong.

Other ghosts will reap their revenge on these new gods when the time is right, but their mother is not one of them. It is not Nerissa's time to wake. For all of our sakes, I hope that does not come for a very long time.

She just might destroy everything to start all over again. If that happens, you have to be there to stop her.

You have to do better than last time.

The people living now don't deserve to be slaughtered, just as they didn't back then.

More than that, I don't know what will happen to us.

The dead.

We're in some sort of holding cell of the gods' design.

If she destroys this too, I don't know where we'll go.

At least here we can watch over you. Though it can be torture sometimes.

We've watched you walk into trap after trap. If the rules weren't so strict and the punishments so harsh, we would find a way to warn you.

But I can already feel myself slipping.

There was a price to pay for coming back when I did. They made sure I wouldn't make a habit of it. It's taken this long to take its toll. I don't know how far it will go before it ends. I hope I'm still here when it does.

This story is already a twisted and messy thing full of betrayal and heartache. On more levels than even you know.

There is sure to be more of it as it continues, but as warped and wrong as it is, the war is coming.

Carling is coming. He feels slighted by you. He means to make an example of anyone who turns their back to the gods. You seem to be the best person to make an example of in his eyes. He won't rest until your story had ended or his has.

As terrifying as it is at times to see the murderous rage in his eyes when he speaks of you, I want to see how the story ends. I want it to be you that comes out victorious in the end, but in order to know, I have to be in this state of in between to know it.

If I could just see you safe, I could pass on without regrets.

Bonus Chapter

The Longest Day

I'm going to do it. I'm sorry you don't like it, but it's our only choice.

Skylar knew she had lost with those words, and she knew she could lose so much more than an argument if Sprin was as dangerous as people said he was.

"If she dies, you will find I am not an enjoyable person at all." Skylar swallowed the fear that rose in her throat and threatened to choke her.

The grin Sprin gave her in response only made her want to kill him more. "Whether she lives or not is not up to me."

The sun was beginning to rise on the horizon. It felt the way funeral bells sounded.

Skylar forced herself to control her breaths.

"Time to go." Sprin dipped into a bow and gestured to the cave.

The dragon had already gone inside. Skylar couldn't see her in the murky darkness of the cave.

Skylar watched as the woman she loved took one step into the dragon's cave, and then another.

As soon as Telyn was inside, a wall of stone sprung up and sealed her inside.

Almost immediately, Skylar could sense her panic, her fear of the dark, and the memories that it brought with it.

"Take down the wall." Skylar could hear the growl in her own voice.

His wicked little grin returned. "I said she had to be locked in. That implies no route of escape."

Skylar stalked towards Sprin, her fists clenched and ready to swing.

"Careful now, if you kill me before nightfall, she'll never make it out." Sprin clucked.

Skylar had never wanted to murder anyone more than she wanted to murder the little man now. Except maybe Piran, and that was a hard bar to meet.

"I swear on anything good in the twelve realms, if she dies, you die. I will enjoy watching the life drain from your eyes as you pay for what you did. Then, I'll kill your dragon too. She's tormented my people enough already." Skylar gripped Sprin by the front of his shirt and lifted him up until his toes barely touched the ground.

"Those are bold words, are you sure you can follow through?" Sprin asked.

He was just as cocky as Piran, with less than half of the misplaced authority.

Skylar held a blade to his throat.

She set him down on the ground and held him there, her blade never once wavered.

"We are going to sit here all day, and you're going to get really friendly with my dagger until you let her out." Skylar seethed.

"You'll fall asleep before long." Sprin scoffed.

"And you'll eat your words when you realize how many days I've stayed awake waiting for her to be safe."

Skylar watched the sun crawl across the sky. The hours passed like they were full days and her hand ached from gripping her dagger so tightly, but she didn't dare shift her grip. If she showed any weakness, any exhaustion, Sprin would take advantage of it.

Skylar should have listened when Portia had tried to tell her what a nasty piece of work he was.

But there hadn't been much of a choice, had there?

Brea needed to wake up, and he, unfortunately, was the only one who could help them.

But it should have been Skylar that was locked in that cave. It should have been Skylar that paid the price for the cure because Brea wasn't Telyn's responsibility.

Brea was like a little sister to Skylar.

Skylar had been there for countless scraped knees and bruises when Piran was too busy being his unfeeling self.

Skylar should be the one saving Brea.

But Telyn hadn't hesitated to give up whatever was needed to help bring Brea back.

That was one of the things Skylar admired about her.

She never hesitated when someone was in need. Telyn had her own agenda, they all did, but she took the time to help others along the way. She did what she could to protect the ones she loved.

And Skylar was failing to protect her.

Telyn had lost people and grown stronger to be able to prevent it from happening again.

Skylar had lost people and hadn't changed at all.

No matter how much she had tried to keep Telyn safe, she was still failing.

She had failed her parents, her own little sister, and she hadn't learned.

She had failed Arlo, and hadn't changed.

Still, she wasn't able to do enough to protect the ones she loved.

She was beginning to doubt she would ever be enough. She must have been cursed to lose everyone she cared for.

No.

She wouldn't lose Telyn.

Her grip tightened on her dagger and Sprin flinched as the blade bit into his skin, drawing a drop of blood.

It's almost nightfall. Skylar tried for a soothing tone, meant to help her as much as she hoped it would help Telyn.

The sun continued on its torturously slow path across the sky until eventually, it vanished.

"Let her out."

Skylar's dagger didn't leave Sprin's throat until the wall of stone was down and Telyn had stumbled out of the cave and into safety.

Skylar didn't see any blood, but that didn't mean Telyn wasn't hurt. Skylar shoved her dagger back into its sheath and rushed over to Telyn.

Skylar knelt down beside Telyn as she crumpled onto the ground.

Sprin was all but forgotten as Skylar ran her hands over Telyn to check for any injuries.

The light had gone from Telyn's eyes.

The dark had done something to her. She had spent too much time with it, and it killed Skylar to see Telyn look so defeated.

"You're not hurt?" Skylar demanded as she cupped Telyn's face in her hands.

"I told you it would be easy." Skylar could see right through the smile that Telyn plastered onto her face.

Sprin stepped around Skylar and gave Telyn a once over.

"Not even a scratch." He mused.

Skylar glared. "So, you did expect her to die."

Sprin shrugged.

"Will you give us what we need now?" Telyn asked.

"Not quite yet. I haven't received my payment yet." Sprin's contempt grin was back.

He had already put Telyn's life in danger and taken something indescribable from her, and he wanted more.

Skylar had half a mind to kill him anyway.

Acknowledgements

Thank you guys so much for sticking with me and the Death's Handmaiden series. I owe the motivation to even finish this sequel to the amazing support I recieved when I released Queen of Swords. I think the one thing they don't really tell you in writing is how hard it is to write sequels, but I did it!

I did it for those of you who fell in love with my characters the same way I did, and for those of you who have yet to.

And once again, thank you to all of my self published friends! You continue to inspire me and show me that with some time and dedication, we can succeed in careers that we love.

Also By

Death's Handmaiden
Queen of Swords
King of Wands

The Darkling Chronicles
The Shadows of Stars
The Rise of Rebellion
The Whispers of Whitmans
The Darklings of Descent
The Lightlings of Lex
The Hands of Hope

Made in the USA
Columbia, SC
25 January 2023